THE
INCONSISTENT
VILLAINS

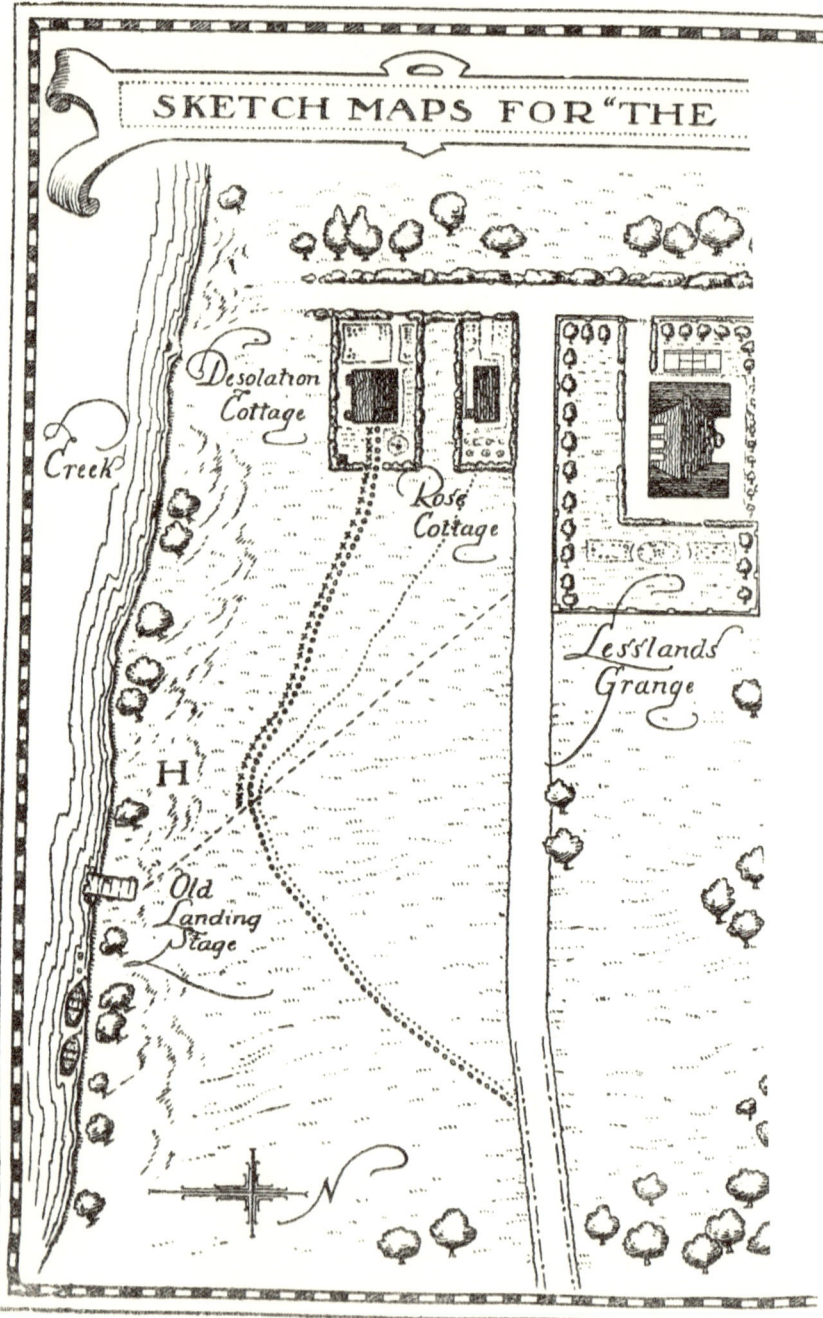

SKETCH MAPS FOR "THE

Creek

Desolation Cottage

Rose Cottage

H

Old Landing Stage

Lesslands Grange

N

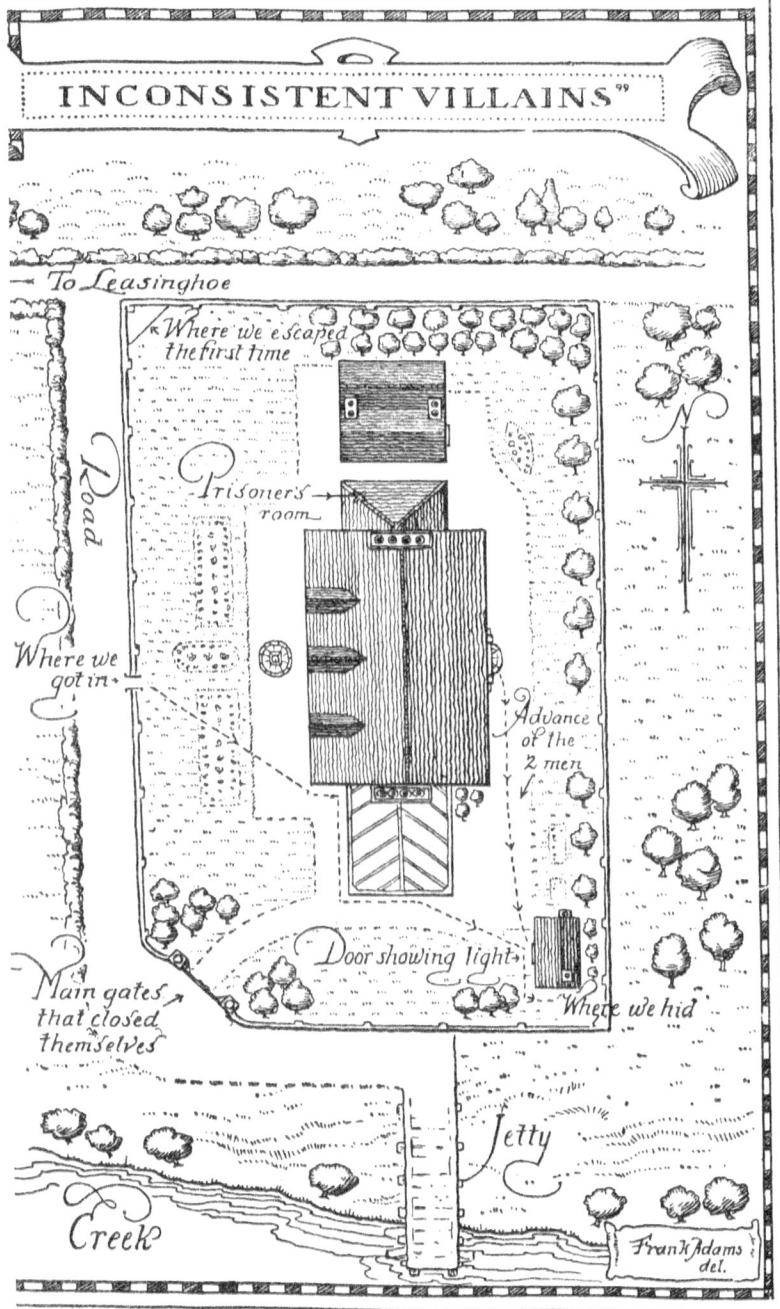

"INCONSISTENT VILLAINS"

To Leasinghoe

Where we escaped the first time

Prisoner's room

Road

Where we got in

Advance of the 2 men

Door showing light

Main gates that closed themselves

Where we hid

Jetty

Creek

Frank Adams del.

THE INCONSISTENT VILLAINS

N. A. Temple-Ellis

COACHWHIP PUBLICATIONS
GREENVILLE, OHIO

The Inconsistent Villains, by N. A. Temple-Ellis
© 2026 Coachwhip Publications edition

First published 1929
Neville Aldridge Holdaway, 1894-1954
CoachwhipBooks.com

ISBN 1-61646-630-8
ISBN-13 978-1-61646-630-5

Note by the Compiler

My share in the production of the following pages has been limited to casting the abundant material supplied into a form that should be easily readable. To that extent I accept all responsibility. Regarding subject-matter, I have been at pains to avoid the least variation from the account of the affair as it was given to me, even where some additional effect might have easily been obtained thereby.

N. A. Temple-Ellis

Note by Sir Edmund King

After a great deal of deliberation and consultation with all concerned I have decided to offer the public this authentic account of a series of recent remarkable events that is still the subject of discussion. For the past few months the air has been thick with rumours, and thinly-veiled and often grossly inaccurate allusions have been of frequent appearance in the Press. Under these circumstances the lady who is chiefly concerned has given her consent to the publication of this memoir, believing with me that a frank acknowledgement of the truth is preferable to the endurance of the varied and outrageous scandals that have been industriously promulgated in certain quarters.

It was thought by those whose advice I took that the presentation of the story in the literary (*sic*) form generally described as detective fiction would enable it to reach the larger circle of readers who would probably have fought shy of it in proper biographical shape. My thanks are due to Mr. Temple-Ellis for his services in making this possible.

Where the narrative deals with members of the general public whose connexion with the case was purely fortuitous, fictitious names have been introduced. My task has been rendered easier by the recent demise of a gentleman who once served in the Indian Army, and by the good-natured permission granted by a prominent member of the Labour Party to refer freely to his part in the story.

Those acquainted with the Peak district of Derbyshire cannot fail to realize that it is difficult to refer the descriptions given in the narrative to that area. The reason for this single act of reticence in what is otherwise a perfectly open account will become apparent to the reader as the story proceeds.

Edmund King

1

In Which We Post a Letter to Ourselves

Arbuthnot himself admits that there was something so amazingly complex about the affair as it presented itself to us in its earlier stages that he cannot quite recollect any real parallel to it, in that respect, in real life. It began with the ringing of the telephone bell as we sat at breakfast that gloomy, chilly, mid-November day. Telephones ring for many purposes, trivial and tragic, but this one rang up the curtain on a play that was to hold us fascinated until dull November was a thing of the past.

My friend discarded his toast and took the receiver off its hook. To the disjointed half-conversation I paid no attention, and with *The Times* firmly wedged between sugar-basin and coffee-pot, continued placidly to feed mind, and body.

Arbuthnot resumed his seat.

"How well it pays," said he, "to keep in with the Press. That was Falcon, of the *Bulletin,* telling me something that makes me fear you have eaten your last meal in London for some time."

I am no sybarite, I hope, but a glance at the drear, grey sky without and another at the cheerful blaze in the grate opposite to me, made me wish that the Press *communiqué* had been delayed till a better day.

"This *would* occur," I said, "just at a moment when it is necessary for me to be within reach of the British Museum every day, if I am to get on with my work."

Arbuthnot failed to answer. Instead, he deftly twitched *The Times* away from under my very nose, consulted a page other than the one whence I had been deriving pabulum, returned the paper to me without apology, crossed the room to a bureau of long, narrow drawers, pulled open one marked 'One Inch Ordnance', extracted a map, pushed the marmalade and an entrée dish in opposite directions, and, in the table space thus made available, spread his map and lapsed into study.

"Do you know Essex?" he asked, after I had nursed my wrath for five minutes over the rape of *The Times*.

"I've seen county matches at Leyton," I volunteered.

"H'm. D'you know Colchester?"

"I went there occasionally when I had a friend stationed in the Cavalry Barracks there years ago."

"Eastward of Colchester, barring the mushroom seaside towns, is a distinctly lonely part of the world," he said: "a land of marsh, and creek, and grey North Sea."

I looked at the leaden sky without and shuddered.

"And what is it that would drive us into that desolation?" I demanded.

"Its name," said Arbuthnot, "is Baxter Creen."

"You mean Sir Baxter Creen, knighted during the War for making munitions or something of that sort?"

"Exactly." There was no need, however, for him to grin, for, even if the King baronetcy does date back beyond the Merry Monarch, I should be the last person to give myself airs on that account.

"And how comes Baxter Creen to drive me away from my work and my fireside?"

"Yes," said Arbuthnot, answering obliquely, "I'm sorry, that while this pleasant Kensington flat and the British

Museum know you, for a while, no more, the great British public should have to wait for your monumental tome on *Shakespeare's Use of Metaphorical Expressions.*"

It was characteristic of the man that he never doubted, any more than I did, that I should accompany him, however much I might grumble over a compulsory divorce from the study that had taken all my spare time for the last three years.

"Three days ago," added he, "Baxter Creen interviewed me and offered me a piece of work—pressed it on me in fact. He is, as I should judge, a man used to getting what he wants, only in the course of years, after many successes, he has become careless as to how he sets about getting it. With me he made the error of assuming that if he offered a sum of money sufficiently large I should be his servant. When I declined, with a minimum of politeness, to handle the affair, he was distinctly annoyed."

"What was his business?" I asked.

"I neither know nor care. He did not reach the stage of divulging it. But I will give him credit for persistence. Falcon rang up to say that, at a Press luncheon yesterday, he by chance overheard some remarks that passed between Creen and Hemingway, from which he gathered Creen had induced Hemingway to write to me and ask me to reconsider my decision. It's not the first time Falcon has done me a good turn since we dragged him out of the Riviera libel case, you remember."

"Well, what then?"

"Simply that Hemingway is a bird of very different plumage from Creen. One doesn't go out of one's way to neglect the wishes of a Secretary of State, especially when he's a good fellow who has turned up trumps in the past, and may be useful again in the future. Hence, rather than concede Creen a triumph, we vanish for a brief holiday and leave him perforce to find another man for his job."

A knock at the door announced Mrs. Holden, most estimable of housekeepers, with the morning mail. Arbuthnot shuffled the letters, dealt me my third, selected a familiar handwriting from the residue, threw the letter bearing it on the table, and began issuing instructions to Mrs. Holden as to our impending absence. "And all letters," he concluded, "you will re-direct and post yourself, as usual, care of Mr. Kaye, Walham Green—you have the address."

"Very well, sir." Mrs. Holden withdrew; she had long ago suffered a complete loss of any faculty for surprise she may have once possessed.

"Sir Edmund King and his eccentric friend now fade from the public eye. A good train leaves Liverpool Street at ten-thirty and will land us in Colchester within a couple of hours, in time to catch Messrs. Morris & Stubbs before they adjourn to lunch," continued Arbuthnot.

"All right," I said weakly. "I'll go and pack."

"And shave," added he.

"I have already done so," I countered indignantly.

"I mean your moustache."

"Good heavens! That's not necessary. We haven't committed a crime."

"Baxter Creen," said Arbuthnot enigmatically, "is a persistent man, so I think you will do rightly to sacrifice your military toothbrush; and when you have adopted a pair of horn-rimmed tinted glasses you will do fairly well as Cyrus G. Monk, Lecturer in Botany at the University of Plymouth, Massachusetts, and now studying for the doctorate of an English university."

"Great Scot! Is this really necessary?"

"Baxter Creen," said Arbuthnot dreamily, "is a persistent man. I shall assume a cherished pair of walrus moustaches, a wing collar, and a gold watch chain, and become a water-colour painter of the old, or Diamond Jubilee, school. Thus equipped we shall spend a pleasant week or so until Baxter Creen has committed his troubles to another's care."

I submitted, remembering that Arbuthnot occupied a unique position and had great difficulty in hiding his light under a bushel.

"But I warn you, that while *you* can paint more or less tolerably, *I* know nothing whatever about botany."

"That's what a new subaltern said about patrolling when I sent him out into No Man's Land, and I answered, "Well, now you've got a damned good chance to learn." I understand the ecology of the Essex marshes with their saltmarsh vegetation is exceptionally interesting."

Little did I dream when he uttered those words of the deadly fascination that those lonely marshes would have for us even before twenty-four hours were past. Before the taxi was at the door I had sacrificed my moustache and Arbuthnot had added twenty years to his age. His last act before we left was to take the unopened letter that was the cause of our hurried departure, and, with a grin at me, drop it into our own letter-box as we passed out.

"Remember, Mrs. Holden, we left last night," he told the good lady as she stood superintending the strapping of a couple of leather cases on the taxi. "I have written a line to Kaye," he added to me. "He will be responsible for forwarding letters as soon as I give him an address, which latter he will keep to himself."

In the train Arbuthnot informed me that he was Mr. Egbert Ponsonby and produced a visiting card to prove his statement. "The best I could do from my collection," he remarked apologetically. "Your inability to produce one we can ascribe to professional absent-mindedness. And now for Morris & Stubbs."

"These being—" I queried.

"Estate Agents, of Colchester, who are prepared to let at a reasonable rate for the winter a furnished cottage near the sea—by which they mean a tidal creek—and not far from the village of Leasinghoe."

Messrs. Morris & Stubbs proved entirely complaisant. Not for them to wonder why two apparently otherwise sane men should wish to bury themselves on that lonely, wind-swept coast so late in the year; it was only their business to let the cottage, so our transaction was very promptly completed. The place, it appeared, belonged to a Colonel Gregory, retired from the Indian Army, and now living at 'Lesslands Grange' near Leasinghoe, and the cottage had been tenanted by a maiden aunt of his, who, after the fashion of some maiden aunts, found it impossible to live in amity in the same house with her nephew. Perhaps, however the Colonel himself was not entirely blameless in the matter. At any rate, the old lady had recently died, and therefore the Colonel sought a more profitable tenant. A deposit in advance was effected by means of what Arbuthnot always called his 'Incognito' account—a special arrangement under which the bank was accustomed to honouring unusual signatures on short notice. Equipped with a letter of introduction to the Colonel, and the name of an elderly dame of Leasinghoe who could cook and clean, and fortified by a good lunch at a decent hostelry in the High Street, we continued our journey as far as possible by a branch line of railway, and then, alighting, were faced by a couple of miles' walk to Leasinghoe.

In this situation the station-master summoned an individual answering to the name of 'George', and the latter produced a hand-cart and agreed to transport our baggage to Leasinghoe for a moderate sum. The short autumn day was rapidly waning and a windless cold seemed to rise from the ground and wrap us round as we trod briskly along the country road. Half an hour's good going, and shouts from 'George' in the rear warned us that the building seen dimly in front was Lesslands Grange. Faced by oncoming darkness, we lost no time in seeking an interview with the Colonel.

The door was opened to us by a manservant whom I might as well call the butler, although, as we found afterwards, he was the only man kept in the house. Seen in the dim light, he was yet an unprepossessing object, short, strongly built, red in face, thick in neck, and with little beady eyes set too closely together. Arbuthnot handed him a card and Morris & Stubb's letter. These he received grudgingly and went away, leaving us standing on the doorstep.

Two minutes must have elapsed before his return and I had time to study the neglected appearance of the garden, even for November. Even the house itself wore an air of gloom to my eyes. Was it merely a lack of paint, an effect of dark curtains and the dullness of autumnal twilight, or was it a manifestation of the soul that some think houses possess equally with human beings? My thoughts were truncated by the reappearance of the butler, who admitted us without relinquishing his grudging air.

Colonel Gregory was tall, thin, grey-haired, and of a dull yellowish complexion. He eyed us gloomily and it seemed distastefully and made no offer to shake hands. The room he stood in had a large blazing fire, which should have made for cheerfulness, and yet there was something inimical in the atmosphere to my mind. House, owner, and servant were equally lacking in attractiveness.

"Mr. Ponsonby?" he asked shortly, and Arbuthnot bowed. "And your friend?"

"This," said Arbuthnot, "is Mr. Cyrus G. Monk, an American university lecturer at present studying in England."

I bowed, and said, "Pleased to meet you," wondering whether my lack of the appropriate accent would pass unchallenged. But, as Arbuthnot told me later, people from Massachusetts have no accent, and it is even doubtful whether they use the form of salutation I employed. As it was the Colonel only glowered at me.

"Are all you confounded Americans ashamed of your second name?" he demanded. "What's yours, anyway?"

I was tongue-tied. It was one of the little events that are always in wait to make the way of deception hard. I thought, almost audibly, for at least twenty seconds and then said "Grover". How the name occurred to me, goodness only knows, but Arbuthnot interposed promptly and cheerfully.

"After Grover Cleveland, the President. You mustn't mind Monk, Colonel. Like all these great students he is capable of forgetting anything outside his own sphere of work."

The colonel continued to glower and then said abruptly, "Well, you seem to have satisfied the agents, so I shan't interfere. Anything is better than the old cat who was there before. I furnished the place for the confounded woman; she insisted on paying no more than a pound a week for it; when I forced her to double that she retaliated by leaving her money to foreign missions. Have a cheroot?" He proffered a box of dark, evil-looking weeds. I declined, but Arbuthnot, never lacking in intrepidity, took one.

"Black Trichinopolies," growled the Colonel. "Cost me fourteen rupees a thousand in India and about twice that a hundred in this accursed country with its swindling duties—and I smoke twenty or more a day. They give a man a beggarly pension and then get most of it back in taxes. Buller!"

The last word sounded like an unusual expletive, but served to summon the same disagreeable-looking servant who had admitted us.

"Whisky," said the Colonel laconically, and it appeared so rapidly that I had no doubt that the butler, through long practice, could anticipate his master's demands with ease.

We declined refreshment on the grounds that we wanted to get settled in before night.

"You'll find the cottage in order," said the Colonel, pouring out for himself. "Though what can possess you to plant yourselves there at this damnable season, God only knows. Desolation Cottage!" he added with a sour chuckle.

"A cheerful name!" I ejaculated.

"The old woman expected the end of the world and the destruction of the unrighteous, especially me, to happen any day. The name was a sort of prophecy. Buller, give these gentlemen the keys and show them out. I can't ask you to dinner—I'm too hard up."

So we came out again to the last weary glimmer of twilight, found the faithful George at the gate, and together marched on along a road that grew steadily narrower and more deep-rutted. George knew where Mrs. Jerrold, our prospective "help" lived, and pulled up at a diminutive cottage, not by any means the first we had passed.

On the East Coast even the women-folk are more taciturn than those elsewhere.

"Eggs and bacon, and enough bread and tea for tonight, I can bring along, also paraffin," she announced when we had made plain the reason for our call. "George Higgins, you slip along quick with these bags and come back for coal and kindling wood."

On inspection, the cottage proved tolerable; it contained six rooms, besides a kitchen, and was sufficient for our needs. The Colonel's idea of furnishing must certainly have been somewhat Spartan and his aunt's choice of picture and ornament made even a pseudo-artist like Arbuthnot wince, but at any rate the essentials of comfort were present.

Omitting details, Mrs. Jerrold had prepared some sort of meal in a surprisingly short time, while 'George', who had apparently become one of the family, laid and lighted a fire, filled lamps, and carried hot water upstairs.

"Ex-service?" asked Arbuthnot, watching him at his tasks.

"Yes, sir."

"What are you doing now?"

"What I can get, sir. Fifty per cent disability. A piece of me back is gone and I couldn't tackle the farmwork again. Odd jobs is my line."

"I see. If occasion arises I'll send for you."

"Thank you, sir. I'm glad of anything that comes along."

"Decent fellow, George," said Arbuthnot later; "he positively demurred at extra compensation for his self-imposed domestic duties."

We polished off our bacon and eggs, and Mrs. Jerrold washed up, settled terms for her future services and supplies, took possession of the back-door key, ordered our breakfast for us at half-past eight, and vanished, leaving an impression of grey hair, keen eyes, a face hardened and toughened by decades of contact with the East Coast of cold sea and bitter winds, and a habit of amazing efficiency. We lighted pipes and drew up to the fireside.

"Did you ever reflect, King," asked my friend, "on the disadvantages of occupying a new place after dark? One's position is analogous to that of a navigator in uncharted seas. He knows his ship: we know our house; but beyond that he and we are equally at sea. We might find our way back the way we came, but a move in any other direction might immediately land us in some predicament."

"Is there a moon?" I asked.

"No." He went across to the window and drew aside the curtains. Something in the view, or lack of it, drew his attention, for he threw up the sash and thrust his head into the outer air.

"Land in sight?" I asked, in terms of his own figure of speech.

"Nothing but the navigator's curse—fog," he answered, and indeed, if he had not spoken I could have told by that sudden cold dampness of the air of the room.

"Well, well," said he, "you will now be grateful to me, in view of the fact that we are clearly debarred from any nocturnal exercise, for having brought the chess-gear."

Arbuthnot and I play chess regularly, and up to now I have never beaten him from a level start. My strong point is defence, and if I can keep that brilliant mind from securing my downfall within an hour I am content. "Your chess does me good," he said once, "for its stubborn defence is akin to the formidable appearance of a problem bristling with difficulties and presenting no good initial opportunities for attack."

I remember very well playing the French Defence that night; a bit out-of-date, I know, but strong in appeal to me because of the massive phalanx of defenders one gathers round the threatened monarch. It was thus engaged that we passed that critical moment of the evening when one is ready for bed. Hence, when my defence was finally shattered and I acknowledged defeat as usual, instead of retiring we lighted pipes anew and began to talk.

"What impressed you most in this day's work?" Arbuthnot inquired. He was always willing to listen to my opinions, alleging brutally as his reason that he thus got to know how the man in the street looked at things.

"The Colonel, undoubtedly. Even apart from his abominable rudeness he was a character."

"The Colonel, his butler, Mrs. Jerrold, George Higgins." Arbuthnot enumerated them as at a roll-call. "Here are four people, met in the space of an hour or so, who all strike one as interesting. It is always the case as soon as one reaches the country. Individuality is swallowed in towns but puts forth strongly in rural conditions, as I think Wordsworth said, more or less."

"That may be so, but I can't help identifying the Colonel with something sinister. It's probably all fancy, but his house, his garden, his servant, his appearance, his manner, all gave me the impression of a solitary evil soul, saturated with savage resentment against the world."

"Very well put, King, but you mustn't forget that we must have appeared to him as beings totally foreign to the men of his world. He probably classed us as nincompoops, pacifists, and bores."

"The butler again," I said, "looked a low bully."

"Prize-fighter. Did you notice his ears, his nose, his knuckles. Probably now has an easy life, augmenting the Colonel's whisky bills and terrorizing the women of the village."

"My sympathies are with the maiden aunt," I remarked, "I shouldn't be surprised if those two more or less urged her into her grave for the profit that might be expected."

"Ah, I'm afraid long acquaintance with me has made you too ready to scent a tragedy. I'm for bed; but first we'll open the window for two minutes and get rid of some of this stale tobacco smoke, even at the expense of letting in a little fog."

As he spoke he pulled aside the yellow curtains and raised the window to its full extent, and the kindly lamplight shone out on what looked like a solid packing of grey cotton-wool. I shivered as wisps of it came floating in, only to disappear in the warm air of the room. On the mantelpiece a little clock, that George had found time to set going before he left, indicated by a sudden whirring noise that it was about to strike one.

"I think it was Tyndall who first proved that fog, contrary to general opinion, serves to intensify sound," remarked Arbuthnot. Never in life was speech so suddenly justified. There came in at that open window out of the

night, through the fog, such a sound as no man might wish to hear twice—a cry of unspeakable terror, of despair, of impending death, rising to a pitch of shrillness, and then—no more.

I believe my first impulse was to fling down the window and snatch together the curtains, for there are limits to what one can endure unshaken, but Arbuthnot was already leaning out, listening intently.

"S-some sea-bird, I imagine," I found myself saying in a kind of husky whisper.

"Perhaps." He withdrew his head. "And perhaps no bird, but a soul taking flight."

"What can we do? What can we do?"

"Exactly nothing. Here is our ship—there are the fog-bound, uncharted seas. It would be madness to venture out. I can't even tell from what direction, nor from what distance, that sound came. Over there, somewhere, is the creek. Six steps, and this light would be invisible, and we should wander aimlessly."

"Honestly, what do you think?"

"That there are more than curlews calling in the marshes to-night."

"But even if our chance to help is the slightest, oughtn't we to go?" I had recovered somewhat from my first panic alarm.

"If that sound came from a human being he is past our help. Do you want to join him?"

"God forbid! But it seems callous to stand by, inactive."

"Bed," said Arbuthnot briefly. "Sleep if you can. It may happen that we shall want clear heads to-morrow."

A few minutes later we had retired to our rooms. I got into bed, leaving my bedroom door ajar, for the feeling of companionship it somehow gave me.

"King?" The voice of Arbuthnot from his room.

"Hullo!"

"As far as I can estimate the tide in this part of the North Sea should just have turned."

"What of that?"

"Only that they say souls go out with the ebb-tide. Good-night."

2

In Which Blood Serves the Purpose of Ink

I suppose it was at least two hours before I obtained some kind of sleep, and when at last my subconscious mind took charge it was only to present the events of the past day in an inextricable medley of the ridiculous and the horrible. I woke to find a November apology for daylight showing dull grey in the window-square. The fog had gone, but the skies were leaden, and I sensed it was still bitterly cold outside.

Every one knows how unpleasant it is to wake with the feeling that something painful is lying at the back of the mind waiting to be remembered. It was not long before I sat up in bed with a start as the memory of the horror of the night before flashed back. My watch showed that it was not much after half-past seven, but I had no desire to remain longer in bed. As I swung my feet floorwards I heard footsteps on the stairs and Arbuthnot, in his dressing-gown, came in. Despite the outrageous and dismal moustache I could see that my friend's face was alive with interest.

"You're awake? Good. Slip on your dressing-gown and come down. There's something below worth seeing."

As I struggled into the garment, I took a hasty glance outside. My window was in the front of the cottage, which turned its back on the road. My view was a garden, or what should have been one, an expanse of rough pasture sloping down to the marshes, and beyond the marshes the land rising gradually on the other side of the creek.

Arbuthnot led me to the front door, and we stepped out on what was probably once a gravel path, now almost entirely grass-grown. I can't really say what I expected he had to show me; I think I had uneasy fears of a corpse; but what we actually saw exceeded in a horrible grotesqueness anything my imagination had called up. Upon the window of the room we had occupied the previous evening—a window of the ordinary type divided into upper and lower halves—was drawn roughly, in some reddish liquid, a figure three. It occupied the whole of the upper portion of the window and reminded me oddly of the enormous figures on the cards used in some shops when a bargain is to be advertised.

"Blood?" I said at last in a voice not much more than a whisper.

"I think so. Mrs. Jerrold noticed it there when she went in to clean our room ten minutes ago. She says she thought at first it was some child's joke, and then realized that it was too high up for a child to reach. There's some sense in that old woman. She called me to see it at once."

"Any footprints?"

"None. The ground has been frozen all night. Well, it's too cold here for dressing-gowns. We'll talk upstairs, as we dress."

So we went from room to room talking, while I checked the growth of my incipient and unwanted moustache.

"The first question always," said Arbuthnot, "is not what to think, but what to do. I propose to call in the police."

"You do! And why?"

"Here we have a very bizarre occurrence. Taken at its best it is a very unpleasant practical joke; at its worst it is something much darker. Certainly even lads in remote

villages, under the stimulus of the cinema, form secret societies and indulge in passwords, daggers, and all the paraphernalia of mystery, but, taken in conjunction with the cry in the night, I am disposed to rank this beyond a boyish prank. Suppose the person responsible is watching our actions, then if we allow the matter to pass unreported we encourage him to think we have something to conceal."

"But who in this lonely spot can have any concern with us?"

"What to think comes after. Our part is a frank attitude of bewilderment."

"Shall you mention the—er—noise we heard last night?"

"Better to do so. Later on we might wish to mention it, and then could not do so without being open to question over our previous concealment. The cry, the figure, and the thumb-mark together make a matter deserving enquiry."

"The thumb-mark!"

"Yes, on the window-sill. So you failed to notice it. It is conspicuous enough."

"In blood?"

"If the other is. I scraped off a little of the red substance where it had run down the pane, and have it in an envelope. It will be posted to Kaye to-day. Fortunately there is now an infallible test for bloodstains, and we lose nothing by making sure."

We went downstairs and outside, and there was the thumb-mark, a large one, I judged, showing as a dull red blotch on the white, wooden window-sill. While I had gaped at that amazing numeral I had entirely failed to notice the lesser mark.

As we sat down to breakfast the figure, reversed, showed distorted through the inferior glass in the window. To me there was something indescribably menacing about it, but Arbuthnot settled to breakfast with that calm assurance of his that almost savours of cold-bloodedness.

Mrs. Jerrold brought in fresh tea, with the air of one whose importance has been enhanced by an untoward occurrence.

"Is there a police-constable in the village?" asked Arbuthnot.

"Yes, sir. A young fellow. Been a soldier. Not that there's even been much for him to do in Leasinghoe."

"Then will you walk as far as the village and ask him to come along?"

"I will, sir. It's only ten minutes' walk."

Five minutes later she had taken off all the impedimenta of breakfast in one immense tray and vanished.

"And now, what to think?" said I as I filled my pipe.

Arbuthnot shook his head. "Too early," said he. "We must continue to act. As soon as we have interviewed the 'young fellow who's been a soldier', I will accompany you to the marshes to begin your ecological studies."

"Criminological studies seem more likely," I said. "What do you expect to find there?"

"I expect nothing."

I sat down by the fire, while Arbuthnot wrote his note to Kaye, and all the time I felt as if that evil figure were impending over my shoulder, till I hardly dared to look round. It sounds rather silly now, but the inexplicable always has special terrors for man, as witness his flinching from the supernatural.

A female voice raised in expostulation, and sounds of boots being violently scraped and rubbed by the back door, announced that our invocation of the law had had effect. Constable Jones, when he presented himself, made a good impression. He was one of those young men whose sound, if slow, intelligence had been polished by variety of war service. Mrs. Jerrold rose even higher in our estimation when we found she had resolutely declined to impart any information in advance.

The constable's eyes opened wide when he caught sight of the window and its strange blazon.

"That's what you sent for me about?"

"Partly that. Now come outside."

While I nodded confirmation, Arbuthnot told him the little we knew, which was not much more than a man could see for himself.

"You reckon it was done with blood, sir?"

"I fancy so. I might have thought it a kind of joke if it hadn't been for the cry we heard in the night."

Thereupon he added an account of what I have already described.

"Well, sir, it's a funny business, and, if you don't mind, I'll get on the 'phone and ask the sergeant to come along. I suppose there's no one you suspect—no enemies like."

Arbuthnot reassured him on that point and he took down our names and was referred to the bank and to Kaye who, as a solicitor, came in very useful, if he wished to prove our bona fides. Then he went, with the air of a man who had found nothing so interesting since the Armistice.

Ten minutes after, when we were ready to go out, Mrs. Jerrold reappeared.

"Mrs. Bessom's in the kitchen," she said, "asking if 'tis true we've had the police in, as she saw him go up the road."

"Mrs. Bessom?" queried Arbuthnot.

"Yes, sir. She lives in the next cottage a little way up the road—and she's lost her lodger."

"Indeed," I said. "Does she expect us to get her another?"

"No, sir, he's not given notice—he's just gone, leaving all his things and owin' her two pounds nine and fourpence."

Arbuthnot took charge of the conversation.

"Bring her into the next room," he said, glancing at the window, "and we'll see if we can help her."

Mrs. Bessom, large, florid, and heavy-featured, was also voluble, apologetic, and evidently vastly gratified at being the centre of a small sensation.

"There, sir, it's very kind of you to take notice of my troubles. Had him three months, I had—came last August —and never a bit of trouble, and now here he goes off without as much as a word." She threatened to become tearful.

"Perhaps we could get at things easier if you answered a few questions," said Arbuthnot. "What was his name?"

"Mr. Percival Hunt, and I never—"

"His age?"

"He was youngish. May have been twenty-four or five."

"What was his occupation?"

"When he come he said, 'There I've gone an' failed my medical examinations, and all through them night clubs in London, and now my only hope is to work 'ere where I can't dissipate'; and he had rows and rows of medical books; some of 'em fair made me blush, old woman or not."

"What were his habits?"

"Reg'lar as clockwork. Study all day, and then a walk last thing at night. He had his own door-key."

"When did you see him last?"

"When I cleared away supper last night, about nine he was sayin' to his brother, 'Well, I going to have one more try', meaning, like as not, the examination, and I went out and shut the door and washed up and off to bed and never set eyes on him since."

"His brother?"

"Yes, his brother came over from Colchester last evening: come by car, and I couldn't help thinkin', 'You'll 'ave a job, my lad, getting home in the fog'."

"Ever seen the brother before?"

"Once before he came. About a month ago."

"Were the brothers on good terms?"

"As far as I know, sir, very good terms."

"Had Mr. Hunt used his bed?"

"No, sir, there it was just as I'd made it. It fair gave me a turn when I took in his shaving-water."

"You don't know what time the brother left?"

"I don't sir, but it must have been later than ten o'clock. That big car is so quiet that it'd take twice that noise to wake me when I'm properly off."

"Has Mr. Hunt left all his belongings?"

"Every stitch, sir. Heaps of shirts, and three or four suits, and books and pipes and everything."

"H'm. Well, Mrs. Bessom, we may be worrying for nothing, but I advise you to mention the matter to the police. If Mr. Hunt was foolish enough to have taken a walk in the fog last night he may have met with a mishap. You have no address to communicate with his relatives?"

"No, sir."

"Well, if necessary, they might be advertised for. But, first of all, see the constable. If a search-party is organized, my friend and I will be pleased to join it. By the way, describe Mr. Hunt."

"Tall, sir, he was—taller than you—and had fair, straight hair and almost blue eyes and a bit of a moustache, and all across his left hand was a big scar where he said he had spilt acid when he was a student."

"I see. And the brother?"

"He was darker, and not as tall as the other and no moustache. I can't say I ever took great stock of him, only seein' him twice."

Mrs. Bessom departed in search of Constable Jones, who was indeed having a red-letter day, and Mrs. Jerrold brought in the post, as she termed it, consisting of one letter. It was, of course, the one which had driven us out from our cheerful fireside. Under a fresh cover and re-directed by Kaye, it now leered at us from the table as if conscious of the imbroglio into which it had driven us.

"No harm to read it now," said Arbuthnot, and he scanned it, and passed it to me without comment. It read thus:

> "My Dear Arbuthnot,
>
> "I promised to write this to intercede for Creen. He tells me he sought your assistance in vain. I've no great use for him, but from what he told me (I am not at liberty to divulge what it was) he is in sore trouble, and if you can reconsider your decision you'll be doing the fellow a good turn. He says, rightly as I think, that you are the only person likely to be of any use to him.
>
> "Yours sincerely,
>
> "R.G.H."

"Now, King," said my friend, "do we shake the dust of this alarming place from our feet and return to the assistance of Sir Baxter Creen, thereby adding a trifle of ten thousand pounds to that Fund which once gave you such an unpleasant half-hour,[1] or do we remain here, looking for trouble in these God-forsaken marshes?"

"Honestly, what do you make of the business here, Arbuthnot?"

"To my mind it may be as bad a business as a man might well care to tackle."

"Then we'll stay."

---

[1] An allusion to the remarkable events, chronicled elsewhere, connected with "The Helpers of Humanity."

Probably Arbuthnot had already made up his mind, but I am always glad to think now that I threw my influence, such as it was, on the right side.

"You have said it. Now for our postponed botanical excursion."

The weather was still cold and the sky leaden when we went out. It was an easy matter to pass through the by-no-means complete hedge of our garden into the rough grassland beyond. I looked behind me, and the only conspicuous objects were the gaunt chimneys of some largish house surrounded by trees. This I judged to be the residence of our unprepossessing acquaintance, the Colonel. Before us all was bare and desolate; the long, coarse grass was brown and frost-bound and rustled to our steps; above our heads some birds were calling dismally as though oppressed by oncoming winter. As we came to a lower level, 'withered sedge', such as the poet sings of, replaced the grass and we could see the creek lying between its low banks.

"It needs a couple of hours to high tide," said Arbuthnot. "You remember that whatever happened last night did so when the creek was full. We will therefore first study the ground round about high-water mark."

"Arbuthnot," I said abruptly, "this affair will get on my nerves. One feels so hopelessly in the dark. Have you formed any conclusions?"

"None. For the present I am content to assimilate any information that comes along and be grateful. Here we are working with little hope. The frozen ground will show no footprints. Hullo!" He pointed to a place where the sedge seemed to have been disturbed and flattened.

"This may mean something, or it may have been done by an animal."

We searched carefully, but there could be no footprints, and we could find no bloodstains.

"Let us make assumptions," said he. "Supposing a man were done to death on the marsh last night, and *supposing* that man were no other than the missing Hunt, we should work backwards towards Mrs. Bessom's cottage, which we see yonder—that is, in the direction from which presumably he came."

I think we saw the scrap of paper simultaneously, but Arbuthnot was the one to pick it out from the clump of sedge.

"Walk on," said he. "You're a botanist. What do you want with scraps of paper? In this open space a dozen eyes may be noting our every movement."

A few steps later on he stopped, and under pretence of blowing his nose, opened the scrap of paper (it was folded in four), inside his handkerchief, glanced at it, raised his eyebrows, and then thrust the paper into a waistcoat pocket.

"Anything?" I questioned.

"I'll show you presently."

As he spoke a curious thing happened. Something metallic rang under my foot. I paused and glanced down, unsuspectingly, and picked up a little box of dull metal.

"Into your pocket, man!" rasped Arbuthnot as I gazed at it in surprise. "Let's get back to the cottage now as quickly as possible, or we'll be finding too much for our own future comfort." He laughed grimly.

Back in the house we found that Mrs. Jerrold had lighted a fire in another room, because, as she put it, "that three do get on anyone's nerves—I can't bear to go in the room". I found myself in silent but hearty agreement with her.

When the door closed after her, Arbuthnot drew the scrap of folded paper from his pocket and passed it to me without a word. I opened it, much as one opens some telegram that must bring good tidings or bad, and stared at it in amazement. Scrawled across the middle was the one sentence, in pencil:

Grierson has gone to Port Said.

"There's a clue for you, King," said Arbuthnot with a dry laugh.

"But—" I stammered. "Do you think this has any connexion with the other matter? Things are rapidly becoming bewildering."

"Well, can you imagine any normal circumstances under which that curious message could have been dropped in the middle of a lonely Essex marsh? Now, let's see your box."

I produced it. It was unusual in appearance, being about an inch square by an inch and a half deep, and composed of some metal that was very likely steel, darkened as rifle barrels are darkened. Arbuthnot shook it without result. However, there was a keyhole, and Arbuthnot, obtaining a hairpin from Mrs. Jerrold on the pretence of a choked pipe, set to work. He is generally very clever with locks, but this one baffled him, and he laid the box down at last with the remark "Whatever may be in there, the owner was extremely anxious to preserve it from prying eyes."

"A valuable jewel," I suggested.

"Possibly. I must take it to London, where I know a man capable of opening it without damage to the contents, whatever they may be."

We had no chance for further speculation, and barely time to shuffle our finds out of sight, for Mrs. Jerrold entered to say that the police had returned in force. They certainly had, for our friend Jones had faded into the background behind an inspector and a sergeant.

"Very glad you've come," said Arbuthnot frankly. "This is an annoying business to two fellows hoping for a peaceful holiday."

"Quite so. It's a peculiar affair. There may be nothing in it at all, but it seems worth looking into," said the inspector. "We have seen Mrs. Bessom, and heard Constable Jones's report. Is there anything to add to your statement?"

"Nothing, I fear."

"Very well, then we will deal with this thumb-mark. We shall get a wire by to-morrow telling us whether it belongs to anyone already known to the police. If it does, and the person Hunt has not reappeared, we shall proceed to take steps. I am leaving Sergeant Wigmore, who, with Constable Jones, will organize a search-party for the missing man."

After dealing with the thumb-mark and granting permission for the elimination of that abominable three from our window, the party went on to survey the marsh. We watched them prowling about for some time, but eventually they went away, apparently unsuccessful.

"Wouldn't it have been more consistent with your previous actions to have handed over our finds to the police?" I asked.

"Not if my theory is correct. The circumstances are by no means identical in nature."

"Then you have a theory?"

"I have a strong suspicion that it must be lunch-time."

So I had to hold back my inquiries and turn my attention to rump-steak, brussels sprouts, and potatoes.

"I must reopen my letter to Kaye," said Arbuthnot, "and ask him to circularize the universities respecting a student named Percival Hunt who failed his final medical degrees this year. If he existed he should be easily traceable. There is only one outgoing mail from here—it goes at four—so we will go as far as the village post office first, and then offer our services to the search-party."

On our way back from the post office we encountered the police sergeant and were warned to assemble with the other searchers at Mrs. Bessom's cottage. Quite a considerable party had been got together. Besides ourselves, the sergeant, and the constable, there were also the curate, the schoolmaster, who must have dismissed his charges early, four boy scouts, and three men of the village who probably belonged to yacht crews in the summer and were paid off for the winter. Hands for yachts are largely recruited from that part of Essex.

The sergeant, who seemed to have his wits about him, divided us into two parties—one to work eastwards and the other westwards, both parties keeping in touch with the creek to inquire if any boats, by which the creek could have been crossed, were missing. I found myself in the party going eastwards, my companions being the constable, the schoolmaster, a companionable fellow who had had the sense to bring a map and an electric torch, two scouts, and one of the villagers. After some delay a hurricane lantern was added to our equipment.

Unfortunately our setting out was marred by a piece of ill-luck. As we filed down the cobbled path from the cottage to the gate, Arbuthnot slipped on one of the smooth, rounded stones and came heavily down.

"My ankle," he said as we raised him up. "Not broken, I think; only a sprain, but I'm afraid it's put me out of court for this little jaunt." We half-helped and half-carried him back to the cottage, where Mrs. Bessom received him with the air of one nerved by disaster to cope with anything.

"I'm sorry about your friend," said the sergeant, as we parted at the gate to go our several ways, "but, anyway, by the look of him, I don't think he was the sort likely to be of much use on a job like this."

I concurred heartily.

Of that search I don't propose to say much. It was at the back of my mind that the most we could hope to find was a corpse, and I had had my fill of sensations for a while. Evening crept on, dull and colourless, and it was colder than ever. We poked in ditches, slipped on frozen pools, interviewed boat-owners who all proved that Mr. Hunt had had nothing to do with them or their boats, and found ourselves at nightfall more than four miles from Leasinghoe.

"That place over there," said the schoolmaster, pointing to what appeared in the dim light to be a collection of buildings enclosed by a high wall, "was a munition factory once, but is now disused. It's four and a half miles from the village, and I propose we go no farther. It'll be a hopeless business by night, for we've nothing definite to go on."

The adults of the party agreed, and the scouts reluctantly acquiesced, so we turned back in the gloom and were glad to see Mrs. Bessom's cottage again. The sergeant's party had returned before us and had equally drawn a blank.

"Your friend's gone, sir," said Mrs. Bessom to me. "George Higgins chanced to come along about an hour ago and helped him home."

I turned my footsteps towards Desolation Cottage, and there I found Arbuthnot, one foot laid on a chair before the fire, a pot of tea and smoking implements by his elbow, and a mocking grin perceptible beneath those egregious moustaches.

"Any luck?" asked he.

"None whatever. How's your foot?"

"Never better."

Mrs. Jerrold entered with welcome provisions.

"Is your foot any easier, sir?" she asked solicitously.

"Well, the pain's a little less, and there's no swelling to speak of, but I'm afraid of a serious lesion of the tendon Achilles."

I stared. "What's all that about?" I demanded, when she had gone.

"I've no idea. But it sounded well. And, anyway, I've spent most of the afternoon studying medical text-books."

"The deuce you have! But it was a nasty slip."

"In my line of business one can't afford to make slips."

I stared again, and his grin broadened. Then I began to smile also.

"Consider, King," said he, "what an appalling waste of time it would have been for me to looking for what I was sure wasn't there. But it would have been most ungracious for me to have refused point-blank to have joined the party, although I believe one of our friends did."

"Indeed?"

"The worthy Colonel unpolitely consigned the sergeant to blazes, the latter tells me, when he was approached to join the party. Neither would he let his bulldog attend."

"I'm not surprised. But what have you been doing in my absence?"

"I fancied an uninterrupted inspection of the abode of the missing Hunt. Mrs. Bessom made me quite comfortable and I said I preferred to wait till you returned rather than seek other help. But it was boring for me to lie on her sofa with nothing to read but medical lore and the *Eastern Daily Press,* so I troubled her, with a hint of remuneration, to go over to our cottage for a blue-covered book, called *The Fundamental Inconsistency of the Pre-Raphaelites.*

"Did she find it?"

"No, but she afforded me a valuable half-hour while she and Mrs. Jerrold looked for it. I was grieved to have to tell Mrs. Jerrold afterwards that, after all, I had left it locked in my case. And there, I fear, it must continue to conceal its non-existence for the remainder of our stay."

3

In Which Arbuthnot Receives Marching Orders

Later on that evening, when the ham and eggs had been consumed in equal partnership and pipes were alight, I found Arbuthnot disposed to talk.

"One minor detail I have cleared up," said he. "Unimportant, except that no investigator likes to leave loose ends. I had been puzzled as to why Mrs. Jerrold never noticed the car that must have been standing by the other cottage when she went home last night. Had she seen it she would surely have mentioned it this morning. But I saw to-day that there is a side-turning next to that cottage and there, no doubt, the car was parked."

"What did you find out this afternoon?" I asked, for I had the feeling that I should welcome even a little light on what was about equally baffling and sinister.

"I found numerous medical text-books. Guess in what condition?"

"With leaves uncut?" I suggested.

"I don't blame you for saying so. It crossed my own mind. But these, on the contrary, were well-used, with marginal notes frequent."

"Then the man was studying?"

"Had studied. I don't know much about medicine, but I guess that many of those books were far more advanced than the cram-books likely to be used by a man sitting for an ordinary medical degree. Our friend Hunt must have been *amazingly* unfortunate to have failed in his examination. I took a page from a book for the sake of the handwriting contained in the margins."

"Anything else?"

"I looked for letters or other documents lying about. There were none. I even ventured upstairs and looked for marks on his underclothing. There were none. His trunks, also, like ours, were innocent of initials, and were lying unlocked."

"I suppose his writing does not resemble that on the message we found in the marsh?"

"No such luck."

"Then you drew almost a complete blank."

"Almost, although there is such a thing as negative evidence."

There was a silence while he refilled his pipe.

"Coincidence is the curse of criminals and criminologists alike," he said at last.

"Meaning?"

"That I found something to which I absolutely dare not attach any significance. How many people called Grierson do you suppose live in this country?"

"Probably hundreds. It's a good old name. For all I know there may be Griersons in the peerage, and others working in the London Docks."

"Precisely. Now I took up one book in which the reader had marked his place by a scrap of paper torn from a newspaper and roughly folded, and I had the curiosity to look at the paper. Here it is." He drew it from his pocket-book as he spoke and passed it to me, and this is what I read:

"Heir to English Peer
    "His many friends will be delighted to congratulate Lord Alresford, of Alresford Abbey,

Hampshire, on the birth of a son and heir to the peerage, which dates from George the First. Lord Alresford, it may be remembered, married, rather late in life, Miss Mabel Decker, daughter of the late Mr. Jabez P. Decker, of Cincinnati.

"The heir apparent for some years had been Lord Alresford's nephew, Mr. Walter Grierson, who was noted as a hockey player at his University, and also achieved distinction by taking a First in the Oriental Languages Tripos. He is at present believed to be game-shooting in Rhodesia.

"Both Lady Alresford and her infant son are reported to be making satisfactory progress."

"Torn from the *Morning Post,*" said Arbuthnot, as I sat pondering.

"Yes, it's an easy thing to do. I've often torn off the corner of *The Times* to serve as a bookmark."

"A corner?"

"Yes."

"But this isn't a corner. You can see that by the fragments left of the adjacent columns."

"My God, you're right, Arbuthnot!" I cried. "There's something in this."

"Maybe. It's work for Kaye, anyway, ascertaining the present whereabouts of Mr. Walter Grierson. He is quite capable of dealing with it, for I don't fancy leaving this quiet little place for a few days yet. It may be very important to know the date of that extract. And now, King, you are obviously dying to hear what I think of the business, so fire away with your questions."

I didn't hesitate to avail myself of this offer, for I had the feelings of one in a dark room, who can see nothing, but who cannot put out his hand in any direction without touching something that in the darkness feels unusual and out of place.

"What do you suppose became of Hunt?"

"In my opinion Hunt went out with the tide, and I think he was dead before he started on that journey. I am sending, through Kaye, a message to a friend at Scotland Yard, who will arrange for a watch to be kept on the coast from here southwards in case the body appears."

"Why only southwards?"

"Because the tidal currents on the East Coast set southwards."

"But I thought a dead body sank at first?"

"In still water it does, but remember there's a strong tidal ebb in these creeks, probably sufficient to sweep it along."

"Now what of that ghastly figure?"

"Two things; if Hunt was number three, there have been presumably also numbers one and two, and failing our intervention there will be also a number four at least. I take the number to be a threat, as well as a gruesome mark of triumph. Secondly, the figure was put there in the fog."

"Ye-es. Well, what of the thumb-mark?"

"The significance of the thumb-mark was in its conspicuousness. I expect to hear more about that thumbmark to-morrow."

"Have you any theory about the business as a whole?"

"My dear King, if I could already fit an explanation to those facts I should be a clairvoyant, not a criminologist!"

"I expect the clue we want is hidden in that box. Suppose Hunt was a doctor who had done something disreputable, and been struck off the register. He may have robbed his accomplices of the proceeds of some theft. They track him down and kill him, but in the struggle the box is dropped in the marsh, where it might have lain unseen for ever, but for chance."

"Splendid! And meanwhile the unsuspecting Grierson placidly continues his trip to the East."

I could see that he was laughing at me.

"I'd forgotten Grierson," I admitted. "What strikes you about that message?"

"The shortness of it."

I suppose the shortness must have extended to my temper at this remark, for I got up and went off to bed, postponing further questions.

"Remember, Ishmael," said Arbuthnot, as I went out of the door.

"What about him?" I asked unguardedly.

"He was disinherited, and became a wanderer," said my friend dryly.

We had barely completed breakfast the next morning, when Mrs. Jerrold intimated that Mrs. Bessom was in the kitchen and would like to interview us.

"Let her come in," said Arbuthnot. "Well, have you found your lodger?" he continued, when the good lady had been ushered in.

"No, sir, I'll never see him again. 'Twasn't for nothin' a white owl was in that tree opposite my cottage last night, and though I'm a Londoner born and bred, I know what's what—he'll never come back, poor young feller. But, as you told me yesterday, it's only right to advertise for his folks, and 'twould be a great kindness if you'd tell me what to put."

"But surely the curate or the schoolmaster, or perhaps Colonel Gregory, would be more suitable persons to ask, as residents here?"

"No, sir. I'm a Wesleyan, I am, and the schoolmaster he don't like me since I called him a blooming upstart; and as for the Colonel, wild donkeys wouldn't drag me near his door."

"Dear, dear." Arbuthnot took a sheet of paper and wrote. "Will this do?" He read out:

> "PERCIVAL HUNT. Will this gentleman, or any person knowing his whereabouts, please communicate with Mrs. Bessom, Rose Cottage, Leasinghoe, Essex. Failing a reply, articles left by him at this address on the 14th inst., will be disposed of to meet expenses already incurred."

"That's fine, Mr. Ponsonby," said Mrs. Bessom approving. "Now what shall I do with it?"

"If you like, leave it to me. I will have it inserted in the 'Personal' column of two London papers, and you can pay me when the goods are sold. If you get any replies you might show them to me, as swindlers often reply to such advertisements."

"Thank you, sir. I will. Poor young feller." She left in her usual state of impending tearfulness.

"Now for my letter to Kaye," said Arbuthnot. "It must go, albeit I have to limp to the post office. Item, Mr. Grierson; item, is there any doctor on the register named Percival Hunt; item, to arrange for a search along the coast."

He had just finished writing when Mrs. Jerrold brought us a letter. Arbuthnot removed the outer cover with its typewritten address and dealt with the enclosure.

"Hullo!" said he, and an expression as near annoyance as he ever permitted himself flitted across his face.

"This is distinctly annoying," he continued. "Here we are involved in a matter which, to the callous mind of the investigator, has singular and abundant merits, and now I am bidden to transport myself to the other end of England to look for a fool who's lost himself."

"Let him remain lost," I suggested. "Surely this case is important enough to justify your remaining here."

"Amply. But this is Hemingway writing again. You'd better read what he says."

He tossed the letter to me, and philosophically turned to his pipe. This is what I read:

"My Dear Arbuthnot,

"I wrote to you yesterday on behalf of Baxter Creen, but on calling at your flat to-day over another business I found you had previously disappeared into the unknown. Of course, I realize that this means you have matters of moment in hand, but I think on reading this you will consider my difficulty transcends in importance whatever else you may be undertaking at present.

"To be brief, you are probably aware that a strike of tin-plate workers threatens in South Wales. It is touch and go whether the men come out or not on the 19th, and a strike at this moment, when industry is already staggering under repeated blows, would be a disaster of the first magnitude.

"At this critical juncture, Herbert Turnbull, a well-known member of the I.L.P., left Sheffield, on the 13th, to conduct a propagandist tour among the tin-plate workers. He was to address a meeting at Birmingham on the night of the 13th en route to Cardiff. When the train reached Birmingham he had vanished, and up to the time of writing (noon 14th) remains undiscovered.

"He was not expected to exert his influence on the side of peace, but you will see that such an occurrence is going to set up far more bad feeling than the most incendiary of speeches could have done, for Labour circles will be only too prone to regard the abduction (if it was one) as a challenge,

"I may say that the more active patriotic associations, one and all, have given me their assurance of non-complicity in the affair.

"The police are exerting their utmost efforts to find Turnbull, but I am anxious to leave no stone unturned, and therefore urgently request your assistance. The enclosed card will make you right with any official investigators you may meet in your search. If you find him telegraph me the code word 'Silver' at once.

"Yours, etc.,

"R.G.H."

"I fear I must go, King," said Arbuthnot, when I passed the letter back to him. "After all, Percival Hunt is almost certainly dead, while Herbert Turnbull is almost as certainly alive, and therefore, politics apart, has the prior claim. But I leave this place with the utmost reluctance."

"For my part," said I, "when you are gone I shall remain in it with the utmost reluctance."

"Well, well, you must be careful not to risk the night air. If anything comes from Kaye, open it and read it, and lock it up till I return. If Turnbull is not found, and the strike is called on the 19th I shall be back on the 20th."

Hired conveyances were not to be found, and Arbuthnot, still limping realistically, was taken to the station about noon by the schoolmaster, who fortunately possessed a motor-bicycle and sidecar. I returned into Desolation Cottage to face my solitary lunch. With Arbuthnot went the message we found in the marsh and the mysterious box.

That afternoon was a lonely one for me. I missed the steady grey eyes, the calm voice, and the air of assurance that marked my friend. Left to myself, the events that had intrigued us assumed their most horrible aspect. I was fascinated by the figure four. Arbuthnot absent, I saw myself as the possible fourth victim, though how a vendetta should have sprung up against us in this remote Essex village passed my comprehension. Were we, by any chance, dealing with the deeds of some curious homicidal maniac? Claustrophobia assailed me, and I put on my hat and coat and walked out again towards the marshes, where in all probability some horrible fate had come, with the suddenness of a thief in the night, upon the wretched Hunt, so that he shrieked once, and no more.

The cold was not so intense, but the skies were grey, and an air of indescribable loneliness hung over everything. I turned my footsteps idly towards a small, disused landing-stage that I had noticed during the course of our search the previous day. It was old, and here and there timbers were missing. A length of ancient rope drooped forlornly from the end. Cautiously I advanced upon the creaking planks. The tide was not far from the turn, and I judged that at high water the stage would be almost awash. In front of me the grey waters lapped against the banks, and I wondered what their turbid depths might conceal.

It is a power that I share with many people—the ability to sense the presence of some person unseen. The feeling came upon me then and I swung, round. There, at the landward end of the little pier stood a man, regarding me. A second glance was hardly necessary to tell me that it was no other than the Colonel's unpleasant servant. He must have followed me across the marsh, and drawn nearer while I stood watching the water.

Honestly, I didn't like the look of the fellow. I remembered Arbuthnot had said he had probably been a professional boxer. No doubt he was out of condition, and I was not entirely unacquainted with the gloves, but the odds, I knew well enough, are always on the side of the professional man. My alarm may appear exaggerated, but the sequence recent events was a disturbing factor in the judgment of any situation.

"Come off there," he growled, when he saw I had noticed him. He spoke with a Cockney accent which I will not attempt to reproduce.

"Don't you know that that there place is private property?" he continued. "Just because you rent a cottage you think you've bought the whole of Essex. That's the worst of you damned foreigners, and you needn't think folks about here will stand it."

Now it was very obvious that the most irascible of property-owners could have taken no exception to my stepping on to his decrepit and clearly abandoned stage, so I concluded that the man Buller was merely finding an excuse for being quarrelsome. It was none of my business to provoke him, so when I stepped again on firm ground I merely said, "I'm sorry. I wasn't aware it was Colonel Gregory's property. Please give him my apologies for the trespass."

"That's all very well," he grunted, seeing the prospects of enjoyable bickering fade; "but there's mighty funny things been happening since you two coves come here, and if I was you I'd keep myself to myself, and not be found shoving my nose in other folks' business."

The man was detestable, but I judged a dispute should be avoided at all costs, and, besides, I was actually rather startled to find some one linking our arrival with the untoward incidents that had followed so closely upon it, so I went my way without further words. To pass time, it occurred to me that I would walk as far as the village and buy some daily papers. These arrived in Leasinghoe at a late hour of the day, and on the two previous days, occupied with our local troubles, we had not bothered to obtain any.

"Papers," said the damsel in the little shop that combined the post office with multiple other activities, "can't be had as a rule, unless you orders, but it happens I have a *Telegraph* and a *Herald* left on me hands to-day."

I took both. As I expected, both gave prominence to the abduction of the unlucky Turnbull, but I could find no reference in either to the affairs that had stirred our neighbourhood.

The *Telegraph* said:

"We are bound to deplore the mentality of those who engineered the abduction (if abduction it be) of Mr. Turnbull. Loyal citizens, in these days of national uneasiness, are, we are fully aware, continually confronted with immense provocation, but they must remember that, unless, a member of the body politic has so far transgressed as to forfeit the privileges of citizenship, they have no right to interfere; while in the latter case the duty of intervention lies with the representatives of the law. As Bacon wrote three hundred years ago, 'When discords, and quarrels and factions, are carried openly and audaciously it is a sign the reverence of government is lost'."

The *Herald* said:

"In this piece of petty spite, devised by those only too well aware that they are fighting a losing battle against the advance of the workers of this country, we detect the malice of the same sort of mind that foisted the notorious Zinovieff letter[1] on an all too gullible public."

Unfortunately, however, neither paper furnished me with any useful information. The unlucky Turnbull had left Sheffield at 3.15 p.m. on the 13th on a train that stopped at several places en route to Birmingham. A large party had seen him get on; no one apparently had seen him get off. The police of six counties and numerous volunteers were searching for him, and there was talk of using troops as well. That was all.

I tucked the papers under my arm and went on, and not far from the cottage recognized Sergeant Wigmore standing in the road. I greeted him with an inquiry for news. He looked at me uncertainly for a minute, and then said:

"Yes, sir, there is news. It'll be public property in half an hour, so I don't see any harm in telling you."

"Come inside," I suggested. "On a day like this a drop of whisky does no one any harm."

"Thank you, sir, but I'm just waiting about here for Constable Jones to come along."

"Never mind that. I'll tell Mrs. Jerrold to keep an eye on the road, and call him in when he comes along."

With that he acquiesced, and after I had poured out a modicum of stimulant and we had imbibed, he tapped his pocket significantly.

[1] Readers may recollect the affair of the Zinovieff letter in 1924.

"You'll not guess what's in there."

"I've no idea."

"Nothing less than a warrant for the arrest of one Charlie Wills, alias William Buller, at present butler to Colonel Gregory."

"Good heavens! What's the charge?"

"Of being concerned in the disappearance of this man Hunt."

"Clearly the police have been busy."

"Mind you, sir, there's nothing like enough to hang him *yet,* but enough for an arrest on suspicion. You see, it was *his* thumb-mark on your window-sill. They had his impressions at Scotland Yard."

"The devil it was!"

"In earlier days," continued the sergeant, "he was Charlie Wills, a promising young boxer, known generally as the 'Bromley Hacker', but after winning a few fights he went the way of many a better man before him and took to drinking. Then one night, under provocation, he smashed his wife's head in with the kitchen poker and got ten years for manslaughter. He did his time without fuss, and when he came out the Salvation Army got hold of him. He had several jobs he failed to keep before they got him in with the Colonel here, who wasn't particular. Of course he took a fresh name, being well known before."

"Dear, dear," said I.

"And that isn't all. We know that Buller was out of the house that night. Jones, being young, is keeping company with the housemaid at the Grange. She got up that night, being mad with earache, and went down to the kitchen for some olive oil to. pour in, and coming back, what with the pain, and the candle not burning well walked into Buller's bedroom instead of her own, and there was no one there. That was about one in the morning, just at the time you heard that noise."

"Did *she* hear it?"

"Not to notice. The Grange, you see, lies much farther back from the marsh. I expect we shall have to call you respecting that sound, your friend, I understand, having been called away."

I sat silent; the prospect of appearing in court under an alias was not inviting.

"I heard that Buller had been seen down in the marshes this afternoon, so I sent along for Jones, and waited here for him, thinking he'd come back this way. But it looks as if we shall have to go up to the Grange after all."

At that moment the constable appeared, and they went off together, while I sat down to think. I found myself unable to believe that the events of the last two days pertained to a brutal but commonplace murder, carried out presumably for gain. Certainly I had been justified in thinking the man Buller a villain, but was he the greater villain? The question of Grierson puzzled me. He had gone to Port Said, which lies, as every one knows, on the way to India, and the Colonel had spent most of his life in that interesting country. Was the man Buller, by any chance, only the tool of a more sinister scoundrel, carrying out a plot of which we had only so far touched the fringe? Yet if one accepted Buller as the arch-criminal one could take that repulsive figure on our window as a clever blind and the thumb-mark as a particularly unlucky accident for him. But stop. Buller had no brain to evolve anything so fantastic as that gruesome symbol. Had a cleverer brain directed him, so that curiosity might be diverted toward two strangers, *whom hardly anyone in the district knew existed?* So far, as I knew only four people were aware that we had occupied the cottage that night, and of these our useful housekeeper and the man Higgons seemed singularly harmless.

I mentally wished Arbuthnot a speedy return, for however I looked at things I failed to derive anything but discomfort from them. It was no good writing to him, for even if Kaye had an address the chances were that my friend would be back at Leasinghoe before the letter had found him.

I had anticipated a lonely evening, but nevertheless I did not hail with any enthusiasm the appearance of a Press representative. He was of the difficult kind who maintain good manners and thus make it awkward for one to rebuff them. I took the line of telling him all I had told the police, consoled him with whisky, was as reticent as I dared over my own identity; and, with what I considered a commendable stroke of daring, established friendly relations by claiming acquaintance with Falcon, the editor of the *Bulletin,* though I saw it meant writing to Falcon the next day and partly taking him into my confidence. No doubt the "Essex Mystery" would soon be competing with the vanished Turnbull for the public interest.

My dissatisfaction was completed by a visit from none other than the Colonel. He came in hard on the heels of Mrs. Jerrold without waiting to be announced, and I saw at a glance that his mood was far from pleasant.

"Here's a pretty business," he growled. "And as far as I can make out it all began with you pair of busybodies. Are you fool enough to think that poor old Buller had the brains to contrive what he's charged with? It's all damn nonsense."

I resented the man's attitude intensely but I was in no position to demur.

"I'll tell you one thing. I shan't tamely submit to losing my only decent servant in this way. I'm very much inclined to make a few inquiries about you and your friend, who seems to have faded away. If it wasn't for the money, I'd have you out of the cottage straight away. Cry in the night! Probably a cow bellowing."

"But the thumb-mark?" I protested meekly.

"Bah! It may have been there for weeks. I know he cut himself when he was here clearing up after the old girl died. It's all a pack of nonsense, and as for that fool Hunt—well, a man who wanders about in a fog and falls into the creek deserves all he gets."

With that he left me, and I finished the day in no enviable frame of mind, for clearly if the Colonel cared he could make things distinctly awkward for us.

4
In Which I Crawl on a Public-House Floor

I find that my hasty notes for the next two days, the 17th and 18th, refer to a variety of matters. I was extremely anxious to miss nothing that could be of use to Arbuthnot on his return. I wish I could say, however, that what transpired in those eventful forty-eight hours served to throw light on what had gone before. Instead of this, fresh occurrences only intensified the mystery in which everything was wrapped.

My first visitor on the morning of the 17th was Mrs. Bessom, who arrived in a state of high excitement, having, I suppose, come to regard me, in the absence of Arbuthnot, as her natural confidant.

"They broadcasted for him last night," she announced. "George Higgins happened to be in the bar of the 'Three Kings' at Wivenhoe, where they've got the wireless, and heard all about it."

"That was a good idea," I said, feeling that Arbuthnot had found time to do a little useful work in London on his way north.

"It was that. And what d'ye think? His sister's a-coming to-day. Telegram only came ten minutes ago."

She produced the document in question from the pocket of her apron and passed it to me. I read:

"Deeply distressed at news of brother. Coming down early as possible. Arriving about twelve. Geraldine Hunt."

Then I returned the telegram to Mrs. Bessom without a word and stood pondering. The man Hunt had seemed so far such a mystery that it was a kind of shock to discover that he had at least one flesh-and-blood relative.

"What I makes so bold to ask is," went on Mrs. Bessom, "will you kindly come in while I'm a-seeing the lady? I feels sort of nervous like alone."

"I'll be pleased to come," said I; "but wouldn't it be advisable to call in a member of the police force? They will certainly be very anxious to get into touch with any of Mr. Hunt's relatives."

"Well, see the police she will certainly have to, but as my poor husband said, 'Police is police, and very good in their place, but the less you have to do with them the better', so, if you don't mind, we might see her to settle my little affairs like and she could see the police after."

I thought it advisable to agree. I imagined that Mrs. Bessom had hopes of a generous pecuniary settlement, and did not desire to carry out the transaction under official eyes. I promised to visit Rose Cottage about twelve.

"George Higgins," said Mrs. Bessom as she left, "has promised to be at the station to show her along."

The next item I find noted is the arrival of a letter from Kaye, confirming our opinion that the writing on our window had been executed in blood. He also stated that he had communicated with all the universities in the British Isles respecting Hunt and was awaiting their replies, but as we were now in touch with a relative this seemed to me no longer of any importance.

I pass on to the arrival of Miss Hunt. I presented myself at Rose Cottage in good time, but had been there no more than a few minutes when a large touring car drove up to the door, and a liveried chauffeur assisted a young lady to alight.

"There!" said Mrs. Bessom, evidently favourably impressed. "She's all in black—veil, gloves, and all," and the good lady hastened to admit her visitor, while I mentally commiserated with the unfortunate George on his useless tramp to the station.

"This is Mr. Monk," said Mrs. Bessom, ushering in her caller. "He and his friend now gone away have been most 'bligin to me in my troubles."

Miss Hunt bowed, in my direction. She was a tall and generously-proportioned girl, but I could only see her features very indistinctly through the thick, black veil she wore. When she spoke her voice was low-pitched and full, and her words were uttered with decision.

"I heard the broadcast report last night when it was then too late to leave London. Besides, my mother was too alarmed to be left alone immediately. She and I are Percival's only near surviving relations. So I came away first thing this morning."

"Deary me," began Mrs. Bessom. "Now let me explain—"

"I don't think you can tell me anything," the girl intervened. "I've had a terrible time reading the morning papers as I came along in the car. My visit is only to arrange my poor brother's affairs here, and I must return as swiftly as possible to my mother, who will be prostrated when she sees this morning's news."

I thought it only fair to support her in her desire to be brief, but added a remark on the desirability of getting into touch with the police.

"I'm afraid it's more than I can face at present. I shall tell the family solicitor when I get back to town to supply them with any information they may require."

She opened a bag she carried and withdrew a photograph which she passed to Mrs. Bessom.

"There!" said the latter. "The very image of him, poor young feller."

I was permitted to look, and saw a healthy-looking young man, evidently fair, and with good features and a pleasant smile. Across the corner of the photograph was written, "Yours, Percival".

"I should like to look over his things," said Miss Hunt, "in case there is anything of family importance."

I took the opportunity of making my departure, well knowing Mrs. Bessom could be relied on to tell me later what occurred subsequently, and indeed it was within half an hour when that lady appeared, alternately tearful and triumphant.

"Yes, she's gone, poor young thing. Between ourselves, sir, she gave me a five-pound note and wouldn't hear of any change—said I must have had a worrying time. She went through all Mr. Hunt's things, and said there was nothing of any importance, but would I send them to her carriage forward, but not to send for a fortnight because her mother would be so upset at seeing them. And not to mention she'd been down because it was a case and the police might think she was interfering."

"Did she leave an address?"

Mrs. Bessom fished in her commodious apron pocket and brought out a slip of paper.

"14, Queen Anne's Mansions, S.W. 1," she read out.

I mentally made a note of the address, and Mrs. Jerrold fortunately appearing with lunch, I was left alone. I wished I had heard more of the unfortunate Hunt, but I reflected that if Arbuthnot wished to investigate in that direction he had only to apply to the address which I noted in my pocket-book as a precaution. On second thoughts I also sent the address in a note to Kaye, in case Arbuthnot on returning to town might see Kaye and thus have a chance of interviewing Miss Hunt if he wished to.

That same pocket-book tells me, though my memory of these occurrences hardly needs stimulating yet, that Sergeant Wigmore called on me that afternoon.

I hastened to make him at home.

"Shall want you to-morrow, sir, at Colchester, at twelve o' clock," said he.

"Wills, alias Buller, was brought up and formally charged this morning, and the police asked for a remand for twenty-four hours."

"Indeed! Why was that?"

"Well, sir, the difficulty is about the body. We're 'oping for it to turn up. It's very awkward to charge a man with murder when there's no corpse. If we did so, and then the supposed deceased was found alive and well and rampaging around the West End of London, the police would be a laughing-stock."

"No fresh evidence, I suppose?"

"Mrs. Bessom has deposed that the alleged victim was in the habit of carrying a considerable sum of money on his person in notes, and, as no money was found among his belongings when we searched them yesterday, it is possible the money was on him at the time."

"Motive, eh?"

"Quite so, sir. Apart from that we can assign no reason for the supposed crime."

He mentioned that a bus had been arranged to take the witnesses to Colchester and that I was to be at the village post office by 10.45 if I wished to travel on it.

My day finished, as far as interest was concerned, with a perusal of the daily papers. I had paid for a telegram to London the previous evening in order to ensure getting a supply of papers. I found Mrs. Bessom's advertisement in *The Times* and *Telegraph*. All the papers gave prominence to the 'Essex Mystery', and I was rather relieved to see myself described as Silas G. Munt, an American professor. They had no fresh information, and I was losing interest, when the sight of the front page of the *Bulletin* reminded me that I had yet to put myself right with Falcon. This meant a hasty rush to the post office with a discreetly worded missive, and I was then free to devote the rest of my time to wondering what sort of figure I should cut in the police court the next day.

On the morning of the 18th I preferred a seat in the bus to a lonely journey to Colchester, and at 10.45 found myself in the company of Mrs. Bessom, Constable Jones, and a half-hysterical housemaid from the Grange.

"Colonel gave her notice when he heard she was a witness. Called her a damned busybody, and she up and said she was going then and there," the constable informed me. "Not that we minds," added he. "She'll go to her mother till such time as we're tied up."

"I don't blame her," said I. "The Colonel seems unable to take a reasonable view of anything."

"True," said Jones. "He wouldn't mind if a murderer went free, so long as there was some one to hand him his drinks regular."

It was a cold journey and the court, when we reached it, proved to be colder still. It was uncomfortably crowded and the Press were very much in evidence. I was glad to encounter Sergeant Wigmore, who seemed like a friend amongst so many unfamiliar faces.

"No luck," he whispered to me, "and there's no chance of the magistrate committing him for trial on the present evidence. We shall ask for another remand. I hear that Colonel Gregory has sent his solicitor to assist Buller."

He pointed across the court to a lean, youngish fellow with cold, fish-like eyes, and I wondered how I might fare at his hands if he chose to be aggressive.

Buller, when he appeared, looked his usual truculent self, and catching sight of me, sent me an evil grin, as if hinting that he would yet find his opportunity to pay me back for interfering.

Sergeant Wigmore gave formal evidence of arrest.

"Did the accused person make a statement?" asked the magistrate, who was, to all appearance, the one person in the court who felt no interest in the case.

"Your worship, he only said, 'You're a lot of bloody fools,'" the sergeant replied, and the prisoner laughed.

The inspector of police testified to being shown the thumb-mark, that Scotland Yard had declared the thumb-mark to belong to Charlie Wills, and that witnesses could be called to prove that the accused was actually Charlie Wills.

"I *am* Charlie Wills," said the prisoner genially. "That ain't a crime, is it?"

That hastened matters, and Mrs. Bessom was put up, perspiring in spite of the low temperature of the room, and making great play with a handkerchief. Nevertheless she told her story fairly well, without bringing to light anything

I have not already recounted, and the defending solicitor limited his questions to the facts relating to Hunt's brother.

"So you can't swear what time his brother left?"

"No, sir; but it must have been after ten."

"I suggest there was nothing to prevent his having remained to a very late hour?"

"Nothing, sir."

"Had you ever seen him before that evening?"

"He came once before—about a month ago."

"Did you ever hear quarrelling between them?"

"Never, sir."

"Has this brother communicated with you since the man Hunt was reported missing?"

"No, sir."

The housemaid at the Grange was the next witness. Her story was a simple one, and after the magistrate had restrained Colonel Gregory's solicitor from suggesting that she had gone to Buller's room with an immoral motive, she was allowed to stand down.

Thus it came to my turn, and it was not till then I realized that I was faced with the necessity for committing perjury. However, there was nothing else for it, and, with an inward shrinking from what might be the pains and penalties attaching, I gave my assumed name, and blundered through my story. Then the defending solicitor rose, and it was obvious that he regarded me as a person to whose relation no possible importance could be attached.

"You consider this cry came from a human being?"

"Yes."

"Might it have been a cow calling after her calf?"

"If you think a cow would have been there on a frosty night in November."

"Can you swear that the thumb-mark was not there the previous evening?"

"Of course. I can't, but it looked fresh."

"Can you suggest any reason why anyone should wish to make marks on your window?"

"I can't."

"Had you ever seen the accused before?"

"Once only, when he admitted my friend and myself to Colonel Gregory's house the evening of our arrival."

"Where is your friend now?"

"In London, on business. He expects to return on the 20th."

"Did you ever see the person Hunt?"

"Never."

"And you know nothing about him?"

"Nothing."

That closed my cross-examination and I sat down, thankful for having come out unscathed.

"Your worship," said the defending solicitor, "I propose to put my client in the witness box."

So Buller was put up and kissed the book, and told a most plausible tale. He had stayed up late the night in question, and just as he was going to bed he had thought he heard a noise outside the house, so he had gone the rounds, and that, no doubt, was when the servant found the kitchen empty and his bedroom unoccupied. As for the thumb-mark, he had been at the cottage cleaning windows and so forth and remembered scratching his hand badly on a nail. That was about a week before the cottage had been let. He had had a clean record since he had been released from prison, and it was hard on a man trying to go straight to be pulled up about nothing.

The spectators, who had come expecting fresh dramatic revelations, were beginning to show signs of failing interest, and I shared the feeling with them, for ever since Mrs. Bessom had given her evidence I had been puzzled at the back of my mind over some inconsistency in what I knew. It was like realizing that some calculation was wrong, and yet being unable to spot the error. It is so easy to miss the obvious when one is living in a case, instead of being a cool and detached looker-on.

At the end the police asked for a remand for a week, upon which solicitor for the defence intimated he would expect his client to be granted bail. It is somewhat unusual for bail to be granted in a case that may involve a capital offence, but the police raised no objection, and the magistrate fixed the surety at two hundred pounds, the Colonel coming forward to provide the amount. I had a word with Sergeant Wigmore as we left the court.

"No more than I expected," said he. "He's loose now to make fresh evidence against himself. You can generally depend on that class of criminal to do it. If he took a good sum off Hunt he'll be drinking and then talking. We're putting a plain-clothes man on to him."

I was very glad when the jolting bus set me down once more in Leasinghoe, and I could sit by the cottage fire, light a pipe, and think. My thoughts, however, were profoundly dissatisfying. We had entered, it seemed, a cul-de-sac. From the time of the initial startling events nothing had occurred to throw any fresh light on the mystery. Hunt, alive or dead, was yet to be found, and the case against Buller remained exceedingly flimsy. Arbuthnot, with probably the only two clues worth having in his possession, was hunting the north of England for a derelict politician. There was also the silence of Hunt's brother to ponder over.

In this mood I went out and walked, risking the baneful effects of the night air. As I walked, and wondered, a sentence I had heard spoken but recently suddenly stood out in letters of fire in my brain.

"She and I are Percival's only near surviving relations."

I stopped in my walk. Fool that I was; that was the thing that had been puzzling me since Mrs. Bessom's cross-examination. Hunt's supposed brother stood out in a sinister light. I visualized him and Hunt in dispute over some treasure, maybe secured in the box we had rescued from the marsh. I saw a struggle in which the precious box was dropped, and pictured the baffled survivor hastily driving away into the fog. Well, it all needed a better brain than mine to cope with it.

At the post office I stopped to collect my daily papers.

"There's a wire for you, sir," said the girl in charge. "It came half an hour ago, but there was no one to send out with it."

It was from Arbuthnot.

Return to-morrow.—Ponsonby.

With a very much lighter heart I left the shop. It would have been wisdom to have returned to the cottage, but instead of that I went gaily along the road, swinging my stick and feeling as if all the cares of the world were no longer on my shoulders. It was thus that about seven o'clock I found myself in the village of Wivenhoe. Man is a reasoning animal, and even when indulging the most casual whim will snatch at a reason to cast an appearance of common sense over his actions, and therefore when I caught sight of that ancient inn, 'The Three Kings', I decided to enter on the off-chance of finding George Higgins there, and directing him to come the following day and impart a little tidiness to our neglected garden. But the inn was empty.

I commented on this remarkable fact to the man who served me with beer.

"Oh, ah, sir. There's a public meeting about some dispute over mooring rights, and I guess all my customers, being mostly seafaring men, are there. They'll be along presently."

He showed me that I could enjoy my drink in comfort in the parlour. It was a curious room, lying directly behind the bar (which itself gave immediately on the street), and was reached by descending three steps at the end of the bar counter. The wall between the bar and the parlour had been partly replaced by a glass window, to admit light into what would otherwise have been a very dark room, and possibly also to allow the barman to see when his customers in the parlour required their glasses replenishing.

I sat on a long wooden seat directly under the window, where no one from the bar could see me unless he was on the barman's side of the counter, and by chance placed my drink on the seat beside me instead of on the table. Hence anyone in the bar would have been totally unaware that there was anyone in the parlour.

I had taken no more than one sip of my beer when I heard the street door open, and the footsteps of the attendant coming to take the order of the newcomer.

"One double Scotch, one pint," said a voice. Familiar words, but even more familiar that low, unpleasant, growling voice that could belong to no one but the man whom I had last seen on the verge of standing his trial for murder. I risked a hasty peep through the window, and it was indeed Buller. His companion I hardly noticed, beyond realizing that he wore a blue jersey, common to yacht's crews, and such as one could see in Wivenhoe fifty times a day in the winter.

The barman served them and then went off about his own business. I heard the two men conversing, but they spoke in low tones and I was unable to catch a word they said. So I sat consumed with impatience, wondering whether I was by any chance missing exactly what we so badly wanted to know. Certainly Buller, who might have been expected to be on duty at that time of the evening, had not come to Wivenhoe for nothing.

"Never again, I says." The words, uttered in a louder tone by Buller's companion, were clearly heard by me. That settled it; hear I must. Dropping on my hands and knees I crept toward the three steps that led up to the bar. If the barman found me there my position would be ridiculous, while if Buller caught me eavesdropping I could foresee unlimited trouble. Nevertheless I crouched on the steps, shielded by the end of the counter, and prayed that a horrible draught that blew through that narrow opening would not provoke a sneeze. In the discussion that was going on their voices became raised without their noticing.

"Well, after being so near swinging, I'd have thought you'd 'ad enough, too," said the other man.

"Bah! I tell you they can't hang me. Don't be so b—y soft."

"It's all very well for you, Bill, but I tell you I've 'ad enough. I 'adn't gone but a little way, drifting with the ebb so as to make no noise, when there 'e was."

"Who?"

"'*Im*. A-bobbing up and down in the water, just for all the world like a bloke bathing. You know, close against the water it ain't as a rule so foggy. Bumped 'is head twice against the boat 'e did. Gawd. I couldn't stand it no longer, an' I took an oar and shoved him off, and a minute after there 'e was again! It ain't natural for a corpse, just drownded, to be that lively."

"Sure 'e was dead?"

"'E'd 'ave shouted if 'e 'adn't been. What did *you* do, Bill?"

"Cut and run like hell, you fool, of course. Well, I must get back. You walk along so far, an' listen to commonsense, and I'll hand you out your bonus."

They went out. I dared not risk another peep, much as I should have liked to see the second man more clearly, for I knew that a man who knew as much as I did had better run no risks. I ordered another drink, and, knowing they would be walking towards Leasinghoe, gave them a good ten minutes to be well on their way before I set off.

I believe my dominant thought was gladness that Arbuthnot would be again with me inside twenty-four hours. Then I pictured the wretched Hunt, flung to the creek, and his dead face "a-bobbin' up and down" as his body followed one of his murderers on that ebbing tide that Arbuthnot had referred to at the very time. I can tell you my walk home was a brisk affair, and I held my walking-stick

as if I wished it were something more substantial. In that
frame of mind I was guilty of a perceptible jump when
some one stationary by the roadside flashed an electric
torch full in my face.

"Strike me pink if it ain't Mister blooming Yankee!"
said the voice I had heard but half an hour ago. "Guv'nor,
don't you go catching no cold. This here night air isn't
good for the likes of you." He chuckled and extinguished
his torch, and I managed a rather unconvincing laugh, as
of one who would humour a drunken man, and made off
homewards, not without sundry glances behind.

5

In Which I am Shown that England is but a Small Country

I have a feeling that those parts of my narrative which do not directly include Arbuthnot are relatively uninteresting, just as *Hamlet* is not quite the same when the Prince of Denmark is not on the stage, so I pass with all rapidity to his return. But first I record a letter from Kaye, which arrived on the morning of the 19th. He stated, firstly, he had been instrumental, as requested, in initiating a coastal search; secondly, that he had so far no news of the whereabouts of Mr. Walter Grierson; thirdly, that he had had negative answers from seven universities regarding an unsuccessful medical student of the name of Percival Hunt; and lastly, that there were two registered medical practitioners of that name, one being a ship's doctor on the Orient Line and at present somewhere between Colombo and Australia, and the other an elderly man practising at Torquay. It appeared to me, therefore, that unless one of the remaining universities produced some information, Mr. Hunt was either not a doctor or not Mr. Hunt, and in the light of what I knew either hypothesis seemed equally absurd.

Arbuthnot arrived about noon, escorted by the invaluable George, complete with hand-cart.

"Gad, I'm glad you're back," said I, unable to resist the impulse to shake him by the hand, although I knew he detested the practice.

"Been having sleepless nights, King?" he asked, grinning at my effusion.

"More or less. Did you find your man?" I fear my interest in Mr. Herbert Turnbull was slight, but it seemed the obvious thing to ask.

"I did not. But there are some failures more inspiring than success."

"Meaning?"

"All in good time. Here comes Mrs. Jerrold to satisfy my craving for tea. After that you can enlighten me as to the course that local events have been taking."

I was nothing loth, and while Arbuthnot sipped his third cup of tea and overloaded the air with tobacco smoke, I set about as complete an account as I could manage of the various happenings that had contributed to my bewilderment during his absence. And indeed it was a tale 'of shreds and patches'. Arbuthnot heard me out mostly in silence, only occasionally throwing in a question.

"The court proceedings seem to have been rather perfunctory," he said. "No doubt the police only wished to implicate Buller, and the defending solicitor only cared to try and clear him. Probably every one knew no conclusion could be reached on the facts presented. Otherwise there would have been more inquiry into the identity of Hunt."

I produced Kaye's letters as a kind of appendix to my report, and after Arbuthnot had perused them he sat silent.

"I suppose you expect me to comment?" he said at last.

"If you choose to. I've thought and thought until my brain nearly refuses to function. Last night, of course, I was convinced of Buller's guilt, but the man isn't more than a tool of some greater villain. It's no ordinary murder."

"Remarkably true. But give me time to digest your heterogeneous budget. Meanwhile I'll tell you, if you like, what I've been doing."

"Very well. But I warn you it must be something extremely interesting if it's to take my mind off this confounded business."

"Good! I promise you you won't be disappointed. Now listen. I found time when I reached town on the evening of the 16th to insert those advertisements you probably saw and to arrange for a message to be broadcast concerning Hunt. Also, and this will interest you more, I had the box opened. But perhaps I'll leave that part till later."

"No, no. Damn Turnbull! The box before everything!"

"Well, well, King, you were always impetuous. Here then is the box that so excites your curiosity. Don't stop to ask who opened it, for that gentleman is happier in a strict anonymity."

Before my fascinated eyes he drew the box, apparently undamaged, from his pocket, took a roughly-made and curious-looking key from another, and, without a word, passed both to me. I believe my hand was shaking as I fitted the key made by Arbuthnot's retiring friend.

"Wait a minute. King," said he, grinning. "It's only fair to guess first."

"Jewellery," said I, "of great value, or possibly, failing that, a phial of some subtle poison." I had been cogitating nightly on the contents of that box.

"Now look."

The key turned easily, and I raised the lid without any effort. Then I saw, projecting toward me, a small wooden handle. A metal bar lay across its top and held it in position. I pushed a finger under the bar and it sprang back to a vertical position. Then I pulled on the handle, and what came out in my hand was nothing but a stamp such as is used in offices for stamping dates, signatures, and so forth. Arbuthnot pushed a slip of paper towards me and I impressed the stamp on it. This is what I saw, outlined in a dull red colour:

"The pad with the colour is fixed at the bottom of the box," said Arbuthnot, as if there were nothing else worth mentioning. I sat staring at that unexpected symbol till the lines began to waver before my eyes.

"What do you make of it, King?"

"It suggests nothing to me. It's just another mystery to add to those we've already encountered."

"H'm. Perhaps so. Shall I continue my story?"

"If you've no more to say about this extraordinary thing."

"All in good time. You saved your puzzles for me. Now I present *you* with one."

"Thanks. Now, about Turnbull."

"The abduction of a person from a railway train in England is no child's play. That Turnbull had been so treated there was little doubt. A man, setting out on what was no doubt to him a kind of holy war does not preface his work by a total disappearance. That he should wilfully vanish, knowing it would embarrass the Government, seemed foreign to the nature of a man who is, I believe, styled by his associates 'Honest Bert'. If he had been murdered on the train his body would have soon been discovered adorning the side of the permanent way. So I assumed that I was dealing with a case of kidnapping, carried out by decidedly clever methods. The police were still at a loss when I got into touch with them at Sheffield. Had Turnbull been dealt with by what I may call knockdown and quick-get-away methods there could have been no concealment. If he had been rendered unconscious an carried off in that state as a fainting case or the victim of accident or illness, the occurrence must have been noted by some one. Clearly some better method had been employed.

"I found the police able to tell me several things. Turnbull had travelled in a third-class non-corridor coach. Twenty or thirty people had assembled to see him off, and the crowd round the door of the compartment had effectually prevented anyone else getting in with him. The first stop of the train was at Ambergate Junction, and there were several subsequent stops of less interest."

"Why of less interest?"

"Consider. The success of the coup showed that it was a carefully-planned affair. No doubt the aggressors relied on Turnbull's having a compartment to himself when the train left Sheffield; it was a fair assumption, especially since 'The Red Flag' has become a popular song on such occasions. But they could have no guarantee that he would be alone after the first stop. Hence, on this hypothesis, he was either taken off the train at Ambergate, or before."

"Before?"

"If the train were stopped by adverse signals. But it was not likely, because such an event could not be allowed for in a prearranged plot. However, the engine-driver and fireman both swore that there had been no such stops, nor any slowing up sufficient for two men to remove another, the other being either struggling or unconscious, from the train."

"Why two men?"

"I am anticipating. I then saw the clerk in the first-class booking office. He could prove from his accounts that three first-class tickets had been issued to Ambergate on that day, and so far as he remembered they were bought by one man. He could not say at what time of day. In the third-class office several tickets had been issued to that station in the course of the day, and beyond that there was no help there for me.

"By this time, for these inquiries took some hours to complete, allowing for delays, it was too late to go to Ambergate, as I had proposed, so that trip was necessarily postponed till the 18th—yesterday."

"Surely the police could have done as much as you so far."

"Certainly, but I am one and they are many. If you are many, the easiest way to find a lost thing is to go and look for it, which is exactly what they were doing. But I was operating singly and therefore required different methods.

"The next morning, by the first available train, I left for Ambergate. It is a lonely place and its sole importance lies in its being a junction. Beyond it is farmland and woodland, stretching away north toward the Pennines. The whole station staff consists of the station-master and one porter. I interviewed the former first. He had nothing to say on the matter and called in the porter, who, he explained, had been on the ticket barrier on the arrival of the train in question. The porter intimated he had already told the police all he knew.

"'He never come off 'ere, that I can swear,' he said, rather sullenly.

"'Who did come off?' I asked.

"'Three gentlemen,' he said. 'Give up first-class tickets. Nobody else at all.'

"'Did you know them?' I asked.

"'One of them I knowed,' he answered. 'T'others I didn't.'

"'Who was the one you knew?' I continued.

"'Sir Henry Tringham, up at the 'All. Everybody about here knows him.'

"'Could anyone have left the station any other way?' I asked.

"'I don't think so,' said the station-master. 'There was a gang working on the next set of rails, changing sleepers. They had good lights, and they would have shouted if they'd seen anyone suspicious-like hop down that side. I was on the platform, and I saw the gentlemen he speaks of. They were down at the far end and went straight off. No one else came off to my knowledge. Sir Henry and his pals had a car waiting, and drove away at once.'

"At this point the station-master said he had to go off for a few minutes to feed his fowls at his house across the road, and I was left alone with the porter. All the time we had been conversing I had had the impression that he imparted his information with reluctance.

"'Look here,' I said. 'I'm not the police, although I produced their credentials. Tell me all you know and I'll guarantee no harm comes to you or yours, and, what's more, it'll be a five-pound note in your pocket.'

"He got very red in the face, and shuffled his feet about, and I believe was hesitating whether to treat me as a friend or hit me in the eye. Fortunately for him he took the former course.

"'My father,' he said at last, 'is gardener up at Sir Henry's place. If it got about that I'd been reporting things about Sir Henry he might get the sack. The truth is, Sir Henry was blind drunk that night, blind—paralytic. It's seldom he's anything but drunk, but he was worse than usual when he come off the train. But I don't know that you want to hear all this.'

"'Everything,' I said, 'if you wish to earn your reward.'

"'Well, he was so drunk that there were his friends supporting of him, one on each side, and he was a-leaning forward, like as if to fall if they let go, and saying, "Ooh-ah-ooh", and his hat knocked over his eyebrows.'

"'So you didn't see his face?' I asked at once.

"'No, sir, and maybe I wouldn't have recognized him first or last if one of his friends hadn't said to the other as they passed me at the barrier, "By Jove, Geoff, old man, poor old Tringham's worse than usual to-night." And so he was.'

"'You didn't recognize the friends?' I naturally inquired.

"'No, sir, they was strangers to me, but gentlemen. I couldn't describe them properly. They was both tall, one had a soft hat on, the other was bareheaded.'

"'And how was Sir Henry dressed?' I asked him.

"'Nothing special. Had a macintosh on, and his usual light 'Omberg hat with a black band.'

"'You saw Sir Henry's car?'

"'No, sir. It drove up just as the train came in, and they rushed him to it and were off sharp, having no doubt had enough of him for one night.'

"Believe me, King, I sat down on a seat in that waiting-room and laughed till I almost cried, while the porter began to look aggressive again."

"But I don't quite see," I objected.

"No, but when I tell you that I was aware that the ill-fated Turnbull had left Sheffield wearing a tweed cap perhaps you will."

"I get you. Sir Henry Tringham was no other than Turnbull, of course."

"Of course. These fellows evidently knew the district, and Sir Henry's little failing. They took three first-class tickets at Sheffield to Ambergate Junction, and got in a compartment as near Turnbull's as possible. As the train drew in at Ambergate they stepped out quickly, opened the door of his compartment, jumped in, and if my supposition is correct, as we shall know some day, one of them gave him a swift jab to the solar plexus. Now to a man well-developed about the waistline and completely out of training such a blow is devastating. I see the unhappy Turnbull bent double, while they pushed his cap in a pocket, and one placed the hat from his own head well down over the victim's eyes. Then they hurried him off. No wonder the porter said he looked likely to fall, and was making curious noises. You've done some boxing, and you know what it feels like to be winded. I expect the man, hurried along so fast that he could not get his breath back, was expecting to drop dead. Then that ostensibly chance remark dropped in the hearing of the porter was almost genius."

"Why do you say almost?"

"Wait. I rewarded the porter and told him to keep his tale to himself. Meanwhile the car I had ordered the day before from Derby to be at my disposal at the station was waiting. The porter showed me which road led to Horndale Hall, Sir Henry's place, and I went off."

"But you didn't know they were going there."

"They weren't. But they would take that road first in case anyone from the station was watching them."

"I see." Despite my preoccupation with the other affair I couldn't help being interested.

"Now at this moment good luck appeared on my side. It's no more than one expects from the laws of probability. The road seemed to go on more or less interminably, climbing gradually all the time, until at last we came to a road fork. One road, leading to the left, was a metalled road, the other was not. At their junction stood a cottage. In front of the cottage, in the road, stood a small boy. In the hands of the small boy were a note-book and pencil. That was the good luck."

"In what way?"

"Twenty years ago, when motoring was relatively in its infancy, and cars were counted in dozens where now they are counted in thousands, it was a favourite sport of street urchins to note down the identifying letters and numerals on the number plates of all the cars they saw. The game is now dead in most places, for cars have become too numerous to be interesting, but, in this remote district, conditions, in that respect, were those of the early nineteen-hundreds in better-populated parts. So this lad flourished his note-book and pencil. I stopped the car at once, and when a woman came to the door of the cottage I advanced and asked to be shown the right road to Horndale Hall. The respect that gained me made it easy for me to inquire if the boy were her son, and what he might be doing.

"'Yes, he's my son,' she said. 'And he's a handful. It's quiet here for a sharp boy. When he's not in school he's always on the look-out for motors. Why, t'other evening after dark he heard one, and run out of the house in his nightshirt.'

"'*And* I got the number,' said the boy proudly.

"'Was that recently?' I asked casually.

"'This is Saturday—then it must have been Monday,' said the mother. The thirteenth! Here was luck indeed!

"'I expect it was Sir Henry Tringham's car,' I said.

"'It wasn't,' said the boy. He opened his book. 'Here's Sir Henry's number,' he said, 'and here's the number of the other car.'

"And he had it down in plainest black and white—LZ 8793.

"'Besides,' said the boy scornfully, pointing, 'the car never went toward the Hall. It went up that way.'

"'Nonsense!' said his mother. 'That road don't go nowhere except up to the moors.'

"'I seed it,' affirmed the urchin.

"'Jump in,' said I to him. 'I've plenty of time. We will go that way and see where the road goes to.' I think what would be nowadays commonplace to most boys seemed a miracle to that little chap. 'Drive slowly,' I said to the chauffeur, 'and answer his questions.'

"So the boy hopped up in front and we went on while the road grew narrower, and cart-ruts became more prominent, and the grass at the sides often almost united to obscure the surface.

"'Sir,' said the boy, suddenly turning round to me. 'I seed a ticket lying on the road.'

"Out of the mouths of babes and sucklings!

"'Stop!' I called to the driver. 'Now, sonny,' I said, 'I'll swear you never really saw a ticket.'

"'I seed it,' said the boy with determination.

"'Get it and I'll believe you.'

"He was down from the car and off back along the road like a shot, and in half a minute he had returned and handed to me—a third single ticket from Sheffield to Birmingham, dated November 13th! No doubt the cold, dry spell of weather had preserved it. All credit to Turnbull for thinking of dropping a clue as he was driven off to confinement! And credit also to my juvenile assistant for his sharpness!

"This was inspiring. We went on, and the road showed signs of an imminent end. It finally terminated as a road, and became a track, still leading upwards towards the moors. At our limit as motorists stood an old stone barn, no doubt a building in connexion with a farm we had passed a mile farther back.

"The car stopped, I alighted, and while the chauffeur began difficult reversing operations, and the boy, from a point of vantage, directed him, I lighted a pipe and strolled about, wondering whether I should leave the car and reconnoitre the moor path.

"It was then that I received the biggest shock this affair has yet given me. This is what I saw, drawn with white chalk on the old wooden door of the barn I mentioned."

Arbuthnot tore a sheet of paper from a pad as he spoke, seized a pencil, and in a moment passed me this:

"The symbol in the box!"

"Precisely. That is what I meant when I said failure could be more inspiring than success."

"But this is incredible!" My voice, I believe, rose nearly to a shout as I said it. "It's impossible! It makes confusion worse confounded."

Arbuthnot listened with his customary grin; I am sure he enjoys working up his effects.

"It's a coincidence," I said finally.

"Then it's the most amazing coincidence that misfortune ever devised to baffle an anxious investigator."

"Go on with your story," I said.

"I had to be another case of acting first and thinking afterwards. Here was I up against something extremely peculiar. Should I go on, or should I stand back and bide my time? I decided on the latter. The country-side was alive with searchers; sooner or later they would cross my path and hamper me; moreover, by going rashly on I might blunder into something much too big to tackle on the spot without a plan. The car's nose pointed downhill, and off we went.

"I restored the boy, enriched by half a crown, to his mother, and took his name and address in case some day I might be able to do something for him, for he was a sharp lad. Then I made the pretence of going to Horndale Hall, but I was no longer concerned to prove that Sir Henry Tringham had not been at the railway station on the evening of the 13th so we went straight on to Derby. There the news I had hoped for had already been received; the strike was settled, and the urgency of my mission a thing of the past. I left immediately for London, getting there about eight last evening."

"Then what about Turnbull?"

"Either he is dead, which is unlikely; or he is being kept prisoner for some purpose we know nothing of; or, the strike being settled, he will soon find himself at liberty."

"What more?"

"I had an interesting evening in town. I first saw Hemingway, and amused him with my story of the abduction. I pointed out that, the strike being off, Turnbull would almost certainly reappear, and therefore, having other urgent matters in hand, I had considered my mission at an end. If Turnbull did not come to light, I would turn my attention to the business again. He agreed. Then he tried to put in a good word for Baxter Creen.

"'It's a pity you're so busy, Arbuthnot,' he said, 'for really that poor devil Creen is in a very unpleasant fix.'

"'He's a millionaire,' I said; 'he can buy a dozen detective agencies if he likes. I don't like that type of man.'

"'He's no friend of mine,' said Hemingway, 'but I can't avoid feeling sorry for him at present. I shouldn't be telling you this, but the truth is he's lost his daughter—the beautiful Iris Creen. An only child and the pride of his otherwise flinty heart. I suppose she could have married almost any bachelor in the kingdom, and therefore she chose to disappear with her chauffeur. He's still hoping against hope to avoid a scandal. He has employed the usual agencies without success, and seems to pin his faith on you.'

"'Very kind of him, I'm sure,' said I. 'When did this happen?'

"'I believe the girl vanished on the 10th. The man had only been employed a week.'

"'Love at first sight, eh?'

"'So it appears.'

"'Police doing anything?'

"'He won't hear of their being employed.'

"'I'm sorry I can't help. Very honestly, if I had time to explain to you what is taking my attention at present you wouldn't ask.'

"With that I went on to see Kaye in his evening retreat, a mansion in Suburbia. Mrs. Kaye, as usual, disappeared as soon as she heard the maid utter my name. Kaye himself sizzled with curiosity, as he had every right to do after the varieties of inquiries he had received. However, there was no time to indulge him.

"First of all he told me that his replies from the universities were complete, and no Percival Hunt could be traced.

"'Right,' said I; 'now let's have a look at the London telephone directory.'

"He brought it and I asked him to find the number of Hunt, 14 Queen Anne's Mansions, S.W. 1.

"'Not on the phone,' he told me, after a search.

"'Good! Now have you a back-file of the *Morning Post?* I know you take that paper.'

"He went to a cabinet and brought me what I wanted without a word. I had only to go back to the 2nd of the month to find that on the previous day Lord Alresford's wife had presented him with a son and heir. Then we sat and smoked, and I asked for news of Grierson.

"'I have none,' said he. 'I am given to understand from his lordship that Grierson went off to South Africa over six months ago on a shooting tour, and has never troubled to communicate his whereabouts. He may be out in the wilds where the dispatch of letters is difficult, if not impossible.'

"By this time I was more than a little tired, but I declined Kaye's hospitable offer of a bed and went back to London in one of those nice little green electric trains the Southern Railway provide, for I wished to settle two little matters in the morning, before coming to see what had befallen my friend King."

"And those were?"

"Firstly, the ownership of the car that drove Mr. Turnbull away from the sight of men. You remember it was registered under a London number, so a visit to Scotland Yard soon proved that it belonged to the Honourable Geoffrey Charteris, address, Lymington Court, in the New Forest. Does that stir your memory?"

"Why, of course!" I said. "The remark at the railway station!"

"Exactly. That is why it was almost genius, as I said but like nearly all the works of man had its one flaw."

"Continue."

"I found *Who's Who* quite informative respecting the said Charteris. Second son of the Earl of Brockenhurst; educated Westminster and Cambridge; soccer blue; and attained distinction in geological studies; has published a monograph on the carboniferous limestone. Now, isn't that interesting?"

"Why specially interesting?"

"Dear, dear, King, I fear long pondering has scattered your wits. And I fear that I am going to disperse them even more. Prepare now for a shock. Was Hunt a doctor?"

"I think so. Don't you?"

"I am morally certain of it. But there is no doctor to fit that name. What follows?"

"That Hunt was not his proper name, I suppose."

"True. Then how could he have a Miss Hunt for a sister?"

Puzzled and bothered over this and that, I had failed previously to see this implication.

"Perhaps a half-sister," I suggested. "Or, more likely, Hunt was the black sheep of the family and had found it convenient to change his name, and she had loyally adopted that name for the occasion. That would explain also his brother's silence."

"Creditable to you, King. Distinctly creditable, but, alas for your blind faith in womankind, untrue. I sent a wire to Miss Hunt from my hotel this morning. I wrote:

"'Am here with small box property of your brother. May I call.—Monk, Leasinghoe.'

"I had my wire back inside an hour, undelivered for reason stated, 'Not known at address given.' Even then I wasn't satisfied, and called round at 14 Queen Anne's Mansions, where I was hospitably received by a certain General Octavius Hopkins, who began by damning me for an insurance agent, and concluded by pressing brandy and soda on me at nine in the morning! Net result of inquiries—nil. And now there's work for you. Go and see that woman Bessom, and tactfully break it to her that she'd better tell the police all she knows about Miss Hunt. Meanwhile, I am not ashamed to say, I shall compose myself to slumber."

So I went out with bewilderment thickening upon me, and succeeded in communicating a small portion of it to the late Hunt's landlady.

"I sent Miss Hunt's address to Mr. Ponsonby, and he called to offer his sympathies. No one of the name of Hunt lived there or was known of there. He says you had better tell the police before things get any worse."

I left the good lady speechless for once, and no wonder, and returned to find Arbuthnot almost offensively comfortable and dormant on the sofa.

6

In Which Arbuthnot Uses Mathematical Skill and the Wanderer Comes Home

Monday, November 20th, brought interesting news. I find I have preserved several newspaper cuttings of that date, and they all deal with the reappearance of Mr. Herbert Turnbull, and are, in essentials, identical.

We received our papers that day through the kindly medium of George Higgins, who "happened to be coming our way", as he expressed it; but my private opinion was that George was none too affluent, and when I suggested some temporary labour on the unweeded paths and neglected plots around our cottage he consented with suspicious alacrity.

I took up a paper at random, and found the most prominent position allocated to an account of the restoration of Mr. Turnbull to society.

"Hallo!" said I. "Turnbull is found."

"You mean set at liberty, don't you?" said a voice from beside the fire. I glanced down the page rapidly and found that it was so.

"Read it out," said Arbuthnot. So I began:

> "General relief will be felt throughout the country over the reappearance of Mr. Herbert Turnbull, who, as our readers are well aware, vanished under remarkable circumstances on

the 13th inst. Mr. Turnbull was discovered
about 9 a.m. yesterday morning, wandering
on the moors above Haworth in Yorkshire.
Rarely can that little village, famous for ever
as the home of the Brontes, have shared in
such a sensation.

"It appears that when Mr. Turnbull was
first accosted by two moorland shepherds,
who, like all the local inhabitants, had no
doubt been on the qui vive for days, he was
totally ignorant of his whereabouts, and was
suffering considerably from anxiety and the
effects of his week's incarceration. Interviewed by a representative of the *Yorkshire
Evening Post* Mr. Turnbull had an astounding
tale to tell.

"It appears that at the moment when the
tram, in which he was travelling to Birmingham, drew up at Ambergate Junction, his compartment was invaded by two men. Naturally
not expecting an assault, he was unprepared
for a staggering blow on the chest dealt him
by one of his assailants, which had the effect of deranging his breathing. In this state,
unable to regain his breath, he found a hat
thrust on his head, and he was bustled, inca-
pacitated against resistance, along the platform, through the barrier, and into a waiting
car. As the car drove off, his arms were pinned
to his sides, and a gag thrust into his mouth.

"In this unenviable condition, he was
transported for what he judged to be several
miles, when the car stopped, and he was required to continue his compulsory journey on
foot. How far he went in this manner he has

no idea, but long after he had grown intolerably weary, footsore, and sleepy, a pad soaked in chloroform was pressed over his face and he finished his travels in a state of unconsciousness.

"Mr. Turnbull says that he came to himself in complete darkness. He was lying on a rough sort of bed, adequately provided with blankets. He was obliged to lie still till the nauseating after-effects of the anaesthetic had worn off, but when he felt better and attempted to move he was securely chained by the leg. Cautious movements showed him that he was fastened to a stone post or pillar, and that his movements were thus circumscribed within a very small area.

"At this stage he heard movement near him and the light from a bull's eye lantern was suddenly flashed in his face. A large mug of hot tea and a plate of roughly-cut bread-and-butter were set down on the bed beside him, and in spite of his acute resentment at his treatment, the captive thought it wise to satisfy his hunger. His attendant shone the light on the food and drink till they had been consumed, and then vanished with the empty utensils, having declined to vouchsafe a word in answer to Mr. Turnbull's questionings.

"So, apparently, matters continued. The silent attendant saw to his prisoner's needs in a rough and ready fashion, even going so far as to produce daily papers and remain with the light while Mr. Turnbull had the melancholy pleasure of reading that his whereabouts remained a complete mystery. But when the

gaoler went away the light went with him,
and so the unlucky captive spent many hours
in the darkness. In these uncongenial circumstances, he states that he preserved his courage, and indeed his sanity, by singing hymns,
a proceeding to which apparently no objection was taken.

"He had naturally been unable to keep any
account of time and indeed was amazed on his
return to human society to find that the date
was only the 19th. Eventually he was removed
from his dungeon in a state of coma, evidently
induced by means of a narcotic administered
through his food. When he awoke, he was lying
alone in a disused and tumble-down barn on
the moors, and the grey light of dawn shewed
that his abductors, with surely unusual courtesy, had left him wrapped in blankets; and had
provided a thermos flask, which he found to
contain coffee, and a packet of sandwiches!

"Naturally Mr. Turnbull is unable to give
an account of his place of imprisonment, but
he believes it to have been a cellar, as it was
always pitch dark there. It was also very damp,
and he distinctly heard the persistent sound
of water dripping from the roof."

I was interrupted in my reading by a shout of laughter
from Arbuthnot.

"Splendid!" he cried, rising from his chair and walking
up and down the room, rubbing his hands together. "You
take the point, King, don't you? This is really most enjoyable."

"I see the poor devil was pretty badly treated," I said.
"I don't see any grounds for pleasure."

"And yet," said he with the grin I preferred to see indulged at the expense of some one other than myself, "you have all the material for an interesting piece of deduction. Is there any more news?"

"Little more. Turnbull thinks that his original assailants were members of what he calls the idle class. There is an editorial which is a curious compound of righteous indignation and barely-concealed sympathy with the villains of the piece. Now I want to know what we are going to do about the news I learnt at the 'Three Kings' concerning Buller. Buller will surrender to his bail on the 25th, and unless there is fresh evidence I don't see how a case can be made out against him."

"Nor do I. The case against him will be withdrawn, no doubt, unless you come forward. I think, as the police seem to have done, that Buller is more useful at liberty."

"Yes, but aren't we running rather a risk with a man like that loose in the neighbourhood?"

"King, when I think about the risk we *are* running the addition of Buller seems a very small matter."

These were comfortable words indeed!

"Then are we to sit still waiting, till we go the way that Hunt went?" I said rather angrily, for no man likes that feeling of being the hunted one.

"By no means. There are four things that require doing while we sit here talking."

"And they are?"

"Firstly to reconcile Colonel Gregory's expenditure with his income. It's a good rule that a man living above his means is to be regarded with suspicion; he is more open to be bought than a man who is financially sound. I hope Kaye will have some facts for me by to-morrow."

"How do you know he *is* living above his means?"

"I don't know at present. It is merely a guess. But his transparent anxiety over money matters, coupled with his

obvious extravagance in the matter of cigars and whisky,
is interesting."

"What else?"

"Secondly, I deem it imperative that we should get into
touch with Mr. Geoffrey Charteris. Again the invaluable
Kaye had his instructions in a letter I wrote before leaving
London."

"Shall you tackle him openly?"

"Circumstances will decide that."

"And?"

"Thirdly, King, I want you to realize that this area,
in some unknown way, is a *locus* of disturbance. The man
who called himself Hunt was not here for nothing."

"No, he was hiding in mortal terror of his life in the
quietest part of England he could find."

"Nonsense. He was here for what he could get. Do
you honestly think that a man in dread of some imminent Nemesis would regularly and by choice take his walks
abroad last thing at night?"

"Perhaps not," I conceded. I had not quite seen the
matter in that light before.

"Of course not. Then, don't you remember the remark
that his landlady overheard, about having 'one more try'.
Isn't it probable that that last try cost him his life?"

"I suppose you are right."

"Then it follows that if we are to lay our hands on what
it was that drew Hunt to this place and so to his death
we shall do well to extend our acquaintance with this district."

I shivered, and agreed.

"Fourthly, in this sermon, we have to make what we can
of the message we found in the marsh."

"Trace Grierson, you mean?"

"No, that is already being done. Passenger lists of the
last month are being scrutinized."

"But I thought he was already in Africa? Don't you think the message meant that he was on his way home via Port Said?"

"If I did I should first require proof that he had ever gone to Africa."

"Then if he has just left England he can be traced, because he must travel under his own name."

"Why?"

"The passport difficulty."

"No. He may have gone in a yacht, or shipped before the mast in a cargo steamer. There are always ways and means of getting ashore without a passport. But I am not thinking of Grierson."

"You said you were!"

"I said I was thinking of the message."

"But the message referred only to him."

Arbuthnot sighed wearily.

"And I gave you the strongest possible hint before I went away," said he. "Who do you think dropped that piece of paper—Hunt or his murderers?"

"It might have been either."

"It might not. If we had found the box only, we might have supposed it had fallen from anyone's pocket in a struggle. But when we find *two* things, and one of them a bit of paper, we begin to see they were intentionally discarded by some one, who, even when faced with death, could remember the necessity of getting rid of them. A heavy object falls easily from a pocket, while a lighter article does not. You doubt me? Then put two half-crowns and a pound note in your hip pocket, and stand on your head. The coins will drop out; the paper will cling to the pocket."

"I believe you," I said. "I don't like standing on my head."

"Then you agree that the paper was of vital importance?"

"There seems no doubt about it," said I.

"Then, King, you old fool, will you tell me why a man kept in his pocket a paper of such tremendous significance that even at the hour of death he remembered he must get rid of it, *when he could have memorized every word on it in five seconds?*"

I don't like being called an old fool, but I forgot that while I stared in amazement.

"What then?" I asked.

"There must have been another message on the paper. The remark about Grierson was clearly some after-thought. Probably you have heard many times of invisible writing. It is a simple matter. One writes in some fluid that only becomes visible after a chemical reaction produced by the action of water, or some chemical, or heat, has taken place."

"Yes! Then we can soon see if that paper had a message!"

"It has been done," said Arbuthnot dryly. "I was not exactly idle while I was away. And there *was* a message."

"Then that's something worth far more than anything we've found yet," I cried.

"Yes," said Arbuthnot slowly. "There was a message—in cipher."

"That's a pity," said I after a pause. "Still, what one man has invented another man can discover."

Arbuthnot jumped up from his chair again. "I shall certainly finish by kicking you, King. One fool makes a remark, and for centuries after other fools waste their time repeating it."

"But surely no cipher is insoluble?"

"Theoretically, of course, you are correct, provided a sufficiently long passage in the cipher used is available, but in practice one may easily make a cipher that defies solution. I believe it was Jules Verne who, many years ago, pointed that out in one of his novels."

"But I thought that one could always base a solution on the comparative frequency of the appearance of the various symbols in the passage, by comparing that with the order of the commonest letters in the English language. I mean that the most frequent symbol would represent 'e' because 'e' is the most frequently used letter of the alphabet, and so on."

Arbuthnot drew a sheet of paper to him and for a couple of minutes wrote busily on it. Then he pushed it across to me and I saw the following:

K	I	N	G	L	E	C	T	U	R	E	S	O	N	C	I	P	H	E	R	S
1	2	3	4	5	6	7	8	9	10	11	12	1	2	3	4	5	6	7	8	9
L	K	Q	K	Q	K	J	B	D	B	P	E	P	P	F	M	U	N	L	Z	B

"The first line," said he, "is a simple sentence in English. In the second line we take a fixed sequence of certain chosen numbers, in this case the ordinary sequence from one to twelve, and set them against the letters in the sentence, allowing no breaks at the end of words. When our sequence is exhausted we begin again. In the third line the letters are obtained by continuing the alphabet by a number of letters equal to the number given in the second row, that is to say, K is replaced by the next letter L, while I becomes K on counting on *two* letters, and so on. If we reach the end of the alphabet in the process we simply go on again at the beginning, as you see in the case of T, which becomes B. The advantage of the system is that no letter is always replaced by the same letter. For example, E occurs three times in the original. The first time it is replaced by K, the second time by P, the third time by L. Hence this kind of cipher cannot be solved unless we can find the series of numbers used in making it."

"One might try a few sets of numbers," I rashly suggested.

Arbuthnot shook his head pityingly.

"Suppose," he said, "that we restricted ourselves to the first twelve numbers, and made series by arranging them in as many different ways as possible. Each arrangement would be the base of a different cipher. Now we could put the number one in any position from first to twelfth, and after we had placed it, we could put the number two in any one of the remaining eleven positions. So that for *every* position of one there would be eleven positions for two. This gives us already 132 positions. Continuing with the number three, for *every* position of one and two, there would be ten possible positions for three. This gives us 1,320 positions. Finally, the number of positions would be expressed by the number which I believe mathematicians call the factorial twelve and which is equal to 479,001,600. Therefore, King, if you attempted a thousand solutions per day you might easily be busy for the next thousand years. Moreover, this is assuming that all the numbers one to twelve were used, and no others. But we have no guarantee that this is so, and the actual number of possible solutions is thus far greater."

"Great Scot!" said I. "And you think this message is in a cipher of that type?"

"Probably. It doesn't respond to ordinary treatment, anyway."

"Then we gain nothing?"

"There is a faint ray of hope. The drawback of the system is that a numerical series is difficult to remember, while, on the other hand, it is not the sort of thing to keep written down. If an easy series to remember, like the one I used as an example, is employed, the danger is that some one may chance on it. The remedy is to have a series that, if once forgotten, can always be reconstructed. The four figures that make the number of the year would make one, or a certain person's telephone number would serve. That is our only chance, some inspiration derived from what we know or may yet find out in the case."

"You might let me see the thing," I said.

Arbuthnot opened a pocket-book and passed me a strip of paper. "Here is a copy," said he. Here I reproduce, from a copy I made of it later on, the baffling message:

i d x f g d m o d v u q w f f s k e s g
y i j f b n m o r k o g d h f l q o o x
n f y f b k f o c x x t h t f a q e g m
t r wl h o x p c o v j l h

As I sat gazing at this concoction, interruption came in the form of Mrs. Jerrold.

"Sergeant Wigmore to see you, sir," she said.

"Good! Bring him in," said Arbuthnot, taking possession of his piece of paper.

"Good day, sir. Pleased to see you back. I thought, having to come as far as Mrs. Bessom's in any case, I'd drop in and tell you we've got him."

"Got whom?" I cried. "The murderer?"

"No, sir. It's Hunt we've got—or rather his body. Came ashore several miles south of here this morning. In the absence of any available relative or friend, Mrs. Bessom has to go and identify the corpse. But I've no doubt it's him, as no other disappearances are known of recently. His clothes correspond to his landlady's description, and the scar she remembers on his left hand is still noticeable."

"Anything found on the body?" queried Arbuthnot.

"Nothing of the sort one would expect to find. No money or papers. Instead of that, something very surprising indeed."

"Really! What was that?"

"Sir," said the sergeant, leaning forward as if to give weight to his disclosure, "we found round his shoulders a pair of water-wings, the sort of thing people wear when they go bathing."

"Dear me! You don't suppose he went bathing in the creek on that bitterly cold night?"

"Well, sir, don't you think, living alone as he did, he may have become a little bit queer in the head?"

Arbuthnot shook his head.

"Were there any marks of violence on the body?" he asked.

"The doctor thought the neck was marked, but couldn't be sure, the body having been in the water several days. There'll be an inquest to-morrow. And now there's more trouble, I find, about this so-called Miss Hunt."

"Yes," said Arbuthnot gravely. "That's a queer business. My friend here sent me her address and I called, as I felt sympathy with her over this distressing affair. No doubt Mrs. Bessom has told you what happened."

"Very queer," assented the sergeant. "Anyway, that unknown female had access to all Hunt's belongings. Certainly the police had already searched them, but it was very improper for Mrs. Bessom to allow her to do so without reference to authority. I don't like it, sir," he added suddenly. "There's something about this business that gets on my nerves. I'm pretty well used to the dirty side of human nature, but all this mystery gives me that creepy feeling that there's something terribly bad about to come out."

"Not worth while attending the inquest," said Arbuthnot, when the sergeant had gone.

"What do you make of this business of the water-wings?" I asked curiously.

"It proves anyway that Hunt wasn't drowned. But consider, King. In the unlikely event of my requiring to commit a murder in Cornwall, I should be very content to leave my victim where I had dealt with him. If, on the other hand, I slew a man in Kensington, where I live, I should much prefer his corpse to be found in Balham or Hackney Wick. I think that whoever dealt with Hunt couldn't leave this area and so preferred that the evidence should leave instead. I tell you, this place is a *locus* of disturbance. The more am I reluctant to leave it, and yet our most fruitful line of research seems at present to lie in London, or beyond."

"You mean?"

"I mean the doings of the Honourable Geoffrey Charteris. Supposing to-morrow's mail is encouraging, I move we go up to town."

The morning mail, if not encouraging, was at least interesting. Kaye wrote to say that Grierson could be traced in no passenger list. He also communicated facts of significance concerning Colonel Gregory. As far as could be ascertained the Colonel had very small private means, if any. He had commuted a portion of his pension towards the purchase of Lesslands Grange and some cottage property nearby, and his income in consequence would be distinctly small. The property was fully mortgaged, indicating subsequent borrowings.

"That man," said Arbuthnot, "smokes twenty cigars a day. Assuming they only cost him sixpence each, that is yet an expenditure of one hundred and eighty-two pounds a year."

"How can he do it?" I cried.

"Exactly. How can he? Suppose we double the amount to include his drink bill, and we then have a sum probably equal nearly to his whole income."

"Hunt's money was never found," I said. "The man I saw in the bar of the 'Three Kings' was to get a bonus. The more I think of the Colonel the less I like him."

"Charteris is in town," said Arbuthnot, reverting to the letter. "Arrived yesterday. Has rooms in the Albany, which he seldom occupies. Spent the afternoon in the Museum of Practical Geology in Jermyn Street."

"You'll never regret that you once did Kaye a good turn," I said.

"No. He's indefatigable. And I believe if he never received a penny for it he'd do equally well. Now, it's boot and saddle, or rather, George and his handcart."

We left Mrs. Jerrold in charge, gave her a cheque for a month's rent to hand to the Colonel, and were in Colchester in time for lunch. From there we were lucky in securing an empty first-class compartment, and when we emerged at Liverpool Street we had effected the trifling alterations to restore our normal appearance. It was a pleasure to see my friend again his real self. I have never considered whether he should be called good-looking or not. The impression his face always gave me was one of intelligent strength, a man always accessible to reason, and always intolerant of nonsense. People have told me before now that they felt in his presence an overwhelming impulse to sincerity, based on a feeling of the uselessness of trying to move him except by the sheer truth.

The taxi drove out of Liverpool Street Station into the dull gloom of a November evening. A cold north-east wind was blowing and occasionally flakes of snow attached themselves to the windows.

"Evil weather for the marsh," said Arbuthnot, glancing out.

I shivered, and gazed with immense appreciation on the orderly succession of lights that flanked our progress. Perhaps particularly in November the soul that is the city's most successfully combats the external influences of nature.

Mrs. Holden, apprised of our coming by a wire from Colchester, had prepared a pleasant greeting. Arbuthnot was as pleased as I was to see again the inside of our flat, for in his journeys in connexion with Turnbull he had had apparently no time to see his own home.

"We've been away one week," I mused aloud, "and in that time we have sampled improbabilities and puzzles enough for half a lifetime."

Arbuthnot chuckled grimly.

"The curtain has only just risen," said he. "Wait a month, and perhaps you will look back on this past week as a period of positive stagnation."

"I've not lived in your company for nothing," said I, "but frankly I never remember quite such an impasse as we seem to be in now."

Mrs. Holden entered with the inevitable tea-tray. It was a standing order that at whatever hour we might return on any occasion Arbuthnot would require tea. Mrs. Holden was evidently troubled. When she had deposited the tray, she fidgeted about at an unnecessary rearrangement of the cups, instead of withdrawing.

"What is it?" asked Arbuthnot bluntly.

"Sir, while I've been with you I've learnt to hold my tongue. All the same, what I see, I see, and it's my belief that this house has been watched since you've been away."

"Proceed," said Arbuthnot encouragingly.

"It's always a quiet street, but this last week, since the 14th when you left, there's been nothing but people about. A match-seller took up his stand opposite for three days, then there was a cornet-player, and a man called and said he'd been sent to examine the telephone. I kept a very sharp eye on him, you may be sure. Then there's Mr. Briggs, of Glasgow, keeps ringing up to know if he can see you. To-day the match-seller came back. He stands by the lamp-post opposite. If you look out you can see him."

We lifted a corner of the curtain, and peeped out. There was no one there.

"He was there a minute before your car drove up, any-way, sir," said Mrs. Holden, rather taken aback.

"You were quite right to tell us," said Arbuthnot, and dismissed her from the room.

"There's my first cheerful evening for a week spoilt," I grumbled. "Where do we come in in this affair?"

"We don't at present, so far as I can see," said my friend. "When we do, we must be careful our coming in is not merely a prelude to our going out." He looked at me meaningly.

"But the figure on the window?" I objected.

"Was done in the fog, as I told you before. Now our business lies with Mr. Charteris."

"You propose to round him up and get what you can out of him?"

"No, no. If you go to a man, the onus of opening the ball is on you, because the man knows you have not come for nothing. It devolves on you to lay at least some of your cards on the table."

"Then what?"

"Clearly Mr. Charteris must be made to come to us."

"How can you achieve that?"

"We must wait for our opportunity. Kaye is having him watched. When the time comes we must so arouse his curiosity, that he feels impelled to know more of us. Then it is our hope that he will give something away that may help us to piece together this puzzle."

"Shouldn't we gain more by following him?"

"H'm. It's hard work following a clever man. I would sooner pick up the trail where I left it at the barn with the symbol. Come now, a game of chess, while we wait for the next move in a bigger struggle."

He had hardly spoken when the door-bell of the flat rang, and he glanced at me with a look of resignation.

Half a minute later Mrs. Holden appeared with a visiting card,

Mr. James Briggs,
299, Sauciehall Street,
Glasgow.

"Show him in," said Arbuthnot, "and be ready to show him out again."

7
In Which We Encounter an Example of Persistence

Mr. James Briggs, when he made his appearance, was a rather remarkable-looking man. He was as tall as Arbuthnot, that is to say, about two inches shorter than myself. His hair was iron-grey in colour, and I judged him to be at least fifty years of age. These are details. What impressed me was his face. Every angle in it—I say angle advisedly, for it was notably deficient in curves—seemed to betoken strength. The heavy lines were those of a man who had come triumphantly out of a hard life. His eyes gleamed from under drooping lids in a way that suggested impetuosity sternly disciplined. His chin was the chin of a conqueror.

So much had I taken in when I heard the voice of Arbuthnot, with that cold steel ring in it that I knew of old meant anger in repression.

"This is an unexpected honour, Sir Baxter."

The two men faced each other, neither flinching, while I stood endeavouring to comprehend what I had just heard.

"So," continued Arbuthnot, "you were content to telephone while I was away, but you favour me with a call in person as soon as I return. I congratulate you on the efficiency of your espionage system."

Then the other spoke, and his voice, though steady, was harsh and grating.

"Mr. Arbuthnot, I sought an interview with you under the name of a business acquaintance because I felt reasonably certain you would decline to receive me, if I came openly. For this I apologize. On the 11th of this month I sought your assistance and had the misfortune to give offence in my manner of doing so. For that I apologize profoundly. My plea in extenuation is that at the time I was acting under a severe nervous strain. I now come again, prepared to lay my whole trouble before you, before I ask you to decide whether you can intervene. If you can do so, there is nothing in my power to offer which I would refuse you for your services, whether successful or not, for I am perfectly confident that in you reposes my only hope."

On the whole, I thought the man had made a very honourable *amende*.

Arbuthnot was speaking.

"Sit down," said he, pulling forward another easy chair toward the fire. "I accept your apology unreservedly. In return for it I will be perfectly frank with you. I have been absent from London on a difficult and important case. During that time a certain person, whom we need not name, wrote to me to ask me to assist you. On another occasion when I was passing through London I saw him, and he personally urged your claims. I was obliged to decline owing to the pressure of this other matter. Conditions are still unaltered, and I see little chance of amending my decision, but if you care to state your business in confidence I will give you a definite answer. By the way, d'you know my friend King?"

We nodded to each other.

"King," said Arbuthnot, "is the repository of many secrets. You will not object to his presence, I take it?"

"Certainly not. I accept your terms. If I can't enlist your help, so much for the worse for me—and for another."

"Proceed," said Arbuthnot, taking a fresh pipe from the mantelpiece.

Sir Baxter Creen went to his subject direct, as if he realized it would pay him well to do so in dealing with Arbuthnot.

"I have, or had, a daughter," he said. "You lead a busy life, but even you may have heard of Iris Creen. I was proud that she should be judged beautiful. She resembles her dead mother in that respect, for I, as you see, have no pretensions to good looks. She is only twenty-three, and for the last two years she has had all London at her feet. She could have married some of the proudest titles in England, and did not. I never interfered. I cared to see her happy, not merely married to some decadent from the English aristocracy. I trusted her, for I fancied I saw in her, not the hardness they charge me with, but a certain inherited power of selection and judgment that would prevent her making a fool of herself. On the tenth of this month she disappeared in the company of her chauffeur."

We both knew the story, of course, but, speaking for myself, it acquired a new impressiveness from his lips.

"Under these circumstances my first thought was to get her back, my second to avoid a scandal. A man doesn't make a fortune in business and remain entirely unspotted, but she was good, and I always showed her my best side. I would take her back without a question asked. But a woman marked by scandal, and yet inheriting the vast sum that will come her way, is doomed to a life on the dubious fringe of society, little better than the demimonde. Therefore I would not invoke police help. I called in two private agencies after you had refused me. So far they have 'found' her four times—at Eastbourne, at Colwyn Bay, in Edinburgh, and in Jersey. In each case they were wrong."

He laughed grimly.

"So I have written and sacked them both," he added.

"Tell me all you can," said Arbuthnot.

"At 3 p.m. on the 10th Iris left my house in Park Lane to pay a week-end visit to some friends at High Wycombe. I was away at a board meeting when she went, so she left a little penciled note, couched in her usual affectionate terms, to say "good-bye'. You can see the note, but there was no hint in it of any unusual intentions. The car was a Rolls, and the chauffeur a new man I had engaged for her only one week previously, on the 3rd. His name was Willaims—Leonard Williams. The same evening, as I was sitting down to a lonely dinner, I had a telephone call. It was for Iris, to tell her that her favourite hunter, which should have been sent to High Wycombe, had slipped up in the loose box and strained a sinew and was therefore not available. She had chiefly gone to stay with the Bur-netts for the sake of a day's hunting, you understand.

"I immediately put in a trunk call to High Wycombe, only to hear that Iris had not yet arrived. I asked them to ring me up as soon as she did so. At midnight they rang up to say she was still absent. I surmised road trouble, and sent off another car to do rescue work if necessary. In the early morning another telephone message announced that the second car had arrived and found nothing. Fortunately Mrs. Burnett is a sensible woman. I asked her to invent an excuse for Iris and keep her own counsel. Then I went out personally and searched the road—in vain. And everything done since has been equally in vain. Neither of them has been seen or heard of. You see, it is very likely that but for the accident to the horse no inquiries would have been made till much later; I did not expect her return until Monday."

"What about the car?" asked Arbuthnot. "A Rolls-Royce isn't exactly easy to hide."

"The car," said Sir Baxter, "was found abandoned on Dartmoor on the 13th. That gave me hope that that lonely area might conceal the missing pair, but search has been fruitless."

"It appears," suggested Arbuthnot, "that there is nothing to settle the question as to whether the flight was an abduction or an elopement."

"I pray the former," said Creen, "for in that case her chances of returning unscathed are so much the greater. But if it were an abduction case I should have expected a demand for ransom before now. On the other hand, if it were an elopement I should most likely have received some request for forgiveness and reconciliation. Instead, there is this blank silence."

"They might fear you too much," said Arbuthnot dryly.

"Iris would not. She knows perfectly well I would not have refused her marriage with *any* man who went to work about it in an honourable way. I have my pride but I have always put her happiness first. I trusted in the level head I have always found on her shoulders. If this is an elopement it's a purely unnecessary one, and shows the man in a bad light."

"You are an unusual parent," said my friend. "It makes your misfortune the more regrettable."

I think Creen took heart from those words. "Can I anticipate your help," he asked promptly.

"The trail is cold," returned Arbuthnot. "I am not a magician. On the other hand, I am bound to admit that you have my sympathy. Allow me to ask a few questions."

"By all means."

"Had Miss Creen any considerable amount of money on her when she left home?"

"She may have had. She had drawn a hundred pounds from her account the day before. One cannot say she did it for the purpose of elopement, for she may have needed it for a dozen reasons."

"The notes have not been traced?"

"They were Treasury notes."

"H'm. Tell me frankly if, supposing this to have been an abduction, you have anyone in mind likely to have organized it?"

I think Creen was guilty of a moment's hesitation. "Men do not succeed in business without making enemies, and I suppose I have my share. But I could not point at anyone likely to have done such a thing. I could mention half a dozen names, but it would probably mean nothing more than so many wild-goose chases."

"You are satisfied that your search of the Dartmoor region was effective?"

"As effective as time and money could make it. Bearing in mind my daughter's exceptional good looks, I fail to see how the numerous enquiry agents could have failed to identify her had she been there. Consider that I was offering ten thousand pounds to the agency, and another thousand to the actual man who found her, and I think you will agree they had some incentive to combing out the neighbourhood."

"Then it is reasonable to conclude that the car was taken to Dartmoor by an accomplice, in which case the abduction theory gains ground."

"What then?"

"If we are dealing with the first degree of cunning we might look for them in the diametrically opposite direction to Dartmoor. I lay a ruler on the map of England so that it passes through London and has the centre of Dartmoor at one end. The other end will reach the East Coast somewhere east of Colchester, if I know my map as I think I do. Yes, if I decide to take up this case I think it might pay me to work in that direction."

It was as well that the conversation did not require my assistance, for I sat dumbfounded. All trails seemed to lead towards that dismal corner of the North Sea coast where I had already spent such unpleasant days. I was divided between admiration of Arbuthnot's skill in throwing out a suggestion that might give him an opportunity of returning where his interests lay, and fear of some Nemesis that seemed intent on driving us eastward to an unforeseen *débâcle*.

Sir Baxter Creen was speaking. "I see your point. But may I suggest it is a very slender basis for a detailed search?"

"Granted. But we are rather in the position of the Meredithian character who threw up his head like a ha'penny and went by the toss! Our only other hope seems to lie in the identity of the man Williams. No doubt that has been investigated."

"The man had an excellent recommendation, but my chief ground for engaging him was that Iris seemed satisfied that he was suitable. I always had faith in her judgment. He was tall, with a keen, determined face, and good manners. I put him down as an ex-officer, fallen on evil days. I took up his reference more as a matter of course, than anything else, and found it quite satisfactory."

"You might tell me the name of his late employer, who recommended him."

"Certainly. His name was the Honourable Geoffrey Charteris."

Crash! An involuntary movement of my legs, stretched out before the fire, had sent poker and tongs into the fender with a hideous rattle. I bent hastily to recover them and to hide my confusion.

"Another twinge, King?" I heard Arbuthnot asking sympathetically. Without waiting for my answer he added, "King received a leg wound in the war, and occasionally during a cold spell of weather it still gives him sudden excruciating pains."

"Damnable," I managed to utter, as I sank back in my chair, and felt the unwanted crimson ebbing slowly from my cheeks.

"Charteris was the name, I think you said?" went on Arbuthnot slowly. "What had he to tell you?"

"Not much. Apparently he keeps a car in town. The chauffeur was taken ill two months ago and Mr. Charteris drove the car himself. This man Williams was a down-at-heel fellow who looked after his car outside a night club on one occasion. Charteris slipped down while dancing and hurt his wrist and found to his relief that this fellow could drive. He was impressed by him as one who was down on his luck through no fault of his own. The man was reticent about his own affairs, but nevertheless Charteris gave him a trial as driver and found him so satisfactory that he retained him till his regular man was available, and then gave him an excellent testimonial. That was all he could tell me."

"How did Miss Creen come to be without a chauffeur?"

"Her former man was drunk on duty and was immediately dismissed. This man Williams must have heard of the occurrence for he applied before the vacancy had been advertised."

"Indeed? Have you been able to learn anything from your servants that might give a hint as to the relations between your daughter and the man Williams?"

"No. It is a delicate question, you will realize. I impressed on my butler, whom I can trust, the need for keeping his ears open, but he reports he has heard nothing."

"That means little. If there had been intrigue, pardon my expression, servants are almost bound to have seen or heard something."

"What can one do? If I interview them they will be naturally reluctant to speak. They love Iris; they certainly don't love me. In addition, the scandal will then be bruited abroad in a dozen objectionable forms."

"Yes. I suppose you haven't lost a footman lately?"

"No. Why do you ask?" Creen inquired, evidently astonished.

"Merely that you might then have possibly found a vacancy for me."

"I see." For the first time in the interview Creen's face relaxed into something like a smile. "No, I haven't lost a man, but I could very well employ an extra one."

"It seems our best hope of picking up a clue. You still have time to get an 'unclassified' advertisement into to-morrow's papers. My name for the occasion will be James Marsh."

"Can you do the work?" asked Creen curiously.

"I can try. You will have taken pity on me as an ex-service man—like Williams. I hope you will allow King to call occasionally in order that I may have the pleasure of waiting on him!"

"I'm immensely in in your debt," said Sir Baxter as he rose to go. "I am reluctant to refer to money matters, but you have my guarantee on that question."

"Well, well," said Arbuthnot enigmatically, "it may cost you a good deal; but, on the other hand, it may cost you exactly nothing at all. Good-bye."

As soon as we were alone I was bound to broach the subject that was naturally uppermost in my mind.

"What the devil do you make of Charteris's coming into this business?" I demanded.

Arbuthnot almost giggled with sheer joy.

"Magnificent!" he said. "I haven't had a case for months that was capable of providing such a succession of stimuli to the jaded brain of the investigator."

"When I was a boy," I remarked, "I remember reading a ghastly story about a man-eating spider. I know now there are no such things, but I have the feeling that we keep on touching, here and there, the web woven by some human equivalent of that ancient nightmare, while the foul creature itself remains hidden, ready to rush out at the critical moment and fasten on yet another victim."

"Very fine," said Arbuthnot, grinning unfeelingly. "*My* chief concern is as to what one does if one should happen inadvertently to shoot the contents of a soup-plate over the dress-shirt of a peer of the realm!"

The telephone rang in time to stop my reply. Arbuthnot answered it. When he had heard the message he turned to me with a shrug of the shoulders.

"The Honourable Geoffrey Charteris has left London by car, going north," said he.

8
In Which I Take Up My Scientific Pursuits

"That's a pity," I responded. "Of course I realize that his connexion with this affair may be of pure coincidence, but when you know a man has been concerned in one kidnapping case, and then hear his name mentioned in what may very well be another, you are bound to take notice."

"Perspicuous as usual, King. The logical mind suggests a probable coincidence, yet some less logical corner of the brain clings to a hope that there may be something else in the matter. Hence the fire-irons get demolished through your habit of jumping to conclusions. Now to act."

"But how?"

"My work is already arranged for the next few days. As for you, you will have to go back to Leasinghoe."

"Ugh!" I had no love for that place—alone.

"Yes, we know the man Buller is in possession of certain information. But to my mind he is a very unlikely person to part with any of it. He has no imagination, judging by the account you gave of the conversation you overheard. Such a man cannot be frightened into a confession. But his accomplice comes into a very different category. His remarks showed him to have a mind capable of feeling terror. Do you think you might recognize him—or at least his voice—again?"

"I hope so."

"Very well. On your arrival at Leasinghoe you will call on Colonel Gregory."

"Indeed?"

"You will tell him that your studies make it desirable for you to have the services of a boatman in order to reach otherwise inaccessible parts of the area."

"Yes."

"He will tell you he knows nothing about any damned boats."

"Most likely!"

"You will then ask if you may consult his butler on the matter."

"I see."

"He will tell you you can do any sanguinary thing you like, as long as you don't worry *him.*"

"Yes."

"You will then interview Buller, tell him you have come to the conclusion he is a much-wronged man, and give him five shillings. Then ask him to recommend a boatman. If we are lucky he will suggest his comrade in crime at Wivenhoe."

"And then?"

"If you can identify the man, send to Kaye the code-word 'Eureka' by wire, and I will come down as promptly as circumstances permit. Go about armed, and remember the night-air grows less healthy towards the end of the month!"

"I am not likely to forget, especially with the cheerful prospect of long boating excursions with a man there is every reason to believe was recently concerned in a murder! Meanwhile, what happens about Charteris?"

"Kaye will continue to have his rooms watched. When he returns to London, if you are still at Leasinghoe, I shall probably recall you to assist me in dealing with him."

It was thus that the 22nd of November saw me journeying back to the place I had left less than twenty-four hours previously. It was with no light heart I went. As the train traversed mile after mile in its inexorable progress I went over an amazing list of persons who had, from our point of view, behaved unaccountably. Beginning with Colonel Gregory of the apparently elastic income, and his vile factotum Buller, there were also Hunt the mysterious, with his hypothetical brother and his mythical sister, the unknown man who was Buller's accomplice, and the three men who had contrived the abduction of Turnbull, including in their number that somewhat sinister figure, Charteris whose name had come on me as a thunderclap in the interview with Baxter Creen. Here was a stage of actors, all apparently playing their parts, and yet, to the baffled onlooker, it seemed no cohesion could arrive from the chaos of events in which they moved. One could devise a dozen hypotheses, and every time one was left in the position of a man who has successfully solved a jig-saw puzzle, only to find a number of seemingly unnecessary pieces left over at the end.

The morning papers contained news of the inquest on Hunt. The medical opinion was that death had probably occurred from strangulation previous to immersion, but, the body being much discoloured from its period in the water, it was not completely certain that this was the cause of death. There were no wounds on the body. Acting on the coroner's direction the jury returned an open verdict of "Found Dead". No evidence as to how the body came to be in the water was offered, and the paper I was reading had a leaderette entitled "Another Undiscovered Criminal: What are our Police Doing?" Taking into account what I knew about the case I thought this was distinctly unfair to the force.

I think Mrs. Jerrold was glad to see me back, and I am sure the faithful George, who had been warned by wire to be at the station, rejoiced on my return. I deferred my interview with the Colonel until I had lunched, and then set off for Lesslands Grange.

Buller admitted me, and it was something of a shock to renew acquaintance with that face of low cunning. He was civil, having probably realized he had been doing himself no good by his behaviour towards me. On the other hand, the Colonel, like Kipling's Sergeant, was distinctly less than kind. The interview was not very different from Arbuthnot's forecast. After I had stated my case the Colonel glared at me and replied unfeelingly,

"Well, I suppose if you're anxious to join our late friend Hunt, Buller will fix it up for you."

I recoiled a step. How was I to interpret that remark? Was I to take it at face-value, or did the ambiguity shroud a warning to keep away from that *locus* of disturbance Arbuthnot talked about? It might merely be the speaker's notorious ill-temper, venting itself in an evil pleasantry— or it might not. However, I had to go on—I wasn't accustomed to neglecting Arbuthnot's wishes.

Buller was complaisant. I told him that I, for one, was certain that the accusation against him was rubbish, I explained my need for a reliable boatman to enable me to study the shores of the creek. I wished him good luck on the 25th when he was due to surrender to his bail, and passed him his *douceur*. It worked.

"I can get you a feller," he said. "Yacht-hand, but paid off for the winter. A very nice quiet chap. Nothing to talk to, you understand, but steady. I'll look him up in Wivenhoe to-night, and tell him to see you in the morning."

This was fortunate. The reference to Wivenhoe, coupled with Buller's obvious anxiety that I should not lure the man into conversation, suggested that he intended to nominate his accomplice for the post. When I went to bed that night I did not know whether I was more gratified or alarmed at the prospect.

Evidently Buller carried out his undertaking, for at ten the next morning, Mrs. Jerrold told me that there was a man come to see me about a boat. When he slouched into the room, clad in the traditional blue jersey, I naturally took a keen look at him. The general impression he gave me corresponded with the indistinct memory I had of the man I had seen in the bar of the 'Three Kings'; more I could not say. His tanned, weather-beaten face, deeply-sunk blue eyes, and stubbly growth on chin, did not make an alarming picture, but I recollected that the man I had seen, unlike Buller, had apparently shown some compunction over his share of the crime.

"You was wanting a boat?" he said interrogatively, fingering his cap.

Did I, or did I not, recognize that voice? I thought I did, but I was on guard against being led astray by a preconceived idea.

"Yes. You were recommended to me by Buller, the butler at Lesslands Grange. What is your name?"

"Josh Reynolds."

"And you come from?"

"Wivenhoe, sir."

"Really, I think I may have seen you before. Did I, by any chance, see you with Buller in the Wivenhoe road last Saturday evening? I'm not sure, because it was only by the light of a street lamp."

"May have done. I did see him that evening, so far as I remembers."

This was confirmation! I ventured one more step.

"I'm sorry for Buller. It seems to me he is being made to suffer just because the police can't lay the hands on the man responsible for that business."

"Well, sir, it's not for me to say, but I'd swear Buller never did it."

"So would I. Now to business. I am making an ecological survey of this area. That means a study of all the wild plants and where they grow. Perhaps you know I'm from an American university. Now in many places it's much easier to reach the marshes from the waterside than from the land. Hence I want a boat, and a man to row me wherever I direct."

"Very good, sir. I'm your man. Being winter I wouldn't ask too much for hire."

"I'll give two shillings an hour, and throw in a pound note when I've finished with you."

It was a high rate of pay, but I wanted to be on good terms with the man, and I knew my supposed transatlantic nationality would account for any undue liberality.

"That's very fair, sir. When will you be wanting me?"

I wished I could tell him I didn't want him at all. Having practically established the fact that he was the man we wanted, it was an anti-climax to have to spend weary hours on the creek engaged in a pretence of scientific work. However, I clearly saw it had to be endured.

"To-day, if possible," I said, "about two o'clock."

"Very good, sir. Perhaps you can find a little old stage down below here on the creek. You can almost see it from this window."

"I've seen it," I replied.

"I'll have the boat there at two this afternoon."

With that he went, cheered up by the prospect of easy money, and I thought I was justified in going to the post office and sending off my code-word 'Eureka', feeling rather proud that I had settled my job so promptly. When I returned I found George Higgins busy tilling the soil in the cottage garden.

"Sir," said he, "I'm taking the liberty of putting in a couple of rows of broad beans, being the only thing in the vegetable line it's any use planting at this season."

"Carry on, George," said I; "even if we're not here to eat them I've no doubt some one else will."

There was something distinctly likeable about Higgins, apart from the fact that I have always a soft spot in my heart for an ex-soldier.

When I had lunched I took the botany case that Arbuthnot had insisted on my having, and supplemented my equipment by some bottles of beer in a haversack. Thus provided I was standing on the decrepit and forlorn stage before two o'clock. The tide was nearly up and the water gurgled uneasily under the planks, washing to and fro weeds as surely as fat as those that rooted on Lethe wharf. I don't know why the memory of those lines should have come to me then, but I think that I had the same sense of impending disaster that the first act of the immortal tragedy conveys. "The curtain has only just risen," Arbuthnot had said. But even then I was such a long, long way from realizing the drama that was to ensue.

Above me the sky was a universal leaden blue, and there was that stillness in the air that seems only to fall in autumn. The cold of the day before had gone, and the air was damp and close. The creaking of oars in rowlocks drove me from my meditations. An ancient black tub was wallowing towards me under the skilful propulsion of the man Reynolds. He came alongside cleverly, and seized the piece of old rope that I had once before noted pendant from the landing-stage.

"Jump in, sir," he said. "She ain't much to look at, but she's roomy, and clean inside."

I passed down my impedimenta, and stepped gingerly in, to find he had not spoken untruly.

"Work seawards," I said. "Keep near the left bank and put in to the side whenever I tell you."

So we set off on about as futile a journey as the mind of man could well devise, and I come to an example of what seemed the dominant characteristic of this case.

Just as Arbuthnot had been detached on another errand and had thus encountered the symbol on the barn; just as we had been interrupted by Baxter Creen and had thereby picked up a remarkable piece of information; so now, when I was steadily killing time, was I to have a sudden reminder that we moved in the midst of mystery.

We had spent some time nosing into the marsh and then pushing ourselves off again. I had accumulated quite a collection of vegetation entirely nameless and uninteresting to me, and I was contemplating opening a bottle of beer and with it endeavouring to dissolve the taciturnity of my assistant when the shock came.

A few yards inland from the creek was. a low bluff covered with the long tufts of autumn dried grass. As my eye chanced to travel towards it I suddenly found my gaze reciprocated. A face, largely masked by a cap pulled down well over the eyes, was looking at me from between two tussocks of grass. The owner of the face in question evidently was lying prone.

"Steady, sir," said a voice behind me. In my astonishment I had made an involuntary movement and the boat was rocking perilously. I glanced at my companion, but his face did not reveal that he had noticed anything. When

I looked again to the bluff the watcher had vanished, having no doubt wriggled backwards. As we were below his level, he had so become invisible. My first impulse was to put ashore and give chase, but I was deterred by a double consideration: the man might be merely a sportsman, or more likely a poacher, and if he were otherwise I was far from sure as to what the attitude of Reynolds would be in a fracas. What annoyed me most was that I had not seen the man clearly enough, to have a hope of identifying him again.

We proceeded downstream till we were in sight of the deserted buildings I had seen on the day of the fruitless search for Hunt. Then I gratified Reynolds with beer before we turned to work back against the tide. It was while his attention was concentrated on the liquor that I saw the man again. This time he crouched behind some low bushes, probably brambles, that came near to the bank. Had I not been alert I do not suppose I should have seen him at all. I could sympathize then with the annoyance felt by Alice when the Cheshire Cat insisted on reappearing at unexpected moments. It was an uncomfortable feeling to know that that individual had been keeping pace with the boat going downstream, slipping from hedge to hedge, from bank to bank, from bush to bush, unseen and watchful.

"Get back as quick as you can," I said to Reynolds. "I've forgotten an important letter I had to post."

The man rowed his best, but it was long past four, the hour for post, when I disembarked. In the cottage a telegram awaited me:

Purchasing shares as directed.—Kaye.

It was a few moments before I saw the cleverness of it in rendering my code-word harmless should there be any interested person with access to the post office. "Eureka" as the name of a mine was distinctly convincing.

I regretted that it was too late to get a letter off to Arbuthnot, because I was now aware, for the first time since some one had chosen to write in blood on our cottage window, that we were an object of interest to some persons in the area. I did my best by dispatching a wire to

Kaye, hoping that its ambiguity, clumsy though it might be would be a sufficient hint to Arbuthnot that I should like his presence. I wrote:

> Unforeseen developments. Suspend purchase. Want advice. Writing.—Monk.

Then I drafted a letter to my friend and walked as far as Wivenhoe to post it in case I might thus catch the train dispatch. I would have relied on "George," but he had taken his homeward way before I returned to the cottage from the boat. I carried a powerful torch as well as my automatic, but nevertheless before I saw my fireside again I had resolved to abstain from evening walks. I saw nothing, but I was perfectly well aware I was followed. It was no wind that caused that stir behind the hedge, no predatory animal that sent the stones rattling down the bank into the road, no water-rat that splashed in some unseen pool. I was half-resolved to make a dash at him, whoever he might be, but it did not seem fair to take such a definite action before I knew how it would accord with Arbuthnot's plans. So I came back to Desolation Cottage, placed the lamp on the table near the window so that no shadows on the curtains should be there to call the attention of anyone who might be outside, and spent a decidedly unhappy evening.

9

In Which a Green Lamp Fails
to Carry Its Usual Significance

The morning of the 24th brought a telegram from Arbuthnot:

> *Exercise great caution over share purchase.*
> *Watch developments. Hope to return shortly.—*
> *Ponsonby.*

I thought the meaning was sufficiently obvious. Being
satisfied that Arbuthnot did not issue unnecessary warn-
ings, I did not view the future with any great degree of
composure.

The morning was wet, and I was not sorry to see it so,
for I had told my boatman I should not require him in the
event of rain, and I much preferred the cheering fire Mrs.
Jerrold had built to a morning's sojourn in the marsh under the surveillance of unknown and inimical eyes.

So I sat by the fire, emulating Arbuthnot in consump-
tion of tobacco, and wishing him back. In my pocket-book
was the man Reynold's address safely noted down. That
had been my task. It seemed the reasonable thing to lie
discreetly low until my friend returned to act. Had I but
known I was merely enjoying the lull before the storm.

Sergeant Wigmore called in the course of the morning.
He was disconsolate.

125

"The case against Buller has been withdrawn," he told me. "He was watched, but nothing fresh could be found out against him."

"Has anything been found out about Hunt?" I asked. "It seems to me that when the victim is an unknown man, investigations of an alleged murder must be exceedingly difficult."

"We've found nothing," said Wigmore gloomily. The papers are shouting about police incompetence. I'm sometimes inclined to think that Hunt was a lunatic who tied on a pair of water-wings and jumped into the creek under the impression he was spending a summer holiday at Margate."

"It's the strangest affair I've ever come across," I asserted.

"Ah, you're right there. I was just wondering if in your travels about the district for your scientific work you've ever seen anything unusual."

I answered negatively. "The place seems to have reverted to its old quiet," I said, and he took his departure without further conversation.

The afternoon brought another wire from Arbuthnot:

Coming down to-morrow.

This was splendid. I set to work mentally composing my report. Arbuthnot could hardly fail to be satisfied. Besides identifying Buller's accomplice I had secured definite evidence that the area was still 'a *locus* of disturbance'.

When Mrs. Jerrold went at nine that night I was extremely careful to see that doors and windows were securely fastened. Then I sat down and tried to concentrate on a novel. The truth was that I was reluctant to go to bed. The quiet day had given me time to picture myself as the object of attentions from that sinister power that still moved so completely unseen. I was alone in the cottage. I heard again in imagination the death-screech of the man whose life had been torn from him in the marsh. A mouse stirring somewhere in the kitchen shook me. In damp weather, like many other people, I am subject to that creeping sensation of the hair at the back of the head. No doubt it is a purely physical effect, but unpleasant. It was one o'clock before I finally took up my lamp and went to bed.

I undressed, extinguished my light, and went to open my bedroom window, which had earlier been closed against the rain. The sky had now cleared, stars shone, but the night was dark. Now I should make it plain that as my window faced toward the marsh, the old landing-stage was visible in daytime, lying about half-right as they say in the army. By craning my head to the left I could just see the upper windows of Lesslands Grange.

It was purely by chance that I should lean out and look towards the latter place. Then I withdrew my head in bewilderment. From one of the windows of the Grange shone a clear *green* light!

I sat down on my bed before the open window and thought furiously. There is nothing in the law to prevent a person's using a green light in his bedroom, even at one o'clock in the morning. Nevertheless, it is indisputable that very few people do so. Was I witnessing some harmless eccentricity of the old Colonel, or was this another trifle to add to that long list of unexplained incidents that occupied my mind?

I returned to the window. The light still shone. A red light is recognized as a warning, but to me there is something far more baleful in green, like the glare of eyes from some jungle animal that moves otherwise unseen. I turned my eyes toward the right, and even as I did so another green light leapt into being in the marsh!

Fascinated, I watched. It is very difficult to form any estimate of distance in the night, but I felt reasonably sure that the second light must be somewhere near the land-ing-stage. I was equally certain that the two lights must be visible from each other. Here was no harmless freak to be idly viewed, but something whose strangeness was as disturbing as those other mysteries the marsh had already offered us.

I looked back towards the Grange. The light that had been there was gone!

I did not need the evidence of those two signals to tell me that there was some unknown link between the Grange and the marsh, but here was a magnificent opportunity to learn something of what that liaison was. By that green glow in the marsh were, without doubt, men, or at least a man engaged in some enterprise that shunned the light of day. The good people of Leasinghoe were one and all fast asleep at that hour. The light burned unchallenged and unnoticed.

I think I am normally a man of action. Down there, cloaked by darkness, something was happening that it be-hooved us to know. Then caution took a turn. *"If you're anxious to join our late friend Hunt, Buller will fix it up for you."* At that hour, and under those circumstances, the only too well-remembered sentence was enough to give me a cold, uneasy feeling in the spine.

So I sat hesitating till a glance at the luminous dial of my watch showed me that twenty minutes had elapsed since I had put out my lamp preparatory to bed. What should I do? I looked again and the marsh light was gone.

I think it was that that decided me. I scrambled coat and trousers on over my pyjamas, thrust my feet into socks and shoes, drew my automatic and torch from their usual abode under my pillow, and rushed downstairs. The house being empty, there was no need for caution indoors. In a few seconds I was outside, with the front-door key in my pocket, and was running across the garden.

Once through the hedge I became circumspect. I fancied I could find my way fairly well toward the landing-stage, though, as I estimated later, I must actually have trended rather too much to the left. As I worked my way forward down the wet, slippery, grass slope, with my hand firmly closed over the butt of my weapon, I kept saying to myself, "You fool, do you want to go the way Hunt went?" Nevertheless I went on, my pace growing slower and slower as I judged I was approaching the position the green lamp had occupied.

The marsh was as silent as the grave. This in itself was disconcerting. Each time my foot came out of some mud-hole with a sucking noise I imagined a silent listener. Once I splashed into a veritable pool, and felt sure I had betrayed my presence.

Perhaps I was within a hundred yards of the landing-stage when I turned my head, and then stopped dead. Behind me, from Lesslands Grange, the green, unwavering light shone once more. But this time, instead of an answering signal from the marsh, there came to my ears the unmistakable rattle of oars in rowlocks. Was this, then, the end of my adventure? The noise of oars grew fainter and ceased, and I began to regret that I had not come out more promptly, even at some risk. A few chance words overheard might have told us more than we could learn by much patient investigation.

It was then that I suddenly realized that I was not alone in the marsh. Sounds that suggested a man running came to me apparently from the eastward, that is to say, from the opposite direction to that in which I had been moving. Splash went his foot in a pool, and twice I heard him stumble. The darkness shrouded all, and it was uncanny to hear those rapid steps towards one and to know that one could not hope to see the runner until he was within ten yards.

Very likely, judging by the sounds, he would run straight into my arms. I was not so very far wrong. A dim black shape appeared, and passed within less than ten yards of my position. I was ready for him, but there was no need. He went by, looking neither to left nor to right. As he ran his breath came in horrible panting gasps, as if he were at the end of his tether. Surely no man ran like that unless the devil himself ran at his heels. I stared after him in astonishment, and that was nearly my undoing. *There were pursuers.*

Two at least of them came on me out of the darkness. They were running faster and much more easily than then quarry. It was only in the last couple of seconds that I saw that I was bound to be mistaken for the man they hunted. Then I was off, with my heart pounding against my ribs and a great fear driving me. Even at school I was never better than twelve seconds for the hundred, but that night I honestly believe I did even time. Even now I lay down my pen and shudder as I think of that race.

They had seen me. A voice shouted, "Stop or we shoot!" But panic fear was driving me; I could not have stopped for an angel with a flaming sword. "You'll—go—the—way—Hunt—went," said the clamorous throb of my head.

Then came the bullets. Crack! Crack! They passed above my head. How often in the old days had I cursed my men for aiming too high at night!

Here was the slope. I scarcely felt the rise in my mad rush. I stopped to look for no gap in the hedge but took a flying leap. A bramble tore at my cheek, a thorn scraped across my wrist, but I was through.

More by luck than by intention I had travelled in a straight line to the cottage. I fancied I might have gained a few yards on my pursuers. In three seconds more I was fitting the key in the front door. Crack came a bullet above my head and a splinter of brickwork fell. The key was in—

it turned—I was inside. Instantly I rammed home the top and bottom bolts with which the door was provided and retreated along the passage toward the kitchen. The passage bent at an angle to go round the foot of the stairs, and in that angle I stood. No bullet fired from any window could reach me there.

Straining my ears to catch the slightest sound, I leant against the wall, and considered the prospect of a vigil lasting till dawn. Certainly these were determined men. That I had indubitably saved a man's life did not at the moment appeal to me as a sufficient recompense for the possibility of losing my own before the night was out. I was not at all sure that I had not unwittingly interfered on the wrong side.

I wondered if the shots had aroused anyone in the neighbourhood. That they had been heard seemed certain, but whether there was anyone bold enough to set out and investigate seemed quite another matter. With the affair of Hunt in memory the bravest man might shrink from reconnoitering the marsh in the hours of darkness. I was certainly not safe till dawn. It was then that I realized with a sudden cold fear at my heart that my bedroom window had been open all this while. The cottage, as usual in the country, had low rooms, and a man, perched on the shoulders of another, could easily have reached the window.

Off came my shoes, and I tiptoed upstairs and stood by the open bedroom door listening. Was that a sound? My heart was still pumping loudly. I controlled myself with an effort. Yes, I could hear a rustling in the stems of the creeper that covered the front of the cottage; some one was coming up that way!

In a moment I was kneeling by the side of the bed remote from the window. The open space showed the darkest of blues, and I thought I should be able to detect the appearance of a head in it. The rustling increased: I heard a grunt, betokening violent effort, and a round black object framed itself in the open window. Without hesitating I fired. I aimed wide of the mark, for how should I be able to explain the presence of a dead man in my garden the next morning? The space showed clear again, and a noise came up from below as if some one had landed heavily upon the ground. Then there was silence.

Throughout the rest of the night, a matter of over five hours, I watched and listened, going to the staircase to light my pipe and returning to the bedroom to watch. I dared not go to the window to fasten it, for I should have been too conspicuous a target. Only as dawn came stealing over the eastern sky, and I, from behind a curtain in the window of the back bedroom, saw Mrs. Jerrold entering by the back gate to take up her day's labours, did I return to bed.

Within half an hour her voice announcing shaving water broke my first troubled slumber. I shouted to her to come in.

"I've had a bad night," I said. "I woke up early this morning imagining I had heard guns fired, and I couldn't get to sleep again so I think I'll stay in bed till about ten."

"'Twasn't no imagination," said the good lady. "I've seen Mrs. Bessom. She's pretty nigh frantic. Guns going off and a man running round her cottage."

"Really," I said with the best imitation of surprise I could manage, "then it wasn't merely a dream. But what a remarkable part of the world this is, to be sure. We seem to live in mystery."

"You're right, sir. Such goings-on is enough to frighten anyone. Well, if you aren't getting up just yet, perhaps you won't mind if I slip back and see that poor soul Bessom. By all accounts she's been in hysterics half the night and not a soul come near her."

"Didn't anyone else hear the noise?" I asked.

"To be sure. I heard them myself, but you couldn't expect a woman to go out at that hour to face men with guns. And the couple next door heard them, but they shoved their heads under the bedclothes. Not till daylight did one of 'em go off to tell P.C. Jones."

I let her go, and settled down again, not to sleep but to think. I had already made up my mind to be ignorant of all that had transpired during the night. What appalled me was that I was now clearly involved in whatever devilment was going on. The pursuers believed they had traced their quarry to my cottage and seen him unlock the door and let himself in. That clearly branded me as an accomplice. Therefore I could quite easily expect to be selected as the next object of their attentions. Who was the man who ran for his life? Whence did he come? Where did he go? Was he a scoundrel escaping or the victim of some plot? I flogged my brain with questions, and got no answer. Thank God Arbuthnot would be here at noon.

I suppose that in spite of all my worries, tired nature finally asserted itself, for I slept, only to wake with a start and realize that I was not alone in the room.

"So you came home in a hurry last night, King," said a familiar voice. It was Arbuthnot, surveying me quizzically.

"Good heavens, yes!" said I, struggling up to a sitting posture. "But how did *you* know?"

"H'm. When a man slumbers till after noon, with a three-inch scratch on his cheeks and another on his wrist it is a fair assumption that he was rather busy the night before."

"Yes," I responded. "Perhaps you also noticed the chipped brick above the front door, where the bullet hit?"

I was always pleased when I could manage a little shock for Arbuthnot, and so reverse the ordinary procedure.

"So it has come to bullets, has it?" said he, his eyes brightening with interest.

"It has. Wasn't Mrs. Jerrold informative?"

"I haven't afforded her an opportunity. When I heard you were still in bed I came straight up, scenting trouble. Now get up and tell me all your news while you're dressing."

I was nothing loth, and in under half an hour I had acquainted him with the substance of what I have already related. Then I proceeded to mention casually that Mrs. Bessom had been prostrated by the shock of hearing the shots and the footsteps of a man around her cottage. I had not supposed it particularly important, but the effect of my last remarks on Arbuthnot was electrical.

"Come on," said he. "We've got to call on that woman *at once*. Don't you see the significance of what you have mentioned? Come quickly, and be ready to sympathize."

He rushed me straight out of the house and up the road to Rose Cottage. The door was opened to us by a neighbour we did not know. In response to our inquiries she informed us that Mrs. Bessom was lying down on the sofa in the parlour, and was still feeling extremely prostrated.

"You tell her our names," said Arbuthnot. "Mr. Monk, Mr. Ponsonby. When she knows who it is she'll see us, I'm sure."

It was even so. We were promptly ushered into the room, where Mrs. Bessom, the usual luxuriant bloom of her cheeks changed to a distinctly greyish colour, lay extended on a couch.

"Dear, dear, Mrs. Bessom," said Arbuthnot, as he spoke, closing the door against the neighbour who evinced an intention to be present at the interview, "this is a sad business. We felt bound to call and offer our sympathies."

"Very kind of both you gentlemen," said Mrs. Bessom feebly.

"Of course," continued Arbuthnot, "we wouldn't worry you in your present weak state for anything, but we are naturally interested in something happening so close home. It might be our turn next, you know."

I wished Arbuthnot hadn't put quite such a note of conviction into his last sentence.

"Yes, sir. And between friends I don't mind speaking at all. I've told young Jones all I know, so there's my duty done and a clear conscience."

"When did all these alarming incidents occur?" asked my friend.

"I think it must have been between one and two. I was lying awake, for, truth to tell, since poor Mr. Hunt went I haven't been sleeping any too well, and I wasn't having no woman in to sleep, neighbours being that nosey when they get in a house. Then I heard two bangs quick one after another. "Lord!" I says, "what's that then?" I was pretty thankful I had a light burning."

"You sleep at the back of the house?" interposed Arbuthnot.

"Yes, sir. And the sounds come from the front."

"From the marsh probably."

"That's what they sounded like. Then there was a few minutes quiet, and my shakiness was just going off a bit when bang went another, sounding a bit nearer to me, and then I heard some one running on the gravel path outside. I tell you I was shaking like a leaf, and what do you think I did? Got up and went round, lighting candles in all the rooms so that anyone would think there was lots of folks stirring."

"That showed presence of mind," said Arbuthnot encouragingly.

"Then I hopped back into bed," the dame continued, "and lay there like a jelly. And just as I was hoping 'twas all over bang went another, and I went under the bed-clothes quick."

"That wasn't all?" suggested Arbuthnot, and I glanced at him in some surprise. How the deuce did he know that there was more to follow?

"No, sir. The worst was to come. I must have waited nigh two hours, and then I thought of all them good candles wasting and plucked up courage to go and put 'em out. So I went first into Mr. Hunt's bedroom in the front of the house. There was the candle burning and the bed made just as if he'd been coming back to it, for I haven't had the heart yet to interfere with his room. And there was his trunks a-lying as he'd left 'em, and some books of his I'd carried upstairs, an" his dressing-gown on the back of the door."

She paused, and despite her condition of shock I could see she was not oblivious of obtaining an effect.

"Then, my God, I looks towards the window, the curtains not being drawn, you understand, and there *he* was with his white face a-pressed against the window-pane!"

"Who was?" I asked involuntarily.

"Mr. Hunt!"

"What!"

"Yes, I know what you'll say. He's dead, and I told the police myself that it was his body they fished out of the water. And so it was, I know. But he'd come back, poor murdered man, asking for justice on them as killed him."

"Could you swear to him?" asked Arbuthnot incisively, for the good lady showed signs of incipient hysteria.

"I couldn't quite do that, sir, for I gave one screech as soon as I saw him, and run to my own room and locked myself in."

"Do you think it might have been that brother of his who came here twice?"

"No, sir, his brother wasn't like him at all and this face was."

"H'm. I suppose Constable Jones had a look at the room to see if it had been broken into?"

"No, sir; he took down my statement and went off to inform his superiors."

"Then no doubt the woman who is here with you went up?"

"No fear. She wouldn't go in there, after what she's heard, for a thousand pounds!"

"Then shall I step up and see if everything's all right? You might have seen a man preparing to break in."

"Thank you kindly, sir. I hadn't thought of that. It's the front room, right at the end of the landing."

Arbuthnot went while I sat and listened to fragmentary repetitions of what I had already heard. Finally I pressed a pound note on the dame, and advised her to buy some comforts to cheer herself up after her very unpleasant experience. Arbuthnot returned. I fancied the shadow of a grin lurked behind his apparent air of solicitude.

"Nothing wrong, Mrs. Bessom," he said reassuringly. "Now I think we've worried you long enough. If we can do anything at any time don't hesitate to send for us."

"Do you believe in ghosts, King?" asked my friend as we strolled back to Desolation Cottage.

"I don't think so. Do you?"

"Not in the kind that presses its nose against window-panes. I always believed it was the privilege of ghosts to pass through closed doors and float airily upstairs. No self-respecting spook would cling to a bedroom window-sill."

"Surely you don't believe Hunt is alive?"

"I believe that some one came to see Hunt this morning, either to obtain sanctuary or to give him a warning, or both. What other interpretation is possible? I suppose he came to Hunt's cottage, despaired of getting in, went away, and hid till his pursuers had given up the chase, and then returned in a last attempt to get into touch with his friend."

"I don't often criticize," I remarked, "but it seems to me you have overlooked the fact that any accomplice of Hunt's would certainly know he was dead and that it was no use seeking him."

"Good for you, King. He would certainly know it, un-less—"

"Unless what?"

"Here we are at the cottage. Let's continue the discussion by the fireside."

We went in and settled down in a couple of easy chairs Arbuthnot continued his remarks.

"As Mrs. Bessom's narrative drew to an end," he said, "I pictured this man creeping back to the cottage, seeing a light in Hunt's bedroom, and laboriously and at imminent risk of his own life climbing up to it. He sees an empty room, but one bearing obvious signs of occupation. No doubt Hunt is out on one of his nocturnal expeditions. The man is surrounded by danger; at any minute he may tumble to the ground with a bullet between his shoulder-blades. He dare not wait for Hunt's return. Yet it is im-perative to get a message to Hunt. How is it to be done? He is unlikely to happen to have an envelope on him, and an open piece of paper thrust in the letter-box might fall into other hands. He retired into a dark corner of the garden, pencils a note on a scrap of paper he fortunately has on him, climbs up again to the window, and wedges his missive between the upper and lower sashes, which no-toriously fit badly in cottage windows. The end projects beyond the upper sash and Hunt will not fail to see it when he wakes in the morning. Then he catches sight of Mrs. Bessom and disappears hastily."

"That's all very well," I said, "but you haven't answered my previous objection. It seems to me that it is far more likely Mrs. Bessom saw one of the pursuers."

"Why on earth should the pursuers go there when they were perfectly sure they had seen him take shelter in *your* cottage? They probably knew Hunt was dead, while they also very likely knew that you are alive—*at present*. Why should they suspect Hunt's cottage?"

I suppose I was nettled. No man likes to hear the possibility of his early decease canvassed so callously.

"You forget," said I, "that had a message been left in the manner you suggest, it would have been there when you inspected the room a few minutes ago."

"It was," said Arbuthnot.

"It was!" I echoed, thunderstruck. "Then why on earth couldn't you tell me so at once?"

"Ah," said my friend, grinning. "Like Mrs. Bessom, I enjoy getting my effects."

"Never mind. I excuse you this time. Go on."

"As we were waiting to be admitted to the house I looked up to the window of the room I already knew to have been Hunt's, having visited it on the day I sprained my ankle. It was then I saw the piece of paper. That was nothing in itself, for the badly-made windows of cottages, with their unseasoned wood, have often to be wedged in that way to prevent their rattling. But after I had heard Mrs. Bessom's story I thought the matter was just worth looking into, and so it proved."

"And the message contained?"

Without a word Arbuthnot opened his pocket-book and passed me a folded scrap of paper.

"Read it for yourself," said he.

I have the original before me now as I write, and this is what I see:

khufdlpgfssushhvdzhvkag
ffyquookcywshfeormtjnb
masamtvkyfhzh.—JIM.

The letters naturally are not well spaced in the original, and in fact overlap here and there, as one would expect a message written in the dark.

"The man was no fool," said Arbuthnot, "to be able to sit down in the dark with the fear of death hanging over him and compose even a short message in cipher. I wish his brain had been a bit poorer, and then he might have condescended to write in plain English."

I had been gazing dismally at the thing as he was talking. The recrudescence of that confounded cipher and symbol gave me a feeling of helplessness.

"However, he committed one little indiscretion—in signing his name," continued Arbuthnot cheerfully.

"I don't see that," said I. "There must be hundreds of thousands of Jims in this country."

"Granted. But to whom do you sign yourself simply "Edmund" when you write?"

"I should to my parents if they were alive, and to my wife if I had one. As it is, only when I write to my brother Philip do I sign that way."

"Your *brother,* eh?"

"I see your point; but Mrs. Bessom swears the face wasn't that of Hunt's brother."

"It wasn't the face of the man she knew as Hunt's brother—a man unlike him in features, and one who has never troubled, as far as we know, to visit the scene of his disappearance. But the face she saw at the window was like Hunt."

I concede the possibility. "You wish to endow Hunt with one fictitious and one genuine brother."

"It is possible."

"Then how, as I asked before, could this brother fail to know that Hunt was dead?"

"Suggest a reason for yourself."

"Of course," I mused, "he might have been lying seriously ill and news was kept from him."

"Really, King," growled Arbuthnot, "that doesn't do much credit to your intelligence. So he got up from what might have been his death-bed, ran like a stag across country, and recklessly climbed up to bedroom windows! Try again."

"I see!" I said excitedly. "He had been in confinement somewhere and escaped."

"Precisely. Somewhere in this locality, a man belonging to the same gang as Hunt has been kept imprisoned since before Hunt's death. We begin to see our problem clearly outlined now, if never before. What is this gang after? And who are the people who seem capable of defending themselves and at the same time taking vengeance on their adversaries, even at the expense of rousing the whole countryside by revolver practice at dead of night?"

10
In Which We Afford Assistance to the Police

After lunch, our privacy was invaded by Sergeant Wig-more. We exchanged cordial greetings.

"Really, you know, Sergeant," said Arbuthnot reprovingly and with a twinkle in his eye, "you fellows must try and keep this district in better order. It isn't safe for people like me and Mr. Monk to go about."

We understood the sergeant to say under his breath that he had had about enough of it.

"No clue?" asked Arbuthnot. "Surely you can hope to find some footprints in the marsh after such a wet day as yesterday?"

"Yes, sir. Having taken Mrs. Bessom's statement, I was about to go down there and called in here on my way first to see if you gentlemen had heard anything last night. Of course, if you cared to step down with me to the marsh you'd be very welcome. Jones is at Colchester over a poaching case."

Did I, or did I not, imagine that the worthy sergeant had no love for a solo expedition to that home of mystery?

"I wasn't here," said Arbuthnot. "My friend was wakened by a sound he thought was a shot, and which was presumably the last one fired, as he remained awake and heard nothing more. That was all. We'll go for a stroll with you with pleasure. It shouldn't be impossible to run at least some of these people to ground, I should think."

"Well, sir, when Hunt disappeared we naturally kept a sharp look-out for any suspicious characters in the neighbourhood. We found no one; in fact there didn't seem anywhere such a person could lie concealed. Begging your pardons, you two gentlemen were the most unaccountable folks about here."

Arbuthnot laughed heartily.

"So what did you conclude?"

"We thought that Hunt's murderer, if he was murdered, must have come down for the occasion, so to speak, and cleared out immediately afterwards."

"H'm. Did you really?"

"Hallo!" said I, breaking into the conversation. "I'd clean forgotten I ordered my boatman for ten, and now it's past two."

"Poor devil!" said Arbuthnot. "Write a post card telling him he'll not suffer financially. I suppose he's not still waiting for you?"

"I can see the landing-stage from my bedroom window. I'll run up and look."

I did so, but the place was clearly seen to be deserted.

"He's gone," said I as I rejoined the others.

"Good!" replied Arbuthnot, with a meaning glance at me. "Now, Sergeant, where do you propose to start?"

"I thought I'd begin at Rose Cottage. We know there was a man there last night and we might pick up some tracks from that point."

"I quite agree. Monk, you needn't post your card till to-morrow. There's no Sunday delivery. Come along."

"Of course," added Arbuthnot, as by an afterthought. "You may not find it quite so easy as it appears. Plenty of people cross the marsh. *My friend here, for example, is often down there* in connexion with his botanical work."

"Well, well," said the sergeant genially, "if we find his footprints we'll only suspect him in the last resort."

I looked gratefully at my friend, for I had overlooked the fact that my own telltale tracks of the night before would certainly be decorating the marsh.

It was Arbuthnot who found a track of footprints in the soft mould of Mrs. Bessom's front garden, which, like our own, faced out on the marsh. It was he also, who pointed to the damaged place in the hedge. Beyond that, progress was not so easy, for a running man does not leave a full foot-impression.

"Look here, Monk," said Arbuthnot to me, "you can that this fellow was in a great hurry. Look at this deep mark, where the sole of his boot rested, with no heel-mark to correspond."

"Possibly so, sir," said the sergeant, "but more likely he was going on tiptoe to avoid a noise."

"Never," was the decisive answer. "A man on tiptoe takes short steps. The distances between the marks we have seen suggest a racing stride."

The sergeant was a genial fellow. He looked at my friend keenly and said, "Well, sir, I'm always willing to learn, but I never thought to learn from you."

"Ah! An artist has to be able to use his eyes."

The sergeant nodded comprehension, and we continued our search, which eventually brought us up against a path, little more than a track, crossing our line at right angles.

Arbuthnot looked left and right. On one side rose the grey chimneys of Lesslands Grange, on the other, about a hundred yards distant, was the old landing-stage that has figured more than once in this narrative.

"Does Colonel Gregory keep a yacht?" he asked. "There seems to be a path here from the creek to the Grange."

"Not that I know of, sir, but the late owner was very keen on sailing and fishing, and I suppose other people may occasionally use the old landing-stage."

"Quite so. I can see traces of recent footprints. Now to pick up our trail again."

It was curious to note how Arbuthnot had become the leader of the party, and how the sergeant fell in behind, apparently without resentment.

We found the footprints again fairly easily. The land rose slightly and the tracks bore away to the left, that is, diverging from the bank of the creek and approaching the by-road that ran more or less parallel to it inland.

"Here's a muddle," said Arbuthnot suddenly. He pointed to a small square patch of ground almost devoid of turf. On it, plainly to be seen, were two overlapping footprints,

"Hallo!" said the sergeant, regarding the marks as he would have a snake in the grass.

"Pursued and pursuer," said Arbuthnot.

"How do you know?"

"A man doesn't normally fire shots at himself. Now we've got a double job. Somewhere about here the pursuers, one or many, diverged from the route followed by their quarry, probably because of the darkness. Are we to continue to follow this man's trail, or see where his pursuer went? I suggest you follow the one we've been on, and Mr. Monk and I will try to save you time by attempting to trace the other. It'll be dark in an hour. If we miss each other, come to the cottage."

The sergeant readily agreed and we parted company, while I hugged myself at the thought that every step of his led away from my telltale path to Desolation Cottage.

"Thanks very much," I whispered to Arbuthnot. "But they'll be found to-morrow, I fear."

"Which way is the wind?" asked he.

"Seems about south-east," I said.

"Precisely. And a south-east wind with a falling barometer denotes the approach of a depression. By to-morrow morning the rain will have made your footprints into little mud-holes of purely indefinite outline."

Very relieved, I willingly turned my attention to a lesson on scoutcraft, my instruction only finishing when we inspected the trampled flower-bed, happily devoid of flowers, under my own bedroom window. In the afternoon light, already dimming down to a dreary, neutral-coloured dusk, a dark blob, our friend the sergeant could be seen about half a mile away.

"Now your bacon is saved, King," said my friend briskly, "we've got to get up to that road where he is before dark. Come on."

He fairly rushed me back through the marsh. It was a race against twilight. We met the sergeant returning towards us, disappointed.

"I traced him to the road," he said, "but I couldn't get any farther. The crown of the road is worn off, showing bare flints and pebbles, which naturally didn't take an impression."

"Exactly. But what did you make of the bicycle tracks on the softer material on each side?"

"Nothing. They went straight past the point where the foot-tracks left the road, so they couldn't be connected with it."

"Well, we'll have a look. One doesn't live in the middle of a first-class cinema film every day of one's life. Will you go into the cottage and warn Mrs. Jerrold we'll be back in ten minutes. Then we'll all have some tea together."

The sergeant went off obediently, and we made for the road at the point he had indicated.

"But, good heavens, Arbuthnot—" I was beginning suddenly, when a shout caused us to turn. It was the sergeant, who showed signs of returning to us.

"Carry on, and we'll catch you up," bellowed Arbuthnot, and the officer turned away again.

"I seem to have interested both of you," said my companion with a dry chuckle. He sprang out on the road as he spoke, and began keenly scrutinizing the edges, where mud and sand washed from the crown of the road had collected.

"Look, King, four tracks, two on each side. Here and there they cross, but it's plain there *are* four. Made, you will observe, in all probability by two bicycles only, since the tyre impressions are duplicated. Now which way did they come from? On principle, we'll suppose the less frequented way, that is, from the east. Then we'll go left."

He trotted along the road for a matter of twenty yards, and then stopped with a little cry. Following behind, I saw the tracks had ceased.

"How annoying!" said I. "And it's nearly dark, too."

Arbuthnot gave me one glance; it may have been scorn or merely commiseration.

"Come on," he said briefly. "Let's go and console the sergeant. I don't fancy the night air."

On the whole, I think I fancied it rather less than he did, and we made good time on our return journey. We found the sergeant eyeing a large pot of tea, substantial slabs of buttered toast, and a corpulent home-made cake with distinct approval. He turned at once, however, on our arrival and addressed Arbuthnot with a mixture of deference and curiosity.

"Come to think of it, sir, how did you know there'd be bicycle tracks in the lane?"

"I didn't," said Arbuthnot vaguely as he made for the tea-pot and waved us to our chairs. "I only thought that they might have chased him on bicycles."

"Yes, I admit 'twould have seemed likely, if the wheel-tracks had stopped where he left the road. But then, heaps of folk around here get about on bicycles. Most labouring men go to their work that way."

"It was only my idea," said my friend. "I'm not in the C.I.D., you know."

"No, sir. But speaking of that, I shouldn't be surprised if they sent a man down here. It isn't a local job. Did you find anything of those other tracks?"

"We thought we did for a short distance. I suppose they realized they were losing him in the marsh, took pot-shots at him as a last desperate resort, and then decamped."

The sergeant nodded.

"Very likely. I must go over the ground myself to-morrow."

"Listen," said Arbuthnot.

There was the steady beat of rain on the windowpanes.

"You'll never see those tracks again."

"That's bad luck. Well, I took a few measurements in case there was ever anyone to fit them to. But we don't know where they came from, and we don't know where they went to. And that's that."

So speaking he took his leave, and Arbuthnot relapsed into an easy chair and a cloud of smoke, and grinned at me.

"Come," said I. "Now he's gone, what about those bicycles—and other things?"

By way of reply he seized a writing-pad and for a couple of minutes drew busily. A copy of the rough sketch he showed me of Desolation Cottage follows.

"I'm not exactly a cartographer," he said, "but the sketch contains the essentials. The line of crosses shows the track you took in the night, the dots indicate the path of the fugitive, and the small circles the advance of his pursuers. The dot-and-dash lines mark the position of the bicycle tracks."

"And the 'H'?" I asked curiously.

"Of no present importance. It just stands on the approximate spot where the unfortunate Hunt was launched into eternity."

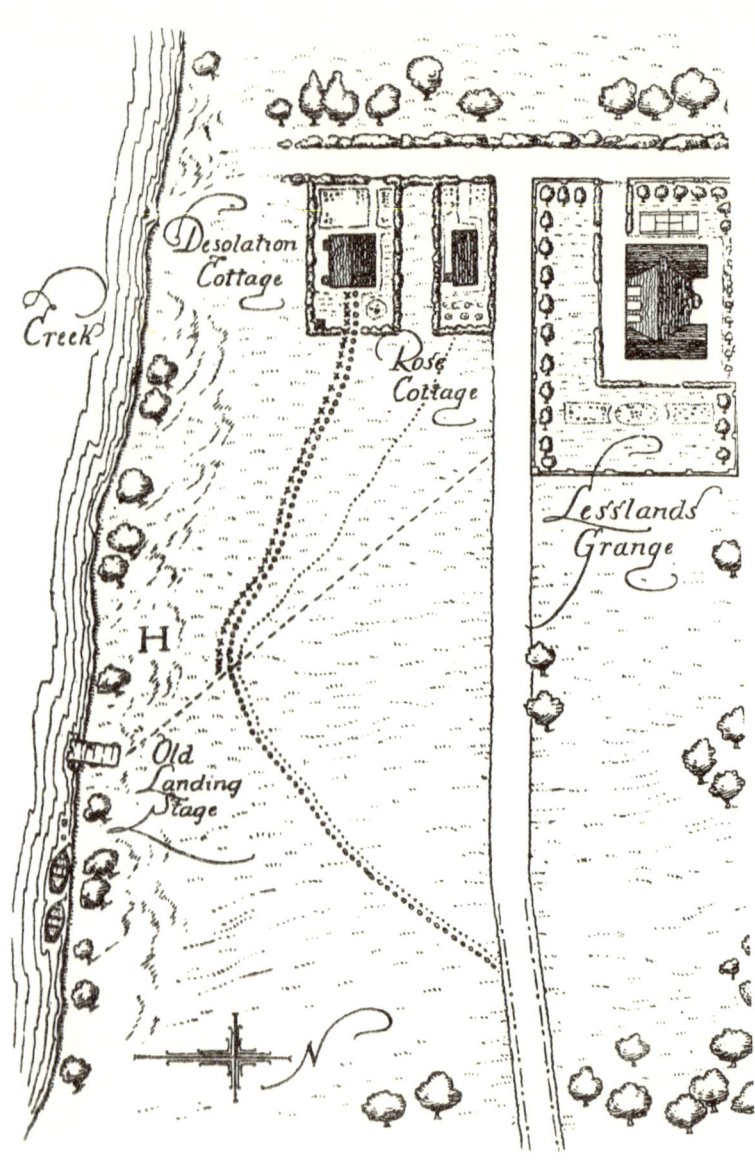

Creek

Desolation
Cottage

Rose
Cottage

H

Old
Landing
Stage

Lesslands
Grange

N

I shivered.

"When you mentioned that the pursuers ran easily, while the hunted one was nearing the point of collapse, I thought of bicycles," continued Arbuthnot. "One can, if one knows the road, ride without lights in fair safety. A car is a noticeable object, while a bicycle is easily hidden, mounted in a moment, and can be ridden almost in silence. Those who watched Hunt, and finally led him to his doom, probably came and went on bicycles. Perhaps, most likely in fact, they were the same men who chased you last night.

"These men, riding abreast in order not to crash one into the other in the darkness, were almost upon their victim, who was clearly making for Rose Cottage, when he, in a last desperate effort, sprang off the road into the marsh. At the rate they were going they naturally could not stop at once. When they did, they rushed back to the point where he had vanished and also entered the marsh. The rest you know."

"We don't know where they came from," I said.

"No, but we know their direction of retreat. Judging from the circumstances of the chase, their abode may be several miles away. And the rain is now busy obliterating those bicycle tracks."

"And where do the green lamps come in?" I continued, my curiosity unsatiated.

"That's just the point, King. Where do they come in? Look at the path from Lesslands Grange to the old landing-stage. It cuts right across the other tracks. It seems impossible, does it not, that the two events, the chase and the appearance of the lamps, could be connected?"

"Then that," I said dismally, "makes confusion worse confounded."

"No, no," said Arbuthnot cheerily. "It's like recognizing two different chemicals in an analysis. One can disentangle the effects of one from the effects of the other. Now, the lamps first."

"Yes?" I said eagerly.

"A green lamp, presumably denoting safety, shows in the Grange. Some one responds—probably a man in a boat lying off in the creek. He comes to the stage, makes fast, and shows his light. The light in the Grange is promptly extinguished and some one goes down from the Grange to the stage. When he arrives, the guiding light goes out. A message, or something more, passes. The man returns to the Grange and exposes his lamp again as a token of his safe return. On sight of it the boatman puts off. At that moment the chase bears down across the marsh. Does it fit in with your experience?"

"Perfectly. Then how do we stand now?"

"In my opinion we have made a great advance. What I suspected before can now be regarded as proved, that is, that Buller & Co. had no hand in the death of Hunt. But they were somehow present on that occasion, and what they know about it we want to know also. To-morrow we indite a letter to Mr. Reynolds that should put him into our hands."

There were still several things I wanted to ask, but I decided to defer them till the time came for the letter to be written.

"How do you enjoy life below stairs?" I asked. "I imagine you pined for your beloved marsh. Were you able to give Creen any help?"

"Not a great deal. Yet my stay was not altogether devoid of interest. My immediate superior, who was, I gathered, the sixth footman, was a jovial fellow and readily amenable to the influence of beer. It was from him I found out about Carpenter."

"Carpenter?"

"The previous chauffeur who was dismissed on a charge of drunkenness. My friend and I had adjourned to the most popular local tavern at my expense. It was a most common den called the 'Falcon'.

"'Hallo!' said the fellow on entering. 'He's not here.' I naturally inquired who might be the subject of his remark. 'An old gent,' he said, 'who's taken to coming in here lately. Very free with his drinks, having been in service once himself, but afterwards going to Australia and making a pile.'

"I took the opportunity of suggesting that he had possibly by his liberality been the cause of the unlucky Carpenter's downfall. He shook his head.

"'No, that's a business none of us prop'ly understands,' he said. 'Certainly the old chap was in that night and he and Carpenter had a drink together at the bar. Then Carpenter went off, saying he was on duty in ten minutes. And the old man told him he had no business to drink then, and gave him a mint tablet, same as he's given me before now to take the smell away. And I swear Carpenter went off as sober as a judge, for though the boss is an old devil we wouldn't let Miss Iris down, none of us. And ten minutes later he was sitting on the front steps of the house saying, "Oh my bloody head." And of course he smelt of drink and got the sack then and there. 'Twasn't no good us saying anything. But Miss Iris sent him fifty quid, she did, though she wouldn't go against her father.'

"Wasn't it all plain as daylight, King? That 'old gent' must have been a remarkably fine actor. The drug did its work and Mr. Leonard Williams stepped gaily into the vacant billet."

"Very clever," said I. "What did Creen think of it?"

"Well," said Arbuthnot grinning. "I think he was a little flabbergasted. You see, it was evidently his own nature that had given these abductors their chance. They knew he never forgave a servant and banked on that fact."

"Did you ever see the 'old gent'?" I asked.

"No. You can guess I paid frequent visits in the hope of doing so. He had evidently come a few times after he had accomplished his purpose to avoid suspicion; also perhaps to meet his accomplice Williams. I tried hard, without rousing suspicion, to find out the dates he had been present, but not unnaturally failed. The only date I established for certain was that he had not been there the night after Iris Creen had disappeared, for by then the servants had all got wind of the matter and were quietly discussing it, and my friend remembered the old man was not among them that evening. Does that suggest anything?"

"I don't see."

"Isn't it possible he was engaged in taking the Rolls-Royce to Dartmoor?"

"It certainly fits in," I admitted. "What did your fellow-servants think of the whole affair?"

"Naturally they knew exactly what had happened. You can't *hope* to conceal these things, as I told Creen, only his love for his daughter blinds him. But they could tell me nothing I didn't know, except one small, yet perhaps vital, point."

"And that?"

"One of the housemaids, whom I took to the pictures—Heaven help me!—had heard Iris Creen address the man by a name that apparently did not belong to him. The chauffeur was in the hall, presumably receiving orders, and this girl heard Iris Creen, no doubt thinking she was alone, say 'Good-night, Dormer.' She swears to the name. The trouble is that it's clearly a Christian name and therefore so far little help, but it shows the friendly terms existing between the two. Hence what we know to have been an abduction is also clearly an elopement."

"But," I objected, "there are a dozen easier ways of managing an elopement than doing it in the guise of a domestic servant. Miss Creen had perfect freedom of movement."

"Certainly. Therefore we may assume that the man in question obtained his position in the household for some other purpose, and there succumbing to the charms of the lady, employed his existing organization to get her away."

"What purpose—robbery?"

"I don't think so. An ordinary thief is not so easily diverted from his purpose by female charms."

"Possibly he planned the abduction from the first and won the girl's confidence to make it an easier job," I suggested.

"I don't think so, for you notice no attempt has been made to make use of the possession of the girl—no blackmailing, for example."

"Did Creen by any chance recognize the name you heard?" I asked.

Arbuthnot chuckled.

"Creen has an iron face," said he. "You may guess I was watching it closely when I told him. I can't say he flinched, but I know he poured himself out a very stiff brandy immediately after. Then he said he'd known a man with that name years ago in South America. The impression I gained was that our friend Creen had received a shock."

"I'll take your word for it," I said. "If you are not a judge of such things then no one is."

"Very well, King. Now note the implication. He knew the name, *but he didn't know the man*. For the man was in his household a week, and, judging by what I am told, could not have been in disguise, for he had no moustache; beard, spectacles, or other of the ordinary media of camouflage."

"Extraordinary," I mused.

"Note the further implication. He was so infatuated with the girl that he told her, if not his real name, at least the name that meant something very serious to Baxter Creen. Suppose, instead of absconding, she had confessed to her father? One can imagine the said 'Dormer' would have been made to repent bitterly of his precipitancy. As it is, I don't care very much whether I do anything more for Creen or not. I don't expect my clients to have led blameless lives, but I do expect their confidence. However, I may get something out of him yet."

I admired the letter that Arbuthnot produced for the edification of the man Reynolds. Done out on the little portable typewriter that accompanied us on our travels it read thus:

> "Do you remember going down the river with Hunt? Next time you may go that way yourself. We can lay our hands on you when we like. Escape is impossible. Your only hope is to come to the old landing-stage by water at one a.m. Tuesday morning. If you can satisfy one who will be there that your business does not concern us you can go free. If you fail to come we will make you number four the same day. Speak of this to anyone and your hours are numbered."

"There," said Arbuthnot. "I think that is sufficiently crude to draw a man of some unschooled imagination and no great will-power, the obvious tool of our friend Buller. Now write your post card and say you have a cold and will not want the boat to-morrow. We'll give him the day free to brood over that message. I trust he won't dare communicate with Buller, who is a hardier villain."

"What do you hope to find out?" I inquired.

"I want to know the whole truth about the business Buller is engaged on. I can make a guess at its nature already, can't you? More important, we have to find out exactly how much Reynolds has seen of the devilment that is going on in this district."

I think that Sunday night marks the end of a period. After we had visited the post office we sat down in comfort by the fire, while a keen north-west wind, that had sprung up after the rain, rattled the windows and tormented the trees, dragging from them their few residual leaves. Yes, it was the end of a period, for to my mind, from the day following dates the piling up of event upon event, of tragedy and denouement, that was to make my life the whirling phantasmagoria of a nightmare. From the time when we laid hold of Josh Reynolds in the marsh till that day when the last reverberations of the final *débâcle* thundered in our ears, I do not think I ever again fully cast off that almost intolerable tension that was to be my lot.

11
In Which We Dispose of a Minor Villain

Monday, the 27th of November, was a fine, clear day. George Higgins arrived and busied himself in the garden. The marsh under the rare sunshine was at peace.

"Arbuthnot," said I, as I stood gazing out on the scene, "aren't we running a considerable risk to ourselves in going down there to-night to deal with this Reynolds?"

"We are. I will tell you what I propose. As far as I know the man has never seen me. I will deal with him and you must keep silent, for otherwise he may recognize your voice. It will be your business to keep a sharp look-out and warn me if necessary. See that you are armed."

"Thank you. I'm always armed at present."

It wanted a quarter of an hour to one that night when we extinguished our lights. By Arbuthnot's arrangement candles had burnt in our bedrooms for ten minutes previous to our departure, so that any observer would suppose we were safely in bed. Arbuthnot manipulated the front door in his silent way and we faded into the night.

It must still have needed a minute or two to one when we reached the old landing-stage. Things were uncannily silent, and I had that feeling that I wanted to face two ways at once. Considering my previous adventure I can hardly be blamed for jumping when the sound of a low cough broke the stillness.

"He's there," whispered Arbuthnot. "In his boat, lying at the end of the stage. Now to stimulate his memory!"

"Reynolds?" he said in a quiet but penetrating voice.

"Yes, sir." The answer came back through the darkness with a quaver in it.

"Come ashore. And mind, no monkey tricks, or, by God, I'll spoil you!"

"C-coming, sir."

We could just see him scrambling on to the planks and coming uncertainly along them. As he stepped to the ground Arbuthnot laid the cold muzzle of his revolver to the man's temples. Reynolds fell on his knees.

"Don't shoot, sir, for God's sake! I've never done you no 'arm."

"Quiet, you fool, and you'll come to no harm. Now answer my questions truthfully the first time. Can't swim, can you, Reynolds?"

"N—no, sir."

"I knew it. None of you seafaring people can. Well, if you go downstream, you won't have any water-wings to keep you up. D'you remember how Hunt came bobbing up and down along with your boat, eh?"

The man was almost speechless with fright.

"Yes, sir. I'll tell the truth, I swear."

"Right! Now we've seen you busy about here at nights. We guess your game. Own up."

"Ye—es, sir. Nothing much, sir. Only bringing a few little things ashore."

"For Colonel Gregory, eh?"

"Yes, sir."

"What sort of things?"

"Mostly cigars. Sometimes a few cases of drink—whisky and such like."

"Ah, I guessed so. Rather risky, isn't it?"

"Oh, 'tis risky, but less than you'd think, because nobody thinks nowadays that anything of that sort is going on. And now coastguards is done away with, who's to interfere?"

"Suppose some one saw your green lights?"

"Yes, sir, they're a risk, but after that night you knows about in the fog we thought we'd risk the lights to be sure all was clear."

"And then you ran into something after all, eh?"

"Pretty near, sir. I was only just away when them guns went off, and I swear I'll have no more to do with it."

"Who started this business?"

"Buller began it about a year ago to get on the right side of the Colonel. The old man was mighty hard up and jumped at the idea. Buller knew me, and I knew some fellows sailing east. I used to take out a fishing boat, go round to the mouth of the Thames and collect what cheroots and such like they'd brought. Then I knew the second mate of a bootlegger sailing from Leith to Nassau, and he was always willing to oblige with a few cases. Risky work and not too paying when every one had had a pick of the profits, but better'n doing nothing. I used to sail up to Wivenhoe and then bring back the stuff at night, as you knows. Used to save the old man a pretty penny on what he smoked and drank, but he had a bee in his bonnet, and I fancy what pleased him most was diddling the Government. Buller kep' egging him on, knowing it put the old man in his power."

So that was that, and I stood confounded. It was like the drawing aside of a painted curtain to reveal something appallingly sinister behind. While the tangible Buller remained as an item in the case I could feel we were linked with reality. With his dissociation from it, it seemed to me we were close up against the unknown power that destroyed Hunt. Arbuthnot was speaking.

"A very pretty tale. There's to be no more of it."

"I swear, sir, I'll have no hand or part in it again."

"And now, Reynolds, we want to know exactly what you heard the night of the fog, and don't lie to me, or, by hell! I'll have your liver torn out with red-hot irons."

It was not so much the threat as the cold ferocity of Arbuthnot's tone that made the man whimper with fear, I think.

"Only the truth, sir, so help me God. Buller and me was on the stage when we heard him scream out and then he sort of went gurgle-gurgle and Buller says, 'Cut it, mate—I'm off', and he run, but seeing where the sound come from he run the other way, not towards the Grange."

"What did you do?"

"I cast off the boat pretty quick, and I didn't dare take to the oars for fear of making a noise, so I let her drift with the ebb till she was a couple of yards or so clear, and then backed water. Then I heard feet on the stage and somebody says, 'My nose is bleeding like a pig where he struck me. Never mind, we'll make a trade-mark for his pal the Colonel with the blood.' Plain as anything I heard it, the, man speaking excited like, as well he might. But why they thought Hunt was a friend of the Colonel I don't know, and neither does Buller, for he wasn't at all. Then there was a splash, and I let the boat go with the tide and that corpse came bobbing along in the water after me till I was fair sick with fright."

"What happened to Buller?"

"He got clean lost in the fog, and I think them other chaps must have got lost, too, for they put their mark on the window of that cottage where them two strange gents is living. Then Buller he comes creeping here and there feeling his way, and he thinks that's how he got his thumb-mark there on the window-sill, for he was round that cottage wondering where he'd got to. Took him a good two hours to find his way home he says."

"I see. Now, Reynolds, don't you think you know a little too much to be allowed to live?"

"Sir, sir!" The man was prostrate on the ground, shuddering in an ecstasy of fear. "I swear by anything I'll never split."

"Well, it's a good thing for you you've told the truth. Get out. As long as you keep your mouth shut and don't cross my path again, I won't hurt you. What's Buller going to do?"

"God bless you, sir! I'll swear I won't meddle no more. But Buller, sir, is a fool. He says if he can get hold of them chaps he'll have a pretty penny out of them."

"God help him if he tries," said Arbuthnot grimly. "Now, get out quick."

The man was gone in an approximation to an instant. He wasted no time. The creak and splash of oars died away.

"A sufficiently despicable character," said Arbuthnot to me, and then, "Hallo, King, what was that?"

That was a loud splash from inland, as if some one had inadvertently stepped into one of the many pools with which the ground was dotted. We stood still, our eyes vainly striving to penetrate the darkness.

"Some animal," I whispered. I spoke too soon. The silence was cut by the startling sound of a loud sneeze.

"Come on," said Arbuthnot, "we're two to one."

We dashed forward; there was the sound of hasty footsteps from in front; then I slipped and fell on my face. Arbuthnot waited for me, for it would have been madness to have separated in the dark.

"Sorry," I said, as I struggled to my feet. "I spoilt a chance."

"Not much of a one, anyway," said Arbuthnot. "Come on; we'll be happier when we're indoors."

I went straight to bed. I was tired and cold, and the interview I had attended had given me a feeling of disgust that I was glad to lose in sleep. Arbuthnot I left busily inditing a letter to the invaluable Kaye.

The same morning saw us holding a post-breakfast council of war.

"I can't get over this smuggling business," I said. "I thought all that sort of thing went out of existence after Waterloo."

"That sort of thing never goes out of existence," said Arbuthnot. "I suppose it's due to a kind of 'something-for-nothing' complex such as makes respectable women become 'red in tooth and claw' at West End sales. What bootleggers can do on a vast scale in the States is surely possible in a much smaller way in this little island? I've heard of such things before being done on a small scale."

"It disheartens me," I said. "I always hoped that in some way or other the unspeakable Buller would prove to be the jackal of a greater villain, and hence a valuable link in the chain. Still, there is that reference to the Colonel to be cleared up."

"More than one Colonel in the world," replied Arbuthnot briefly. "As I supposed, the fog is the key to what puzzled us most in that night's happenings. Considering our short acquaintance with the district it was inconceivable that anyone should so soon have had grounds for honouring us with attention. What then? In the fog, the *wrong* window was decorated with that charming little trademark."

"Yes," I said. "It seems very likely. But whose window, then, did they intend to decorate with the gruesome mark of their triumph? Not Hunt's, for it would be useless there, seeing he was already dead and gone."

"Yes, Hunt's," said Arbuthnot. "The two cottages are close together. In the fog the mistake was easy."

"I don't yet see your point," I said.

"Well, how was Hunt taken? Could they hope to stumble on him by chance in the fog? Hardly. Yet they came prepared with something to strangle him, and something else to buoy his body and float it out to sea. In the fog, most admirable of screens, *they watched the cottage that night,* and took him as he went out on his 'last try'. What follows? Probably they came upon the car in the side lane and guessed he had a visitor. Then they risked a peep at him in some way we don't know, perhaps between carelessly-drawn curtains, and recognized who he was. So when they had disposed of Hunt they returned to gratify his associate with the sign of their achievement. Most likely they supposed he would, on account of the fog, be remaining there till morning. So I assume 'the colonel' was none other than Hunt's mysterious 'brother.'"

"Weren't they running a gratuitous risk in thus flaunting their evil success?"

"So it would appear. And that makes me think that had the person, whom that numeral was intended to edify, seen it himself, he would not have been in a position to risk drawing attention to it."

"In other words, we have thrust ourselves into a combat between two packs of rogues."

"If we have, King, all the more reason for keeping on until we have rid society of the lot."

"Technically correct," I said, "but personally rather disquieting."

"Well, well," said Arbuthnot grinning, "we have been in some tight corners in our time."

"And the thumb-mark?" I queried.

"No doubt arrived there in the way we have been told. It was too conspicuous for anyone to suppose that the

people who had so neatly disposed of Hunt had been careless enough to leave it there. And the suggestion that it
was an old one was futile, because I had the sense to look
up the weather reports, and so found that there had been
two days of heavy rain that week, which would have effectually obliterated it in that case."

"And what do you propose to do about Buller?" I asked.
"After all, the man has been breaking the law."

"Certainly he has. But he will do so no more, for his
necessary accomplice Reynolds is far too frightened to
continue in the business, and without him it seems to me
the arrangement falls to the ground. Moreover, it's quite
likely that Buller will sample more than a just retribution
if he meddles, as he proposes to do, with what is going
on around us here. I propose we leave him alone. As for
that poor old devil, the Colonel, who aroused in you such
violent suspicions, I think he has made his own hell quite
satisfactorily, so why not leave him in it?"

"Very well," I said. "That clears the stage anyway."

"It does. Now we have to realize that we are now definitely in the same danger that Hunt was. You appeared on
the night of the green lamps to be giving shelter to a man
whom we know to have been one of Hunt's gang. What
looks more likely than that we are two other members of
the same gang? We must assume we are marked men. What
shall we do?"

"Clear out," I said hastily. "Follow up Charteris, or try
to find Miss Creen. I have had my fill of this marsh and its
secrets." I spoke irritably, for no man likes to be followed
and shot at by hidden rascals.

"No, King, I think not. Clear out we shall eventually,
and perhaps in haste, but not just yet. Let me recall to you
five separate occurrences—the murder of Hunt, the man
watching you when you were on the creek, the signs that

you were followed from Wivenhoe that same night, the chase in the marsh, and finally last night's watcher. Such related actions almost inevitably radiate from some local focus: they could hardly be carried out except by operators living nearby. This is our first business, to find whence these people come on their unpleasant errands."

"It sounds suspiciously like putting one's head in the lion's mouth," I said none too cheerfully.

"I fear so. You know what big-game shooters do when they want a pot at a tiger?"

"Yes, I believe they tie up a goat."

"Exactly. King, you will, on this occasion, have to be the goat."

I have always thought that Arbuthnot might sometimes wrap up his remarks in a more tactful garb.

"And most likely suffer its usual fate," I said resentfully. "I'm sure I could perish with more dignity if I weren't feeling the comparison with the horned creature of your metaphor."

Arbuthnot grinned unfeelingly.

"It amounts to this," said he. "If people want to follow us about, let them follow *you*. At the same time I will endeavour to follow *them*, taking care to intervene before the tiger springs. Remember we've never seen a single one of these busy gentlemen. If we met one in the street we should pass him unknowing. We can only recognize them by catching them at work."

"This means risking the night air," I suggested.

"I suppose so. Fortunately we are now entering on the moonlit half of the month. The moon does not set to-night till nearly one o'clock. Supposing you set out to explore the marsh, and draw the attention of certain interested persons thereby, it will be fairly easy for me to keep you in view without betraying my presence."

I nodded.

"What course shall I follow?" I asked. As usual Arbuthnot had gained his wish. He drew the Ordnance map, his inseparable companion, from his pocket.

"Trouble comes from the east," he said as he unfolded it. "Here you see the road on which we found the bicycle tracks. Here is the creek. Here we have a considerable group of buildings, which I understand to be an explosives factory now closed down, and on a 'care and maintenance' basis, with a caretaker in sole charge."

"Yes," I said. "I saw that the day we looked for Hunt, and again when I went down the creek with Reynolds. The place is quite near the creek, and has a jetty belonging to it. I shall know it again."

"Good! Now I propose that you move eastwards in a direction parallel to the road until you reach this place. I shall follow you in whatever fashion seems best. When you reach the buildings halt till I rejoin you. Do not on any account vary your course, but aim to keep a hundred yards from the road. Is that clear?"

"Perfectly."

"Very well. If after you have waited a quarter of an hour at our rendezvous I have failed to appear, make for the road and return direct to the cottage that way."

"Then you intend to capture the watcher, if there be one, single-handed?"

"On the contrary, I am not at all sure I want to capture him at all."

"Why?"

"Consider. If we caught him we should have to release him again. We should have no grounds for detaining him, and in addition we should have presented him with valuable information as to our identity. I wish to see his face if possible, but, more important still, to find his refuge."

"I see."

"There is our night's work—or, by Jove! King, why not make it an afternoon's work?"

"An afternoon's work?" I queried, distinctly taken aback.

"Yes. Look."

I looked. Stealing across the marsh, like floating scarves of some amazingly ethereal muslin, came the forerunners of the fog. Before my eyes outlines blurred and shapes vanished. A marsh bird cried above the silence.

The first wisp of the air foam drifted across the window. In spite of the fire I shivered.

"Come outside," said Arbuthnot. "We can then get a better impression as to its density."

In the garden George Higgins was dimly visible, toiling at the garden he had redeemed.

"It's visibly thickening," said Arbuthnot. "A man would be barely visible at fifty yards. You will have to be careful not to lose your way."

I agreed, not fascinated by the prospect. To move in danger in a fog, is I have always thought, more nerve-racking then to run risks in darkness. We returned indoors.

"Good!" said my friend. "Now what more likely than that those who are watching us should seize this opportunity to carry out at least a reconnaissance? They could move as safely as in darkness, and with less difficulty."

"It is possible."

"It is probable. After the fracas of the night on which you were shot at they would deem it expedient to lie low for a little while in case a watch was being kept. But they would be all agog to resume operations. We were watched last night. Is it incredible that the watch will continue in the fog?"

"You make it appear very likely," I said.

"We'll give them a couple of hours to come out about their business. I don't imagine this fog is likely to disperse before night—there is not a breath of wind. After lunch we'll set our trap."

My lunch that day must have resembled the condemned man's last breakfast. There was no point in arguing with Arbuthnot; he had made it plain we were bound to run risks if we were to progress. It must have been about two o'clock when I finally sallied forth into the wall of mist.

"Keep a steady rate of about three miles an hour and don't look behind," Arbuthnot said as I went.

The garden was deserted; George Higgins had probably found conditions too dismal to remain at work. As I strode down the narrow grass path, beaded with the drops of fog-rain, and stepped through the gap in the hedge, it was as if I had, inside a minute, cut myself off from humanity. The clammy, white, inscrutable bank of mist swallowed me as a vortex draws in the unlucky mariner. At ten yards I could still see objects, at twenty a vague outline, at thirty a mere blur.

I worked across the marsh, keeping rather to my left, so as to hit the rising ground nearer the road than I was at my starting-point. Obeying orders not to look round, I listened eagerly for sounds of Arbuthnot's movements. There were none. That man could move without sound.

It might be supposed that as I went on I gathered confidence, but actually the opposite was the case. After all, I had had various nerve-racking experiences in connexion with this case. I knew the men I was up against did not scruple to shoot. I could not feel sure that Arbuthnot, even with his highly-developed sense for topography, could keep on my track. Every bush concealed, to my imagination, a possible armed man; every piece of dead ground harboured its quota of evil watchers; the sudden snort of a grazing pony set my heart thumping thunderously against my ribs. By the end I was strung up to snapping point.

The fog was patchy; generally it was denser on lower ground and thinned out slightly wherever I came to any small eminence. It was thus that I caught sight of my objective, after I had been walking for about an hour and a half. I congratulated myself on having kept good direction. Before me loomed a high brick wall. The buildings behind were invisible. I stopped, at about thirty yards' distance, opposite a pair of massive iron gates.

I was surrounded by a great silence, and suddenly, like a wave, panic terror swept over me. As long as I was moving I had it under control; it was the act of stopping that set loose all my worst imaginations. I glanced round here and there like a hunted hare and saw, to my astonishment, that the great gates were half ajar. Curious I had not noticed it before! But here, at any rate, said my feverish brain, was a kind of refuge. Behind those gates I could crouch by the wall and peep out for a sight of Arbuthnot. People could not come on me from all sides at once; at the worst I could make a fight for it.

I went forward none too slowly, passed the gates, and entered a grass-grown courtyard. Tall buildings showed but dimly on the far side of it, for inside here the fog was denser than outside.

Perhaps I had gone half a dozen paces inside before I heard the shout, and then I stood still in my tracks as if I had been suddenly petrified. The words had sounded like "Look out, sir!" but that seemed unreasonable; I had no friends in the vicinity. I swung round to see if I could catch sight of the shouter. *The ponderous iron gates were closing!*

No man's hand touched them, yet slowly and inexorably they drew together. I had to make my decision in a flash. The danger within or the danger without? I chose the latter. As I hurled myself through the narrow remaining space the gates seemed to accelerate, as though vicious at losing their prey. Smash came one of them against my heel, and, losing balance, I pitched forward on hands and knees.

Shaken mentally and physically, I sprang again to my feet, determined to lose no time in hiding myself in that previously unfriendly fog. It was then I saw the man. He stood perhaps thirty yards away, looking no more in the fog than some relict gate-post or pillar. The devil and the deep sea! I preferred the evil I could see to the other I knew not of. Drawing my automatic I rushed on the unmoving figure. It was a rash act, for he could have shot me down as I came, but barely had I moved five paces when I saw Arbuthnot creeping stealthily but swiftly up behind him. It was all over quicker than I can write it down. With a bound my friend was upon the unknown, had flung something over his head, and pinioned his arms. I dashed forward.

"Cover him," said Arbuthnot to me. "We must be out of this quick," he added to me in a swift whisper.

I pressed my automatic into the man's back between his shoulder blades.

"Don't speak or you die," said Arbuthnot. "Quick march!"

The captive, unresisting, shambled away, a quaint figure with his head, wrapped in Arbuthnot's coat. My shirt-sleeved friend followed by my side.

"Did it to prevent his seeing me," he whispered to me. "It's better not to give away information unnecessarily."

Unmolested we marched on in the fog until, after half a mile, Arbuthnot called a halt.

"I don't think we were followed," he said to me in an undertone. "I judged it better to collar the fellow, even though we shall have to let him go again. When I heard him shout I feared at once we were in a trap and I determined on securing a hostage in case you had been captured."

"I nearly was," I whispered back.

At the back of my mind some ancient memory persisted in stirring. That shout I had heard in some marvellous way evoked a remembrance something wrapped in the mist of bygone days. It tantalized me. It was as if a curtain had been half-lifted on a very different picture from that of my present life. However, Arbuthnot was talking.

"Now, my friend," he was saying, "it suits me to keep your face covered up for the present, although I intend to take a farewell glance at it by and by. Judging from your humble attire I doubt if you are sufficiently big game to atone for the loss of my colleague Hunt, but we shall do our best with you."

"You do what you like, sir," said a muffled but unmistakable voice from under the folds of the coat.

Arbuthnot stared in amazement. I have rarely seen him so completely taken aback. With a swift movement he twitched the covering from the head and shoulders of our captive. There stood revealed—George Higgins!

"Good God!" I said half to myself. "Then it *was* 'Look out!' that he shouted?" My mind went back to an evil day in those war years. I saw myself marching up through old Vermelles, shell-smitten and horrible, at the head of my company. Then I heard that voice shout, and had my sudden vision of the toppling wall of the shattered building next to the Brewery. The shout has saved me by inches only. Arbuthnot's voice cut through the revelation of memory.

"Kindly explain, Higgins, why you should follow my friend about in this fashion. It will be better for you to tell me no lies." The voice had the ring of steel.

The man drew himself up to attention.

"Sir, I followed him over the top at Loos to do my best, and that's why I'm following him now. I wouldn't see my old company officer going into danger alone."

"Is this true?" asked Arbuthnot turning to me.

"Perfectly. He was in the Second Battalion—in my own company. I remember him now. What's my real name, Higgins?"

"Sir Edmund King," came the response without hesitation. "I knew you, sir, nearly from the beginning, but it wasn't my business to say anything. Then when I saw you were running risks I couldn't help standing by."

"Then," said Arbuthnot curtly, "it was you who watched Sir Edmund when he was on the creek, who followed him to Wivenhoe, and who watched us in the marsh last night."

"Yes, sir."

Arbuthnot stood silent a moment. Then he relapsed into silent laughter.

"Well, well, you've given us a shock, and we owe you an apology. We hoped to find something on this little expedition, but hardly expected to discover a helper. But surely you ought to know me if you were in the Second Battalion?"

Higgins leant forward and scanned my friend's face closely. Then he suddenly stiffened like a ramrod.

"My word!" he breathed softly to himself. "It's Captain Arbuthnot. It was them whiskers that done it, else I should have known him before."

There was a new note of reverence in his voice, and my mind jumped back to that distant day in '15 when Arbuthnot had been haled from the front line to go and undertake some peculiar work that no other person apparently could be found to do, leaving an irate commanding officer, a dejected friend, and a unit as nearly mutinous as a Guards' battalion could ever conceivably be. He was already adjutant then, and I believe the men would have followed him a little beyond the gates of hell.

"Come," said he. "It is getting dark and I don't like this neighbourhood overmuch."

As we went along Arbuthnot cross-questioned Higgins, without much result. It appeared that the latter had never seen anyone else following me. Then, while Higgins fell a few paces to the rear, I detailed my remarkable experience. Arbuthnot listened with keen interest.

"Could you swear the gates had not been open all the time?"

"I couldn't. It was merely my impression that I had first seen them shut. In the fog and my state of nervousness I couldn't be certain."

"You saw or heard no one?"

"Not a soul. The place seemed deserted."

"Very interesting indeed. Did you—this is important—form any impression as whether the walls were scalable or otherwise from the *inside?*"

"I couldn't say. I was only inside a matter of ten seconds at the most."

"I see. We had better, I think, enlist the assistance of Higgins. You remember him as a useful man? One never knows when a little help may be necessary."

If he had known, they were prophetic words.

"Higgins?"

"Sir."

"We are here on a difficult and dangerous business. We are up against people entirely devoid of scruple. Your first duty is silence. Your second is to be available whenever wanted. You will draw pay at the rate of a first-class warrant officer. Is that clear?"

The man grinned.

"Very good, sir," he said, and so was added to our available forces.

12

In Which I Lose My Balance,
and Another Man His Life

Pipes went furiously that same evening while Arbuthnot was engaged in going over matters in the light of the afternoon's unexpected denouement.

"It does one good occasionally to get a blow in the face like that. It reminds one that, however careful one may be, there are always some factors that are beyond the wit of man to allow for. Our watchers having proved to be the faithful Higgins indicates one thing at any rate."

"And that is?"

"That we are at present not receiving the obvious attentions of this local gang. What then? Either their energies have been drawn off in a different direction, or they are meditating some different form of treatment to meet our case, something really cheerful, like poison or arson!"

"What do you make of the affair of the gates?" I asked.

"I have been cursing myself for my failure to investigate that factory, but this affair has been so complicated from the first that I have never had time to act on mere speculation. I fancy we shall have to pay that place a visit. Suppose now, that the gates actually opened after you first saw them, as seems most likely. Then some one saw you, recognized you, or imagined he did so, and opened the gates by some mechanical device, hoping you might be tempted inside."

"But how was he to know that I should fail to see the gates open themselves in such a suspicious manner?" I objected.

"Quite so. How was he? If you had seen it happen it is not likely you would have been tempted inside hence the operator would appear to be giving away an important secret for a problematical gain, would he not?"

"He would."

"But suppose he were by his act giving away no secret at all?"

"I don't follow."

"Suppose some one of the Hunt fraternity had already been entrapped that way, and had subsequently escaped and undoubtedly warned his associates. What then?"

"Clearly it would be useless expecting another of them to fall into the same snare."

"Quite so. Unless there was an overwhelmingly strong temptation to risk it in the fog, always provided he had not seen the gates opening."

"What sort of temptation?"

"The presence of a prisoner inside, for example."

"Don't you think it rather far-fetched to invent a prisoner to bolster up your hypothesis?"

"My dear, old, fat-headed King" (such were his words, I regret to say), "I'm not inventing a prisoner. Haven't we already seen that Hunt was number three?"

"Yes."

"Isn't it more than probable that the escaping man you saw in the marsh was number two? He must have been captured before Hunt's death, because he was ignorant of it."

"I agree."

"Then isn't it at least an even chance that number one may still be incarcerated in that factory, whence, I have no doubt, the other man escaped?"

"It's reasonable. But he may, like Hunt, be dead."

"Certainly he may."

"Certainly he may. But while a live prisoner has value as a hostage, a dead man is no more than so much cold mutton. It is possible that for some reason he may have been kept alive. Perhaps Hunt would not have died—at least not just when he did—if he had submitted to capture. You now see the importance I attach to the question of whether the walls are scalable from the inside. They are easily so from without—so much I saw to-day; but before one gets in it is advisable to consider whether one can also get out again."

"Provided the ground on both sides is the same height, as it is in this case, it should be possible," I said.

"Have you ever been to the Zoological Gardens?" Arbuthnot demanded in reply.

"Yes," I said in surprise.

"Next time pay more attention to the iron railings with incurved tops overhanging the enclosures. A catproof fence is made on the same principle. If that wall is so fitted inside it is a pretty trap."

"By heaven!" I said, jumping up. "The gates are, at any rate. I remember—only a fleeting glimpse—downward curving iron spikes inside. That sounds as if you are right."

"H'm. I must go into the ownership of this place when I get to town. There's a point involved here."

"To town?" I echoed.

"Yes. I expect to be recalled to town either to-morrow evening or Thursday morning."

"Indeed!"

"Yes, probably Kaye will forward a message."

"From whom?"

"From Baxter Creen. I suppose you'll select my time of absence, as usual, to get into some scrape. But before I go I should like to see a little more of our rendezvous of this afternoon."

"Inquiries might be made about the alleged caretaker in charge," I suggested.

"They are being made. I put Higgins on to that job this afternoon, and he will report here as soon as Mrs. Jerrold is gone home."

It was about half-past nine when a cautious knock on the front door drew our attention. We, on our side, were equally cautious. Arbuthnot knelt and spoke through the letter-slit.

"Who's there?"

"Private Higgins, sir." We exchanged smiles.

Higgins, it appeared, had not been idle. He had, as he expressed it, "dropped in on two or three people", and had also visited the local inn.

"Dawson, the man's name is, sir," he said. "Commonly called Sandy Dawson through, the colour of hair and beard he has. He's an elderly man, don't often come into the village, and hardly has a word for anyone. His provisions is sent him from London, and all he buys is a couple of loaves twice a week and a pint of beer now and again. I can only call to mind ever having seen him but once myself."

"How long has he been here?" queried Arbuthnot.

"Over a twelvemonth, sir."

"Do you remember who was here before him?"

"No one, sir."

"Indeed? This is interesting. Are you certain?"

"Yes, sir; the place was absolutely empty for a good two years. Before that some firm had been using it for breaking down shells and small arms ammunition. Then they finished and there wasn't a soul there till Dawson came."

Arbuthnot looked at me.

"The mystery of the superfluous caretaker," said he, grinning. "King, I think we are bound to pay that place another visit."

"To-night?"

"Why not? To-morrow night may be wet, and the night after I shall probably be in town."

"What do you hope to do?" I asked.

"Little enough. Still, we can examine the possibility of getting in and out again."

"The obvious thing would be to waylay this caretaker and take his keys from him," I suggested.

"Quite so. That is so obvious that one is inclined to ask whether it has been done before."

"Who would do it?"

"I presume that Hunt and the other members of that gang were here in order to get into that factory, which appears to be so well protected against intrusions. One at least was probably imprisoned there. We are bound to look upon Hunt and his comrades as the aggressors, as they were in the Turnbull case; otherwise why should they thrust themselves into danger, as we know they did? I think if the caretaker carried his keys they would have got them from him before now."

"If he doesn't carry them there must be another person there to readmit him on his return," I said.

"Exactly. What more likely, in view of what we know? I think we must rule out any hope of getting the key of the gates. A light ladder would be useful. I estimate the wall to be about sixteen feet high, and it may be capped with glass fragments."

"I can bring a ladder, sir," said Higgins promptly. "I does a bit of window cleaning occasionally, and I've a small ladder easy to carry about."

"Good. Taking turns, it should not be impossible for three grown men to transport it four or five miles to the scene of action. You don't possess a fishing-rod, Higgins?"

"No, sir. But I have a sweep's pole for pushing up chimneys. It's in parts and you joint it together. It's a good length."

"Splendid. I need something to poke about on the inside of the wall. We shan't dare use a torch. Higgins, you run along and get your paraphernalia and meet us in half an hour on the road that runs towards the factory, at a point about two hundred yards east of Lesslands Grange. This house may be watched."

Higgins went off, and I sighed for the comfort of the fireside. After the previous late night, and nine miles or so of rough going that afternoon, plus the various alarms I had experienced, I could willingly have dispensed with another nocturnal expedition. However—

When we set out the fog had cleared somewhat but it was very dark. Higgins we found faithful at the rendezvous. Arbuthnot and I shouldered the ladder, for we knew that the other, in spite of his willingness, was not physically strong. Higgins carried the sections of his pole and a length of rope. It was a weary tramp, but I was in a mood to bless the monotony. Heaven knows I had had little enough of it of late.

"You and I will inspect the wall at various places, King," said Arbuthnot, "while Higgins mounts guard below. Whether it will be possible to lower the ladder on the inside of the wall remains to be seen."

Thanks to Arbuthnot's leading we came to the factory without having lost direction. By his instructions we were left twenty yards away while he crept forward to the gates.

"No lights visible," he whispered on his return, "and it's much too dark to see anything. We'll mount the wall a little to the left of the gates. Then Higgins will pass up his pole for us to take soundings."

The ladder was planted in silence; it reached to within a foot of the top. Cat-like Arbuthnot mounted and worked his way along the wall to the right of the ladder to give me room to ascend to a position beside him. I flattered myself that I had managed my ascent very discreetly. It was the last occasion for self-gratulation for some time! What followed was over so quickly that my pen must necessarily lag behind my recollection.

I felt a gentle push against my back as I sat looking down into the darkness of the courtyard, with my feet hanging on the inside of the wall. It was Higgins intimating that the pole was ready. I twisted round and took hold of my end. It was then a question of getting the pole into Arbuthnot's hands in the easiest way. It seemed best to me to swing it over the wall on my left, and then by bringing it round in a semicircle it would eventually arrive in Arbuthnot's hands. This would obviate the danger of striking him with it by accident, which might occur if I drew it straight up. It all sounds very simple, but in the thick darkness it behooved one to take no risks.

Cautiously I swung up the pole till it was horizontal and slightly above the level of the top of the wall. Then I began to pivot it round. It was with a shuddering fear that I realized I had hit something, and *that* no brick and mortar either, but a more yielding substance. There was a startled exclamation, some one gave the pole a strong thrust in the opposite direction, and I realized there was another man on the wall! Whether he had been aware we were there we shall never know. My end of the pole, thus pushed, struck me a violent blow in the back. To my horror I felt that I was slipping. I made a convulsive grasp at the wall, failed to get a hold, dropped on to some metallic projection that vibrated at the blow, slid down it, and alighted on hands and knees in the courtyard.

At the same moment I saw out of the tail of my eye the strong light of an electric torch flash suddenly on the wall to my left. Then there was the sharp crack of a bullet, a strangled cry, and the thud of a heavy body crashing to the ground not more than a couple of yards from me. Instinctively I sprang back, on the grass-covered ground, making no sound. Fascinated, I watched the light creep down the wall, waver slightly, and finally come to rest on a huddled-up mass lying on the ground. It was interesting to realize that if the operator of the light swung it as little as three yards to one side I probably then had exactly one more second to live Noiselessly I drew out my own weapon. But the light never moved; evidently my own fall had passed unnoticed during the other happenings.

"King!" said a thin whisper in my very ear.

Good God! It was Arbuthnot. I put out my left hand and touched him. Voices!

"Another one?" queried some one in quick, guttural tones.

"No—only that damned interfering servant from the Grange."

"Dead?"

"Near enough."

The light still shone on the body. Then a figure came between and bent over it. Had I raised my arm I could almost have touched him, but, outside the ellipse formed by the rays of the torch, the darkness was profound, and we were as invisible as if we had been on the other side of the wall.

"Got to be got rid of," said the first voice.

"Yes, that's all very well. I'm getting scared. We're making this place too hot to hold us. It isn't fair for only two of us to be left here to face everything," grumbled the second voice.

"No good grousing," said the other, with a voice of authority. "Go and get a wheelbarrow. We must move him from here. He'd better go downstream."

"All right." A brushing sound denoted footsteps over the grass. The torch went out.

We stood in an amazing position. Within three yards or so was a man totally unaware of our presence, a man who would certainly blaze at us if he, by any chance, caught sight of us. As far as I could judge in the darkness I had him covered, and Arbuthnot told me afterwards that he was also prepared, but it was about as nerve-racking an experience as ever came my way. I estimate that we stood so not longer than three minutes, but it seemed that number of aeons before we heard the rumbling that told of the approach of the wheelbarrow.

Then the light flashed out again. It was hideously weird to see a little, sandy-bearded men prosaically trundling that commonplace barrow for such a ghastly purpose. The light again came to rest on the body. I guessed by the horrible angle at which the head lay that the neck must be broken. So Buller had paid the penalty of his rashness! The light went out.

"We can shift him in the dark," said the guttural voice. "I'm not easy about the light. The man used to have a pal to help him, and there's no knowing if he's about here."

I felt Arbuthnot's hand pressing me back a pace as in darkness they began to fumble with the body of then victim.

"Suppose he's not dead," said the voice that I now identified as belonging to the subordinate, sandy man.

"All the same. Soon will be," was the answer. "You'd better come back here afterwards with some sand in case there's bloodstains about. Heave!"

A dull thud betokened that the inert burden had been placed in that most unusual substitute for a hearse.

"Get hold of the handles. I'll guide you. Come on," said the voice that had issued all the orders.

With that the gruesome procession moved off. Strange as it seems now, I could only think at that moment of the undignified removal of the inebriated Mr. Pickwick. Actually I was on the verge of hysteria and could have shrieked with unnatural laughter.

"Well, we're in," said Arbuthnot dryly in my ear.

"How do *you* come to be here?" I managed to ask, biting my lips to keep down that silly inclination to giggle.

"I couldn't stay on that wall to be potted at. I came down almost simultaneously with you. It was either that or dropping the other side and leaving you to your fate."

By way of reply I grasped his hand.

"Come," said he. "We've a few minutes before the ghouls return. Let us take our intended view of what we can. Higgins can be trusted to stand by. Did you notice the down-curved spikes on the inside of the wall? We may have a devil of a job getting out again."

Keeping me in touch, he struck off across the courtyard until we encountered what was evidently the wall of the building. Arrived there it was a toss-up whether we moved left or right. We chose the former, chiefly because the funeral party had gone off towards the right. Feeling our way along by the wall we came to a break in it. It seemed we had reached the end of the main building and were looking into the black recess of a covered-in alley that separated it from an adjacent smaller building. Here we paused.

"D'you hear that?" whispered Arbuthnot to me suddenly. *That* was the sound of a groan, faint but unmistakable. Without a word Arbuthnot dived into the alley. Again that low note of despair, this time from above our heads! And then very plainly, "My God! My God!"

"There's evidently a window above us," whispered Arbuthnot again. "Apparently open, but most probably barred. Let me get on your shoulders."

In the darkness I hoisted him up. I could see nothing, but he appeared to have found the window, for his feet suddenly left my shoulders.

"Hist!" said he.

"Who is it?" said a new voice, sharp with excitement.

"Better for you not to know for the present. I'm a recruit. Listen."

"Yes. For heaven's sake go on."

"Jim got away. He's gone north."

"Yes, yes! Thank God for that, anyway."

"We can't rescue you for a few days. But you're perfectly safe. It's only a matter of patience."

"How do you know I'm safe?"

"We've got a hostage. They won't dare touch you."

"The deuce we have! Who is it?"

"Never mind. Better you shouldn't know too much till you're free."

"Is Roger Gordon with you? Since Jim got away I've been hoping every night he'd be able to do something."

"He couldn't come."

"Why?"

"He's dead."

"No! Oh, the hounds—the vile hounds! How did they get him?"

"In the marsh; during a fog. But, look here, I must go now. This isn't a healthy resort. Stick it. You'll be free in a week."

"God bless you! I'm trusting you're what you seem to be."

"Don't worry about that. Have I tried to get anything out of you? Look out for me in a week's time."

"Did they shoot at you? I swear it was a shot that woke me."

"No, that was— Good-bye."

A light shone at the far end of the passage. I seized Arbuthnot as he swung from the window-ledge, and helped him to come silently to the ground.

"Quick, King! They're coming back this way. Into the courtyard and pray heaven they never spotted us. Keep away from the spot where Buller died."

Crouching in a corner, ready to shoot, we saw the light travel across towards the outer wall, saw something being scattered on the ground, saw the light recede, and breathed again. Time passed and still Arbuthnot remained immobile. After a lapse of what I judged to have been at least fifteen minutes he returned to life.

"Don't think they're coming back. Now to get out. Plain voice that prisoner had for a mere figment of the imagination, hadn't he, King?"

I conceded his triumph.

"You're not going back to him are you?" I asked.

"Not to-night. I don't know enough yet to sustain a safe conversation. Now what is Higgins doing?"

We had not long to wait for an answer. From the top of the wall came the plaintive mew of a cat.

"Good for him," said Arbuthnot.

We made toward the sound.

"Higgins?" It was but a whisper, but it carried.

"Sir."

"We can't do anything here. Move along to the left with your ladder and rope till you reach the angle of the wall. That's our hope," said Arbuthnot. "Here the rope would merely hang between the spikes and we should pull ourselves up underneath them. If he lowered the ladder it could not rest against the wall."

We made for the corner. Higgins, having had to descend and move his ladder, was a minute later, but soon a husky "Sir" announced he had arrived.

"Listen, Higgins. Pull your ladder up and balance it across the wall. Fasten your rope firmly on it at the middle—not merely to the rungs. Then lay your ladder across the corner so that one encl is on each wall and see that the rope hangs clear. Be careful and don't hurry."

"Very good, sir."

"Splendid," I whispered.

"So long as the ladder doesn't give way," was Arbuthnot's cheerful answer.

Higgins being little more than a war-wreck, I thought it a great credit to him that he was ready in so short a space of time.

"I'll go first," said Arbuthnot. "Then there'll be one to steady each end of the ladder for you. You're heavier."

He seized the dangling rope as he spoke and began to ascend hand-over-hand. Then I heard the ladder creaking as he moved along it.

"All ready, King."

In my turn I seized the rope. I could hear the light ladder straining ominously, for I am no small weight, but it held. I clawed my way desperately on to it and shuffled along to join Higgins on the wall. Then, as if we had not had our fill of sensation for the night, a long feeler of light from the far side of the courtyard suddenly fastened itself on the top of the wall and came creeping along in our direction.

"Drop!" hissed Arbuthnot.

We wasted no time in obeying. With one sweep of his muscular arm he sent ladder and rope tumbling off the wall on to the ground outside. It was a matter of a mere fraction of a second. As our feet touched the ground the beam of light passed above our heads.

"A narrow squeak. We might have shared Buller s fate," said Arbuthnot.

I said nothing. For one thing, the ladder had hit me on the shoulder in its fall, and for another I felt a recurrence of the sensation of impending hysteria.

"Bedtime," said my friend whimsically. "Even if they heard the ladder fall I doubt if they will dare follow us in the open. They've enough on their minds for one night."

He led off. A long time will have to pass before I forget that tramp back. My head ached, my bruised shoulder throbbed, every nerve in my body seemed on edge. Higgins marched on uncomplainingly and made me feel ashamed of myself. It was, I suppose, about three o'clock in the morning before I finally crawled bedward.

"Sleep well, King," called Arbuthnot after me. "I don't imagine we are in any serious danger to-night."

It was excellent advice, but hard to follow. The events of the past thirty hours or so had been such a strain as to drive me momentarily beyond the reach of sleep; that is the condition when men go mad. I had seen many men die in the war, but yet the death of Buller, scoundrel though he was, was indescribably nauseating. Shot down while in a position incapable of defence, thrown dead or dying in a wheelbarrow and trundled away to the creek, he seemed a mere innocent compared with these unknown men who pursued their vendetta with such complete disregard for life. And the prisoner? Who was he, poor devil? What were his hopes? How could he possibly be rescued? I must have got some sort of slumber eventually for Mrs. Jerrold had to awake me at ten o'clock, but I was inexpressibly weary when I dragged my way downstairs to find the imperturbable Arbuthnot making his accustomed substantial breakfast.

"Hallo, King! Feeling cheery?" said he, glancing up.

"Like one who has toiled all night and caught nothing," I answered.

"On the contrary, we had a very good catch last night."

"My God! The wretched Buller!" I shivered.

"Yes, *he* soon paid the penalty of his rashness. I suppose he must have got on the track of these people on the night you saw the green lamps. There is bound to be a hue and cry for him before long. I hope it won't hamper our actions. Possibly the old man at the Grange may connect his absence with their own little private enterprise and stay his hand for a while."

"What did you make of the prisoner?" I asked.

"Spoke like a gentleman. I had a difficult conversation to maintain. It is troublesome when the person one's addressing automatically assumes one has knowledge that one doesn't really possess. However, I took a risk and was rewarded."

"How?"

"By learning Hunt's real name. He was evidently Roger Gordon, and it is a fair even chance that the other man you met in the marsh was Jim Gordon, his brother. They should be traceable, either in the archives of crime—or elsewhere."

"I see. What else do you gather from last night's episode?"

"The opposition gang seem to be in deadly fear. They shoot at sight and thereby run risks. That shot very likely was never heard by anyone but us, but there was the risk following so closely upon other events. You noted, I suppose, that there are now definitely only two of that gang left at the factory. We know there must have been more at one time both by our own observation and their remarks. Where are the others? Judging by what we heard I should say they have left the district altogether. There's a puzzle for you. And what is the secret of that place? That's another."

"What did you mean by speaking of a hostage?" I asked curiously. "Was it merely to cheer the fellow up?"

"I meant something—or nothing. Perhaps to-morrow will show. Love is the incalculable element that plays havoc with the careful labours of the investigator."

"If you choose to be mysterious," I said, "that's your affair. Meanwhile, pass the marmalade."

Arbuthnot grinned.

"When love comes in at the door, logic flies out at the window," he said. "And so am I reduced to doing other people's work."

"Oh, go to blazes!" I said angrily. I think my nerves were very raw that morning.

13

In Which I Entertain a Devil Unawares

The next morning, that of the last day of November, brought a telegram for Arbuthnot. He scanned it, and passed it to me. Thus it read:

Expected dividend declared.—Kaye.

"Continuing our Stock Exchange series," remarked Arbuthnot.

"What does it mean?" I asked.

"It means my departure by the mid-day train."

"Indeed. On what grounds?"

"I arranged when I wrote to Kaye on Monday night that if a message from Baxter Creen urgently requiring my presence was sent on to him by Mrs. Holden, he should send me this code wire."

"What about that poor devil, the prisoner?" I asked.

"He must wait. We don't even know that he is deserving of sympathy. I leave you with the more assurance because after the events of the night before last night it is extremely unlikely that danger will threaten from the factory. Of course that doesn't prevent it appearing from other quarters."

"I picture Colonel Gregory as the disturbing factor in the near future," I said.

"I shouldn't wonder. He must be feeling uncomfortable at present, wondering if Buller has been caught on one of his 'free-trade' trips."

Arbuthnot duly took his departure, and I was left to pass the time by traversing again and again the amazing sequence of events that bade fair to render my life a misery. While Arbuthnot remained things were tolerable, but in his absence I found myself clinging to the fireside, while I heard again the death-shriek of Hunt and saw the corpse of the foolhardy Buller topple from the wall. It was pleasant to have the companionship of Higgins.

"Depend upon it sir," he growled confidentially in my ear as I stood beside him in the garden, "if Captain Arbuthnot's in charge 'twill come all right in the end."

I cheered up a little as that day waned into a cold starlit twilight. It was a day of respite. A telegram came in the evening:

Anticipate early return.—Ponsonby.

So December came with a bitter frost and brilliant sunshine, and with it came Mr. Jennings. I was meditating a stroll in the sun about eleven that morning when I heard the purr of a car die down and cease in the lane outside. That in itself was unusual. Then came the sound of feet on the gravel path, a steady succession of blows with the door-knocker, and noises of Mrs. Jerrold's hastening forward in response. She brought me a visiting-card:

Mr. C. J. Homerton Jennings

I motioned her to close the door after her.

"What sort of man is he?" I questioned.

"He's dressed like a gentleman," she answered noncommittally.

Here was I straightaway in a pretty quandary. I remembered Arbuthnot's half-humorous suggestion that I always chose his times of absence to get into a scrape. I had little doubt that this was some subtle move, on the part of one or other of the gangs whose operations we had been studying to find out more about us. On the other hand, I was an armed man, sitting by my own fireside, in broad daylight. Surely there could be no very grave danger in seeing the fellow. I should certainly strengthen suspicion if I refused to do so. I had only ten seconds to decide; one cannot keep a caller loitering

"Show him in," I said.

Mr. Homerton Jennings appeared. He was rotund and immaculate, with a clean-shaven face, gold pince-nez, and incipient baldness. A pair of pale grey eyes searched my face.

"How d'you do?" I said vaguely. "To what am I indebted—"

"For this intrusion?" he broke in brightly. "I know your time is valuable, Professor Monk. Let me explain myself at once. I am here representing that well-known scientific periodical *Research.*"

I recoiled a step. "Indeed!" I muttered. Here was a pretty kettle of fish. My plan of dealing curtly with a plausible rogue collapsed; instead I was confronted with a far more formidable adversary in the shape of an inquiring scientist.

"Our attention was only drawn to the fact that England had such a scientifically distinguished visitor by references in the popular Press respecting some local trouble; otherwise, let me tell you at once, we should have anticipated this call by some days," said Mr. Jennings earnestly.

I growled something in reply to this semi-apology.

"Many of our readers," he continued, subsiding gracefully into the seat which, in my perturbation, I had failed to offer him, "would be immensely interested in some little account of your investigations in this interesting area."

I pulled myself together. This man must be squashed at all costs. If he came to suspect I was an impostor he would be bound to talk, and the upshot might be a descent of the police on us, or a hurried change of abode which would hamper our future plans in the locality.

"Very likely," I said, "but there are two objections to that."

"Yes, yes," he said anxiously. "Please be quite frank with me."

"Firstly," I said, "I have been so bothered and interrupted by local events external to my usually well-ordered life that my work has necessarily suffered."

"Ah, yes," said he sympathetically. "I can well understand that. Nothing is more disturbing to the scientific mind than to be embroiled in outside annoyances. But, if you will forgive my saying so, any little account of your labours you may choose to give me will, to some extent, be enriched in the eyes of our readers by your purely fortuitous connexion with events of popular interest. We have a varied body of readers," he added apologetically.

"Secondly," I went on, his speech having given me a breathing space, "you must be aware of the natural reluctance of a man engaged in research to make any anticipatory announcement of his aims, for he thereby runs the risk of being forestalled."

"Quite so, quite so," he murmured, "and I would not for a moment expect you to proceed beyond generalities. I am not a botanist myself, but merely a person whose position obliges him to keep abreast of current knowledge. I do not ask for detail—in fact, I fear I should not understand it. But, being under the necessity of visiting Colchester to see Professor Chamberlain, whose experiments on the axolotl have aroused such widespread interest, I could not resist the temptation of extending my journey to include you."

The man talked like the Press itself. Still it was encouraging to know that he was no botanist, but only a kind of specialized journalist. He produced an elegantly-bound notebook: no mere reporter's pad, this.

"Well?" he asked expectantly.

I was half-inclined to tell him to go to the devil; but I reflected I could possibly find refuge in a string of vague statements, which if ever printed would merely reflect the secrecy of the investigator.

"My main purpose is ecological," I said.

"Exactly," said he, writing it down forthwith.

"Grave possibilities have been suggested as to the actual distribution of the characteristic plants of the area. It is thought this distribution has varied during the past few years.

"Ah, yes," said he. "Very interesting. And may I ask whether your researches support this opinion?"

I hesitated.

"It is a bad time of year for field-work," I said at last. "But I had no alternative but to come here now or not at all. My opinion is that there have been changes, but of what nature I would prefer not to say."

"Quite so, quite so," said Mr. Jennings. "Professor Monk was naturally reluctant to go into details," he murmured, as if he were saying aloud what he was writing down. He turned to another page of his notebook while I felt my spirits rising. What had Arbuthnot said? "It is troublesome when the person one is addressing automatically assumes one has knowledge that one doesn't really possess." Surely Arbuthnot himself would be prepared to allow me a little credit for the way I was conducting this.

"One little point," my interviewer said deferentially. "I was told to ask you particularly about one marsh-loving plant. I have the name written here somewhere." He fumbled with the pages of his notebook. "Ah, yes, here it is—*Oryza sativa.*"

He eyed me expectantly. I was triumphant. The man was as great an ignoramus as myself. Without his notebook he would have been as devoid of knowledge as I was of this plant, which was apparently of special interest to botanists.

"I have naturally made a special point of the habitat of this fascinating little plant," I said in my best style. "I prefer to be sparing in my comments, but my general opinion is that the plant is spreading, distinctly to the detriment of some of the other flora of the neighbourhood."

"Good!" said Mr. Jennings to my surprise, rising and closing his notebook, instead of making a copious entry as I had expected.

"And now it is about time this nonsense came end," he added in an entirely new, incisive voice.

"I don't understand you," I stammered, while the hair on the back of my scalp rose. What had I done? I cursed my vainglorious confidence of the previous moment.

"Naturally you don't," he said smiling very unpleasantly. "An alleged botanist who talks gravely about the distribution of *Oryza sativa,* the common *rice* plant, in an Essex marsh, cannot be expected to understand much!"

I mentally reeled. How completely I had been trapped! How artfully he had led me on with his insinuations of his ignorance of the subject! What the devil was I to do? "Bluff" said a voice within me. "Bluff for all you're worth."

"I'm not interested in your comments," I said, with the best assumption of disdain I could achieve under the circumstances. "If you make a parade of your ignorance you must expect to get your leg pulled."

"A good try," he said, shaking his head slowly, "but it won't do, Professor—er—Monk. Ardent scientists are not leg-pullers."

"You appear to assume that ignorance of botany is a crime," I said, and not till I had spoken did I realize the folly of my words.

"Not at all," said the abominable man, his smile developing into a sneer. "At the same time, ignorance of botany in a professed botanist is surely remarkable."

"I don't propose to continue the discussion," I remarked.

"Nor I. All I trust is that you will see the wisdom of accompanying me without any fuss, which I assure you, would be entirely useless."

"Accompanying you?" I echoed.

"Quite so. You must realize that your powers of bluffing and air of geniality may have stood you in good stead with the local police, who are not expected to deal with individuals of your type. There comes a time, however, when superior powers are invoked. You may have heard of the C.I.D.—you now meet one of its representatives."

This was appalling. The journalistic busybody vanished: a cold, alert, purposeful detective took his place. Thoughts raced through my mind. Resistance was futile. Should I try to take him into my confidence? If I did was he likely to believe the fantastic tale I could tell? What would be the attitude of Arbuthnot towards any revelations I might make?

On the other hand, if I were arrested, I could hardly clear myself without revealing my identity, and the almost inevitable publicity would certainly react badly on Arbuthnot's schemes. Shortly, the disappearance of Buller would certainly become public knowledge; the "Essex Mystery" would leap to fresh notoriety in the Press, and the smallest item of news would be eagerly canvassed. I even got so far as to visualize the evening newspaper posters in the London streets: "Mystery of Masquerading Baronet"; "Essex Enigma: Amazing Development"; and so forth.

The voice of the detective intervened: "To a man of your undoubted intelligence, the foolishness of resistance is obvious."

I had reached the same conclusion; I must choose the lesser evil of submission.

"You propose to arrest me?" I asked abruptly.

"That is my duty. My orders are to take you to Colchester, where you will be formally charged and will be free to make a statement if you so wish."

"Charged with what?"

"With being concerned in the disappearance of the man Gordon."

"What nonsense!" I managed to utter.

"I have no time to waste," said the detective. "It is not my business to give you information, but it should be evident that the death of Gordon, following immediately on your arrival in Leasinghoe, and your preposterous device to divert attention from yourselves by painting your window with blood, would have attracted the attention of a department much less alert than the C.I.D. And there will be other charges."

The little clock on the mantelpiece struck twelve, and my heart jumped. Arbuthnot's wire had told me to expect his early return. Supposing he travelled by the train he had used previously he would be at the cottage by about half-past twelve. If I could play out time the situation might yet be saved.

"I submit," I said.

"Very well. I take it there will be no necessity for handcuffs. One naturally desires to avoid humiliation where possible."

"I won't resist, if that's what you mean," I said. "At the same time I feel bound to warn you that you are making a colossal mistake which may have unfortunate reactions on your own career."

He laughed tolerantly. "Really, I am beginning to have a sneaking admiration for you, Monk. It is a pleasure to deal with anyone who can accept an unpleasant situation with such good grace. I had thought perhaps the presence of Sergeant Wigmore might have been necessary, but as I have your assurance of good behaviour we can, I think, dispense with his services."

Wigmore! Of course it was he who, not so long ago, had told us that the aid of the C.I.D. would be sought. No, I rather preferred that the worthy Wigmore should not witness my undignified exit from Leasinghoe.

"You can spare me a few minutes to make some necessary arrangements, I trust?" I asked as courteously as I could manage. The hands of the clock had already progressed beyond 12.5. There was hope. If I could get in touch with Arbuthnot I knew there was every chance that things could be adjusted, without the contretemps of a public revelation of my identity, and possibly of his also. I think Jennings must have intercepted my glance at the clock.

"Provided you do everything promptly and in my presence," he answered.

I summoned Mrs. Jerrold.

"I find I have to go away unexpectedly with this gentleman," I said, as carelessly as I could. "I shall return shortly. I will give you a note to hand to Mr. Ponsonby when he returns. That's all." She left the room.

"Quite so," purred the abominable Jennings. "Let everything be done decently and in order. The only fly in the ointment is that the police will take possession of this cottage as soon as we leave it."

The time was 12.10. I sat down to produce a note to Arbuthnot. It was risky in a way, but it seemed imperative that I should lose no opportunity of resuming contact with him. I wrote slowly, partly because I was anxious to waste time, partly for fear of including any indiscreet statement. My note said:

> "Dear Ponsonby,
> "I have been arrested (noon, Dec. 1st) by a member of the C.I.D., on a cock-and-bull charge of being concerned in local troubles. I am being taken to Colchester to be charged. I shall decline to make any statement until I have been afforded an opportunity of consulting a solicitor.
> "Yours,
>
> "C. G. Monk."

"Excellent," said Jennings over my shoulder. "Unfortunately, it is very doubtful indeed whether your friend Ponsonby will be allowed to return here. However, the note is quite harmless."

As I was placing it in an envelope, the clock marked 12.20. If Arbuthnot had travelled by his usual train, and if that train were punctual, two very big "if's" indeed, he would now have left the railway station on his two-mile stroll to the cottage.

"Will you have a drink?" I asked.

Mr. Jennings smiled. "I regret I can't accept your hospitality. Drinks have been known to be drugged."

I summoned Mrs. Jerrold again.

"Give this note to Mr. Ponsonby when he arrives," I said.

"Yes, sir. You might see him yourself if you're going Colchester way. Higgins went along to meet the twelve o'clock train, expecting he might be on that."

"Time we were moving on, Monk," said Jennings.

"We'll keep an eye open for him on the way."

The time was 12.25. I took my hat and coat. Mrs. Jerrold vanished to open the front door.

"Hurry up," said Jennings. "I don't want your precious friend on my hands as well. Others have that job in hand."

I saw no further way of extending the time, unless I wished to leave the house as an obvious prisoner. Mrs. Jerrold's innocent remark had evidently worried the detective. There was a note of menace in his voice. I went without demur.

Outside a chauffeur sat in a large open touring car.

"Get in at the back and sit on my right," said the detective to me curtly. "We shall go fast. If you are foolish enough to try and jump out, your blood be on your own head."

"Will you have the hood up, sir?" asked the chauffeur, preparing to descend.

"Should have been done before. Never mind now. Drive on," snapped Jennings.

Within three seconds the car was nosing its way along the lane. I sat in a turmoil. There was the chance of meeting Arbuthnot, but he would certainly be walking, and could not possibly stop the car. All I could do would be to stand up and shout to him if I saw him. At the most the man beside me could only be angry. A very little warning would suffice for Arbuthnot to realize that he had better be on the alert. It was a godsend that, through the carelessness of the chauffeur, the hood was not up.

As we passed Lesslands Grange a figure in blue stood by the roadside. I recognized Sergeant Wigmore. Jennings waved to him and the sergeant saluted. It was evidently the signal for the police descent on the cottage. I wondered whether they would burst open our trunks. My keys still reposed in my pocket, together with a lethal weapon would be awkward to account for when I reached Colchester. Fortunately Arbuthnot had with him all the documents—letters from Kayc and so forth—relating to the case.

A short distance beyond the Grange we came out on to a straight stretch of road extending for perhaps nearly a mile. "Open her out," said Jennings to the chauffeur.

At his word the car accelerated until it must have been averaging thirty. The distance was swiftly eaten up. Then I saw spring to view some quarter of a mile away two black dots, one slightly larger than the other, conspicuous on the dry white road in the cold December sunshine. I held my breath. In a quarter of a minute I was certain. The smaller dot had become Arbuthnot; the larger was George Higgins with his hand-cart.

When I judged we were no more than a hundred yards away I suddenly sprang to my feet, waved an arm frantically, and shouted for all I was worth.

"Damn you—sit down," yelled Jennings, seizing my coat. "Full speed!" he shouted to the chauffeur. I felt the car jump beneath me.

As I calculated it out afterwards Arbuthnot must have had approximately eight seconds in which to decide and act. For that man it was enough. As in a dream in which everything happens at an impossible speed, I saw Arbuthnot seize the handles of Higgins cart and swing it round broadside across the road. On it reposed the trunk which Arbuthnot used in his travels, a substantial article made to resist the inquisitive. The road was narrow. I saw like a flash we could not pass. So did the chauffeur. There was a grinding of brakes—too late.

Jennings and I were flung forward and his grip on my coat relaxed. I glimpsed Arbuthnot and Higgins leaping sideways to safety. Then came the crash. I felt the near wheels mounting—mounting—mounting. She would overturn! In that instant I took a flying leap into the road. Anything better than being pinned under an overturned car!

I sensed rather than saw that Jennings did not seek to interfere with me. I believe that as he was flung forward his over-rotund stomach came into such abrupt contact with the back of the front seat that he was momentarily knocked out.

I came down on to the hard road anyhow, with a sickening jar to my spine and one leg doubled under me. Vaguely I realized that the car had not overturned. The chauffeur must have been consummately skilful. Then I think I achieved something in the nature of a faint. Hedge, road and splintered fragments of a hand-cart oscillated before my eyes, some one coming towards me suddenly swelled up to monstrous proportions, and I found myself tumbling into an abyss where a noise rumbled unceasingly like falling water in my ears.

When I came to myself it was to find the neck of a flask between my teeth and a familiar voice saying, "Dear, dear, King, I do wish you would not so frequently indulge your natural propensity for getting into mischief in my absence."

14
In Which a Life of Service Brings Its Reward

"Arbuthnot?" I cried, trying to struggle to a sitting position.

"He. Don't try to sit up until you feel steadier."

I subsided again on to what was evidently a roadside stretch of grass.

"Feeling better, sir?" asked another voice. It was Higgins.

"Yes. Here let me sit up, Arbuthnot. There's something devilishly important I must tell you."

They assisted me to sit up and I stared, blinking in astonishment. Apart from the remains of Higgins's vehicle and Arbuthnot's trunk with one corner sadly crushed, the road was empty.

"Where's the car?" I asked, gaping stupidly around.

"Your friend seemed in too great a hurry to stop and assist you," said Arbuthnot dryly.

"Assist me! Do you know who that was?"

"I have some sort of idea," admitted Arbuthnot.

"It was a C.I.D. man. I was off to Colchester to be charged with murder if you hadn't intervened. And now, I suppose, there'll be the devil to pay—interfering with the police in the execution of their duty."

Arbuthnot looked at me. Then a smile came on his face and gradually broadened into a grin of his most pronounced type.

"Don't let that worry you," said he. "But we'll postpone discussions till later. Let's consider how best to get back to the cottage."

"You'll find the police there," I said.

"Very pleased to see 'em," answered my friend, chuckling.

He and Higgins assisted me to my feet. I was shaky, but had suffered less than had seemed probable. The leg I had fallen on was badly bruised, but not otherwise injured. My head sang like mosquitoes in the Arctic summer, but my face was not scarred. One hand, the left, was rather cut about; I twisted a handkerchief round it and thrust it into my coat pocket while Higgins did his best to brush the dust from my outer garments. I was grateful it had not been a wet day.

"The story is this," said Arbuthnot. "You met us, and changing your mind decided to return to the cottage and leave the business till to-morrow. Walking along, Higgins had an accident with his cart; being old it collapsed under the weight of my trunk. We threw the wreckage to the roadside as being irreparable." He began to suit the action to the words. "I very kindly consented to compensate Higgins for his smashed cart," he added, with a twinkle in his eye. "Monk, wishing to be helpful, offered to shoulder the trunk, but, being clumsy, let it slip, thus tearing his hand and bruising his leg. Hence I had no alternative but to become my own porter."

With a single muscular movement he swung the heavy trunk to his shoulder, while I, in spite of my headache and uneasiness, could hardly forbear to smile. We moved off, Higgins giving me an arm for the first hundred yards or so until I felt steadier. Then he petitioned to be allowed to carry the trunk.

"March at attention," said Arbuthnot, smiling, to me, and obediently Higgins fell silent.

As our procession rounded the corner which brought us into view of the entrance of the Grange I stopped, startled. A figure in police uniform had emerged into the road.

"There's Wigmore!" I ejaculated.

"Nice fellow, Wigmore," said Arbuthnot.

"I hope you find him so to-day," I muttered. The sergeant had seen us approaching and was standing in the centre of the road, waiting.

"Good day, Sergeant," called Arbuthnot jovially. "Everything quiet in the little burg of Leasinghoe?"

"Far from it, sir," said the sergeant shaking his solemnly, while I grew red in the face and wished myself elsewhere. "But what's happened to your party, sir, if I may ask? I saw Mr. Monk here driving off with a friend in a car not so very long ago."

"Yes. They met us, and Mr. Monk decided to defer his trip till to-morrow. He had not been expecting my return to-day. Then Higgins's cart came to grief through excessive old age, and so you have the whole story."

"Hard lines," said the sergeant. "We all seem to have our troubles."

"Walk along with us," said Arbuthnot. "This trunk is confoundedly heavy, and I shan't be sorry to put it down."

I fell in behind, speechless. A variety of thoughts rushed through my brain. Here was the man who by rights should have been at the cottage waiting to arrest Arbuthnot when he arrived, walking along and chatting most freely with him. Was it part of the sergeant's guile? Surely not. He must know that I should have informed Arbuthnot at once of the impending trouble. Perhaps he feared to tackle the two of us together. Perhaps a strong contingent of police even now awaited us at the cottage. I shrugged my shoulders, left it to my friend, and listened.

"Yes, sir," the sergeant was saying, "the Colonel's in a terrible state. The man's been missing since the night of the 28th, but the Colonel was slow to call in the police, because, as he honestly enough said, he thought the man was up to some private devilment of his own, and would be dealt with when he returned."

"Indeed?" replied Arbuthnot. "I can quite believe the man Buller was capable of a good deal. No clue, I suppose?"

"None, sir. Must have gone out after he finished his duties on that night, for his bed wasn't slept in, and vanished clean away."

"Dear me, what exciting times we do live in, to be sure."

"Too much for me," said the sergeant frankly. "We've been asking for a C.I.D. man to be sent down, but so far they haven't spared us one."

I was glad I was in the rear where my start of astonishment passed unnoticed.

"Coming in?" asked Arbuthnot, as we reached the cottage gate.

"No, thank you, sir. Not at present. I've got to get busy."

We passed in. I walked like one in a dream, only half-conscious of Mrs. Jerrold's mild astonishment at my unexpected return. I sank into a chair by the fireside, hearing dully distant sounds of her commiseration with Higgins on his misfortune. The note I had left for Arbuthnot lay conspicuously on the table. He opened it, read it, and tossed it on the fire.

"To think that I should have rescued my old friend from the hands of the law," he said, with an air of mock-heroism.

"It's no joke," I said.

"It isn't. I shudder to think what might have happened if we had not happened to come along when we did. I can just picture Sir Edmund King figuring as number four!"

"What do you mean?"

"Simply that you had fallen into the hands of an extremely clever scoundrel, who no more belonged to the C.I.D. than I do to the Holy Rollers."

I nodded feebly.

"I am beginning to think so myself," I said. "But in self-defence I must say he was extremely plausible and convincing. Why, confound his audacity, he even waved to Sergeant Wigmore, as we passed him on the road, and the sergeant saluted. No doubt he saluted me, but I didn't guess it at the time."

"Tell me all about it."

I did so, my narrative being punctuated with little snorts of laughter from Arbuthnot. He became seriously attentive, however, when I mentioned the reference the pseudo-detective had made to "the man Gordon".

"That alone should have told you, King, that the man was not what he pretended to be. Who, except presumably the members of these two gangs and ourselves, know that Hunt was really Gordon? The police don't know it. It was either a slip on his part or a very daring trap for you. Did you admit that you recognized Hunt under that name?"

"I didn't challenge it," I said miserably. "By that time I was horribly muddled up. Had the man come to me as a detective I should have been on my guard, but I was so staggered by this botanical business that it seemed as if my brain were temporarily atrophied. I'm very sorry."

"I'm not," said Arbuthnot brightly. "As it has turned out, his visit was much more useful to me than to himself. A clever rogue, King. His methods strike me as having a distinct touch of genius. Such a man does not turn his attention to crime without the reward being commensurate with the risk—don't forget that."

"What happened when I jumped out of the car?" I asked.

"Nothing of note. For a moment I thought the car was going to overturn. I don't mind admitting I was feeling distinctly awkward. I had stopped the car on your signal, judging matters must be serious, but I didn't fancy the prospect of fatalities, possibly including yourself. The man Jennings glared at me as he passed, and I returned the look with interest. The car went on, driven at a great speed."

"Did you get the number?" I asked.

"I did, but I don't imagine it will be of much use The car was probably a hired one and will be found abandoned somewhere to-morrow. Mr. Jennings is no fool."

"We are now definitely on the defensive," I remarked.

"Never in your life, King. Don't forget your chess. The man who merely defends is bound to be eventually beaten."

"Perhaps your London experiences were more inspiring than my Essex ones," I said.

"I'm not totally dissatisfied. First of all, I have traced Roger Gordon and his brother Jim."

"Oh, good—very good!"

"Their father is Sir Alexander Gordon of Forres, a Scottish baronetcy older than your own. Roger did brilliantly in medicine at Edinburgh. He is returned officially as not practising. Were he alive now he would be twenty-eight. Jim is two years younger, and in his time broke nearly every athletic record at Fettes."

"Where do the family suppose Roger Gordon is?" I asked.

"Kaye put in a telegraphic inquiry to find that out. He is supposed to be in Bengal, studying that unpleasant tropical disease called *kala-azar.*"

"Indeed? It doesn't sound like a family of criminals to me."

"Nor to me. But the information is amazingly significant, nevertheless. My chief business was with Baxter Creen."

"No news in that quarter, I suppose? I mean, the girl is not found?"

"No. The rumour is pretty well spread over London now, but Creen is as obstinate as ever about not invoking the aid of the police."

"What did he want of you?"

"He had received a threatening letter. Would you like to see it?"

"I would."

I studied the half-sheet of typescript carefully.

> "If you retain any interest in your daughter's welfare, you will do well to secure the release of him you know of."

That was all there was on the paper. I stared at it. Then suddenly it was as if a great light had broken in on my brain.

"By heaven!" I said. "Suppose 'him you know of' refers to the man imprisoned at the factory. He was a friend of Gordon's, who was connected in some way with Charteris, whom we know to be an enemy of Baxter Creen!"

Arbuthnot smiled.

"So far it fits," he said. "Then who do you suppose sent that note?"

"Obviously one of the Charteris gang," I said at once.

"Wrong!"

"What?" I recoiled in disappointment. "Then you found out who sent it?"

"No. I knew."

"Then who was it?"

"Myself!"

I don't think Arbuthnot will ever lose his power of surprising me.

"You sent it! How the deuce could *you* send it?"

"It was a shot in the dark," he said, almost apologetically. "There was no risk. It was a case of 'heads I win, tails you lose'. If Baxter Creen didn't take alarm at the missive as I thought he would, there was nothing lost. On the other hand, if it scared him, there was the hope that in his perturbation he might tell me something I wanted badly to know. He is a strong man, but his Achillean heel is his daughter."

"What did you want to know?" I asked eagerly.

"Something more about the man 'Dormer'. Therefore I wrote to Kaye and told him, a respectable solicitor, to dispatch this blackmailing missive! The upshot was Creen's frantic call for help."

"But how did you know enough to send such a letter?" I asked incredulously.

"I didn't. *Toujours de l'audace,* you know. After the escape of Jim Gordon I always thought it possible that the second man was also imprisoned and not dead. There was also the thin link connecting him with Baxter Creen. Creen can only be struck through his daughter. Hence my action."

"Then," I said, as I thought, acutely, for my wits were always sharpened by contact with Arbuthnot, "if what you suggest is true, why haven't the Charteris gang adopted the method you used of frightening Creen?"

Arbuthnot looked at me. "Do you remember resorting to vulgar abuse of me the morning after the night on which Buller received his quietus?" he asked smilingly.

"I may have done," I conceded.

"That was a pity, just when I was explaining this very business to you." No more would he say on the subject.

"Then what did you get from Creen?" I asked.

"I found him, in spite of his self-control, in a state of almost obvious panic. He showed me at once the letter you have just seen. I asked him whether he regarded it as serious.

"'I am bound to,' he said.

"'Then,' said I, 'to be perfectly frank with you, you must have information that you have not so far confided in me. I don't require a man who seeks my help to have been a Galahad all his life, but it is necessary that he should not conceal relevant facts.'

"He nodded.

"'That is perfectly just,' he said. 'News has recently reached me through private channels from abroad that the head of a gang of international crooks has come to England and is masquerading here under the name of Dormer Strang.'

"'Indeed?' said I, beginning to enjoy myself. 'And of course you immediately connected the name with the word "Dormer" that the housemaid overheard.'

"'No, I did not,' he answered. 'It is certain there are plenty of men in England called "Dormer", and it is not beyond the bounds of possibility that one of them has the surname Strang.'

"'Quite so,' I said. 'Then what aroused your suspicions?'

"'Nothing until the reception of this threatening letter. Let me explain. As you probably know, I am head of an important munitions firm. We are always engaged on research relating to new explosives and other material of war. This man who now calls himself Strang is one of those people who earn a precarious and not altogether honest living by stealing secrets that are vendible elsewhere. Hence it is more than possible that he should favour me with his attentions.'

"I agreed. I was beginning to admire Creen.

"'Now, remember, I have never seen the man, but I have asked for a description of him to be furnished me at once. That will be confirmatory—or otherwise. It should arrive shortly.'

"'Were your informants some foreign police authorities?' I asked.

"'No, the news came from my own agent in Vienna. Let me be frank with you, Mr. Arbuthnot. It pays us occasionally to have foreign representatives capable of snapping up any trade secrets that may be offered, without being too curious as to the legality of the bargain. Between ourselves, you are probably not surprised to hear there is quiet but extensive scientific activity in certain European States. Man is a revengeful creature.'

"'In plain words,' I said, 'your agents repeat, on the Continent, the operations of Mr. Dormer Strang in England.'

"He was not annoyed. He laughed openly.

"'You have hit it on the head,' he said. 'After all, the end in view is laudable.'

"'Do you think the English police are aware of Strang's being in the country?' I asked.

"'I very much doubt it. In any case, as I told you before, I don't want the police involved in this in any way. I have your assurance on that point?'

"'You have,' I said. 'Now you can explain the reference to the "release of him you know of." That is evidently the crux of the whole affair.'

"'It is,' he said, 'and at the same time it is my real worry. Only a short time ago an international agent named Klortz was captured and sentenced to a long term of imprisonment in Paris. The information that led to his downfall was obtained by a man acting for me in that city. I am now told on reliable authority that this person and the man styling himself Strang were members of the same gang—'

"I was just digesting this remarkable piece of news when a cablegram arrived. Creen muttered an apology and tore it open. Then he sat back with a curse on his lips.

"'As I feared,' he said and passed me the wire. I read:

"Parwitz six feet fair clean shaven mole left cheek muscular pleasant expression occasionally stammers English perfect.

"The cable was dated from Vienna.

"'Isn't that a damned good description of Williams?' asked Creen.

"'Judging from what I gathered when I was here, it fits him exactly,' I admitted.

"'So,' said Creen, and a spasm of almost unimaginable hatred crossed his face, 'that is the unspeakable scoundrel who has entrapped my Iris.'

"He rose and paced the room; his agitation was obvious.

"'You must find her, Mr. Arbuthnot—and quickly. I know I can't egg you on with offers of money, but, good God, you're a man and can realize what I'm feeling. I want her back. It's immaterial what may have happened in the meantime. She's my daughter and I'll face the world for her. I suppose *you* have no news?'

"'Nothing to tell you,' I said. 'I don't want to raise any false hopes, but I think there's a chance of getting her back relatively unscathed.'

"He fixed me with his eyes. He is a strong man, this Baxter Creen—a good enemy, I should think.

"'Will it hurt you to tell me what you know?' he asked abruptly.

"'I want a free hand,' I said definitely, and rose to go. I think he was momentarily annoyed, but he smothered the feeling and bade me a cordial *au revoir*.

"Then I made another descent on Kaye and searched his newspaper files. You guess what I was looking for."

"No."

"Naturally to see if one Klortz had been lately sentenced in Paris for espionage."

"Well?"

"He had."

"Then Creen was telling the truth."

"On that point, at any rate."

"Do you suspect him on other points then? Surely his anxiety about his daughter is genuine?"

"I am certain it is perfectly genuine. But he is inconsistent."

"How?"

"He talks of taking back his daughter whatever trouble may have come her way, and yet, to avoid scandal, as he says, he refuses to call in the police. Yet the police, if only by reason of their numbers, are clearly most likely to be useful in a disappearance case."

"That reminds me of Turnbull," I said slowly.

"Expound," said Arbuthnot, blowing out a huge cloud of smoke and assuming an expression of rapt interest.

"Well, if this Charteris-Strang-Gordon gang include international secret agents, that indirect attempt to foment a strike in a great British industry takes on an ugly significance."

Arbuthnot slapped his knee.

"Upon my word, King, there's hope for you yet. But I shall be better able to evaluate your theory when Kaye has established the existence, or otherwise, of Dormer Strang."

"Do you expect Kaye to hunt an international crook?" I asked.

"No, no. I only expect him to make an intelligent use of reference books."

It was at this point that Mrs. Jerrold bore in a belated lunch. Arbuthnot did it justice—I couldn't. He looked at me keenly.

"King, you're feeling life a bit hard at present. Lie down on the sofa and hog it in comfort. I assure you I will keep excellent guard."

The invitation was too tempting to be declined. I slept for nearly three hours, my first perfectly quiescent slumber since the night we dealt with Reynolds. I had settled with that individual, by the way, by sending him a couple of pounds and a note to the effect that my health prevented my out-of-door work for a time. I awoke refreshed, to see flickering flames on the hearth and Arbuthnot brandishing the teapot. I sat up.

"By Jove," I said, "I had dreamt myself back into our flat and out of all this imbroglio."

"Come and have tea. Tea is always good."

"By heaven, I'm stiff," I added as I limped to the fireside.

"A walk to the factory will soon work that off."

I jumped. "Do you mean it seriously?"

"Certainly. But not to-night. We must, however, consider plans for freeing the prisoner. I can imagine his proving distinctly useful. That's why I took my large trunk to town with me."

"That's what?"

"I have brought back a small, self-contained oxyacetylene blowpipe and a light sectionalized steel ladder that can be set up in an inverted V shape so as to clear those iron spikes. I had to move heaven and earth to get them, I assure you. Even now, I frankly admit that it is improbable those things were originally manufactured for purely lawful purposes. Perhaps to-morrow night, if it is sufficiently dark, we might try."

"Then you expect that if you release the prisoner Iris Creen will be set at liberty?"

"I don't. For all I know Iris Creen *is* at liberty."

"I don't follow you. If she's at liberty, how is it that no one knows where she is?"

"Some one does know where she is."

"Only the members of that gang."

"And I."

Forgetting my stiffness I jumped up. Then I sat down again.

"I don't believe it," I said. "How did you find out?"

"By using knowledge common to us both," he said, smiling and lifting the teapot lid hopefully, in case of any poor remainder.

"Then why don't you go and get her?" I demanded naturally.

"You know where the moon is. Why don't you go and get it?" he asked insultingly.

I smothered my annoyance.

"Then I take it—"

"She is in a very safe place."

"One might break in through a window."

"There aren't any."

"Then a door."

"There are no doors."

"Even hell has doors," I said, feeling that Arbuthnot in some obscure way was making fun of me.

"Oh, I don't say she's gone as far as that," he answered. With which somewhat ambiguous remark I had to be content.

"Do you think there's any chance of our tracing the abominable Homerton Jennings?" I asked.

"I am asking Kaye to try and ascertain the ownership of the car. It's not very likely it can be done, nor is it so vastly important."

"I'm rather surprised," I added, "that no attempt was made on you either yesterday or to-day."

"I'm not. You see, when I leave Liverpool Street Station I am a very different person from the elderly and rather shambling artist who wanders about Leasinghoe. I imagine that had you been taken they would have hoped to trap me while I was attempting your rescue."

"Yes, I grant your disguise, for all its simplicity, is thoroughly effective, but I shall be glad when the necessity for those whiskers is a thing of the past."

"Well, well, they served me in good stead to-day, at any rate."

"How was that?"

"Without them there is just the possibility that Mr. Jennings would have recognized me, as I recognized him."

"You recognized him!"

"I did. I have been told more than once that a life of service brings its reward. It did in this case."

"What do you mean?"

"It was while in service that I last saw that amiable person. To be exact, I once handed him a whisky-and-soda while I was acting as footman to Baxter Creen!"

"The devil!"

"One of his emissaries, at any rate."

"But is Jennings a friend of Creen's?"

"I couldn't say. They were together in his study. I heard nothing. Even the keyhole was denied me, for the butler happened to be in the hall to which the room opened."

I sat back and endeavoured to assimilate what I had heard. A nightmare is one of the few things in which variety is not charming. Arbuthnot lighted a fresh pipe, and my confused current of thought was broken by the entrance of Mrs. Jerrold. The buff-coloured envelope she held was to me like a danger-signal. Arbuthnot read the message.

"No answer," said he, and passed the paper to me. I saw:

Drop in Midlands—Kaye.

"Hullo, what does this mean?"

"It means that the Honourable Geoffrey Charteris has returned to London," said Arbuthnot, "and that my good friend King and myself are about to endeavour to shake some information out of that very wily gentleman."

15
In Which Words Break Glass

The next afternoon saw us thundering Londonwards in an otherwise empty first-class compartment that we had seen fit to reserve. Arbuthnot was engaged in changing; I was brooding over a pipe in a corner of the carriage.

"Of course," I said at last, "your having seen Jennings at Creen's house does not necessarily inculpate the latter. Creen may be marked down as a victim the same as I was."

"Granted. I should be very slow to condemn Creen because I happened to find a scoundrel visited his house. He admitted that he is bound to have dealings with all sorts and conditions of men. Nevertheless—"

"Yes?"

"Did you pay particular attention to the account I gave yesterday of my conversation with Creen?"

"Naturally."

"Did anything in it strike you as peculiar?"

"No. I am bound to say I thought he gave a very straightforward story. It was confirmed by the arrival of that cablegram and by your inquiry about Klortz."

"Possibly. It was an exceptionally well-told tale, at any rate. It had only one flaw, and that such a startlingly obvious one that I wager you entirely failed to notice it."

"I did fail," I admitted. "It seems to me that any suspicion of Creen must rest, so far, on your impression that when you originally mentioned the name Dormer, Creen recognized it."

"It *did* rest on that, and that was very unsatisfactory, for what I took for a nervous flinching might only have been due to, let us say, a sudden abdominal pain. *Now,* it rests on that no longer."

I sat back and pondered, not very successfully.

"How do you propose to deal with Charteris?" I asked at length. "You said he would be an awkward man to follow."

"I still think so. Fortunately, however, Kaye has found out that Mr. Charteris, for a man of his monadic disposition, has one extremely regular habit. When in town he invariably dines at Lunkin's, a very quiet, respectable, and expensive restaurant in the Haymarket. Do you know it? They say the original Lunkin would have been an earl but for the bar sinister."

"I know it. It is the kind of place where a cigar and a liqueur add half a guinea to the bill. I go there once a year, when old Uncle Theodore comes up from Shropshire for the May meetings. He sits interminably over Napoleon brandy, and talks about the Anglo-Catholic menace."

Arbuthnot chuckled.

"I see you know it," he said. "Charteris, like a few other men, would appear to prefer it to his club. It is a fine advertisement of respectability. He has his own table rigidly set aside for him, after the fashion of old Tom Cogglesby at the 'Aurora'."

"What follows?" I demanded.

"To-night the next table is also reserved. Kaye was instructed by telegram this morning. You and I dine at Lunkin's at great expense. We thereby hope so to excite the curiosity of Mr. Charteris, by a method I will detail later, that he will walk into our trap."

"You interest me immensely," I said, and with that the train slid into that concatenation of light, noise, smoke, and grime that is called Liverpool Street Station. We had a certain bulk of luggage, for we had thought it inadvisable to leave anything in the cottage that might afford any information to an unlawful visitor, so conversation hung fire while we dealt with it. Once back in the flat, however, with Mrs. Holden discreetly beaming as she bore in the almost sacramental teapot, Arbuthnot became communicative.

"This, you must understand, was all arranged with Kaye some time ago in anticipation. To-night we sleep out."

"Really! Well, any place is better than Desolation Cottage."

"Yes, we have palatial quarters, consisting of two bedrooms and an adjacent sitting-room, in the 'Tristram'. My name is Marsh; you are Mr. Judson."

"It all sounds sufficiently intriguing. What is the programme?"

"Firstly, we assemble enough miscellaneous baggage to allay suspicion. This we take along to the hotel, where we dress for dinner. We arrange to arrive at Lunkin's at 7.45, that is to say a few minutes later than Charteris normally commences to dine. We have a small table for two next to his. In the holy calm of Lunkin's sound carries very easily, as you know. We sit down and talk about the progress and the prospects of the rugger season. I seat myself where I can easily see his face. Then at a given signal from me—let us say when I pour out the last glass of the Latour—you make the very innocent remark, 'Fancy that young fool Grierson going to Port Said. Much good may it do him.' Remember to speak loudly. I shall be studying Charteris. Unless I am hopelessly wrong, he will feel impelled to know more about us. I hope he will invent a pretext for following us to our hotel. That is our opportunity."

"Grierson," I said thoughtfully. "I had forgotten about him."

"Had you? It's difficult to know what niche to allot to Grierson in this particular temple of mystification."

"The same might be said of some others. For one thing, there seem to be so many of them."

"There are. Let's make a list. Like individually trivia household expenses, they may assume quite a different, even a surprising, appearance when considered in the mass."

He took a sheet of paper and began to write. This is the list as it was at its completion:

> *Roger Gordon,* aged twenty-eight, of good
>   family, brilliant doctor.
> *Jim Gordon,* aged twenty-six, his brother,
>   public school athlete.
> *'The Colonel',* Gordon's supposed 'brother',
>   youngish judging by description given.
> *Walter Grierson,* aged twenty-four, of good
>   family, linguist, hockey player.
> *Prisoner at factory,* speaks like a gentleman.
> *'Old gentleman from Australia',* a good actor.
> *Geoffrey Charteris,* aged twenty-nine, of good
>   family, geologist and soccer blue.
> *'Miss Hunt',* impressed King favourably.
> *Unknown Man,* who helped to kidnap Turn-
>   bull. Appeared to be a gentleman.
> *Dormer Strang* impressed Iris Creen *very* fa-
>   vourably.

"There's a list for you, King! Granted that some may only be duplicates of others for all we know, it is yet very suggestive. Hardly looks like a roll-call of criminals, does it? And yet all these are linked in some way."

"We live in the age of Raffles," I said dubiously. "Many men have been hard hit by the war. There's been a loosening of moral fibre."

"Who ever heard of a geologist's having his moral fibre loosened?" interjected Arbuthnot with a grin. "If a geologist transgressed it would, I think, be an event unique in the annals of crime. Still, it's a remarkable list. These people are young; they are of respectable origin and good education so far as we have details; three at least are athletes; and we have among them a doctor, an actor, a linguist, and a scientist, besides other possible talent. The list is fairly homogeneous, is it not?"

"I suppose it is."

"Yet is there one serious difficulty about all this."

"That being?"

"The position of Charteris. We have good reason to suppose that he and Strang are in collusion. Yet the name of one shakes even the iron nerve of Baxter Creen, whereas he accepts a reference given by the other without a qualm! Other people on this list are shot at, imprisoned, and even murdered, while Charteris continues serenely on his way. The thing isn't consistent."

"Then do you think it is merely a coincidence that Charteris should be concerned in one abduction case and at the same time give a character to Strang, who was concerned in another?"

"I don't. I am not impressed by that kind of coincidence."

"Then, must we fall back on the assumption that Creen was not familiar with the name Dormer when you first mentioned it to him and that you were mistaken in thinking he was?"

"As I told you before, I was not mistaken. That is now proved."

Arbuthnot's voice sounded as if he were a trifle annoyed.

"It's not proved to *me,*" I said.

"Really, King! Do you remember my account of the last conversation I had with Creen?"

"Very well."

"He told me he had heard there was a secret agent in England masquerading under the name of Dormer Strang, you remember?"

"Yes."

"I asked him whether he had connected the name at once with the name Dormer I had told him?"

"Yes."

"Do you remember his reply? He said he had *not*, because it was certain there were plenty of men in England called Dormer, and it was not beyond the bounds of possibility that *one of them had the surname Strang*. Now do you see it? He could not have made that last clause of his remark unless he already knew that the chauffeur's name was Strang! Another man would have said, in his place, that the coincidence of identical Christian names was no sort of clue, when surnames obviously need not tally."

"Heavens, yes!" I said excitedly. "I see it now. How did he come to make such an error?"

"Clever men overreach themselves. He wanted to prepare against the eventuality that I might discover the genuine Dormer Strang. He wanted me to feel I was up against a very perfect villain in the form of this redoubtable Parwitz."

"It is still possible," I said, as I fancied rather brightly, "that he knew all the time that Strang was Parwitz, but could not bring himself to the point of telling you until he got frightened."

"Answer the 'phone will you?" said Arbuthnot. The whirr of the instrument had almost drowned my concluding words.

"Hallo!" I said. "Oh, it's Kaye. Yes, King speaking. Mr. Arbuthnot is here. Particulars of Dormer Strang? I see."

"Repeat what he says and I'll take it down," interposed Arbuthnot. So it went on:

"'Aged twenty-seven; educated Eton and Balliol; took his First in Greats; two years in the University eight; family originally Scottish, now domiciled in Wiltshire; father Conservative M.P. for Cricklade division'; at present where? Oh, yes, 'Yucatan. Excavating Maya remains.' What's that? Personal description? Oh, yes. 'Tall, quite six feet, and fair; no moustache; well-built and good-looking; slight stammer.' That all? Thanks. Good-bye."

"I told Kaye in my wire this morning to ring me at half-past five. Remarkable resemblance between Strang and Parwitz, isn't there?"

"Remarkable."

"That must have been an expensive telegram that Creen sent to Vienna the morning of the day I saw him."

"What telegram?"

"The one with the description of Strang to be cabled back to him for my edification."

I shook my head. "We are getting into deep waters," I said.

"We are," said Arbuthnot cheerfully. "Unless I'm greatly deceived we shall have to strike out our very best before we touch dry land again. Now, pack up, and let's get away to the 'Tristram'. Unless we are very unlucky, to-night's work is going to add to our knowledge."

We found the rooms were quite good—a sitting-room communicating with a bedroom and bathroom on either side. Acting on Arbuthnot's directions I placed three arm-chairs in a semicircle around the fireplace. He put a small table carrying an electric reading-lamp beside the chair nearest the door.

"Here I shall sit," said he. "You will be next. Mr. Charteris, should he honour us, will have the seat facing the light."

"Hallo! What are you doing?" I asked. He had commenced to dismantle the electric fitting of the lamp.

"These people are so mean with their length of flex," he explained. "I feared it might be so, and therefore brought my own supply. I need the flex to hang from the table in a loop so that I can catch my foot in it if necessary. If the wall-plug is not too tight and the lamp standard sufficiently heavy, as I think it is, the result will only be sudden darkness."

I watched his preparations in silence; he evidently took Charteris very seriously.

"Now," said he as he rose to his feet, "time to dress, and then a taxi to our own private theatre, for comedy, tragedy, or first-class melodrama."

As we left the hotel, feeling ourselves as immaculate as Lunkin's expects its devotees to be, I bought an *Evening News*. There was only a couple of minutes in which to glance at it, but in that little time I received something of a shock; my eye caught sight of an arresting headline:

SHOCKING FATALITY IN THE PENNINES

Glancing down the column I was horrified to see that the news referred to the death of none other than "Toby" Winstanley, one of the best men going, who had passed through school, form by form, with me. Then our paths had diverged, as he went to Oxford, while I, following, rather against my will, a family tradition, went to the sister university. I had hardly seen him for years, and I believed he had been out of England since the war on some work of exploration, but the news was sufficiently distressing. It appeared that he had been on a walking tour and had tumbled over a cliff. So much I had gleaned from the account when the taxi drew up at the door of Lunkin's, and, my mind hastily switching back to the affair of the moment, I dropped the paper and descended to the pavement.

Arbuthnot led the way with assurance; presumably he had reconnoitered the ground previously on one of his recent visits to town. A stately person, whose very deference subtly intimated his transcendent importance, heard our names in a kind of hushed ecstasy, as though we had been angels visitant, and led us to our table.

There was only one person dining anywhere near us; he sat at the next small table. This then was Chatteris. I shot a glance at him as I stepped to my chair—and was disappointed. What I glimpsed was a round face that looked capable of laughter, but was not smiling at the moment, positively chubby cheeks, flaxen hair well brushed back from a face otherwise devoid of anything hirsute, and a monocle. The man was busy dissecting a bird; the wine at his elbow looked like a choice vintage from the Côte d'Or. Once I was seated I could not very well look at him again without doing it noticeably, for Arbuthnot had appropriated the better position for observation. I sat and pondered on the unlikeliness of Charteris to what I had expected, and his puzzling resemblance to some one I had once known and since forgotten, while such scraps of dialogue as "pheasant" and "Yes, sir, '14," I suggested that Arbuthnot in his order to the waiter was not anticipating that excitement would destroy appetite.

So we settled down to talk, and roamed from sport to literature, and from literature to wine, while Charteris finished his bird, and attended for a while to a piece of Stilton, and imbibed port, and then relapsed upon a liqueur brandy and a cigar. At any other time I should have enjoyed my dinner—even when with Uncle Theodore I found much that was pleasant in Lunkin's; but that night the food could easily have been sawdust for all the attention I gave it. Our wine came to an end. Arbuthnot looked meaningly at me.

"Fancy that young fool Grierson going to Port Said. Much good may it do him." In my excitement I had pitched my voice unnaturally high; the sound must have carried twice as far as we needed it to. I felt a blush rising to my cheek; I am, after all, but a poor conspirator. I sensed rather than saw—for I did not dare look that way—that the man at the next table had turned his attention to us with something of a start.

"Exactly," said Arbuthnot dryly. "Much good may it do him."

There was a pause. The situation was tense. I felt impelled to say something to break that silence, and chose the first subject that entered my head.

"So Winstanley's gone," said I, still in that poorly controlled voice. "That's another. There aren't so many left now—" I was going to say "of those who left the school when I did", for the war years had not spared us more than other foundations, but I was cut short by a half-strangled exclamation from the next table and the tinkle of broken glass. Involuntarily I swung round. Charteris sat still, the fingers of his right hand still holding the stem of his broken ballon glass, while those of his left drummed on the tablecloth. His face matched the cloth for whiteness. I turned back to find Arbuthnot regarding me with something akin to amazement.

"I don't like your choice of subject, Judson," said he. "Talk about something more cheerful—the possibility of January, at Monte, for example."

How I got through the remainder of that meal I shall never clearly know. Arbuthnot insisted on cheese and port and a liqueur. Charteris sat on, and, as he did so, consumed at least three more brandies. However mysterious the way in which I had shaken him, I had shaken him badly indeed. It was clear, even to me, that he did not intend to lose sight of us. At last Arbuthnot rose, while a demurely satisfied waiter withdrew.

"Where shall we go?" he asked.

"I'm indifferent," I said, striving to sound casual.

"Better go to the 'Tristram' first. There may be a wire," said Arbuthnot, as we strolled away, leaving Charteris regarding our receding backs.

"Now," said he swiftly a few moments later, as the taxi began to move, "who is this Winstanley?"

"He was a school friend of mine—one of the best fellows going."

"Was? He's dead, then?"

"Yes, poor devil!"

"How?"

"Fell over a precipice somewhere up north."

"Recently?"

"I saw it in this evening's paper."

"Of course you noted the effect of your chance remark on Charteris?"

"Naturally. One couldn't miss it. What the devil does it all mean?"

"Let me see a paper before I try to answer."

The taxi drew up at the 'Tristram'. Arbuthnot sprang out and hastily collected papers from three separate vendors. Then he rushed me into the hotel and up to our suite.

"Unless I'm vastly in error we shall have Chatteris down on us in less than five minutes, and I badly want to see these papers before he comes," he explained as we entered our sitting-room.

His hopes were vain; we had scarcely switched on the electric light and fire when a knock sounded on the door.

"Come in!" shouted Arbuthnot.

An hotel servant appeared. "Gentleman to see you sir," he said. "Thinks he has picked up something one of you gentlemen dropped."

"Show the gentleman in," said Arbuthnot.

Charteris advanced. His assumption of composure I felt to be distinctly better than my own.

"Excuse this hasty irruption," he said genially. "I was dining at the next table to you at Lunkin's just now, unless I've made a mistake, and the moment you'd gone out I noticed this lying on the floor."

He fumbled in his waistcoat pocket and drew out a little gold pencil-case with the end broadened to form a seal.

"I rushed straight out after you. Fortunately Lunkin's know me and didn't think I was absconding without paying my bill! Your taxi had gone, but the commissionaire told me the address given to the taxi-driver was the 'Tristram', so I bagged another taxi, came on here, and chanced on the lift attendant who had just taken you up. From his description I judged I was on the right track."

"Very good of you, indeed," said Arbuthnot. "It's a great pity that the thing doesn't belong to us. At least it's not mine. Is it yours, Judson?"

I shook my head.

"May I see it?" asked Arbuthnot. "Ah, there's a crest on the seal. Surely those two wyverns must belong to the Brockenhurst family. Lunkin's, of course, entertain far more of the aristocracy than they do of plebeians like Judson and myself."

"I don't know much about heraldry," said our visitor, receiving back the pencil-case. "Lunkin's have such a magnificent pile on their carpets that I thought it most likely one of you might have dropped the thing without hearing any sound. I'll take it back there; some old diehard is sure to roll up and claim it. Sorry I bothered you for nothing."

"Not at all," said Arbuthnot. "It was extraordinarily decent of you to trouble. I'm sorry you should have done it for nothing. Stay and have a drink."

"I won't drink, thanks; but I'd be glad to sit down for five minutes. I fear I treated my dinner rather discourteously in thus rushing about, and I dread its retaliation."

Arbuthnot waved him to the selected chair and produced cigars.

"That's better," said Charteris, sinking luxuriously back and heaving a sigh of relief. The air began to fill with the blue haze of tobacco smoke. I sat in a kind of dream. Was this the meeting of two great antagonists, or was it a peaceful Saturday evening after a round of golf?

"I see the Harlequins did badly again to-day," Arbuthnot was saying.

"Ah, did they? Afraid I'm a soccer man myself—or was. By the way, awfully remiss of me, I never mentioned my name—Curtis."

"We were equally bad," said Arbuthnot. "I'm Marsh, my friend is Judson. We're on leave from Ceylon—planters, you know. Just wasting a little money in trying to be civilized again."

"Just so." Charteris nodded sympathetically. "I've heard lots of unkind things said about a planter's life. Dashed good fellows, planters, though, and since you're a couple of them I don't mind making a confession."

"Indeed?" said Arbuthnot laughing. "What's that?"

"That I listened to part of your conversation at dinner this evening."

"Good heavens! I hope you found it edifying! We only talked because to bring out the *Sporting Times* and read it in Lunkin's seemed somehow sacrilegious."

"It was like this. I was sitting dreaming to myself—in fact I had gone right back to the war. Somehow couldn't get it out of my mind at all. Once, thinking over a particularly unpleasant incident, I involuntarily snapped the stem of my glass and thereby destroyed something far more valuable than any wine that could ever be put in! Perhaps you noticed?"

"We did," said Arbuthnot, grinning. "But I'm bound to say we put it down to a different cause."

"Shame on you then! I'd been remarkably abstemious. But now and again scraps of what you said broke into my own thoughts, and I fancied I heard once the name 'Grierson'. It wouldn't have been Walter Grierson, by any chance? I knew him, and have lost touch with him lately."

"Yes, Walter Grierson, until recently next-of-kin to Alresford."

"That's right. 'Pup' Grierson we always called him. He was my fag at school. He's gone off, goodness knows where, owing no end of money in town. The story has been put about that he's big-game shooting, but that's all piffle. In the vulgar tongue, the only thing he has 'shot' is the moon! Some of us are trying to get the matter hushed up."

"We heard the same tale," said Arbuthnot gravely. "We didn't know the fellow; but a friend out there in Ceylon, who I gather is interested in Grierson's sister, asked us to look the chap up. We couldn't find him; but a man who was also home on leave and went back a fortnight ago knew we were after him, so when he met Grierson by chance in Port Said he cabled us, knowing we should be interested. He is supposed to be out on some wildcat scheme of growing cotton without capital in the Sudan."

"Damned young fool!" said Charteris frankly. "It's funny you should be helping me, when I came here with the idea that I was helping you."

"One good turn deserves another," I said sententiously. That was practically my sole contribution to the conversation, and Arbuthnot had the audacity to laugh.

"Anything special in the papers?" asked Charteris casually. "The doctor has forbidden me to read at meals, says it takes all my brains to digest my food, so I haven't yet seen one this evening." He eyed the pile that lay on a side table.

"Nothing much. Labour member suspended. Rise in the franc. Some poor devil smashed while hill-climbing."

"Indeed? Usual foolhardiness, I suppose. Do you mean motor-cycling or mountaineering?" No one not on the alert for it would have detected that trifling change of tone in the speaker's voice, the slight note of anxiety that had crept in.

"I didn't read the details," said Arbuthnot lazily. "It was a fellow called Winstanley, doing a walking tour. Queer time of year to do it, I should say. Tumbled over a precipice somewhere up in the Pennines, or else was pushed over."

"Dead?"

"As mutton." I could see Arbuthnot was shaping his remarks to drive the other to an explosion.

"Hard luck!"

"I don't know. Some people go round asking for accidents to happen to them."

"Yes," said Charteris slowly. "I seem to have met a couple of such people to-night. Don't move!" The last two words were tapped out like machine-gun fire.

Speaking for myself, I had no intention of moving. The muzzle of the baby automatic that Charteris had whipped out was much too near my ample body to be at all encouraging.

"Hands up!" he added.

"Quite in the approved style," said Arbuthnot, laughing. "Were you ever on the films?" He flung his arms wide, and I saw with a thrill that one of them had, as it were accidentally, come to rest on the base of the lamp standard. I hoisted mine on the back of the chair and felt foolish.

"Damn your insolence!" said Charteris. "I am a fairly useful shot, and I advise you not to move."

"Nonsense!" said Arbuthnot. "No one fires off pistol-shots in London hotels, except jealous women and ruined financiers."

"It is your misfortune to encounter the exception," said Charteris dryly.

"Splendid! Now isn't it about time you began to explain your remarkable behaviour? I do you the credit of assuming you are sane."

"You will find I am perfectly sane. Let me remind you of Treloar and Roger Gordon and Jim Gordon—though he escaped you, thank God—and now poor Winstanley."

"Very interesting, I'm sure; but what it's got to do with us I can't imagine."

"If you wish to avoid these visitations you should keep your loud-voiced friend under better control. His remarks were quite conclusive."

Feeling very unhappy, I began to see the ambiguity of my commentary on my old friend. It had certainly drawn Charteris, and I began to wish it hadn't.

"Well, well," said Arbuthnot genially, "if you wish to avoid these fatalities you should keep your amorous friend under better control. His action was quite provocative."

"Damn your insolence!" said Charteris again. I could see that his temper stood at white heat.

"Come," said Arbuthnot. "This is getting boring. What do you propose to do? Will you march us captive out of the hotel?"

"Something much simpler than that. I propose to incapacitate you pair of scoundrels for a considerable period. Let us say a broken wrist for one, and a shattered knee-cap for the other. That would produce a considerable hiatus in your activities."

"More easily described than done," said Arbuthnot dreamily.

Charteris laughed and stood up.

"Not in this case," he said. "Let me explain to you. You did not, I presume, believe all that nonsense about the pencil-case. There is plenty of evidence, however, that I left Lunkin's to-night in order to restore some article you had dropped. When I arrive here I find I have fallen into the clutches of a pair of confidence men who had purposely laid the trap for me. I threaten to hand them over to the police. They attack me. I shoot in self-defence. My overwhelming advantage is that I am well known, of perfectly good reputation, and above suspicion; on the other hand, I have no doubt you two rascals are under false names and have not a leg to stand on in a court of law."

"Very pretty," said Arbuthnot with a sneer. "Is there any alternative?"

"None. Do you think you can put me off with a bogus confession?"

"Your troubles will begin," said Arbuthnot, speaking very slowly and distinctly, "when I stand up in a court of law and explain how I was asked by the Honourable Geoffrey Charteris whether a pencil-case bearing the crest of the Earl of Brockenhurst was my property."

"Nonsense!" said Charteris, though I fancied in the midst of my own agitation that I detected alarm in the ring of his voice. "Lay not that flattering unction to your soul. The pencil-case will never be seen again. The court will treat it as your invention. I shall describe the gold cigarette-case that I saw the amiable Judson produce earlier this evening as the article I found."

"You are clever," said Arbuthnot softly, "so clever that it seems a pity to—"

Darkness!

16
In Which Psychology Affords a Clue

"Smash you," were the last two words, suddenly rapped out. What followed was too rapid for description. All I heard, and I could *see* nothing in the pitch blackness, was a startled exclamation from Charteris, a swift movement past me, and suddenly a loud crash as some heavy object came up against the door of the room. Then a switch clicked, and the room was immediately bathed in light.

Arbuthnot stood near the centre of the floor. Charteris lay, a huddled-up heap, by the door. His automatic lay beside him. Arbuthnot stooped, picked it up, and pocketed it.

"I was mortally afraid of that thing going off, either accidentally or otherwise," he said, "but the risk had to be taken. I know a determined man when I see one."

He bent over the silent figure.

"He's only stunned. He'll probably wake up in an hour or so, and have a fearful headache for a week. Come, let's lug him into the next room and lay him on the bed. We can lock him in there while we hold a council of war. I trust that unholy crash hasn't aroused any attention in the hotel."

Together we raised the unconscious Charteris, no light burden, and carried him into the adjacent room. Arbuthnot removed his collar and tie and opened the front of his dress-shirt, while I dipped a towel in water and wrapped it round his head.

"Coals of fire," said Arbuthnot grinning.

"Somehow I've a sneaking respect for the fellow," I said.

"So have I. He's certainly a man."

"What happened when the light went out?" I asked.

"I simply tackled him low and flung him over my head. He was naturally taken by surprise and therefore it was fairly easy. Now for those— Hallo!"

There was a knocking proceeding outside the sitting-room. Arbuthnot led back into that room and threw open the door. My nerves were frayed; I had visions of our unwanted guest being discovered in the bedroom.

"Sorry to trouble you, sir," said the voice of some functionary in the passage. "It was reported that a loud crash had been heard in your suite, and I was sent up to inquire if everything was all right."

"Perfectly all right. My friend and I were moving a heavy trunk and carelessly dropped it. That was all. I hope no one was disturbed by the noise?"

"No, sir. That's all right." He withdrew. I breathed again.

"Now," said Arbuthnot to me, "get the papers and read me the best account of Winstanley's death you can find. Meanwhile I'll just replace my own wiring by the official one: attention to detail is, we are told, one of the essentials of genius."

He set to work on the lamp, which had come unscathed through the fracas; I noticed that one leg of the table was so placed with the flex round it that when the gradual pull from Arbuthnot's foot grew too great the plug was jerked straight out from the wall; he was nothing if not thorough.

The fullest account of the end of Winstanley seemed to be in the paper at which I had already glanced. I began:

SHOCKING FATALITY IN THE PENNINES.
Ex-Officer's Headlong Fall to Death.
Pathetic Dying Utterance.

"Stop a minute," said Arbuthnot. "Perhaps we'd better lock up our young friend first. We don't want him interrupting."

We went into the next room. Charteris still lay unconscious, so we returned, Arbuthnot locking the door behind him.

"Carry on, King," said he.

I read:

"General regret will be felt at the accidental sudden death of Colonel Claude Winstanley, known among his many friends in town as 'Toby', who met a tragic fate yesterday while on a walking tour in Derbyshire. The unfortunate officer was found this morning by two shepherds lying at the foot of a steep part of Axe Edge, over which he had presumably fallen, probably through missing his way in the dark the previous evening. He was severely injured and unconscious when found, and expired shortly afterwards. We are informed there is no evidence of any foul play.

"Colonel Winstanley had had a distinguished career. While at Oxford he was a prominent member of the O.U.D.S. in which branch of university activities he showed great promise. His rendering of the title-part in *The Second Mrs. Tanqueray*, will long be remembered by those who saw it.

"During the war he achieved the distinction of being the third youngest Colonel in the British army, and gained the C.M.G. and the D.S.O. Subsequently he took up the work of exploration, and served with expeditions in the Libyan Desert and the Sinai Peninsula.

He was an indefatigable walker to whom all climates and seasons were alike, and it must be regarded as remarkable ill-fortune that after so many adventures he should meet his fate on the slopes of our own little Pennine Hills.

"When almost at the point of death Colonel Winstanley momentarily recovered consciousness and uttered a few words to which a pathetic interest attaches. They were, 'Tell them I died for England'. A well-known psychoanalyst, interviewed by our representative, was able to give an interesting explanation of how such a remark, meaningless under the circumstances, came to be made. Colonel Winstanley was once very seriously wounded during the war, and at the time was not expected to recover. When he came to himself at the foot of the cliff his mind must have 'thrown back' to that previous occasion and he imagined he was dying on the battle-field."

"That's all," I said.

"All?" echoed Arbuthnot. "It's the most interesting thing I've heard for a very long time. It's startling, in fact. You feel perfectly sure Winstanley was a straight man?"

"As sure as I feel it about you," I said promptly. "He wouldn't have hurt a fly. I don't suppose any human being living is the worse off for him."

"Indeed? And yet his death roused the redoubtable Charteris to almost ungovernable rage. He jumped to the conclusion that Winstanley had been quietly done away with, and was ready to revenge him on us at considerable risk to himself. Was it pure anger at the loss of his friend?"

"We don't know."

"We do. It was, partly at any rate, rage at some interference with his schemes. What did he say? 'Treloar—Roger Gordon—Jim Gordon—Winstanley.' That means clearly enough that Winstanley was in with the rest."

"I can't believe Winstanley was engaged in any dirty work," I said definitely.

"Perhaps not, but he's gone 'the way Hunt went', for all that. Treloar, of course, must be the man at the factory. Knowing his name is going to be very useful. Just glance into the next room and see if Charteris is still comatose."

He was, but his breathing was less laboured, and I judged it would not be long before he returned to consciousness. It is well known that an illness or a shock of any kind will temporarily accentuate the more striking features of a person's face, so that one then notices things that normally attract no attention. As I looked at Charteris I was again assailed by that feeling of recognition, as if at some time or other he and I had been in contact. I found I was mentally fitting him with a service-dress cap. It was, of course, possible that we had run up against each other during the War. Then in a flash I had it. The cap I remembered was no military one, but a chauffeur's, and the man beneath it was the man who had driven "Miss Hunt's" car to Leasinghoe! I had only passed him in the road that morning as I left Rose Cottage, but I had taken note of him because he was so exceedingly spick-and-span and businesslike in his appearance. There was a corollary. It was quite possible that he had also recognized me.

"Arbuthnot," I said hastily returning to the sitting-room, "I've seen Charteris before."

"Very likely. He's a man about town to some degree."

"No, I mean in connexion with the case."

"Indeed?"

"Yes. He was the driver of the car that brought Hunt's sister to Leasinghoe. It's just dawned on me."

N. A. Temple-Ellis

"Sure?"

"Positive."

"Better—and worse," said Arbuthnot.

"How?"

"Better because it's another small link in our chain. Worse because it deepens the puzzle as to how Charteris goes about his schemes unmolested while his accomplices encounter all sorts of misfortunes. Winstanley, I take it, was 'the Colonel' who called on Roger Gordon the night he was murdered. Those other people clearly knew who he was. Then in his turn he meets the same fate as Gordon. But Charteris stays untouched."

"Except by you, damn you!" said a croaking voice behind us.

We spun round and saw Charteris standing in the bedroom doorway surveying us. In my haste to tell Arbuthnot what I had remembered I had clean forgotten the door.

He was a curious figure as he stood there clutching at the doorpost for support and swaying from side to side. Without collar or tie, his face deathly white, his hair dishevelled, he looked almost a ghost. Yet from somewhere he had produced his monocle, and was regarding us with a glassy stare suggestive of a man in the last stage of intoxication.

"What—do you—propose—to do—now?" he asked with laboured precision.

"Put you to bed," responded Arbuthnot swiftly, going towards him. "You're not in a fit state to be wandering about."

For a moment I thought Charteris would show fight; then he collapsed, and we half-led, half-carried him back to the bed. Arbuthnot made a rough bandage for his head by tearing up a shirt, which I afterwards discovered to have been one of my own. Charteris regarded him with

a gaze in which I think bewilderment mixed with resentment. I wondered how much of our conversation he had
overheard. Arbuthnot went to a case that belonged to his
luggage, and presently produced a phial from the small
collection of useful drugs that always accompanied him
on his travels. He took the phial into the bathroom, and
returned bearing a glass containing a small quantity of
liquid.

"Drink this," he said to Charteris.

The other waved it away.

"Kindly do as you're told. It's a much pleasanter way of
putting you to sleep than the last one I tried."

Charteris hesitated. He was evidently puzzled. Then he
took the glass, drained it, and closed his eyes.

"He'll probably sleep for several hours. Help me to
carry my bags into the next room, and we'll lock him up
again and let him sleep in peace."

We did so, and in five minutes were sitting quietly by
the fireside. It was growing late, but neither of us thought
of sleep.

"A remarkable evening," I said. "What the superbly-
respectable management of the 'Tristram' would say if they
knew, Heaven alone can tell. How on earth are we going to
dispose of Charteris?"

"Let that wait," said Arbuthnot cheerfully, settling
down to his pipe. "Now, King, listen. You remember the
list we made?"

"Naturally."

"It included an actor, did it not?"

"Certainly—you mean the old man who gave Carpenter
the drugged drink?"

"Yes. Now Winstanley was an actor."

"Quite so."

"Moreover, he was an impersonator of female parts.
What was he like to look at?"

"Dark; medium height; clean-shaven; good voice. Quite a handsome man."

"I see. Now, when Gordon was murdered his accomplices were very anxious to find out whether certain things he had in his possession were stolen?"

"You mean the box and the letter in cipher?"

"Precisely. They sent some one to try and recover them. Who would be best to send? Naturally some one who had been there before at least twice. But the man would be running a big risk. He might be detained by the police. He might fall into the hands of Gordon's murderers. Let him disguise himself. To appear as a woman would be easily the safest disguise he could adopt. King, I think your 'Miss Hunt' was none other than your unfortunate friend Winstanley."

"Good heavens!" I said. "It's more than probable. Wonder if the poor old chap recognized me. We shall never know, worse luck."

"But that's not all," went on Arbuthnot, biting his pipestem and staring fixedly into the fire. "There's a flaw in that newspaper report."

"Very likely," I said. "They must have been pretty sharp to get in an account at all, seeing that the poo fellow was only found this morning. Most probably some of the facts are wrong, though I don't see how you know it."

"No, King, it's not an error of fact I mean, but that more significant thing, an error in psychology."

"Then I don't follow."

"Consider. His dying words were, 'Tell them I died for England.' Some one suggests that at his last moments he thought he was again on the battle-fields of France where once he had lain at the point of death. That's all nonsense. Winstanley, I take it, was a very fair sample of everything connoted by the word 'gentleman'. He would never have made such a remark on the battle-field or anywhere else.

That sort of thing isn't said, except on the films. I've watched more men die than I like to think of, and so have you. One said, 'By Jove, I'm sleepy', and another, 'Tell the C.O.M.S. to see about those boots'; the bravest man I knew died as he was saying, 'Pity there's no time for another gasper'. 'Tell them I died for England'! Rubbish! No one would suppose they were dying for pleasure, or to help the Germans."

"Absolutely true," I said, hanging on his words.

"What follows then? What Winstanley said must have been a message for some one. At his last gasp he thought of others, just as Gordon did when he got rid of the box and the paper in the marsh. King, were these men criminals?"

"Heaven only knows. I'm all at sea," I said. Finding Winstanley connected with the affair had upset all my preconceived notions.

"What message then could it be?" he continued. "How could those words mean anything special to anybody, beyond the obvious and ridiculous explanation we have read. Only in one way."

"And that?" I asked, feeling somehow that we had reached a critical point.

For answer Arbuthnot took a sheet of paper from the bureau and drew.

"There," said he, handing it to me. What I saw was only the symbol that had puzzled so many of my waking hours.

"I don't get you," I said.

"King, I deserve kicking. I have sought elaborate interpretations of that symbol for weeks. Now I know that it means exactly what it says."

"But what does it say?"

"Look again."

I shook my head.

"It is merely a reversed F combined with an E. And its meaning is 'For England'!"

I let the paper flutter from my fingers. I sat down heavily in my chair. I took out a handkerchief and mopped my brow.

"Yes," continued Arbuthnot, "I think we may say that half of our troubles are over."

"But are you positive?" I stammered.

"I am, because there is no other possible way in which Winstanley's last words can be made to mean anything at all."

"Go on."

"I've suspected this for some time. The case of Turnbull was a pointer. Consider that list again. Here we have a set of people, all young, all probably well-to-do, all recruited from a certain class, all educated, athletic or intellectual, or both, and most likely totally disinclined to a routine occupation. It occurs to some bright spirit amongst them to form a kind of league in secret to counteract by unorthodox methods the activities of England's alleged enemies. He gradually gathers kindred souls around him. They get their amusement, although I am bound to say that I personally detest such actions, for they almost invariably do much more harm than good. The symbol and the cipher are both indications of rather youthful exuberance, allied, I willingly admit, to a certain ingenuity of mind, since one baffled us until this evening and the other continues to do so.

"Eventually this lively society come up against some thing really serious. They bite off more than they can chew. Their fun changes to a matter of life and death for at least two of them. What it is we don't know but evidently it is something appallingly sinister. This is where we come in. We have to stand by these youngsters until this business is over. Then, if any of them survive, they shall have a more colossal blowing-up than a commanding officer ever gave to a subaltern."

As he spoke there remained not the faintest shadow of doubt in my mind that he had found the truth.

"I'm with you," I said promptly. "Granted that probably they've behaved like young idiots, yet there's murder on the other side, and I, for one, know where my sympathies lie. Can't we get something out of Charteris?"

"Hardly likely," said Arbuthnot, grinning, "after I tried to throw him through a door. Charm we never so wisely, he will be suspicious, and I don't blame him either. That young man must have been living in a particularly choice kind of hell for the last few weeks, with all his friends one by one disappearing. No wonder he was desperate to-night."

"What is our programme then?" I asked.

"We have to get Treloar out of the factory. He is the man from whom we can obtain by bluff what we want to know. And he can be made to lead us where I want to go."

"Where's that?"

"Not Park Lane." He sat forward, still gripping his pipe-stem with his teeth and looking unseeingly in front of him. "Have a look at the prisoner, will you, King?"

I tiptoed into the bedroom. Charteris was fast asleep. The jaunty smile gone from his face, I thought I could detect marks of care. Once or twice he mumbled in his dreams, but I could catch no words. When I returned Arbuthnot was pacing the room, smoking furiously,

"King," he said with a laugh, "I'm going to stake my professional reputation on a throw of the dice. I *think* I can solve that cipher now. Get a piece of paper."

I obediently did so.

"There must be some connexion," he went on, half to himself. "They didn't choose a chance set of numbers and make a memorandum of it on their shirt-cuffs. Ready, King?"

I intimated that I was.

"Write down in one line the letters of the phrase 'For England', spacing them evenly. Got that?"

"Yes."

"Now underneath each letter place the number that gives its position in the alphabet—6 for F and so on."

I did so; the result was as follows:

```
F   O   R    E   N   G   L   A   N   D
6  15  18    5  14   7  12   1  14   4
```

"Here," went on Arbuthnot, producing a slip of paper from the pocket-book that had bulged his dinner-jacket the whole evening, "is the cipher message that Jim Gordon left for his dead brother. It will be sufficient if we try the first few letters. We shall soon know whether we are on the right track. Write down the first dozen letters."

I copied them on to my paper.

"Now place that sequence of numbers underneath, to every letter a number. When you get to the end begin again."

I complied.

"Now for the test. Starting from the letter given in the upper row, count backwards through the alphabet a number of letters equal to the number below the letter. Write down the letter you reach. If you finish the alphabet before you reach your letter, begin again at Z. Is that clear?"

"Perfectly."

I began on my task. The first letter was K. Its number was 6. Then I must count back 6—J, I, H, G, F, E. I wrote down E. So I went on till I had got ESCA.

"It's coming out," I said excitedly. This was my result:

K	H	V	F	D	L	P	G	F	S	S	V
6	15	18	5	14	7	12	1	14	4	6	15
E	S	C	A	P	E	D	F	R	O	M	F

We promptly set to work on the rest and soon had the whole thing.

> Escaped from factory. Treloar retaken. Great danger. Informing Strang.—Jim.

"Good!" said Arbuthnot. "I felt certain that, whatever sequence they used, it must be one that if forgotten could be at once reconstructed from some unforgettable basis. Certainly the message tells us little we didn't know before. It does, however, establish beyond question that Strang is involved with the others, and that serves to clarify matters. Now for the message that Roger Gordon discarded at his dying moment."

Out came the second slip of paper from the capacious pocket-book. I marvelled as I thought of all that had been crowded into our lives since we had first seen that scrap of white lying in the marsh.

"I'll tackle this one," said my friend. "I think I can do it mentally. You take down the letters as I call them out."

He began. "C, O, F, A, S—"

"Hallo," said I, looking up from my writing. "That doesn't sound very encouraging."

"Carry on," said Arbuthnot. He continued:

"W, A, N, P, R, O—"

"No good," I said despairingly. "There isn't a bit of sense in it."

"Kindly continue," said Arbuthnot. He sounded as if he considered my remarks redundant. When he finished dictating I had down the following:

cofaswanprobearlydecstrangandgirlcreenathq
gandtnotreportedsincegthlookoutc.

"Why," I cried, "some of it is sense, and some isn't!"

"Impossible," said he. "One cannot solve a cipher of this nature only partially; it is all or nothing. Let me look."

At any rate, I make nothing of the first few letters, I said.

"Perhaps I can. Let's separate them out a bit." He took the paper and wrote 'c of aswan'.

"What does that mean, then?"

"'C' I take to be an abbreviation for 'city', 'Aswan' is the modern spelling of a town name in Egypt."

"I see. Then it refers to a place."

"No, it doesn't."

"I beg pardon."

"It refers to a ship."

"How do you know?"

"If it referred to the place no one would have bothered to add 'c of' at the beginning."

"A ship?" I said wonderingly.

"Yes. Don't remark, as you frequently do, that you're all at sea, or in deep water, or something of that kind.. Now the rest is easy. 'G' and 't' refer obviously to Gordon and Treloar who were caught and shut up in the factory. The 'g' before 'th' evidently means a date; 'g' is the seventh letter of the alphabet, so most probably, especially in view of what we already know, the date is November 7th. The 'c' at the end is almost beyond doubt an abbreviation for 'Charteris'."

The message expanded into readable form now became:

"'City of Aswan', probably early December. Strang and girl Creen at H.Q. Gordon and Treloar not reported since 7th. Look out.—Charteris."

"Iris Creen was abducted on the 10th," said Arbuthnot thoughtfully. "Probably Treloar and Jim Gordon were then already in captivity. This is all very interesting."

"What do you think of it all?" I asked.

"What do I think? I think that the *City of Aswan* won't sail so early in December as was intended."

"One little point," I said. "Why was this message sent at all when Winstanley could have delivered it by word of mouth?"

"Quite so. I don't suppose it was sent by him. It probably reached Gordon through the post. Then Winstanley was sent down to report. Remember he had probably been engaged in taking Baxter Creen's Rolls-Royce to Dartmoor. On his return, Charteris, nervous about Gordon, sent him to Essex to inquire into things."

"It's quite probable," I said. "What are we going to do with Charteris?"

"Let him sleep for the present, I'm going to do the same. I shall be quite happy on the couch here. I fancy we may have a busy time in front of us."

I also went to bed, but found it hard to get to sleep. Things were happening too quickly for me, but I could see that all this ferment was bound to come to a head before so very long. Where was Iris Creen? What game was her inscrutable father playing? What of this mysterious ship? Had Buller's body been found? Was the wretched Treloar still alive? There was no end to the questions that tantalized me. Yet through it all I sensed the coming of the storm that should dim the daylight and rock the heavens. Forces were at work that must eventually clash. The time for joining open battle must be close at hand. Now I had the personal stimulus of the loss of a man the world could ill spare, and whom it had been an honour to call friend, I trusted that I also might play my part without flinching.

Finally I slept.

17

In Which Arbuthnot Risks an Old Friend and Gains a New One

I felt that I had only been sleeping for a few minutes when Arbuthnot woke me by shaking my shoulders. He was already shaved and partly dressed, though it was obviously not yet daylight.

"Come," said he. "We have a certain amount of work to do to-day. I want to be back in Essex by the evening."

"Has Charteris waked?" I asked.

"No; he's quite comfortably asleep, but he'll have to wake up now to hear what I've to say to him."

Together we went into the other bedroom, where Charteris still lay as we had left him overnight. Arbuthnot tapped him gently on the shoulder.

"Hallo! What the— Oh, it's you, is it?" Realization had come swiftly on awaking. He struggled to a sitting position and blinked at us.

"Still undecided as to my fate?" he asked with a sneer.

"Not at all," said Arbuthnot politely. "That is already settled. Feeling more cheerful this morning?"

Charteris put his hand to the back of his head and winced. "Yes, all things considered. Your work was not quite so complete as it might have been."

"Here is your pistol," said Arbuthnot, laying it on a bedside table as he spoke. "I have taken the liberty of removing the cartridges, being a peace-loving man myself."

"What follows?" asked the other. "Do I make a speech of thanks?"

"You were very drunk last night," went on Arbuthnot, disregarding the remark. "We were obliged to let you remain here after you had tumbled down once and damaged your head. I shall make that right with the management. There is a lounge suit here that should be a tolerable fit, together with the usual accessories. You have fifteen minutes for your bath; a barber will come and attend to you as soon as you have had it; breakfast will be in the next room at eight o'clock sharp. I regret that for convenience it will be necessary temporarily to store your dress-clothes in my luggage, but they will be restored to you by this evening if you are still in London."

With that he walked out of the room and I followed, leaving Charteris, I should imagine, digesting his bewilderment. Arbuthnot proceeded to summon the manager and to favour him with a lugubrious account of the follies of youth which had given the "Tristram" an additional resident. That was easily squared when the manager realized that a person of noble blood was concerned. We parted with mutual expressions of esteem, as I think some one remarked once.

Breakfast appeared punctually at eight, and with it Charteris, looking passably well in a suit of Arbuthnot's tweeds. He had regained his grip of things, and greeted us casually, as if it were an ordinary matter that he should share a meal with his enemies.

"You're looking fagged out this morning, Judson," he said sympathetically. "Had rather a thick night last night, I suppose. I never heard you fellows go to bed."

I felt like confounding his impudence, but Arbuthnot chuckled.

"We stayed up late thinking over what you had told us," he explained.

"Told you?" The answer came in tones of surprise. "I told you nothing."

"On the contrary, you told us more than I ever expected you would."

Charteris shrugged his shoulders. "You must be easily satisfied," he said.

It was one of the most curious meals I have ever attended. Only Arbuthnot found time to eat much. To sit at table with a man who believes he is breakfasting with a couple of the biggest villains going is no everyday experience.

"Now," said Arbuthnot when the meal was over, "I think we have no further claim on your society, Mr. Charteris. For your own convenience, I think it will be better if you leave the hotel with us. After that you will, of course, proceed as you wish."

"Thank you," said Charteris gravely. "It is pleasant to find the elements of courtesy under such unlikely circumstances."

Within ten minutes our luggage had been sent down and we had followed it. Charteris stood on the steps of the hotel entrance and watched us getting into our taxi. At the last moment Arbuthnot leant out and handed him an envelope.

"My address," he explained.

"Ah, quite so. Well, by-by Marsh; ta-ta Judson. We may meet again."

"That is very likely," said Arbuthnot, and we drove off.

"It would be interesting," said my friend a moment later, "to see Charteris's face when he discovers I have used his own symbol in that note, and given my name and address in his own cipher! Now we'll dump these bags at the flat, and then Kaye should have some news for us."

Kaye certainly had news to reward our invasion of his Sunday seclusion in suburbia.

"The car you reported," he said, "has been found abandoned by the roadside near Chelmsford. It had been hired for a week, without chauffeur, from West End Garages, Limited. There is no trace of the occupants, but the description the garage people give of the man who hired it tallies with yours of Mr. Jennings."

Arbuthnot nodded. "I expected as much," he said. "Jennings must have known I'd got his number, and therefore did not risk returning the car. Now, are your inquiries complete respecting this Essex factory?

"Yes, as far as I can make them so. The factory was built in 1908 by Explosives and Allied Products, Limited, a firm in which the controlling interest has been held for many years by Sir Baxter Creen."

"Oh!" said I involuntarily.

Kaye looked at me curiously and continued:

"They built it in that lonely place, as a suitable situation for carrying out experiments with new and possibly dangerous explosives. During the War the place was naturally the scene of great activity, and was considerably enlarged. After the War the firm used it for breaking down ammunition of various kinds. After that, things in the munitions trade presumably being quiet, they put it on the market. It was cheaply acquired by a man called Gilbert Scarsdale; he probably bought it as a speculation, and never seems to have done anything with it. I can't find out much about him; he is at present said to be touring the Pacific Islands for his health, having retired from business."

"You'll never find out much about him," said Arbuthnot.

"How so?"

"He never existed."

"Really?" I could see Kaye was itching to ask more. "Upon my word this must be a remarkable affair you are engaged upon. It would make an interesting story."

"It would," said Arbuthnot, grinning. "But not now. Dine with me on Boxing Day and you shall have it from A to Z. Now we must be off; we have to commit a burglary this evening."

Kaye shook his head and gave us a comical glance. "You'll be getting me struck off the rolls before you've finished," he said. "Is there anything else I can do for you?"

"Yes. Find out all you can about a ship called the *City of Aswan*. With any luck we'll call in on you again to-morrow."

"*City of Aswan,*" said Kaye, making a memorandum of the name. "It shall be done."

That same Sunday afternoon saw us roaring eastward to Colchester in an express train. I spent my time reading the papers. The news of the disappearance of Buller had leaked out; the "Essex Mystery" once again loomed large; I saw a brief and fairly accurate recital of the "string of events that had shocked the serenity of peaceful Leasinghoe"; it was followed by a scathing denunciation of the police, who were urged to be up and doing. It seemed to me high time that we rescued the prisoner unless we wished to be anticipated. It was dusk when we reached the cottage. George Higgins, equipped with a brand-new hand-cart, had been duly in attendance at the station and had been warned to report for duty at eleven that night. Arbuthnot briefly detailed his plans to me.

"There will be a moon," said he, "but judging by the look of the weather it is not likely to worry us much. A faint light is all to the good, since our adversaries know the ground better than we do. Higgins will operate the ladder. When we are inside he will disconnect it, and I shall take the section inside the wall and use it to reach the prisoner's window. First, however, we shall have to reconnoiter to be sure that Dawson and the other men are out of the way."

"What then?"

"Then we bring Treloar back here, rest him for a few hours, and leave with him for town by the milk-train before dawn."

"I see."

"By the way, no disguises and assumed names with Treloar. We tell him the truth, except that we let him believe that we have joined the league in place of Roger Gordon and Winstanley. After all, we *have* joined it in a certain sense."

"Quite so. Now how do we stand at present?"

"You know exactly as much as I do, King. If there is no more tea left in the pot I propose to sleep for a few hours. We shall need to be fresh to-night."

It was good advice, and I spent the time till Mrs. Jerrold appeared with the evening meal, dozing by the fire. Remember that what is set out here as a more or less orderly narrative seemed at the time a succession of strange events, each one with its element of mystery, disquietude, and tragedy, and do not wonder that I was tired physically and mentally.

Arbuthnot devoured his supper with zest. "Not exactly Lunkin's," said he, "but perhaps a better preparation for a hard night's work, for all that." It was shortly after eleven when the three of us marched under a sky of leaden clouds, suffused with a dim, wan light that betokened the hidden moon. Arbuthnot carried his oxy-acetylene outfit, which he technically termed the "gadget"; Higgins and I shared the sections of the ladder. I suppose it may have been about half an hour after midnight when we raised our ladder to the wall of that enclosure where Buller, and God knows who else besides, had met their fates. The place looked sinister, uncanny, even malevolent to my eyes.

It was not long before we had assembled our ladder into two strips of equal length. Obeying Arbuthnot's instructions we placed them side by side against the wall so that

their tops failed by a few inches to project above it. Then
we mounted, while Higgins kept guard below. Remembering the sudden doom that had come upon Buller, we did
not show more than our heads above the level of the wall.

Below all was as silent as if human life had never passed
that way.

"It looks clear," whispered Arbuthnot to me; "but one
can never tell. These people are probably about at all
hours of the night. We mustn't go near the prisoner until
we have made a thorough reconnaissance."

With that he left his ladder and transferred himself to
the wall. Then, with Higgins aiding from below, the ladder was pulled up and let down on the other side. Finally
the two halves were joined at the top and the wall was
bridged.

"Good! It clears the spikes below very nicely. Now we'll
get on—the top of this wall isn't healthy."

Inside a minute we were back in the courtyard where
I had spent such fear-stricken moments. Higgins was
promptly up on the wall and disconnecting the two por-
tions of the ladder. We lowered our half gently to the
ground.

"Lay it on the ground close under the wall," said Arbuthnot in my ear. "It'll never be seen there." Indeed, the thin
metal framework, for reasons best known to its maker, was
coloured a dull black and would have been inconspicuous
anywhere.

On our previous visit, you may remember, we had moved
to the left and so found the narrow alley between the two
buildings, the main one and its smaller adjunct. Now we
bore to the right. Arbuthnot aimed to reach the angle of
the main building. The courtyard was mainly grass-grown
and our progress was quite silent. We reached the main
building and skirted that wall of it that faced toward the
creek.

"There's the gate that leads down to the jetty," whispered Arbuthnot. So it was, dimly outlined on our right.

Still the silence persisted. There can be silences that last too long. I wondered if the birds were flown. In that case the miserable Treloar had no doubt followed Gordon and Buller down the creek. What more likely than that, in alarm at the interest their operations had aroused, they had disposed of their prisoner and fled the district?

Suddenly Arbuthnot's hand gripped my arm.

"Look!" said he in my ear.

I looked hastily here and there. Nothing.

"What is it?"

"Can't you see? Stand where I am."

We changed positions. Then I saw. A tiny, needle-shaped shaft of light pierced the darkness. I moved my head slightly; it vanished.

"From a keyhole. That's why we can only see it from one position. Then there must be an occupied building over there. Tread softly."

Without more words Arbuthnot led toward the light. It came from a small detached one-story building that stood in the far angle of the enclosing wall. Probably it had been the porter's lodge and was now occupied by the caretaker. He stopped me within five yards of the building.

"Problem," he muttered, "are they in or out?"

As if in answer there came, from somewhere in the main building, the sullen crash of a door slamming.

"Quick, King! Round here between the house and the wall!"

I was not slow in obeying. Together we crouched there in comparative safety. There was a sound as if some foot had kicked a loose stone. Then I heard the murmur of voices.

"They're coming to the door where we saw the light," said Arbuthnot in my ear. "Better be ready to shoot in case of need; these people waste no time on preliminaries."

I needed no such warning. The voices came nearer. Their owners halted by the door we had noticed. I have made a little sketch from memory to show the position; it does not pretend to be correct in detail, but it is sufficient.

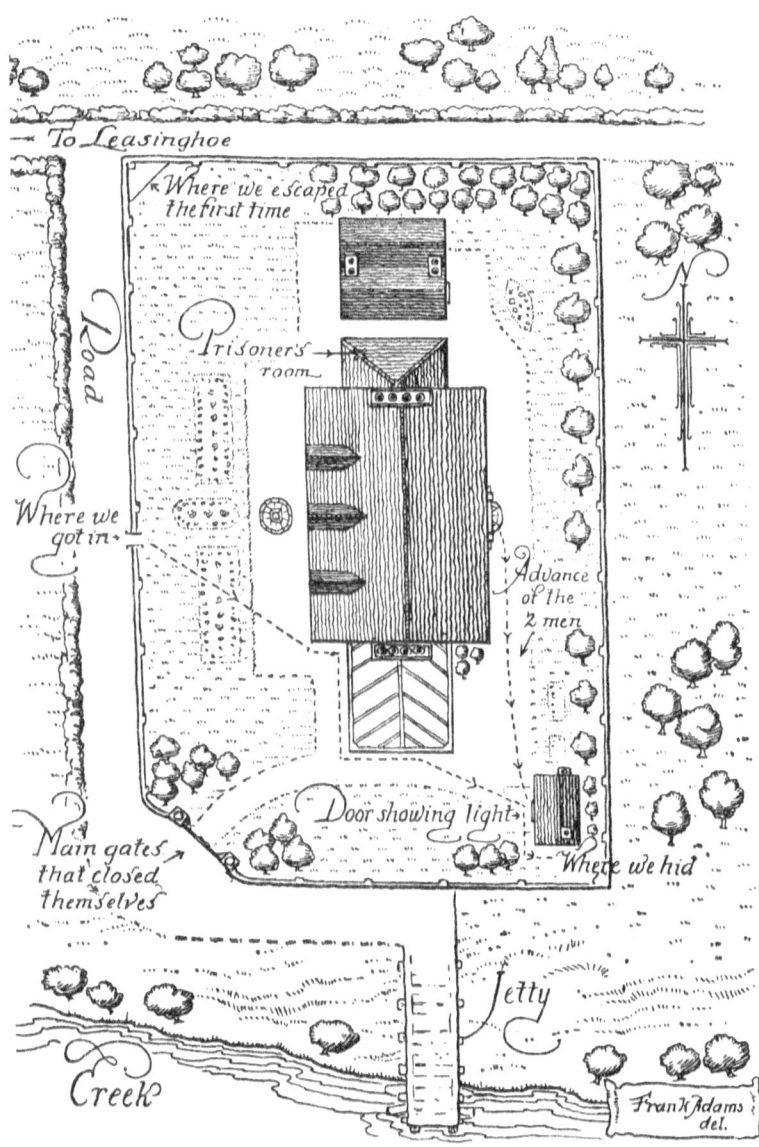

Situated as we were, in the dead stillness of that December night nearly every word the men uttered came clearly to our ears.

"It's nearly one," said the guttural voice that I remembered from our last tragic visit. "Don't forget the car will be here at half-past two. You've got to be ready by two."

"Don't worry," said the other voice, whose tones of subordination I knew belonged to the sandy-haired Dawson. "I'll thank my lucky stars when we're out of here. Suppose he kicks up a fuss, though?"

"Stun him. We've got to get him as far as Cambridge by dawn anyway, by hook or by crook. Then it's some one else's business."

"D'ye suppose the police will raid this place?"

"Shouldn't wonder."

"What if they tumble to the stuff that's here?"

"They won't. It's well locked up, isn't it? They won't burst open rooms that for all they know haven't been looked into for years. They'll wander round the place and find all quiet and go away. Besides, the body of that interfering fool ought to be found any day now, and that'll take their attention off."

"I suppose you're right, Schnurr. Anyhow, it's not our affair."

"Everything O.K.?" asked the man who had been addressed as Schnurr.

"Sure! I've been everywhere."

"Good! We might as well be warm for the last hour. Let's go inside. It'll be mighty cold on the road. And don't forget those two boxes we've got orders to take."

We heard the door open and close. Arbuthnot nudged me.

"Sounds as if we've got the grand total of one hour for our little job," he said. "Come on."

Together we tiptoed past the door and made round the back of the main building for the little alley we had found before. It was pitch dark between the high walls. Arbuthnot used his torch for a bare moment to identify the barred window of the prisoner's room.

"Hoist me up," he said. "I don't want to bring the gear until I'm sure he's still in this room."

I obediently took my friend on my shoulders. Again for a moment his torch flashed out. This time its light was directed into the room.

"He's there!" he whispered down to me. "And sleeping."

Suddenly there was a startled exclamation inside the room.

"Hallo! Who the devil's that?"

"Sssh. Listen, Treloar."

"Yes, go on. I'm listening." The speaker had evidently jumped out of bed and come to the window.

"Get dressed as promptly as you can. We've very little time. We'll be back here in a minute with our gear. But for heaven's sake, before you do anything else, find the pipe I threw at you to wake you up—I wouldn't lose it for anything."

Dangerous as the situation was I could scarcely forbear to laugh. I lowered Arbuthnot to the ground, and together we made off back to the point where we had scaled the wall. It was the work of a moment to re-erect our ladder.

"Higgins?"

"Sir?"

"Pass down the gadget."

"Very good, sir."

Arbuthnot received it into his hands. "You for the ladder, King," said he. With that he led back, while I shouldered the ladder and followed. Treloar was naturally on the watch. I could dimly see his eager face pressed against the bars of his prison. The ladder went up and Arbuthnot climbed it.

"God knows how you'll get in and out," whispered Treloar wonderingly. "You're sportsmen whoever you are, but I fear you'll never cut these bars."

"That's my job," said Arbuthnot. "Are you very fat, Treloar?"

"Good Lord, no! Not at present anyway."

"Then one bar should do. Is there any water in the room?"

"Yes," came the wondering reply. "There's a jugful."

"Right. Stand well back and have your jug handy in case of fire. Pass me up the gadget, King."

I complied. It was no very light article. Arbuthnot balanced it on the window-ledge.

"Keep a sharp look-out, King, and don't hesitate to fire if you still have an interest in life. Look out, Treloar, and keep well back or you'll be frizzled."

I saw Arbuthnot was assuming some kind of mask. There was a pause, apparently while he manipulated taps in the apparatus; a match was struck; and suddenly a tongue of flame leapt out and fastened on to the middle bar of the window. I was bound to keep a sharp look-out for foes, but out of the corner of one eye I saw the fierce blast of fire eat into the massive iron bar as if it had been touch wood. The metal reddened, whitened, became liquid. The heat was intense. There was a smell of singeing cloth, and I did not envy Arbuthnot his post. Then I saw the bar was severed. It set up a fierce hissing as Treloar, obedient to a sharp command, threw water upon it. Then the flame leaped out again, this time seizing upon the lower end of the bar. Gradually as the end melted the bar inclined more and more from the vertical. It was over! The flame vanished. There was the renewed hiss of water on the fiery metal.

"Cool it well," said Arbuthnot, "or you'll be badly burnt getting out. Get hold of anything you want and be quick. And don't forget my pipe!"

He descended the ladder, carrying his precious apparatus.

"Hot work, King," said he. "And, since it couldn't be altogether noiseless, the sooner we're gone the better."

Next I saw Treloar squeezing himself through the aperture that had been made. Unlike the unfortunate Stuart he had *not* grown fat in captivity. In a few seconds he had squirmed out and was feeling his way down the ladder. I guided him to the ground.

"Get hold of the ladder, Treloar. King, you cover the retreat. It's not nearly two, but one never knows."

Carrying his gadget, Arbuthnot led unerringly back to where Higgins was awaiting us. Our half of the ladder went up. Higgins made fast and then descended on the outside to make way for us. Arbuthnot, with his load, mounted. It was at that precise moment that our ears caught an unmistakable sound—the purring of a car!

It was all a matter of seconds, though I must necessarily take longer than that in telling of it.

"The car! Before its time," hissed Arbuthnot. "Over the wall, quick, you fellows!"

His decision was almost instantaneous. The car was certainly close at hand. Anyone who looks at the diagram I gave will see that the car was bound to come along the road that skirted the wall of the enclosure in order to reach the main gates. Across that road our ladder extended. There was no time for us to get over and for the ladder to be disconnected and removed as well. On the other hand, if Treloar and I stayed in the courtyard, then when the noise of the car brought out Schnurr and Dawson we should be in a tight corner indeed.

By the time I had reached the top of the wall Arbuthnot was on the ground outside. The sound of the engine was very near. I caught sight of a faint shape; the car was evidently coming on without lights. Something moved in the road, there was the flicker of a match, and instantaneously a tongue of flame leapt out in the path of the advancing car. As I dropped to the ground, missing the last few rungs, I guessed what he had done.

There was a startled cry, a grinding of brakes, and the car pulled up. I rushed forward. Arbuthnot was already on the step of the car. I saw he had his automatic pressed against the side of the chauffeur's head.

"Here!" said he, as I arrived. "Cover this man while I get my gear. You keep your hands up if you want to live. I can drive a car quite well myself."

The hint was sufficient; the man was evidently very desirous of living. Sounds behind told me that Treloar and Higgins were busy dismantling the ladder. Arbuthnot came swiftly back and dropped his precious gadget in the back of the car. Then he jumped into the front seat beside the driver.

"All right," he said to me. "I'll deal with him now. Get in behind."

I hastened to obey. Treloar and Higgins came rushing up and bundled in beside me. With all our apparatus we were somewhat of a tight fit, and I heard Treloar curse audibly as he inadvertently laid his hand on a hot part of the blowpipe. I heard more. Farther along the road the rattling of gates and the sound of voices.

"Into reverse," came in Arbuthnot's curtest tones, "and back out quick. If it comes to shooting you'll go first."

The driver needed no second bidding. The bravest of men would have had no option but to obey. The car began its backward course.

"Watch the road," said Arbuthnot to me over his shoulder. "I think we can keep them off if they follow."

The car could travel but slowly. I riveted my eyes on the road, expecting every moment to see two figures leap into sight. They did not come. Evidently they did not suspect anything wrong until it was too late to act.

After a tense period that lasted perhaps a very long two minutes we backed into the Leasinghoe road. Arbuthnot gave directions. They were promptly obeyed. The next minute we were creeping cautiously homeward along the narrow lane where Jim Gordon had run for his life. Perhaps we had gone a mile when Arbuthnot leaned forward and clicked on the lights. Thence progress was more rapid.

Treloar sat still without speaking; I think he was still wondering if it were all a dream. With me, reaction had set in, and I was shivering with cold. About half a mile from the village Arbuthnot stopped the car and bade us alight.

"Now," he said to the driver, "you can use this cart-track here to turn in. Get away back to your friends and tell them that next time we come we'll send them down the creek after Buller. If they hesitate about going without their prisoner that may decide them," he whispered in my ear. "The man isn't armed. We can clear off in safety."

He led us off the road, and I saw we were following the same route that Jim Gordon had taken the night of his escape. Treloar was silent and stumbled as he walked. The man was at breaking point, and no wonder.

"Higgins?"

"Sir."

"Report here at five sharp, with hand-cart."

"Very good, sir."

"Now," said Arbuthnot to Treloar as we found ourselves once more in our cottage parlour, "you've got three hours to rest, and then we must be on the move again. We can talk afterwards. Sleep soundly; one of us will be on guard the whole time."

"God bless you!" said the other. He staggered across the room, dropped on to the couch, and was asleep inside a minute. Arbuthnot, muttering something about tea, set to coaxing a moribund fire into activity and sent me to rummage for a kettle.

18
In Which We Begin with Tea and Go on with Milk

"That's better," said Arbuthnot, as the kettle poised on the revivified coals in the grate set up its first, thin, sibi-l-ant note. He walked across the room and inspected the sleeping Treloar. That man lay like a log. Reaction takes some people that way. No ordinary earthquake would have shaken him from his slumbers.

"Good! Now we have enough material to sustain our share of the conversation I think we can get from him nearly all we want to know. I hope, even more, that he lead us where we want to go."

"And where's that?"

"Where Turnbull sang his hymns, and where Iris Creen now lies hidden."

"And that is?"

"Somewhere in Derbyshire, I should fancy."

"You said you knew where she was," I objected.

"I do, within certain limits. But I should not like the job of finding her."

"I don't quite see."

"King," said my friend, taking his pipe from his mouth and speaking very deliberately, "you remember, no doubt, the fifth act of *Hamlet* in which the fencing scene occurs?"

"Of course," I said, wondering where this trail led.

"In it the Queen says of Hamlet, 'He's fat and scant of breath'."

"She does."

"What did she mean by saying that he was fat?"

In spite of my fatigue, I was like the famous Dr. Middleton, "roused for judicial allocution in a trice".

"It has often been supposed," I said, "that the remark was introduced as a joke at the corpulence of the celebrated Elizabethan actor, Richard Burbage, who played that part. That, I should say, is nonsense. Shakespeare would not have introduced such a feeble and irrelevant allusion at such a tragic climax, especially in a play in which he complains bitterly of the 'gags' used to cajole the 'groundlings'. Curiously enough, recent inquiries seem to show that the Elizabethans made use of the word 'fat' in the sense of sweaty or perspiring, and that seems to be a very reasonable solution of the difficulty."

"Excellent!" said Arbuthnot. And then, in a different tone, "What a repository of useless knowledge your head must be!"

"How?" I protested.

"You know a thing like that, which is of no possible importance either to God or man, and yet I'll swear you are entirely ignorant of the essential fact that the commonest geological formation of the Pennines is the carboniferous limestone."

"If I knew it," I said aggrievedly, "what earthly use would it be to me? I'm not a geologist."

"No, but Charteris is, and, as we know, has published a monograph on this very formation."

"Well?"

"Remember Turnbull. He was taken into, and out of, his prison in a state of unconsciousness. While incarcerated he was never allowed to see or feel the nature of the place in which he was. Don't you remember his account?"

"Well?"

"Why were these precautions taken? Because if Turnbull had been allowed to use his eyes or hands he could not have failed to recognize what kind of place his prison was."

"What kind of place was it, then?"

"Remember," went on Arbuthnot, disregarding my question. "They allowed him to sing. They were sure, therefore, that the sound would never reach anyone. He also noticed that no daylight ever penetrated into his dungeon. What does that suggest?"

"Turnbull himself thought he was in a cellar," I said.

"It wasn't a cellar, King."

"What then?"

"One of the outstanding characteristics of the carboniferous or mountain limestone is its readiness to become hollowed out into caves or series of caves through water action. There are examples at Cheddar that are famous, and that remarkable Yorkshire pot-hole, Gaping Ghyll, leads to an underground labyrinth. I believe that Charteris in his investigations found some previously unknown system of such caves and is using it as his head-quarters. In a cave of this nature water percolating through the roof deposits lime and so builds a downward projection called a stalactite. More lime deposited on the floor where the water-drops fall builds up a stalagmite to meet it. Turnbull was chained to a stone pillar which I am certain was no other than a stalagmite. He noted the pervading damp; he heard the dripping of water. The thing is a certainty."

"And Iris Creen is there?"

"We may assume so."

"Do you intend to try and get her away?"

"Not I. I hope to be able to deal with some others who are on that game. The centre of attraction shifts north and, by Jove, that confounded kettle is boiling at last!"

I was grateful for the strong tea that Arbuthnot brewed. He had started upon his second cup when he went on talking.

"The case has been an object-lesson in inconsistency," he said. "Firstly, we had Roger Gordon and his colleagues, apparently engaged in criminal acts, and yet never fitting the description of criminal. Then there is Baxter Creen, capable, I should judge, of most things, and yet honestly and frantically concerned for his daughter; so much so that he calls in my aid instead of using the ruffians whose services he commands, whose action might conceivably betray to the girl that her father was not all she supposed. Then we find that the people who have been kidnapped the girl will not use her even to secure the release of one of their own comrades, because Dormer Strang loves her and will not hear of it.

"Last of all, Creen moves heaven and earth to destroy his enemies, and yet never questions a reference supplied by one of their number. What do you make of this last inconsistency, King?"

"That Charteris has been clever enough to escape detection."

"So one would naturally think. And yet it doesn't fit properly. We are here largely driven back on conjecture, and yet we can make out some line of argument, surely. On the 24th of November, the night I told Creen of the name Dormer I had heard and which we know now he recognized, the same night you were shot at, there were undoubtedly several men at the factory. By the 28th, when we visited the place and found Treloar, there were only two left; even these are now being withdrawn. Did Creen's fresh knowledge make him change his course of action, and in desperation set his own rascals on to find his daughter? It is more than possible. Where did these men go? We don't know, but the next we hear is that they have murdered your friend, Winstanley, in the Pennines. There is no doubt about that. They are therefore hot on the scent of Iris Creen's hiding-place."

"That is all quite reasonable," I said.

"Very well. Now how did they get on the track so after the abduction happened? There is one likely way. The name Dormer warned Creen whom he was dealing with. He is a clever man. His active brain lighted on the total disappearance of Turnbull, that had very probably been engineered by the same agents. He acted on that supposition."

"So far, so good," I said.

"Yes. Now we reach the limit to which hypothesis dare go unsupported. As long as he believed it was a common elopement based on the man's physical attractiveness there was no reason to question the validity of the reference that had been given. But when he found that an enemy was at work, would you not have expected him to look with suspicion on the man who had made it possible for Dormer Strang to get the post?"

"I should," I said promptly. "In this state of anxiety I should have expected him to take that line at once. It would be the natural procedure."

"Quite so. And yet he did nothing of the kind. In other words, *he knew who his enemies were, and Charteris was not amongst them*. He was so sure as to neglect even to consider the possibility. How did he know so much?"

"How did he?" I echoed.

"H'm. Even the twelve apostles had their Judas, you know."

"You don't mean Charteris?"

"I don't. His action the other evening cleared him. Wait till Treloar has spoken and I hope we shall know. There are already indications."

"Do you think we are likely to be raided?" I asked.

"I don't. The chauffeur will be able to tell our friends at the factory that there are four of us, all probably armed. I take it they will deem it wiser to get away according to programme. Now we'll set about packing up. It's better not to leave anything here, I think, except our ladder, which Higgins can look after."

At a quarter to five we shook Treloar out of his slumbers. He was very reluctant to return to consciousness. He stared round in a startled way at his unfamiliar surroundings; then he jumped suddenly to his feet.

"Come," said Arbuthnot. "We march in fifteen minutes. There's some tea here, and some bread and cheese. We shall, I trust, breakfast in town."

"Good!" said Treloar. He fell on to the food and drink with avidity. "Forgive me," he said, between mouthfuls, "if I'm still a bit dazed. I suppose you're keen to hear what I have to tell, and I can tell you I'm desperately so to hear what's been happening since the 8th of November."

"The day you were captured?" asked Arbuthnot.

"That's it."

"Yes, it's probably more important for us to know what happened to you, although you shall have *our* story in due course."

I studied Treloar while the conversation went on. Now he had regained some vitality he was distinctly prepossessing; tall, thin, dark, grey-eyed, and alert, but with the pallor of imprisonment still marking his face.

"Dear, dear," continued Arbuthnot, "I'm very neglectful. Of course you don't even know our names. This is my friend King—more accurately Sir Edmund King. My name is Arbuthnot."

Treloar looked at him.

"Not *the* Arbuthnot—the criminologist?" he asked with widely opened eyes.

"The same."

"That's one to us, anyway!" cried Treloar exultantly. "Who raked you in, Strang or Charteris?"

"They both contributed, but I think it was really Roger Gordon who influenced me most," said Arbuthnot gravely.

A discreet tapping on the back door cut short the conversation.

"There's Higgins. We must be off. We can talk on the road."

In a few minutes we were trudging stationwards; the darkness of night still held and Leasinghoe was a village of the dead. We were all tired, but the cold night air and the possibility that we did not march unwatched quickened the nerves.

It crossed my mind that we were leaving Leasinghoe and its dark shadow of tragedy for the last time. Arbuthnot and Treloar broke into a low-toned conversation.

"Tell me now how they first got hold of you and Jim Gordon."

"It was those infernal gates. We had been put on to watch the factory, you understand, and verify what it was being used for. Roger Gordon had been quietly watching the place for some time, but was to be withdrawn for another job. We lived at Clacton-on-Sea and used to cycle to the factory. We concluded, wrongly as it turned out, that we had only the caretaker to deal with. We speculated on knocking him down while he was on one of his trips to the village, in the hope of getting his keys. As if our intentions had been sensed, he stopped going out. We were nonplussed. Jim Gordon—you know what a hothead he is—actually climbed the wall in daylight, and saw plainly enough that though we could get in we should have no chance of getting out again. Then one night as we watched we saw the caretaker go out. After some discussion we decided to wait at the big gates and waylay him as he returned. Picture our amazement when we found he had

left the gates open! I suppose we ought to have smelt a
rat, but we didn't. Jim urged that the opportunity was too
good to lose. I consented, and we were half-way across the
courtyard when we heard the gates clang together behind
us! Even then we did not suspect the truth. We thought
that the caretaker had remembered his error and returned
to rectify it. 'Now we're in,' said Jim, 'we'll have a good
view of all there is to see, anyway.' We made for the main
building and found a door unfastened. That should have
warned us, I suppose. We went from room to room and
found nothing of note. We were using a torch, you understand. Finally we got into an inner room of considerable
size whose floor was almost covered with large, piled-up
packing-cases. Then we knew we had found what we were
looking for. At the same moment there was a click, the
room was flooded with electric light and three men stood
at the door covering us with rifles. We had to surrender.
We had walked blindly into their trap. They must have
anticipated everything we did, and those three men had
undoubtedly been crouching behind packing-cases near
the door, waiting for our appearance. In that inner room
they could have shot us down unheard if we had resisted.
For a moment I thought they were going to do so in any
case. Then a fat, smiling man with gold pince-nez rolled up."

"Jennings!" I ejaculated.

"I never heard his name. He ordered us promptly into
confinement. There we stayed, without a hope of getting
away, for sixteen days—that is, up to the 24th. Once in
that period—it was on the 15th—there was excitement of
some kind, for some of the gang came in and gagged and
bound us."

"That was the day we were searching for Hunt—I mean
Gordon," I interposed.

"I see. Well, eventually Jim Gordon hatched a hair-
brained scheme for getting away. It was based on the fact

that the caretaker always came in last thing at night to see that everything was all right. He carried a lantern, for they had taken away the electric bulb from the room. In his other hand he invariably had a revolver, for he is a cautious man, this Dawson. His practice was to throw open the door and look and see where we were before he came into the room. If we were in bed, as was generally the case, he would advance and look at us and then go away. Jim's idea, no new one of course, was to prepare a couple of dummies made of bedding and so on to represent us in bed. I was to hide under one of the beds, while he took station where he would be behind the door when it was opened. If, in the dim lantern-light, Dawson was deceived by the effigies in the beds and walked unsuspectingly in, Jim would spring upon him from behind. With my assistance he would be bound and gagged and his keys taken from him. We arranged beforehand that, if the worst came to the worst, one should escape even if it meant leaving the other behind; we judged it imperative others know what had happened. Of course, if Dawson wasn't carrying the key of the gate we had to face failure, and retribution as well.

"All went well up to a point. After the apology for a meal that we received about eight every evening had been handed in we felt safe to set to work on our dummies. Gordon is a bit of an artist; he produced quite good life-like models, even going so far as to scrape soot down from the chimney to add features to the heads. Dawson was late in coming in that night. We began to fear he was going to neglect his duty for once. It was long after midnight when at last we heard his feet shuffling on the stairs. I was under a bed like a shot; Gordon tiptoed to his post. Then the door opened, I saw a gleam of lamplight on the floor, there was a pause, and then feet moved across the room. Gordon was on him with a bound that sent him crashing to the ground, but, to our horror, as he pitched forward his revolver went off. He must have actually had his finger on the trigger when he was attacked. Now he lay stunned with his head against the bars of the empty grate, but we knew the report of the gun must have aroused the rest.

"'Come on!' said Gordon. 'It's now or never!'

"He stooped to Dawson, dragged a bunch of keys from his pocket, and we dashed out of the room. Our error was in not bringing the lamp, which had not been smashed by the fall. On those unfamiliar staircases and corridors we lost time. It seemed ages of stumbling and scrambling before a draught of cold air told us we had found the entrance Dawson must have used. We came out into the courtyard, almost opposite the point where we escaped to-night. 'Make for the gates,' said Gordon. We set off at a run. On our left we heard the sound of voices and there was a light showing from the little house in the far corner of the wall. Gordon must have looked out the most likely key as he ran, probably judging by size, as we knew the gates had a very massive lock. I'll say for him he was as cool as a cucumber. In a trice he had the gate moving. We heard a shout and the sound of men running. The gate was about eighteen inches ajar; it moved sluggishly owing to its weight. Gordon slipped through. I essayed to follow. To my horror the gate moved against me, apparently of its own volition. I dragged at it; it tore itself from my hands and slammed home. I guess now it was some sort of automatic control which one of the gang had had sense enough to apply when he realized what was happening. The courtyard seemed alive with men. A torch was flashing here and there. I lost my nerve and ran wildly about like a fool until somebody sprang out of the darkness and knocked me down."

"Here's the station, sir," observed Higgins respectfully.

Dawn as yet showed no sign; the lonely platform was illuminated by a solitary lamp. A single drowsy porter was noisily marshalling milk-urns at one end. We stood and shivered in the little waiting-room. We had equipped Treloar with a spare overcoat and a hat of sorts, but his teeth chattered with cold in spite of that. Arbuthnot produced a flask and passed it to him.

"What happened then?" asked my friend.

"Then they gave me a hell of a time: cut down my food to a starvation level, and frequently threatened me with a speedy and uncomfortable death."

"Did they try to wring information out of you?"

"Curiously enough, no. They made no attempt of that kind whatever."

"Perhaps they even failed to ask your names?" suggested Arbuthnot.

"Ask our names? They knew them! The head scoundrel your friend called Jennings simply ticked them off on a list he had in his pocket-book."

"That's very interesting—and conclusive," murmured Arbuthnot, half to himself. "Did you form any opinion as to the amount of stuff there was there?"

"I should say that at a low estimate there were not less than ten thousand rifles in the room we visited, presuming all those cases were full. We know he sold rifles to the Riffs, and he probably sold them before that to the Sinn Feiners. Now Egypt is the market."

So that was it!

It was a blinding light of revelation to me, a baleful glare that shone suddenly and luridly on the sinister activities of Baxter Creen.

"Do you mean to say—" I was beginning excitedly, when Arbuthnot tapped my arm unseen in the darkness, and I desisted, realizing suddenly that we were supposed to know all about this already.

"You can guess," went on Treloar, "what a hell it was for us to lie imprisoned there and know that the stuff might be shipped off any day and perhaps no one able to prevent it."

"I somehow think," said Arbuthnot slowly, "that that stuff never will be shipped."

As he spoke the shrilling of a whistle announced the approach of the train. We were the only passengers. We gave Higgins a message for Mrs. Jerrold and Arbuthnot bade him be on the alert for our return. The little local train shook itself into activity by a series of jerks as the last of the milk-urns was bundled in. I glimpsed Higgins standing at attention on the platform—one of the most reliable men I have ever come across.

"Tell me what happened to Jim Gordon," said Treloar, as he shivered in his corner.

Arbuthnot recounted the story I have already told. "Apparently," said he, "they chased him on your own bicycles, which no doubt they found after they had captured you." Then he had to go through the story of the death of Roger Gordon and explain what had happened on the night Buller was murdered. Treloar was amazed.

"By heaven, we're up against something!" he exclaimed.

"We are," said Arbuthnot. "And that's not all, either."

"How so?"

"They got Winstanley the other night."

"What! No!"

"Yes, toppled him over a cliff and smashed him up."

He went on to tell the story as we knew it. Treloar sat in mute rage and sorrow. He was deathly white and his fists clenched and unclenched themselves. No man could have known Winstanley without caring for him.

"My God!" said Treloar softly to himself. "Aren't we going to get even with these beasts?"

"That is our mission at present," returned Arbuthnot. "We are on the verge of great things. If we had not rescued you, you would by now be northwards bound with Schnurr and Dawson. We dined with Charteris in town the night before last. By now he will probably be at head-quarters. Strang is already there, as well as others. The vultures seem to be gathering." He gave a dry laugh.

Treloar seemed puzzled. "Then does all this mean that the gang have got scent of our head-quarters?" he demanded.

"It seems so."

"I should have thought it barely possible," said Treloar. "At any rate, they won't have an easy job finding it," he added more cheerfully.

"Neither should we without your guidance," said Arbuthnot boldly. "We've never been there yet. Ever since we came in on this business we've been busy over the affairs of the factory."

"You couldn't have a better guide," answered Treloar, "if you'll pardon my cheek in saying so. Charteris found the place, but I had the job of fixing the entrance. That's in my line of business. I was at Bedford Modern and then went on to Engineering at London University, and honestly I'm very proud of the way I fixed things in our little bolt hole."

The train terminated its jolting progress at Colchester. Dawn was in the sky; a cold, grey, unhappy light brooded over the site of the old Roman colony; to me it looked foreboding. I was chilled and sleepy, and only kept awake by the tension of the drama in which we played. We had twenty minutes to spare and used it to snatch some hasty refreshment. Then, in more comfortable accommodation, we were rolling off the miles Londonwards.

"Time presses," said Arbuthnot. "Treloar, is there any place in town where you can get a change of clothing?"

"Yes, I always keep some spare kit at my brother-in-law's."

"Good. I want to be away north as quickly as possible. What's our station?"

"I recommend Buxton. It's only a five-mile tramp from there."

"Right. That means the midday train from St. Pancras. We'll meet on the departure platform at 11.45 prompt. We ought to be there by dusk. We'll fix ourselves up with rucksacks and make it look like a walking party. I have a spare revolver I can lend you."

"You expect immediate trouble?" asked Treloar.

"I do. I think when the news spreads that you have been rescued there will be trouble of the very gravest description."

"I don't get you. I'm not such an important person as all that."

"You were, until your rescue, the most important person in the whole business."

"How the deuce could that be?"

"Simply because you represented the last chance Baxter Creen had of getting his daughter back without fighting a pitched battle for her."

"Getting his daughter back! What on earth have I to do with his daughter?"

"Surely," went on Arbuthnot, his voice growing quieter and yet clearer with every word he uttered, "you were aware that Dormer Strang obtained a post as chauffeur to Iris Creen."

"Good Lord! That's news to me. I knew nothing about it."

"That's almost incredible," said Arbuthnot dryly.

"Not a bit of it. You see, Strang and Charteris run the show between them. The rest of us get our jobs and carry on. We hear about everything eventually, of course, but it is thought not good policy to divulge information beforehand. This will tell you. Grierson came down to us at Clacton a couple of days before we were captured. He brought instructions, but he knew nothing about the affair you mentioned or he would certainly have told us about it. How did you come to know of it?"

"Only after the event, of course," said Arbuthnot promptly. "In any case, we didn't come into the affair until Roger Gordon was murdered."

"For heaven's sake, tell me about it!"

"Charteris, Winstanley, and Strang worked it to get the latter into Creen's household as I've already mentioned. Once there, Strang promptly fell in love with the girl and they absconded together. Strang naturally took her to head-quarters. At present I hold a commission from Creen to find the girl at all costs!"

"The devil you do!" shouted Treloar, torn between amazement and laughter.

"That's not all. Creen has discovered that Strang is connected with the people who have been watching his operations at the factory. He is therefore doubly embittered. Moreover, he has a shrewd idea of where our head-quarters are. It is my belief that he will strike a blow at the first available chance. Hence our rush north."

More conversation naturally followed, mostly interrogatory on the part of Treloar.

"I suppose you know Grierson's gone East?" asked Arbuthnot.

"Has he? I supposed he would go back there. His fluent Arabic makes it the most useful place for him. Of course you know it was he who first got wind of this business, in some obscure way or other, in Alexandria?"

"Is he still up to his ears in debt?"

"I imagine so. He was growling about it when we saw him, and hoping he would get away before things got too hot for him. You know he got a nasty knock over the Alresford baby?"

"Yes, but that is nothing to the knock I shall enjoy giving him if ever we meet," said Arbuthnot grimly.

"I don't understand you." Treloar wrinkled his brows.

"I mean that Grierson was the man who sold your secrets to Baxter Creen!"

"Never!"

"I fear so. He was badly in debt. The appearance of that baby ruined his chance of the title. As you say, he wasn't aware that Strang was trying to get into the Creen household or no doubt he would have sold that secret too. Creen and his gang know all your names except that of Charteris. They didn't find them by tracking you, for Strang was never recognized while he was in his chauffeur's post. The names were betrayed. Only Charteris, who otherwise should have been the first man suspected by Creen, was not betrayed. Why? This is the crowning inconsistency. Grierson was fag to Charteris at school. There is no such thing as a perfect villain. Grierson hadn't the heart to sell Charteris when he sold the rest."

"Good heavens!"

Thus the last fold of the curtain of mystery that had concealed so much was drawn up upon the penultimate act of our complex drama. The actors were mustering in the wings.

"Half an hour to London," said Arbuthnot.

19
In Which Death Comes by Sound

At Liverpool Street we parted from Treloar, to meet again as arranged. He went off to get rid of the untidy and prison-stained remnants of his clothing and to re-apparel himself. We made for our flat, and in half an hour had revelled in baths and were attending to an excellent breakfast. Arbuthnot ate more than I did; I think I was occupied in digesting all that had come to light in the past few hours. I felt a sensation of strain as if my brain had more than it could cope with.

"Do you feel positive about Grierson?" I asked.

"I do. I suspected Charteris till the night he tackled us. As soon as Creen knew that the alleged chauffeur was not a chauffeur at all he should have jumped to the conclusion that Strang was acting in collusion with the man who supplied his reference. He did not. The rest is obvious. Now a more pressing problem offers."

"What's that?"

"We have to go among people who without doubt have been informed by Charteris that we are their enemies. Charteris will take a deal of convincing that we are not so."

"There's the evidence of Treloar," I suggested.

"We may be using him as a decoy."

"You gave Charteris your real name and address."

"How is he to know they were genuinely mine?"

I was puzzled.

"No, King, we can only prove our bona fides by our actions. We must take our chance. Now I must speak to Kaye on the 'phone. You go and turn out some suitable kit."

In half an hour I had donned some semi-respectable plus-fours, found my favourite ash-plant, and rescued from oblivion the rucksacks that had gone with us on that memorable walking tour when we had fought with beasts not at Ephesus, but on the desolate Yorkshire coast.[1]

"The *City of Aswan* has been traced," said Arbuthnot when I returned to him. "She's a two-thousand-ton tramp belonging to the Levantine and Western Steam Navigation Company, a concern whose shares are not quoted on the Stock Exchange. She sailed from Alexandria on November 14th for Channel and Baltic ports and is now lying at Dunkirk. Please God it'll be a long time before she gets the cargo she came for. I rather fancy that illegal trade in munitions of war does not rank first in Baxter Creen's thoughts at present."

We reached St. Pancras punctually, but Treloar was already there awaiting us, and dressed similarly to ourselves. He was walking up and down the platform as if eaten up with impatience. Since he had learnt of Winstanley's death and Grierson's treachery his face had worn a grim look that boded ill for some one. We had no luggage other than what we carried on our backs. The train was already in. We secured three seats in an empty third-class compartment, and then descended upon a bookstall opposite, for in the event of fellow-passengers appearing we could not hope to talk much of the only subject that seemed worth discussing. When we returned to the carriage Treloar was the first

---

[1] The story of this tour has been told elsewhere under the title of *The Black Hounds of Hunmanby*.

to jump in. I was about to follow. Arbuthnot stood on the platform waiting his turn. Suddenly his hand gripped my arm as in a vice. I naturally swung round.

"On your left," said his voice in my ear. Standing at a door about three compartments away, his monocle fallen from his eye, his face a study of anger and amazement, was the Honourable Geoffrey Charteris!

"Get in," said Arbuthnot. I entered the compartment mechanically, my brain in a turmoil. What would he do? Clearly he could not do much on a railway platform. Then I saw him again. He had passed our window, throwing in the most casual of glances as he did so. I fancied he was smiling.

Arbuthnot buried himself in a newspaper. Treloar sat drumming impatiently on the far window. There was a bustle on the platform, a whistle shrilled, doors slammed, and the train almost imperceptibly began to move. Nothing had happened. I sat back in my corner and thought hard.

Charteris had certainly seen Treloar in our company and under no restraint. He would therefore argue that we were deceiving him. For what purpose? Evidently in order to lead him to an unconscious betrayal of the hiding-place of Iris Creen. What then would Charteris do? He would leave the train at some stopping-place before Buxton, and attempt to reach his head-quarters before us so as to arrange for us a particularly warm welcome when we came along.

"Derby, I should think," said Arbuthnot's voice from behind his paper.

"Oh!" said I.

"What's wrong?" asked Treloar.

"Derby—good place to get tea," said Arbuthnot.

There was silence. The train rolled on rhythmically. My thoughts went forward to the complication that seemed inevitably impending.

"Here's something in your line, King," said Arbuthnot, bringing his paper and crossing to sit beside me. "'Bacon —Shakespeare Controversy Revived: Alleged New Evidence'."

I looked, and then I saw the slip of paper held in position between his left thumb and the newspaper.

"Indeed?" said I, bending to scan it.

I read:

> "Charteris knows we recognized him. Therefore he knows we shall not dare go below ground without further help. Therefore he will attempt to capture us above ground. If we resist it may give the third party their chance. Surrender and leave things to me."

"I quite agree," I said. "That's the only way to look at things."

"Suppose we're too late," said Treloar suddenly. "Suppose the place has been found and rushed."

"Suppose nothing of the kind," responded Arbuthnot cheerily. "They will only know to-day that you have been rescued. They, no doubt, had hoped to use you as an instrument of barter. Only now will they consider action in force. It is one thing to destroy a solitary man like Winstanley; it is quite another to enter an underground den in the face of armed resistance."

"True, and they won't have an easy job finding their way in. Would you like to hear how I fixed things?"

"Very much."

"The entrance is where a dry valley—you know, one made by a stream, but now no longer containing water— terminates in a basin-shaped depression. At the lowest point of the basin, in the centre, is a hole barely large enough to admit a man's body. Here in old times the stream must have plunged underground. It is such a small affair that before Charteris apparently no one thought it worth while investigating—or else funked it. At any rate, he went down and found it not more than about thirty feet deep. At that depth a sloping way led downwards into the earth—we've cut rough steps in it now. Then he came to a remarkable series of caves, equalling, I should think, any of the well-known ones. Charteris says the caves can't be due entirely to the water that made the pot-hole entrance—more he can't say about it. He never published his discovery, because he intended to explore the place fully later on and then base a treatise of some sort on it. Meanwhile the league was formed, Charteris offered the caves as an ideal head-quarters, and so they proved."

Treloar gave vent to a chuckle. "It was there that we bottled up the unspeakable Porlock[1] for a whole month, until the inquiries into his absence revealed what he had been up to. But to continue. I was put on to devise a proper closure to the entrance. It was no end of a job but good fun. We first had to level part of the sloping way with concrete, into which we fixed two parallel steel guides, railway metals to be precise. On this we had to raise a strong wooden framework. Then we cut away a mass of rock in the roof, having first provided it with a flat steel base with grooves—no end of a job. When the rock was free to fall except for the frame beneath we gradually lowered it on to the steel guides. Result, to all appearances, a fall of rock that had entirely blocked the entrance. Then we worked our rock back along the guides, cut a side tunnel round it, brought it forward again to cover the entrance to this tunnel—and there you are. I'll make you a plan of it."

---

[1] Porlock, founder and secretary of the All-British Association, who misappropriated over £50,000 of its funds in 1925.

He produced the following, which I still have in my possession.

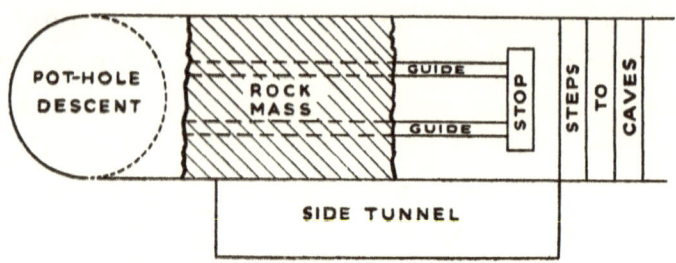

"We keep the guides well greased," he went on. "As it is, it takes the full effort of an ordinarily strong man to move the rock. Now, what stranger, however inquisitive, is going to push for all he is worth against what looks nothing but a solid rock face? Hence you see the place is practically undiscoverable except by treachery. In the last resort the stop is movable, and when fixed forward of its present position the place is impregnable except to blasting."

Arbuthnot studied the diagram attentively.

"I don't think Grierson can have divulged this secret," he remarked. "It would have meant betraying Charteris with the rest."

The train ran into Derby. Arbuthnot sprang to the carriage window.

"No need to get out," said he. "They bring tea along the train. I'll negotiate for some."

In a couple of minutes he had collected twice as many trays.

"One each for you—two for me," he explained. "Pour me out a cup, King. I must jump out and get some tobacco."

The train had drawn in to the main down platform and we were almost opposite the station exit. I saw Arbuthnot visit a kiosk and then, with a word to the ticket-collector, pass through the gateway. In another minute he was back in the compartment.

"Same number," he said to me on returning.

"Same number of what?" I asked stupidly.

"Same number of lumps of sugar in my tea as usual," he answered.

I complied; then I realized what he had meant.

"I suppose," he added to Treloar, "there is a certain risk at present in going as far as Buxton by train. It might have been safer to have got out here and chartered a car. However, we must risk something, and I expect we shall find our redoubtable foes a bit closer home than the railway station."

Dusk was upon us as we left civilization behind and stepped out across the moors. My promise to Charteris made later precludes me from going into details of our route, even if that were necessary. Treloar had been served out with a revolver in case of need, but we marched without incident. We had missed lunch owing to our unconscionably late breakfast, but I was unaware of any feeling of hunger. My nerves were taut; I felt an unusual craving for alcohol, but Arbuthnot would not even allow smoking. We were going into the presence of friends who I thought us foes, and foes who knew us not, at any rate for what we were. Was ever stranger situation? The last faint line of sunset light had long gone when Treloar at last called a halt.

"Steady now," said he in a whisper. "Here we dip down into the hollow. I'll lead or you may fall into the hole."

Slowly and quietly we descended, Treloar feeling his way step by step. Finally we stopped against his outstretched arm.

"Now I'm going down," said he. "It's easy if you've done it a few times, but I've brought a ball of string for you fellows."

"String?" I whispered.

"Yes, you keep one end up here. Pull on it when I'm down and a rope will come up with a knot midway. Pass it round the big boulder. You can't see it, but it's just on your left. Then lower yourselves on the double rope and pull it down after you. That's all. By-by. See you down below."

The whispering tones ceased; there was the clatter of some little stone dislodged, and then silence.

"Now," said Arbuthnot to me, "they ought to try and rush us." But nothing happened. My eyes strained in vain to penetrate the darkness. After what seemed a long time, though very likely it was not more than three minutes, Arbuthnot began to pull on the string he held. Shortly the end of a serviceable rope emerged. We found the boulder without difficulty, and drew our rope round it till we came to the knot. Still the silence around us persisted.

"Curious," muttered Arbuthnot. "I shouldn't have thought they would have missed this opportunity. However, it's safer down below. Here goes." With that he seized the doubled rope and began to lower himself, stood alone, waiting my turn; Then I bent down, thinking I heard a sound from Arbuthnot below.

At that moment something cold pressed against the side of my head and familiar voice said, "I'm not quite sure whether you're Marsh or Judson, but in either case put your silly hands above your head."

"Charteris!" I ejaculated.

"He," said the voice. "It is a pleasure to meet you again so soon."

I felt a hand touching my pockets and finally withdrawing my automatic from one of them. There was no point in resisting.

"I hardly thought your associate would have had the temerity to go below," continued the voice. "However, he will find those there amply capable of dealing with him. I am now going to descend. You will follow and you, Sanderson, bring up the rear."

"Right-ho. Carry on the good work," said a boyish voice.

By straining my eyes I could just see Charteris disappear over the lip of the pit on his downward journey.

"Sanderson? Sanderson?" I said, more loudly than I intended, for a thought suggested by the voice had suddenly slid into my brain. "Not Phil Sanderson, by any chance?"

"The very same. Good Lord, who on earth are you?"

For a second only my eyes blinked in the strong light of an electric torch that played on my face.

"Upon my sainted avuncular relative, it's 'Drowsy'!"

He knew me! And in him I recognized a young cub of a subaltern who for my sins had once been foisted upon me. The nickname was a relic from a school day when I had fallen asleep and toppled backwards off a form; the title had pursued me to the university, and turned up again in the army.

"For the love of Mike, what are *you* doing in this here bag of tricks?"

"Same choice vocabulary, I see," I said. "At present I'm suffering from a misapprehension on the part of your friend Charteris."

"Holy lawgiver of Israel! And who's your pal who went down?"

"Arbuthnot."

"Phew! I'm off below. He'll probably kill the lot of us if he isn't stopped quick. Follow on, Drowsy!"

Without more words this bright young spark swung himself downward, leaving me to rejoice at his intervention and deplore his impudence.

"Is that you, Dormer?"

I spun round as if I had been shot. A woman's voice— and one of the sweetest I have ever heard. I could do no

more than make out an indistinct form, although she must
have been close at hand.

"It is not," I said.

I half-expected her to shriek, or to run away. She did
neither.

"I don't know you," she said, in her low but clear voice,
"but I am ready to put a bullet into you, whereas, whoever
you are, you will certainly not dare to do the same to me."

This, beyond doubt, was Iris Creen, previously unseen
but yet, in a way, very centre of all the tragedy that had
befallen!

"I am a friend," I said. "Charteris and Sanderson have
just gone down. I was about to follow. I am a recruit to the
cause. Have I the honour of addressing the lady who is, or
was, Miss Creen?"

"Who is. We don't run to priests in our society. That
matter awaits adjustment. There's Dormer!"

I heard the brushing of feet on the turf. A tall figure
loomed up.

"Who's w-with you, d-dear?"

"A new arrival," she answered. "Came to-day with Mr.
Charteris."

"My name is King," I said. "I presume I address Mr.
Strang?" I had noted the slight stammer already.

"You do. Glad to have you here. We came out for breathe
of fresh air; it gets rather boring below, but we can't show
our faces by day."

I have not thought it necessary to insist on Strang's
stammer, which, indeed, was only slight.

"I'm not of much account," I said, "but my friend who
is already gone down is in a different category."

"Indeed. Who's he?"

"He is Montrose Arbuthnot."

"By George. You need say no more. We move in exalted
circles indeed. But how come you fellows to be concerned
with us?"

"By accident. Quite independently we got on the track of—er—" I hesitated.

"We understand," said the girl in a voice that never wavered.

"Quite so," said Strang. "But we'd better go on talking below. I don't think this place has yet been spotted, but it's better to be on the safe side."

As the words left his lips a powerful ray of light sprang out of nothingness and fastened upon our faces. There was a shout, and the sound of men running. When I think of how Iris Green acted then it makes me smile to hear men who say a woman goes to pieces in an emergency. Her voice cut the air like a steel blade.

"Stop or I'll shoot to kill!" Then to us:

"Down below quick! They daren't touch me, but they'll kill you if they can."

Mind you, she was standing in front of us as she spoke. I hesitated, as anyone would have done. The rush had apparently stopped. I heard low voices engaged in argument.

"She's right," said Strang in my ear. "Come on; the rope will bear two."

As we moved to the pit mouth, Iris Creen moved with us. No one would have dared risk a shot. Like a flash Strang was on the rope and had vanished.

"Don't trust the rope only—they may cut it," he breathed, as he went out of sight.

"Get on!" said the girl to me. "This isn't a funeral—*yet.*"

So I swallowed my scruples, grabbed the rope, and dropped into the darkness. My knuckles smashed against the rock face; I sought feverishly for places to anchor my feet in case the rope suddenly ceased to support me. Once I swung outward and the back of my head crashed against the rock behind me.

"Here you are," said the voice of Strang.

My dangling feet touched ground, my aching arms relaxed. A torch shone on a narrow opening on my right.

"Inside, and keep to the right," said Strang.

I squeezed past him, bumped my already aching head, and edged into the darkness.

"That you, Drowsy?" asked a voice.

"What's left of me," I said.

"Come on then, and mind the steps."

"Do you vouch for this man, Sanderson?" asked another voice sharply. It was Charteris.

"Drowsy? He couldn't say 'bo' to a goose—that is, except in strictly legitimate warfare. You're a good little boy, aren't you, Drowsy?"

"Confound your impudence," I said. "But, look here, Strang's at the pit bottom and Miss Creen's at the top."

"All serene. She can climb like the graceful squirrel."

"She's not alone."

"How so?" cut in the voice of Charteris quickly.

"They were going to rush us," I stammered. "She held them off while we came down."

"Good Lord!"

"Yes, I know," I said unhappily. "But you disarmed me, and anyway Strang said it was all right."

"I'm not blaming you. But what a woman!" He brushed past me into the narrow opening through which I had just come, and disappeared.

"Where's Arbuthnot?" I asked.

"Last heard of plaintively demanding tea," was the unexpected answer. "When I got down here I found him getting quite annoyed with poor old Lovat, who had been told off to capture him, and Treloar seemed to be helping him. If I hadn't chipped in I believe *they* would have captured Lovat, for Charteris was too dumbfounded to say anything." He chuckled heartily.

Voices faintly came to us; it sounded to me as if one of them belonged to Iris Creen.

"She's down," said Sanderson. "Get down on these steps or there'll be a crowd."

He clicked on a torch, and I stepped downward between white limestone walls. Figures emerged above me.

"That's all right," said the girl's voice. "I suppose I ought to have shot down two or three of them first, but I couldn't quite bring myself to do it. I must have been about a third of the way down, when they found the rope and started pulling me up!"

"What!" said I loudly, from my post on the steps.

"What!" echoed Sanderson from beside me, for once startled out of his nonchalance.

"Of course I let it go at once and came down in approved mountaineering style, wishing my arms and legs had been a bit longer, however."

"Well done!" said Charteris.

I was silent. This was a little more than marvellous. I could see now why Strang had been so ready to leave things to her.

"So we are run to earth at last," said Charteris. "Now we can close the entrance and stand a siege. None of our party is now left outside."

"I don't like that," said Strang. "They could starve us out eventually, and besides, if we shut ourselves up they would be left free to carry on their other business."

"Moreover," said Iris Creen, "if we close the place they can get to the bottom of the shaft and start cutting their way in."

"True," answered Charteris. "I propose then that we leave the entrance open and a man on guard. They'll have to come down one by one. As soon as one arrives, the guard can shoot him in one of the less vital spots and they can pull him up again. They'll soon get sick of that."

"That's stalemate," said Iris Creen.

"Right as usual. But we can leave it at that till we've held a council of war. Sanderson, will you take the first tour of duty?"

"Forward, Horatius," said a flippant voice beside me. "Drowsy, you're on next. Keep awake, in case the orderly officer is sober to-night."

"I'm afraid," said Strang to me, "that I only gathered a vague idea as to who you are, in our hasty meeting upstairs."

"He's a blinkin' barrownite," declaimed Sanderson before I could speak. "Yclept Sir Edmund King, alias Drowsy; clubs, the Athenaeum and Brookwood."

"Indeed," said Charteris, "I'm more concerned with that friend of his who tried to throw me through a door, and very nearly succeeded."

Iris Creen laughed. "What I have missed through becoming a troglodyte! I trust you are now reconciled."

"Hostilities are suspended for the present," said Charteris gravely. "Allow me to lead."

Using his torch he stepped past me down the steps, while Sanderson edged past him to go to his post.

"*Te morituri salutamus,*" said the flippant voice.

"Good night, boy," said Iris Creen. Then we commenced our journey downward.

After about a dozen irregular steps had been negotiated a steady light suddenly replaced the flickering torches, and I saw above my head the glow of an electric bulb that had been switched on. It was the first of a long succession of such.

"Treloar's work," said Charteris over his shoulder to me. "He's got his own plant down here; brought it down in bits and assembled it on the spot."

Now we marched in comparative ease, sometimes down steps roughly hewn, less often up others of the same nature, round about a dozen times, sometimes touching the are rock and sometimes finding timber struts supporting danger spots, until we came to a thick curtain. Charteris pulled it aside, and I stepped into fairyland.

The cave may have been as much as thirty feet square and its walls were chiefly of a glistening white. Stalactites had grown into contact with stalagmites to form three monstrous pillars that seemed to support the dimly-seen roof. The whole was illuminated by the soft light of no less than six electric lamps, masked by hanging shades of translucent material. The floor has been swept clear of rock fragments and roughly levelled. I discerned on the far side a group of persons standing around what proved to be a heating stove. They turned toward us as we entered.

A buzz of conversation sprang up; I was introduced to two men named Lovat and Rawlinson, and then, with something of a shock, I realized that Treloar had brought me up to speak to Jim Gordon.

"I hear I have to thank you for giving me my chance the night I got away from the factory," he said, wringing my hand.

We naturally lapsed into reminiscences of that night of wild escapades. Out of the corner of an eye I saw Arbuthnot being presented to Iris Green. I saw no reason to disagree with Baxter Creen's description of his daughter. I am no judge of female beauty and must leave it at that. She was clad in riding breeches and a jumper and had pulled off a rough tweed hat to reveal black hair, closely-cropped about the neck. When later I looked into her eyes I ceased to wonder about quite a number of things.

Discussion waxed. Treloar had a tale to tell; Charteris had another, and then Arbuthnot briefly took up the running. Yet I, for one, had the feeling we were skating on thin ice, with Jim Gordon there to have his feelings lacerated by a careless word, and with the black shadow of Baxter Green hanging over all.

"Resolved," said Charteris suddenly, "that this meeting form itself into a council of war. Other things can wait."

There were seats of some sort for most there, and a half-circle was formed round the stove, while others perched on a table behind.

"This seems to me how we stand," went on Charteris. "They can't get at us, and we have enough food for several weeks, even with our reinforcements. On the other hand, it seems abominable to let ourselves be cooped up by a pack of rogues."

"Any other exits?" queried Arbuthnot.

"None I have been able to find. Of course the ramifications of the place are tremendous and no one has been fully through it. There must be other vents, for there is a distinct circulation of air, but these openings may be very likely mere fissures along bedding-planes or joint-planes."

"How about the course of the water?"

"There's very little water now, and what there is is only the result of percolation. I imagine the main entrance to this place must have been blocked by a fall of rock which probably diverted the original stream elsewhere.

"Then we are certainly bottled up."

"Yes, but in safety."

"Still, they have one force on their side."

"You don't expect them to call in the police, do you?" interposed Treloar laughing.

"No, I mean the force of gravity," answered Arbuthnot quietly.

At the moment he spoke a distant, low, booming sound smote on our ears, the electric lights momentarily flickered and a small rock fragment from the roof dropped to the ground amongst us.

"Hallo! What's that?" I asked.

"A fall or rock," said Charteris, "in some far-off gallery. I have heard such a sound before. Fortunately most of the caves we use are safe, although there are one or two weak points in the tunnel that leads here."

"I too, have heard such a sound before", I said, and as I spoke I felt that all eyes were focused on me. "It was the explosion of a bomb underground."

"Good God, he's got it!" shouted Arbuthnot. "Those two boxes Schnurr and Dawson had to bring—they guessed we were underground. I suppose the entrance is closed?"

"It isn't!" said Charteris leaping up from his seat. "Sanderson is on guard there to catch anyone coming down."

"Then they've caught Sanderson!" I cried.

"More than that. *They're in!*" said Arbuthnot.

Boom! Another explosion! This time it sounded louder and nearer.

"The old game," said my friend calmly. "Chuck a bomb round each corner, wait till it explodes, and then dash forward. Can you control the tunnel lights from here?"

Charteris jumped to a switchboard. "Out now," said he, "but they'd probably gone in any case."

"What's to be done?" asked Strang. Even in that tensest of moments I marvelled at the way Arbuthnot had come into the lead, even among men each capable of being a leader himself.

"We can't fight bombs in a tunnel," said Arbuthnot decisively. "At the last they won't dare throw for fear of hitting the girl. They'll corner us and expect those who are left to surrender in some distant cavern, or else starve. Our chance is to make a stand here. They must come to the certain to throw in. We must take our chance of shooting them down as they come. Strang and two others take Miss Creen to the safest place you know."

"I stay here," said Iris Creen, smiling.

"You do as you're told," said Arbuthnot, and, I believe for the first time in her life, she did so.

Boom! This time the air shivered with the sound.

"I'm going forward a little way," said Arbuthnot. "We need to know all we can. Switch off these lights. I'll whistle 'Highland Laddie' when I return so that you shall know who it is."

He slipped through the curtains and vanished.

"And that's the man," said Charteris solemnly, "whom I supposed was a jackal of Baxter Creen. King, here's your gun. Can you shoot?"

"More or less."

"Good! You and I will lie down and cover the entrance. You, Treloar, and Gordon, stand aside to take our places in case of accidents. These people haven't to come any farther."

Together we lay down on the rocky ground and watched the curtain. Treloar had momentarily restored the lights so that we could get the direction in which to aim. Then darkness reigned again. Boom! The cavern seemed to vibrate. A small piece of stone hit me in the small of the back.

"They must be about half-way here," said Charteris. "Time your friend was coming back."

Boom! This time much louder. Surely that was a shout? Then came a sound that did not so much enter the ears as strike one a physical blow. I felt as if my body had been suddenly lifted and then flung again to ground. Sickness came over me. The sound was indescribable, but I knew it. Once before, in the evil days when men even fought underground, I had heard it, and I believe every individual hair rose on my head. It was the sound of collapse, of earth and stone and timber crashing to helpless ruin. The whole cave shuddered, a rain of little fragments pattered on the ground. For a moment I could not get my breath.

"The tunnel!" I gasped weakly.

"Lights are gone!" called Treloar.

Silence reigned while a man might count twenty. Then arose in that terror-stricken hush the sound, quiet but distinct, of a voice whistling that strangely heart-stirring tune to which all Highland regiments must march past as long as there is a kilt left in the British Army. The spell was broken.

"Arbuthnot!" I yelled, and stumbled toward the curtain.

20
In Which Sound Comes by Death

Charteris and Treloar brought their torches to bear on the scene. Their light glinted on dancing dust disturbed by the explosion. Then the curtain was swung aside and Arbuthnot stepped into the rays.

"That has settled one of our difficulties," he said quietly, flicking white powdery spots from his garments.

"You mean?" cried Charteris.

"That the fall of rock has entombed the attacking party and incidentally has cut us off from the outside world."

We were half-prepared for that news; nevertheless a cold fear crept to my heart.

"I'm afraid," went on Arbuthnot, as calmly as if he had been detailing the incidents of a cricket match, "that I am partly to blame for the sudden death that overtook them. As they dashed forward after their bomb exploded, I shouted, and that had the effect of checking them for a moment. In that moment the roof fell. One or two may have escaped at the far end, but I doubt it."

"I gather," said Charteris dryly, "that you were not a great way from the spot yourself when it happened?"

"I was quite near enough."

"I can believe it. We'll say no more about that door."

In the eerie light cast by the torches over that chamber that might well become our tomb the two shook hands, and it was not often that Arbuthnot could be brought to do that ceremony.

Voices. It was the other section of our divided forces returning.

"What's happened?" said the voice of Strang.

"A change from the frying-pan to the fire," answered Charteris. "The attacking party have blown the roof in on themselves."

"Good heavens!"

"Do you think—" began a woman's voice.

"I don't," said Arbuthnot promptly. "It's very unlikely indeed."

Which remark temporarily disposed of an idea that had probably been lurking in all our brains.

"This," said Treloar, "is where I come in, I think. We carry a stock of spades and picks and some timbering."

"Excellent," said Arbuthnot, "but for my part I resolutely decline to do anything to save my life until I have had some tea."

The remark saved the situation. For my part, I believe I had been trembling on the verge of hysteria. I was shivering like a man in a bad attack of fever. Treloar went to see if his beloved lighting-system could be put in order. Some one else relighted the stove. Others went hither and thither producing a kettle of water, utensils, and food.

Suddenly the soft radiance of electricity once more flooded the cave. I saw that those who had gone to and fro with torches had succeeded in laying out quite a tolerable meal on a rough table that had been brought into the centre of the floor-space. A second kettle was established on the stove. In a few more minutes Arbuthnot was indulging his craving, but few of us had appetites. Treloar began detailing his plans of rescue. He was in his element.

"I shall want you in reliefs of two to work at the rock-face," he said. "One to excavate and the other to carry

away what is dug out. I shall be in charge of the timbering, and Arbuthnot can help me. He's an authority on the
art of escaping. If you want to get out in reasonable time
you'll have to be satisfied with a tunnel only big enough
for crawling."

"I think," said Arbuthnot, "that we should aim to get
out quickly. Supposing one of the party escaped, he will
have gone to fetch more help. We don't want to crawl
through only to be knocked on the head at the other end."

How we slaved that night! Strang, a man of great muscular strength, dug at the crumbled mass of rock for half
an hour, while I accumulated what he got out and dragged
it, on a travelling rug for want of anything better, back to
the cave and piled it in a corner. He broke two pickaxes in
his tour of duty, but fortunately there was an ample supply
in Treloar's store. After half an hour we exchanged duties.
I welcomed the hard manual labour as a sedative to my
over-wrought brain. After half an hour more Charteris and
Gordon relieved us, and in turn they were relieved by the
other two men. Iris Green remained in the cave constantly
preparing tea; I was not ashamed to have mine strength-
ened with whisky. Even when we were nominally off duty
there was work to be done, supplying Treloar with timber
and sawing it in lengths to his requirements, and sometimes I thought, as I watched him at work, that the engi-
neer is the most wonderful product of our civilization.

As the work progressed it became increasingly arduous.
The excavator had to crouch in the part of the tunnel already excavated and used his tool with difficulty. Still we
went forward, backs aching, faces grimed, finger-nails bat-
tered and torn, and knuckles scarred and bleeding. Moreover, we were half-choked with the white calcareous dust.
I was in the cave when the work was finished. My wrist-
watch, minus its glass, indicated a dubious six o'clock. I
heard a shout, and then Charteris came into the cave.

"We're through," said he, "and there's no sign of danger at the other end."

One by one the workers trooped back into the cave. We were a sorry-looking lot. I don't think one could boast of intact garments or bloodless hands.

"It remains to settle who shall go through and explore," said Charteris.

"That is settled," answered Arbuthnot. "I go."

"I think you've done your share," said Charteris bluntly. "Why should *you* go?"

"Because I'm the one man who stands a chance of remaining alive if there should be anyone at the other end," was the answer.

"How so?"

Arbuthnot glanced at Iris Creen and disappeared beyond the curtain. Then I realized whom he thought he might possibly find at the other end.

Charteris and Strang went forward to guard our end of the cutting. In five minutes all three had returned.

"All clear," said Strang.

"Hallo!" I said to Arbuthnot, sighting his shirt-sleeves, "I thought you put on your coat before you went."

"I did."

"Then where is it?"

"I left it behind."

"What on earth for?"

"Sanderson—was not nice to look at."

"Ah!" A choking sound caught my ears. Iris Creen, previously firm as a rock, had burst into a flood of weeping. It was all too easy to guess the train of thought that had inspired it. Certainly Baxter Creen had more to answer for than any six men would have cared to take before their God.

"Let's make a move," said Arbuthnot. "Our nerves would be all the better for a little fresh morning air."

There was mute acquiescence. In single file we went forward again to the point where we had to crawl. Arbuthnot led. When my turn came my knees shook and my throat was parched. Once before in my life—in 1917—I had had to crawl over dead men to safety, and the memory made the present all the more terrible. The timber supports naturally were not continuous in such hasty work, and between them my torch shone on bare rock debris. Then I shuffled forward more hastily; at one point a human chin decorated with sparse ginger-coloured hairs had jutted grotesquely out into my field of view. I did not need to ask whether Dawson was amongst the dead. At last I came out into the undamaged part of the tunnel. Arbuthnot, Charteris, and Treloar were already there.

"Throw your coat over this before the girl comes along," said Arbuthnot. "It's not pleasant to see."

He threw the light of his torch on to the tunnel floor, and I looked and recoiled hastily. At my very feet was the head of the late Homerton Jennings. He had evidently been last in the procession of villains, and the fall had caught his body, crushing it to pulp, but had missed his head. His face was set in horrible distortion and by some freak his pince-nez still gripped his nose. I hastily covered the horror. Then I remembered Winstanley, and grudged my coat. We went on.

At the entrance we passed another silent figure, laid reverently to one side of the tunnel.

"The last, so please God," said Charteris, his hands mechanically going up in salute.

Arbuthnot stooped and picked up something. It was a small spiral spring.

"From a Mills bomb," said he. "There may be some left in the debris, Treloar. You'd better be careful when you clear the place."

Why dwell longer on the horrors of that night? In a few minutes we were all assembled above-ground in the cold night air. Dawn was yet to come. A chill wind blew across the moors, but it was welcome after the air of the charnel-house. Then we held a brief council of war.

"Where's the car in which you came from Derby last night?" asked Arbuthnot of Charteris.

"I left it in a lane a mile from here, in my haste to intercept you," said the latter.

"Good! It will take us to London. We should attract too much attention in the train in our present disreputable condition. We can pack five into the car—Miss Creen, you, Strang, King, and myself. Miss Creen will stay with my housekeeper while we attend to certain business. I suggest Treloar, Gordon, and the others remain here to get things in order."

"Right!" said Treloar. "I quite agree. We can seal up poor Sanderson in some distant cave till there is a chance to give his bones Christian burial. The others can go down the bottomless pit—you know, the place where we hear the water rushing far below."

"And perhaps pollute the water-supply of half a county," said Charteris. "No, you must find some other way of disposing of them. One of you must come to my rooms in town to report when you have finished."

No one disputed any of the arrangements. In the wan light of the winter dawn those southward bound set out to find the car that should carry them away; the others waved us farewell and turned to descend to their duties. It was bitterly cold, but sweet to be once more under the open sky.

The car was found. Three of us crowded together on the back seat; Charteris and Arbuthnot took turns to drive, and they must have accomplished some very good work, for it was not more than three o'clock that afternoon when four cold and incredibly filthy individuals escorted Iris

Creen into the presence of Mrs. Holden. She, good woman, would not have quailed at the sight of double that number; she promptly took charge of the shivering girl, while the rest of us crowded to the fire.

"This is our best opportunity to talk business," said the indefatigable Arbuthnot. As he spoke he drew a folded sheet of paper from his waistcoat pocket.

"When I reached the end of the fallen part of the tunnel." he said, "I found, wrapped round a stone, this piece of paper. It contains a message for us."

"From him?" asked Charteris.

"From him."

I still have that piece of paper, put away with other relics of terror and tragedy, but, if I hadn't, I think I could reconstruct from memory the sentences it bore:

> "I acknowledge defeat, but I know you will not desire publicly to expose the father of my daughter. I shall be at the factory at Leasinghoe from the 6th to 8th. You can come and see me on any of those days. The place will be open during daylight, and I shall be alone in the office on the upper floor of the main building. There we can talk privately. I am prepared to accept your dictates in every respect and to hand over to your charge all the war material there, destined to illegal purposes, for your disposal. I desire to strike no bargain, but I refuse responsibility for the death due to my agents exceeding their instructions.
>
> "Come in what numbers you like and fully armed. If you finally decide to distrust me bring the police with you and hand me over. I am finished.
>
> "Baxter Creen."

"Well, I'm blest!" said Strang. "That's a peculiar message."

"A document in madness," quoted Arbuthnot. "Remember his Irish descent. There's morbidity and secret love of melodrama there."

"Looks as if we bent him at last," suggested Charteris.

"Creen may break; he will never bend," was the answer.

"What action ought we to take on this?"

"We must go," answered Arbuthnot.

"Creen must have felt very sure we should succeed in getting out," suggested Strang.

"Yes. I suppose he must have been near the spot waiting for news, and when his minions failed to reappear, must have descended into the tunnel, discovered what had happened, and waited there till sounds told him we were cutting our way through."

"Do you look upon this message as perfectly genuine?" demanded Charteris.

"The significant thing about it is its signature," responded Arbuthnot.

"In what way?"

"It makes the letter enough to ruin Creen for ever. He knows that as well as we do. Then why did he sign what amounts to a confession? Because what he says in his last sentence is perfectly true. He is finished. His gang are dead, his evil deeds are known, his daughter is irrecoverable, and he guesses she knows of her father's crimes."

"What then? It appears we have only to step in and insist on his vanishing as the price of our silence."

"That's not quite all."

"What more?"

"It seems to me," said Arbuthnot slowly, "that Baxter Creen does not wish to die alone."

As he spoke there was a knock on the door and the voice of Mrs. Holden was heard saying, "The bathroom is empty, sir."

We looked jealously at each other. Arbuthnot laughed, pulled open a drawer, threw a pack of cards on the table, and said, "Low—bath." It fell to me, and, like the man in Kipling, I 'wallered'. An hour later we were all once more decently clad and seated at a meal that combined the functions of breakfast and afternoon tea.

"What's going to happen next?" asked Iris Creen bluntly in the middle of the meal.

"We are going down to Essex for two days. There we shall do the best possible under the circumstances, I promise you."

"And I?"

"You must remain here, indoors. The telephone is available for you to order clothing to be brought to you from the shops in case you should tire of your present kit. You will not use your own name. Here are three signed but blank cheques. My credit is perfectly good."

"It is quite evident," she answered haughtily to Arbuthnot's very business-like instructions, "that your cleverness does not extend to women."

"It is quite evident," replied Arbuthnot, "you ought to be in bed. Give me two days and I will unreservedly apologize. Meanwhile I require your exact obedience."

Iris Creen walked out of the room without another word. But for the seriousness of the situation I could have chuckled. I saw Charteris hiding a smile and Strang looking vastly perplexed.

"At six o'clock," said Arbuthnot, "the last train that will get us to Leasinghoe to-night leaves Liverpool Street. We will leave this house in half an hour. To-morrow we interview Baxter Creen."

At ten o'clock that night we once more, and for the last time, sat by the fireside in Desolation Cottage. Higgins had been warned by telegram, and in turn had instructed

Mrs. Jerrold to prepare for our arrival. Outside a fog from the sea had rolled up; the marsh was swathed in white. To me it was uncanny, prophetic. We had had a fog curtain for our first act—what of the last?

"On such a night as this Roger Gordon went down the creek, and Buller, stumbling in the fog, laid his thumb on our blood-marked window," I said. Naturally Charteris and Strang had been keen in their demands to be fully informed of our past actions in the case.

"Higgins tells me that Buller's body was found to-day at the mouth of the creek," Arbuthnot said. "That means more police activity. It is as well we came at once."

"You expect to finish things to-morrow?" asked Charteris.

"I do. And then there must be an end to all this damned nonsense."

"What nonsense?"

"Your league must be dissolved. The day is past for such things. We live in England—an old, old country that for a thousand years from Saxon Witanagemot to the Royal House of Windsor had been building up a tradition of sense, of order, of decency—a foundation on which she stands firm when the world rocks. Your league violates that tradition. I grant the purity of your motives, your tenacity of purpose, your skill in execution of your plans. I admit the dangers that threaten, the abuses that linger, the canker of destructive elements. But they are not to be dealt with in your way. England, my friends, is wiser than her people—than you, than me, than any of us. She has a soul, and that soul calls us to service—but in her way, not ours. England moves, like the mills of God, exceeding slow, but she moves on, impelled by the concrete wisdom gathered of her past. Serve in the spirit of England, not in your own. Take up the burdens of patience and toleration and striving she lays upon you. There lies your road."

A silence fell. Once a coal tumbled into the grate. Once the hoot of an owl made me start, as if Roger Gordon had once again cried his death-cry. Then Strang spoke.

"I've finished," he said slowly, staring into the fire as he spoke. "In any case my duty is fairly clear for a little while."

Charteris nodded.

"I had begun to think much of this for myself," he said. "We have lost three good men—I question now the wisdom of it all. The league shall go. Only I ask you to keep the secret of the caves; they are still of immense scientific interest to me, and I want to work unhampered."

"Of course," said Arbuthnot. Readers of this narrative will realize how Charteris's wishes have been respected.

"Now," he continued. "I suggest you all turn in. I must wait up till Higgins reports. He has had to find a large boulder."

"A large boulder!" I echoed. "What for?"

"For to-morrow."

I went off to bed, but sleep failed me. In my mind's eye I was at the factory, where a strong man, crushed, was raving in hatred and despair, awaiting the coming of those who had triumphed over him. I imagined those torments to be terrible to behold. What then? Would he Accept our dictates without striking one more blow? Hardly. Yet what could he hope to do? Not more than perhaps a shot at the man he must hale most. I came to the conclusion that we ought to keep Strang well in the background on our visit.

I was roused from fitful slumber at eight the next morning. A weak, greyish light pervaded the room; outside lay the fog-bank. It seemed appropriate to my mood. The wheel had come full circle. Here, where we had begun, we should finish. Arbuthnot was already breakfasting when I arrived downstairs. The others followed me at a short interval.

"We march at ten," said Arbuthnot. "Higgins will meet us on the road."

"Don't you think," I asked, "that a special danger attaches to Strang?"

"That is very likely. When we find Creen Strang must be left outside the room till we have satisfied ourselves that the other is unarmed."

"Isn't it possible," "suggested Charteris, "that Creen may not be there at all, but has prepared there some kind of trap for us?"

Arbuthnot nodded. "We have to take care," said he.

We were rather a silent party as we crossed the marsh and struck the lane that should lead us to the factory. I think the surroundings, and the tragedy linked with them, affected most of us. After a mile or so we came upon Higgins waiting. Upon his handcart lay a grey stone slab.

"Hallo! What's that?" I asked.

"Couldn't find a boulder anywhere, sir, so I took the liberty, seeing things was urgent, of borrowing this."

"But surely it's a gravestone."

"Yes, sir. It belongs to some one who killed himself a good many years ago and was buried outside the churchyard walls."

"Heavens! What's it for?"

"The automatic gates," answered Arbuthnot. "I don't fancy running round that courtyard like a caged animal with some one potting at me from the windows of the building."

We marched on, the handcart rumbling behind like a tumbril of the Revolution. Strange forebodings filled my mind. I remembered the fate that too often comes to those who follow up a wounded tiger. Presently, through the fog, loomed up those same forbidding walls that had frowned on me on that other day of obscurity. We marched on. Even as on that day the gates were ajar.

Arbuthnot went forward with Higgins, while we watched, and planted the gravestone where it could not fail to prevent the closing of the gates. I may be abnormally sensitive, but the placing of that thing in position gave me a cold shudder of fear.

"Bring your cart inside, Higgins," said Arbuthnot, "so that it will not be noticed should anyone pass."

We marched on, now in single file, Arbuthnot leading, and Strang, by order, in the last position. So we came to the great door of the main building. It was open.

"When we reach the room," said Arbuthnot in an undertone to Strang, "remain outside until I call for you, and be on the alert."

The other nodded. We marched on, this time up a broad staircase and along an echoing corridor. Arbuthnot stopped at a door and struck his fist upon it.

"Come in!" rumbled a voice.

The room was still equipped as an office, with a massive flat-topped desk in the centre of the floor and filing cabinets around the walls, but that I hardly realized till later, for at the desk sat Baxter Creen, the lines on his face a little deeper, the angles a little more defined, and with a light of unreason gleaming in his eyes. Villain though he was, I felt a second-rater beside him.

It was a dramatic moment. Remember he could not have expected to see any of us.

"Mr. Arbuthnot! This is an unexpected visit." The tones grated; the words had come through set teeth.

"And an unwelcome one," said Arbuthnot bluntly. "You chose the wrong man for your task, Sir Baxter Creen. I am glad of this opportunity of throwing it up, for at the moment I represent Donner Strang."

"Indeed?" Oh, the hatred behind the simple word. "And who is this person?" He indicated Charteris.

"Mr. Charteris," answered Arbuthnot coolly. "He once recommended a chauffeur to you."

For a moment I thought Creen's iron self-control would have smashed under this last blow. Then he rallied.

"Where is Strang?" he inquired.

"Outside the door."

"Afraid to face me?" sneered Creen.

"No, but we wish to satisfy ourselves that you are unarmed before we admit him."

Creen laughed, and stood up.

"Search me," he said.

"Do so, Charteris," said Arbuthnot. "It may be calling a bluff."

Charteris, his own revolver handy, went over the other's pockets and reported a blank.

"Now," said Creen, with cold savageness, "having calmed your fears, perhaps we may get to business."

"Come in, Strang!" shouted Arbuthnot.

It seemed to me that the air was so surcharged with its burden of hate that I could hardly breathe. The two men faced each other. For a long minute not a word was said.

"Well," said Creen at last, "it appears that I have been beaten all along the line. All that remains is to make my exit as gracefully as possible. And yet, can you give me any valid reason why I should go to hell alone?"

"None," said Charteris, "except that none of us proposes to accompany you."

"Ah!" said Baxter Creen swiftly, with a sudden change of tone and what was almost a leer on his face, "that decision does not rest with you. I am quite prepared to die if the scoundrel who seduced my daughter dies with me. Unhampered by either of us, she yet has a chance of happiness."

His left hand went suddenly below the level of the desk.

"You're covered," said Charteris sharply.

"So I perceive," said the other with a fearsome joy shining in his eyes, "but what you have there is of no avail against me. In my left hand I now hold a wooden handle which was previously hooked to my desk. From the handle a wire leads through what was once a speaking-tube into the room below and supports there a steel bar. So long as the wire is taut the bar is held. Release the wire and it falls into position to complete an electric circuit. A spark passes into a length of instantaneous fuse, thence to a detonation, and thence to a quantity of high-explosive sufficient to blow us as high as we are ever likely to go."

He laughed a horrible gurgling laugh. His madness was fully upon him. Then silence fell.

It has been my misfortune to have had to face death in many forms, but this turned me suddenly sick. It was unreal in its ghastly finality.

"If you shoot me," croaked Creen, "the handle automatically slips from my lifeless hand."

He began a horrible game of pretending to let the wire slip and then seizing it again. Oddly enough I found time to notice that Charteris was sweating profusely. Strang had not said a word since he came into the room; the scene for him had its peculiar horrors. I tried once or twice to get a grasp on some sort of philosophy that would enable me to face what was to come. I did not want to break down. But my thoughts were like spinning leaves on a torrent. To die; to sleep. Was that all?

"Get it over," said the voice of Strang suddenly.

"Ah! It hurts, does it? She is no more for your arms, scum of a degenerate country."

"That's about enough, Creen," said Arbuthnot curtly.

"No, you wait now upon my pleasure. There is much to tell you. You need time to brood upon your fate."

The objects in the room were blurring before my eyes. A pulse hammered maddeningly in one temple. I found myself leaning on Arbuthnot.

"Enjoy it to the full," went on that gurgling, unclean voice. "Was it for nothing that I spent busy hours last evening carrying ten tons or so of amatol into the room below?"

"It was," said Arbuthnot casually.

"It was!" The answering voice rose to a mad scream.

"I fear so, since George Higgins and I spent nearly all last night carrying it out again!"

I rocked on my feet. A loud singing arose in my ears, and through it I heard a startled cry from Charteris.

Then Creen again. Foam was at the corners of his mouth.

"Liar! Damnable liar! I call your bluff!"

The handle slipped from his hand with a tang from the released wire. From the room below came a kind of loud pop—the detonator. Then silence.

Creen never spoke. His face was twisted almost out of all human semblance. I turned my head away. It was unbearable.

"Stop him!" came the voice of Charteris.

I turned back my eyes, fascinated. Creen was fumbling with a phial he must have drawn from his pocket.

"Why stop him?" said Arbuthnot sternly. "Would you save him for the gallows?"

It was done. There was a choking sound. Creen drummed with his fingers on the desk, swayed, recovered, swayed again, crashed to death. The half-empty phial smashed on the desk.

"What a smell of almonds!" I said with a kind of silly twitter in my voice.

"Prussic acid. Come, let's get out of this."

Like drunken men—I speak for three of us—we staggered into the corridor, downstairs, and out into the fog.

"He must have come in a car," said Arbuthnot quickly. "Charteris, run round the building and see if you can find it." His cool tones were like a tonic. Charteris went off obediently. He was back inside a minute.

"Yes, there's a big Daimler the other side."

"Right! Bring it round to the gates. Higgins!"

"Sir!"

"Everything all right?"

"Yes, sir."

"Good! Load up your gravestone. Help him, King."

Together we lifted it back on to the cart.

"Hallo! What's this?" I stammered.

"I spent my time cleaning it up a bit," said Higgins. Outlined on the face of the slab were the staring initials 'B. C.' It was uncanny. On such coincidences does superstition live. I moved hastily away.

"Higgins," said Arbuthnot, "get off straight away and dump your tombstone in a safe corner. Give this note to Mrs. Jerrold. Collect our luggage from the cottage and bring it to London to the address on this bit of paper. Here's a five-pound note for expenses. Get away quick—and remember Lot's wife."

The Daimler came quietly nosing up through the fog.

"What's to be done now?" asked Charteris. "Can we leave him there?"

"No," said Arbuthnot. "Get the car outside the gates and all on board. Have your engine running so as to get away the moment I come back. Plenty of petrol?"

"Heaps."

"Then carry on."

He vanished back into the building. We negotiated the gates and pulled up outside.

"What's he up to?" asked Strang.

"Heaven knows!" I said. My teeth were still chattering as I spoke, and that not from cold.

"One thing I know," said Charteris solemnly. "In future I'll take off my hat whenever I hear the name of Arbuthnot."

Sounds of a man running. Arbuthnot appeared. He jumped to the vacant seat. We moved off.

"To the right at the turn," he said. "We can strike the main road from Clacton. It's better to avoid Leasinghoe, I think. Get all the speed you can?"

"Do you expect police interference?" asked Charteris

"No, but I'm expecting the bigger part of the factory to go up in dust and smoke in another minute and a half or thereabouts," he answered, glancing at his watch. "Keep your mouths open; it prevents the ear-drums being damaged."

"Good God! So that's what you were doing!"

"Best thing. It casts doubt over everything."

Charteris drove furiously. I craned my head out of the car. The doomed factory faded from sight in the enveloping fog.

"It all began with a sound in the fog," said Arbuthnot dryly. "Let it finish with one."

As he spoke earth and sky were suddenly rent by a mighty roar. I felt as if my neck had received a sudden blow. My breath would not come. My heart paused and then hammered. There, unseen by anyone, the body of the arch-villain must have been flung skyward in a volcano of smoke, flame, and debris. Then came the thudding of falling fragments in the fields around us. Fortunately none of any size struck the car.

"Take the wheel," said Charteris suddenly. "I'm all out."

Dusk was falling over London Town as we threaded our way through the light-bejewelled streets, heading westward.

"We live again," said Charteris reverently, and half to himself.

"Nearly tea-time, *I* think," said Arbuthnot.

Little remains to be told. Arbuthnot had explained to us on our journey Londonwards how he had obtained a set of the keys of the factory from Jim Gordon, who had fled with them; how he had reasoned that Baxter Creen must be planning a general *débâcle* or he would not have inserted the reference to the police in his letter—a few policemen sacrificed to his vengeance would not have worried such a man; how he and Higgins had gone to the factory, found the automatic gate-control against them, and got over by the ladder; how they had discovered the trap, shifted the explosive, and rigged the lock so that Creen could not re-enter that room if he had tried. Fortunately for their operations, Creen had spent the night in the porter's lodge, so they had worked undisturbed. He told also, what I had not previously known, that Jim Gordon had made one abortive attempt to rescue Treloar after his own escape.

Higgins duly reported to us, drew his last pay in the rank of 'sergeant-major' and went away to a job Arbuthnot had found which was worthy of him.

Iris Creen and Arbuthnot made peace over that dreadful scene when the full truth had to be told her. That was an event there is no need to write of. Strang took his hastily-wedded bride away to the south of France and nursed her through a three month's breakdown.

Treloar repaired the tunnel, but until this account is published the remains of Sanderson must await removal to the place where they should rest under some silent yews in the old county of Berkshire.

We duly entertained Kaye at Lunkin's on the 26th of December. It was no more than he had earned. If he had the misfortune, like Charteris, to snap one of Lunkin's wonderful crystal glasses, it must not be ascribed to the strength of the wines we gave him.

In January, in common with the rest of the country, we read of the death of Grierson, stabbed by a fanatical Druse in the streets of Damascus, but up till now only a few people know that the assassin was really an equally fanatical Egyptian. For a man who had so many debts in London it was remarkable to hear that he had left nearly twenty thousand pounds on deposit with the P. and O. Banking Corporation.

Charteris comes in to see us sometimes, for a respite from his scientific pursuits. Some grey hairs look odd above his still boyish face. Sometimes, not often, we look back to those strange days I have written of.

"Poor Winstanley," he said one evening, apropos of nothing. "He was our scout that night. From the point where he died I know he must have wilfully led them away from the tunnel, giving his life rather than betray his friends by a dash to safety. I doubt if it hurt him very much to die."

"Ah!" said Arbuthnot. "So it was like that, was it?"

I hear the rattling of the tea-tray outside. I must lay down my pen.

The Author

N. A. Temple-Ellis was the pseudonym for Neville
Aldridge Holdaway (1894-1954). He taught for
many years, including in the Isle of Wight and in
India, and was deputy head master at a boy's school
in Surrey at the time of his death. During World
War I, he earned the Military Cross. He authored
ten mysteries, published between 1929 and 1941.
His first mystery novel, *The Inconsistent Villains,*
won first prize in the $2,500 Dutton-Methuen
detective mystery contest, judged by A. A. Milne,
H. C. Bailey, and Ronald Knox.

SINISTER CARGO

STANLEY HART PAGE

THE RESURRECTION MURDER CASE

STANLEY HART PAGE

TRAGIC CURTAIN

STANLEY HART PAGE

FOOL'S GOLD

STANLEY HART PAGE

Coachwhip Publications

CoachwhipBooks.com

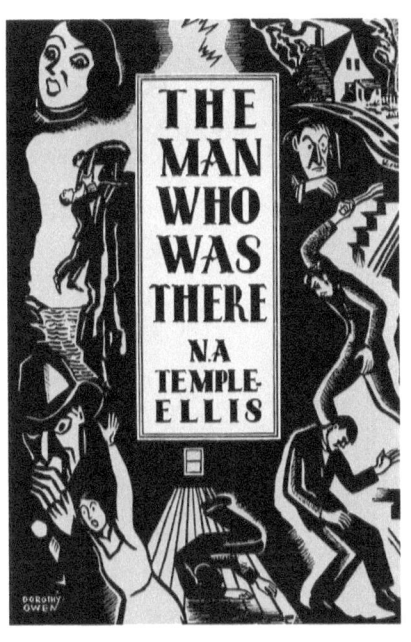

Coachwhip Publications

CoachwhipBooks.com

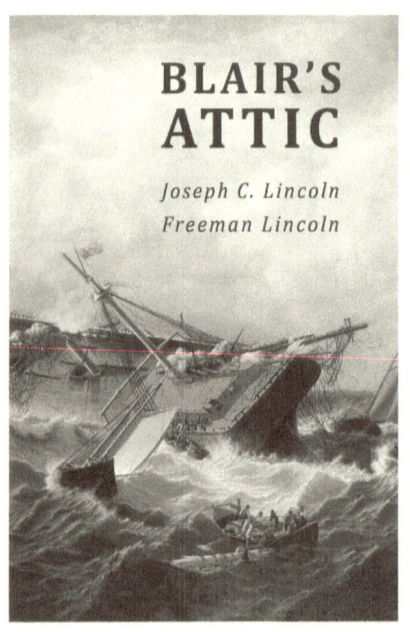

BLAIR'S ATTIC

Joseph C. Lincoln

Freeman Lincoln

MURDER

IN A WALLED TOWN

KATHERINE WOODS

THE CASE OF THE
UNCONQUERED
SISTERS

TODD DOWNING

LOUIS F. BOOTH

THE BANK VAULT MYSTERY

BROKERS' END

Coachwhip Publications

CoachwhipBooks.com

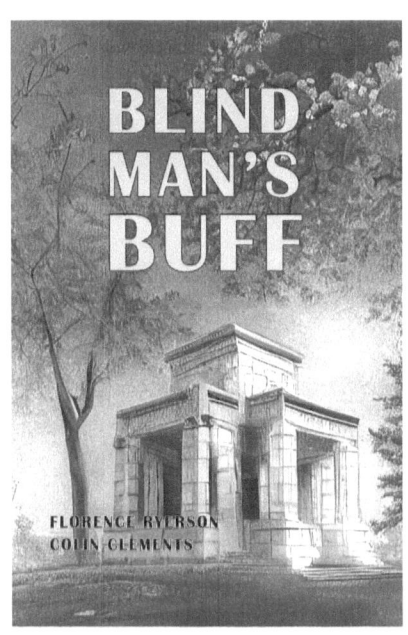

BLIND MAN'S BUFF

FLORENCE RYERSON
COLIN CLEMENTS

POISON CASE
NUMBER 10

MURDER CASE
NUMBER 33

FROM THE FILES OF
THE MICHAEL JOYCE AGENCY

LOUIS CORNELL

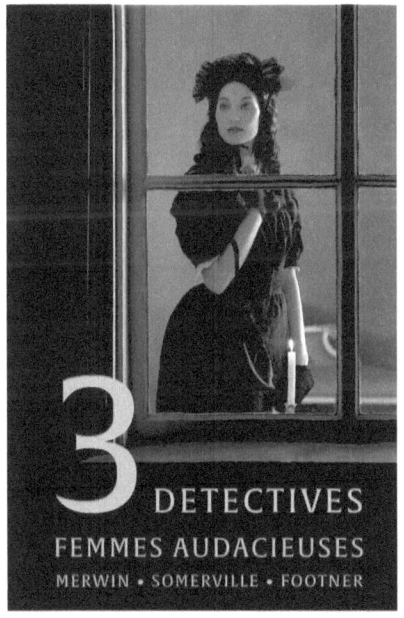

3 DETECTIVES
FEMMES AUDACIEUSES
MERWIN · SOMERVILLE · FOOTNER

MEDORA FIELD

WHO KILLED
AUNT MAGGIE?

Coachwhip Publications

CoachwhipBooks.com

GOLD BULLETS

CHARLES G. BOOTH

The Jekyll-Hyde Murder Case

MADELON ST. DENIS

VIRGINIA RATH

DEATH AT DAYTON'S FOLLY

Death at Windward Hill

Murder in the French Room

HELEN JOAN HULTMAN

Coachwhip Publications

CoachwhipBooks.com

THE
BEACON HILL
MURDERS
&
THE
BACK BAY
MURDERS

THE ROGER SCARLETT MYSTERIES
VOL. 1

THE
SARA ELIZABETH
MASON
MYSTERIES

MURDER RENTS A ROOM

THE CRIMSON FEATHER

HELEN BURNHAM

THE MURDER OF
LALLA LEE

THE TELLTALE
TELEGRAM

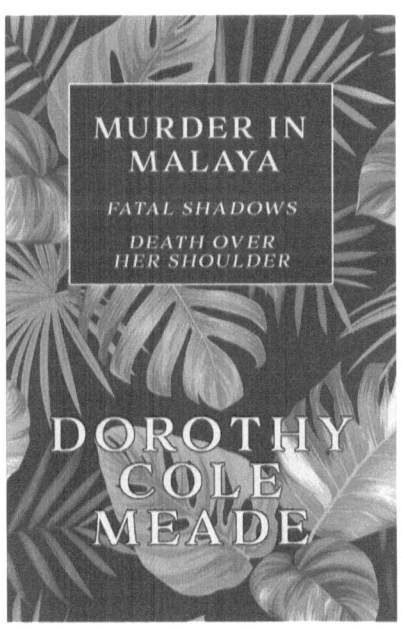

MURDER IN
MALAYA

FATAL SHADOWS

DEATH OVER
HER SHOULDER

DOROTHY
COLE
MEADE

Coachwhip Publications

CoachwhipBooks.com

MURDER AT DRAKE'S ANCHORAGE

E. LEE WADDELL

MAUDE PARKER

MURDER IN JACKSON HOLE

PATTERN IN BLACK AND RED

FARADAY KEENE

3 DETECTIVES
MURDER ON THE RAILS
WHITECHURCH • THORNE • TORGERSON

Coachwhip Publications

CoachwhipBooks.com

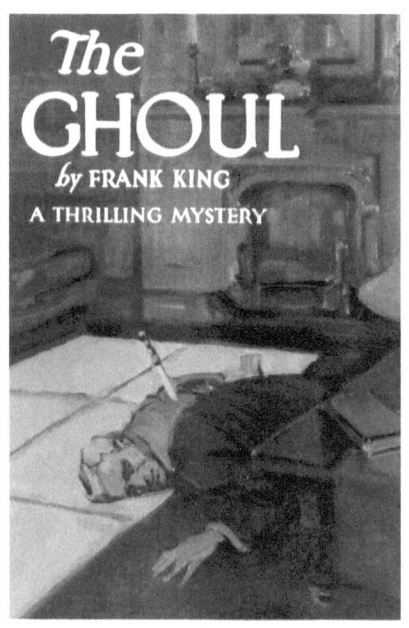

Coachwhip Publications

CoachwhipBooks.com